BY STEPHEN HUNTER

Hot Springs

Time to Hunt

Black Light

Violent Screen: A Critic's 13 Years on
    the Front Lines of Movie Mayhem

Dirty White Boys

Point of Impact

The Day Before Midnight

Target

The Spanish Gambit

The Second Saladin

The Master Sniper

STEPHEN HUNTER

Hot Springs

A NOVEL

SIMON & SCHUSTER

New York London Toronto Sydney Singapore

SIMON & SCHUSTER
Rockefeller Center
1230 Avenue of the Americas
New York, NY 10020

Simon & Schuster and colophon are registered trademarks of Simon & Schuster, Inc.

Designed by Jeanette Olender
Manufactured in the United States of America

10   9   8   7   6   5   4   3   2   1

Library of Congress Cataloging-in-Publication Data
Hunter, Stephen, date
Hot Springs : a novel / Stephen Hunter.
p. cm.
1. World War, 1939–1945—Veterans—Arkansas—Hot Springs—Fiction.
2. Gangsters—Arkansas—Hot Springs—Fiction. 3. Hot Springs (Ark.)—Fiction.   I. Title.
PS3558.U494 H6 2000
813'.54—dc21   99-088530
ISBN 0-684-86360-X

Cover and title page photograph of Central Avenue and the Southern Club in the 1940s courtesy of the Garland County Historical Society.

Lyrics from "Choo Choo Ch'Boogie," words and music by Vaughn Horton, Denver Darling and Milton Gabler, © 1945 (renewed) RYTVOC, Inc., are reprinted by permission. All rights reserved.

Lyrics from "On the Atchison, Topeka and the Santa Fe," by Harry Warren and Johnny Mercer, © 1945 (renewed) EMI Feist Catalog Inc., are reprinted by permission of the publisher and Warner Bros. Publications U.S. Inc., Miami, Fl 33014. All rights reserved.

For my brothers, Andy and Tim,

and my sister, Julie,

who already know the story,

and for my children,

Jake and Amy,

and Julie's children,

Hannah and Sarah,

who will only read it.

My country! America! That is it!

Audie Murphy, *To Hell and Back*

Hot Springs

Wet Heat

CHAPTER

1

Earl's daddy was a sharp-dressed man.

Each morning he shaved carefully with a well-stropped razor, buttoned a clean, crackly starched white shirt, tied a black string tie in a bow knot. Then he pulled up his suspenders and put on his black suit coat—he owned seven Sunday suits, and he wore one each day of his adult life no matter the weather, all of them black, heavy wool from the Sears, Roebuck catalogue—and slipped a lead-shot sap into his back pocket, buckled on his Colt Peacemaker and his badge, slipped his Jesus gun inside the cuff of his left wrist, adjusted his large black Stetson, and went to work sheriffing Polk County, Arkansas.

But at this particular moment Earl remembered the ties. His father took pride in his ties, tying them perfectly, so that the knot was square, the bows symmetrical and the two ends equal in length. "Always look your best," he'd say, more than once, with the sternness that expressed his place in the world. "Do your best, look your best, be your best. Never let up. Never let go. Live by the Book. That's what the Lord wants. That's what you must give."

So one of the useless things Earl knew too much about—how to clear the jam on a Browning A-3 when it choked with volcanic dust and the Japs were hosing the position down would be another—was the proper tying of a bow tie.

And the bow tie he saw before him, at the throat of a dapper little man in a double-breasted cream-colored suit, was perfectly tied. It was clearly tied by a man who loved clothes and knew clothes and took pleasure in clothes. His suit fitted him well and there was no gap between his collar and the pink flesh of his neck nor between his starched white shirt and the lapel and collar of his cream jacket. He was a peppy, friendly little man, with small pink hands and a down-homey way to him that Earl knew well from his boyhood: it was a farmer's way, a barber's way, a druggist's way, maybe the feed store manager's way, friendly yet disciplined, open so far and not any farther.

"You know," Harry Truman said to him, as Earl stared uncertainly not into the man's powerful eyes behind his rimless glasses, but at the perfect knot of his bow tie, and the perfect proportioning of the twin loops at either end of it, and the one unlooped flap of fabric, in a heavy silk brocade, burgundy, with small blue dots across it, "I've said this many a time, and by God I will say it again. I would rather have won this award than hold the high office I now hold. You boys made us so proud with what you did. You were our best and you never, ever let us down, by God. The country will owe you as long as it exists."

Earl could think of nothing to say, and hadn't been briefed on this. Remarks, in any case, were not a strong point of his. On top of that, he was more than slightly drunk, with a good third of a pint of Boone County bourbon spread throughout his system, giving him a slightly blurred perspective on the events at which he was the center. He fought a wobble that was clearly whiskey-based, swallowed, and tried to will himself to remain ramrodded at attention. No one would notice how sloshed he was if he just kept his mouth closed and his whiskey breath sealed off. His head ached. His wounds ached. He had a stupid feeling that he might grin.

"Yes, sir, First Sergeant Swagger," said the president, "you are the best this country ever brought forth." The president seemed to blink back a genuine tear. Then he removed a golden star from a jeweler's

box held by a lieutenant colonel, stepped forward and as he did so unfurled the star's garland of ribbon. Since he was smallish and Earl, at
six one, was largish, he had to stretch almost to tippy-toes to loop the
blue about Earl's bull neck.

The Medal of Honor dangled on the front of Earl's dress blue tunic,
suspended on its ribbon next to the ribbons of war displayed across his
left breast, five Battle Stars, his Navy Cross, his Unit Citations and his
Good Conduct Medal. Three service stripes dandied up his lower
sleeves. A flashbulb popped, its effect somewhat confusing Earl, making him think ever so briefly of the Nambu tracers, which were white-
blue unlike our red tracers.

A Marine captain solemnized the moment by reading the citation:
"For gallantry above and beyond the call of duty, First Sergeant Earl
Lee Swagger, Able Company, First Battalion, Twenty-eighth Marines,
Fifth Marine Division, is awarded the Medal of Honor for actions on
Iwo Jima, D plus three, at Charlie-Dog Ridge, February 22, 1945."

Behind the president Earl could see Howlin' Mad Smith and Harry
Schmidt, the two Marine generals who had commanded the boys at
Iwo, and next to them James Forrestal, secretary of the navy, and next
to him Earl's own pretty if wan wife, Erla June, in a flowered dress,
beautiful as ever, but slightly overwhelmed by all this. It wasn't the
greatness of the men around her that scared her, it was what she saw
still in her husband's heart.

The president seized his hand and pumped it and a polite smatter-
ing of applause arose in the Map Room, as it was called, though no
maps were to be seen, but only a lot of old furniture, as in his daddy's
house. The applause seemed to play off the walls and paintings and
museumlike hugeness of the place. It was July 30, 1946. The war was
over almost a year. Earl was no longer a Marine. His knee hardly
worked at all, and his left wrist ached all the time, both of which had
been struck by bullets. He still had close to thirty pieces of metal in his
body. He had a pucker like a mortar crater on his ass—the 'Canal. He
had another pucker in his chest, just above his left nipple—Tarawa, the
long walk in through the surf, the Japs shooting the whole way. He
worked in the sawmill outside Fort Smith as a section foreman. Sooner
or later he would lose a hand or an arm. Everyone did.

"So what's next for you, First Sergeant?" asked the president. "Staying in the Corps? I hope so."

"No sir. Hit too many times. My left arm don't work so good."

"Damn, hate to lose a good man like you. Anyhow, there's plenty of room for you. This country's going to take off, you just watch. Just like the man said, You ain't seen nothing yet, no sir and by God. Now we enter our greatness and I know you'll be there for it. You fought hard enough."

"Yes sir," said Earl, too polite to disagree with a man he admired so fervently, the man who'd fried the Jap cities of Hiroshima and Nagasaki and saved a hundred thousand American boys in the process.

But disagree he did. He couldn't go back to school on this thing they called the GI Bill. He just couldn't. He could have no job selling or convincing. He could not teach because the young were so stupid and he had no patience, not anymore. He couldn't work for a man who hadn't been in the war. He couldn't be a policeman because the policemen were like his daddy, bullies with clubs who screamed too much. The world, so wonderful to so many, seemed to have made no place in it for him.

"By the way," said the president, leaning forward, "that bourbon you're drinking smells fine to me. I don't blame you. Too many idiots around to get through the day without a sip or two. This is the idiot capital of the world, let me tell you. If I could, if I didn't have to meet with some committee or other, I'd say, come on up to the office, bring your pint, and let's have a spell of sippin'!"

He gave Earl another handshake, and beamed at him with those blue eyes so intense they could see through doors. But then in a magic way, men gently moved among them and seemed to push the president this way, and Earl that. Earl didn't even see who was sliding him through the people, but soon enough he was ferried to the generals, two men so strong of face and eye they seemed hardly human.

"Swagger, you make us proud," one said.

"First Sergeant, you were a hell of a Marine," said the other. "You were one goddamned hell of a Marine, and if I could, I'd rewrite the regs right now and let you stay in. It's where you belong. It's your home."

That was Smith, whom many called a butcher or a meat-grinder, but who breached the empire on Marine bodies because there was no other way to do it.

"Thank you, sir," said Earl. "This here thing, it's for all the boys who didn't make it back."

"Wear it proudly, First Sergeant," said Old Man Schmidt. "For their sakes."

Then Earl was magically whisked away again and, like a package at the end of a conveyor belt, he was simply dumped into nothingness. He looked around, saw Junie standing by herself.

She was radiantly pretty, even if a little fearful. She had been a junior at Southeast Missouri State Teachers College, in Cape Girardeau, he the heavily decorated Marine master sergeant back on a bond drive before the big push for the Jap home islands. She was a beautiful girl and he was a beautiful man. They met in Fort Smith, at a USO dance, and got married that weekend. They had four days of delirious love, and then he went back to the war, killed another hundred or so Japs, got hit twice more, lost more men, and came home.

"How're you doing?" he said.

"Oh, I'm fine," she said. "I don't want anybody paying me any attention at all. This is the day for the hero, not the hero's wife."

"I told you, Junie, I ain't no hero. I'm just the lucky sonofabitch who walked away from the shell that killed the ten other guys. They're giving me the medal of luck today, that's all."

"Earl, you are a hero. You should be so proud."

"See, most people, let me tell you. They don't know nothing. They don't know how it was. What they think it was, what they're giving me this thing for, see, it had nothing to do with nothing."

"Don't get yourself upset again."

Earl had a problem with what the world thought as opposed to what he knew to be true. It was always getting him into trouble. It seemed few of the combat men had made it back, but because he was a big hero people were always stopping him to tell him what a great man he was and then to lecture him on their ideas about the war.

So he would listen politely but a little bolt of anger would begin to build until he'd be off and some ugliness had happened.

"You can't be so mad all the time," she said.

"I know, I know. Listen to me. You'd think the Japs had won the way I carry on. When is this mess going to be over?"

He slipped around behind Junie and used her as cover, reaching inside his tunic to his belt line and there, where Daddy had carried his sap for putting down the unruly nigger or trashy white boy, he carried a flask of Boone County bourbon, for putting down unruly thoughts.

He got it out smoothly, unscrewed its lid, and in seconds, with the same easy physical grace that let him hit running targets offhand at two hundred yards with a PFC's Garand, had it up to his lips.

The bourbon hit like bricks falling from the roof. That effect he enjoyed, the impact, the blurred vision, the immediate softening of all things that rubbed at him.

"Earl," she said. "You could get in trouble."

Who would care? he thought.

A young Marine captain without a hair on his chin slid next to them.

"First Sergeant," he muttered, "in about five minutes the car will take you back to the hotel. You'll have a couple hours to pack and eat. The Rock Island leaves at 2000 hours from Union Station. Your stateroom is all reserved, but you should be at the train by 1945 hours. The car will pick you and your luggage up at 1900 hours. Squared away?"

"Yes sir," said Earl to the earnest child.

The boy sped away.

"You'd think they could supply you with a combat fellow," said Junie. "I mean, after what you did for them."

"He's all right. He's just a kid. He don't mean no harm."

In fact the young man reminded him of the too many boys who'd served under him, and never came back, or if they came back, came back so different, so mangled, it would have been easier on them if they hadn't come back at all.

"You should be happy, Earl. I can tell, you're not."

"I'm fine," he said, feeling a sudden need for another gigantic blast of bourbon. "I just need to go to the bathroom. Do you suppose they have them in a fine place like this?"

"Oh, Earl, they have to. Everybody goes to the bathroom!"

A Negro servant was standing near the door, and so Earl made his inquiry and was directed through a hall and through a door. He pulled it closed behind him, snapped the lock.

The toilet was of no use to him at all, but he unbuttoned his tunic and slid the bourbon out, and had a long swallow, fire burning down the whole way, rattling on the downward trip. It whacked him hard. He took another and it was done. Damn!

He took a washcloth, soaked it in cold water and wiped down his forehead, almost making the pain there go away for a bit, but not quite. When he hung the washrag up, the pain returned. He dropped the flask into the wastebasket.

Then he reached around and pulled out his .45 automatic.

I carried this here gun on Iwo Jima and before that on Tarawa and Guadalcanal and Saipan and Tinian. He'd done some killing with it too, but more with his tommy gun. Still, the gun was just a solid piece on his belt that somehow kept him sane. The gun, for him, wasn't a part of death, it was a piece of life. Without the gun, you were helpless.

This one, sleek, with brown plastic grips and nubby little sights, was loaded. With a strong thumb, he drew back the hammer till it clicked. He looked at himself in the mirror: the Marine hero, with the medal around his neck, the love of his country, the affection of his wife, with a full life ahead of him in the glamorous modern 1940s!

He put the gun against his temple and his finger caressed the trigger. It would take so little and he could just be with the only men he cared about or could feel love for, who were most of them resting under crosses on shithole islands nobody ever heard of and would soon forget.

"Earl," came Junie's voice. "Earl, the car is here. Come on now, we have to go."

Earl decocked the automatic, slipped it back into his belt, pulled the tunic tight over it, buttoned up and walked out.

CHAPTER

2

They walked out to the car in the West Portico of the White House.

"Your last official duty as a United States Marine," said the young captain, who seemed a good enough kid. "You should be very proud. You accomplished so much. I should salute you, First Sergeant. You shouldn't salute me."

"Son, don't you worry about it," Earl said. "You'll git your chance, if I know the world."

They reached the car, an olive-drab Ford driven by a PFC.

The captain opened the door for Earl and Junie.

Suddenly Earl was seized with a powerful feeling. When he got in the car, the door slammed shut, then it was all over, forever—that part of his life. A new part would start, and where it would lead he had no idea. He was not a man without fear—he'd lived with fear every day for three years in the Pacific—but the fear he felt now was different. It wasn't a fear that threatened to overwhelm you suddenly, to drive you into panic, into letting your people down, that sometimes came under intense fire. It was deeper; it was fear down in the bones or even the soul, it was the fear of the lost. It came from far away, a long time ago.

He shook his head. The air was oppressive, like the air of the islands. The huge wedding cake of the White House office building rose on the left; around, the green grass and trees moldered in the heat. Beyond the gate, black fleets of cars rolled up and down Pennsylvania.

Earl grabbed Junie. He held her hard and kissed her harder.

"I love you," he said. "I really, truly do. You are the best goddamn thing ever happened to me."

She looked at him with surprise, her lipstick smeared.

"I can't drive back," he said. "I just can't. Not now. I don't feel very good. Tell the kid. I'll see you tonight in the room, before we leave for the train."

"Earl. You'll be drinking again."

"Don't you worry about nothing," he said with fake cheerfulness. "I'm going to take care of everything."

If there was pain on her face, he didn't pause to note it. He turned, reached to his neck and removed the beribboned medal, wadded it and stuffed it in his pocket. He reached the street, turned to the left and was soon among the anonymous crowds of a hot Washington late afternoon.

REDS KILL 4 MARINES IN CHINA, a headline on the *Star* screamed.

Nobody cared.

"UNTOLD MILLIONS" LOST IN WAR FRAUD the *Times Herald* roared.

Nobody paid any attention.

NATS DROP TWO yelled the *Daily News*.

OPA OKS 11% PRICE HIKE announced the *Post.*

Earl pushed his way through it all, among anonymous men in straw fedoras and tan suits and women in flower print dresses with their own huge hats. Everybody seemed so colorful. In his years in the Marine Corps he had adjusted to a basically monochromatic universe: OD and khaki and that was it. Yet America was awaking from its long commitment to wartime austerity, the windows were suddenly full of goods, you could buy gas again, makeup on the women was expected, and the men wore gay yellow ties against their white shirts, as if to speak to a springtime of hope.

The medals on Earl's chest and the darkness of his deep blue tunic excited no attention; everybody was familiar with uniforms and the medals meant little. They'd seen heroes. Many of them were heroes. He joined their anonymity, just another nobody meandering up Connecticut toward who knows what. Soon enough he came to a splurge of freedom, which was Farragut Square, with its trees, its benches, its stern admiral staring toward the White House. Pigeons sat and shat upon the naval officer and young men and women sat on the park benches, talking of love and great hopes for tomorrow.

A low growl reached the park, and people looked up, pointing.

"Jets!"

A formation of the miracle planes flew high overhead, southwest to northeast, each of the four trailing a white feathery contrail, the sunlight flashing off the sleek silver fuselages.

Earl had no idea what specific type of plane they were and found the concept of a silver airplane fairly ridiculous. In the Pacific, the Japs would zero a bright gleamy bird like that in a second, and bring it down. Planes were mottled brown or sea-blue, because they didn't want you seeing them until they saw you. They weren't miracles at all, but beaten-up machines for war, and there were never enough of them around. But these three P-whatevers blazed overhead like darts, trailing a wall of sound, pulling America toward something new. Pretty soon, it was said, they'd be actually going faster than sound.

"Bet you wish you had them babies with you in Berlin," a smiling bald guy said to him. "You'd have cooked Hitler's ass but good, right, Sarge?"

"That's right," said Earl.

He walked ahead, the echo of the jets still trembling in his ear. The walls of the city closed in around him, and the next exhibit in the freak show of civilian life was something in a window just ahead, which had drawn a crowd. It appeared to be a movie for free streaming out of a circle atop a big radio. On its blue-gray screen a puppet jigged this way and that.

"Look at that, sir," said a Negro woman in a big old hat with roses on it and a veil, "that's the television. It's radio with pictures."

"Don't that beat all?" said Earl.

"Yes sir," she said. "They say we-all goin' own one, and see picture shows in our own homes. Won't have no reason to go out to the movies no more. You can just stay home for the picture show. They goin' show the games there too, you know, the baseball and that like. Though who'd stay home to see the Senators, I declare I don't know."

"Well, ma'am," he said, "the president himself told me it's just going to git better and better."

"Well, maybe so. Wish my Billy was here to see it."

"I'm sorry, ma'am. The war?"

"Yes sir. Someplace in Italy. He wasn't no hero, like you, he didn't win no medals or nothing. He was only a hospital orderly. But he got kilt just the same. They said it was a land mine."

"I am very sorry, ma'am."

"Hope you kilt a lot of them Germans."

"No, ma'am, I did fight the Japanese, and I had to kill some of them."

"Same thing," she said bitterly, then forced a broken smile upon him, and walked away.

Billy's death on some faraway Neapolitan byway stayed with Earl. Billy was part of the great adventure, one of the hundreds of thousands who'd died. Now, who cared? Not with jet planes and the television. It was all going away.

Get your mind off it, he told himself.

He was feeling too much again. He needed a drink.

He walked along until he found stairs that led downward, which he followed into a dark bar. It was mostly empty and he bellied up to the edge, feeling the coolness of the air.

A jukebox blared.

It was that happy one about going for a ride on the Atchison, Topeka and the Santa Fe. That damn Judy sounded like she was about to bust a gut with pleasure. A train ride. A big old fancy train ride.

> Back in Ohio where I come from
> I've done a lot of dreamin' and I've traveled some,
> But I never thought I'd see the day
> When I ever took a ride on the Santa Fe.

The only trains he remembered took him to wars or worse. Now he had a few hours that would take him back to a train ride to—well, to who knew what?

"Poison, Sarge? Name it, and it's yours. One drink, on me for the USMC. Made a man out of my son. Killed him, but made a man out of him."

It was the bartender.

"Sorry about your boy," said Earl, confronting another dead man.

"Nah. Only good thing he ever did was stand up to the Japs at Okinawa. You there?"

"Missed that one."

"Well, he was a bad kid, but he had one good day in his life, when he didn't run from the goddamned Japs. Marines taught him that. I never could. God bless the Marines. What'll it be?"

"You carry Boone County?"

"Never heard of it."

"Must just be an Arkansas liquor. Okay, I'll try that Jim Beam. With a bit of water. Some ice."

"Choo choo ch'boogie," said the barkeep, mixing and serving the drink. "Here's your train, right on time."

Earl took a powerful sip, feeling the muted whack of the booze. It made his fears and his doubts vanish. He felt now he was the equal of the world.

"No, he wasn't no good," said the bartender. "Don't know why he was such a yellow kid. I rode him but good, but he ran from everything. How he ended up in—"

"Mister," said Earl, "I much appreciate this here free drink. But if you say a Marine who stood and fought on Okinawa was no good one more time, I'm going to jump over this bar and make you eat this glass, then the bar, then all the stools."

The bartender, a very big man, looked at him, and read the dark willingness to issue endless violence in Earl's eyes, and swallowed. Earl was a big man too, made almost of leather from his long hard years under a Pacific sun. He was dark and glowery, with leathery pouches under his eyes from too much worry, but he had a bull's neck and those eyes had the NCO's ability to look through you and pin you to the wall behind. His jet-black hair was close-cropped but stood up like barbs of wire on his skull. Under his tunic, his rangy body, though full of holes, was well packed with lean muscle. His veins stood out. His voice didn't speak so much as rumble or roar along, like the Santa Fe. Heated up, he would be a fearsome sight and then some. When he spoke in a certain tone, all men listened, as did the bartender now.

The bartender stepped back a bit.

"Look, here's a twenty," Earl said, peeling off his last big bill. "You put the bottle on the bar, then you go be with some other folks. You can tell them how bad your son was. You can't say it to me."

The bottle came; the bartender disappeared.

. . .

Earl worked on the bottle; the bottle worked on Earl. By the time it was a third gone, he was happy: he had forgotten who he was and why he was there. But by the time he reached the halfway point again, he remembered.

Choo choo ch'boogie, came another train song off the juke, driving rhythms, so full of cheer and hope it made him shiver.

> I just love the rhythm
> of the clickety-clack
> Take me right back
> to the track, Jack.

Trains again. What he remembered about trains was they took him to ships and then the ships took him out into the sea.

He remembered the 'Canal, that time it got to hand-to-hand, and he and his young boys on the ridge were fighting the Japs with entrenching tools and knives and rocks and rifle butts. There was no ammo because the planes hadn't come in weeks. The Japs were crazy then; they came in waves, one after the other, knowing the Marines were low on ammo, and just traded lives for ammo until the ammo was gone. Then it was throat-and-skull time, an exertion so total it left you dead or, if you made it through, sick at yourself for the men whose heads you'd split open, or whose bellies you ripped out, or who you'd kicked to death. And you looked around and saw your own people, just as morally destroyed. What you did for something called your country that night! How you killed! How you gave your soul up!

Then, Tarawa. Maybe the worst single moment of the whole thing: oh, that walk in was a bitch. There was no place to go. The bullets splashed through the water like little kids in an Arkansas lake, everywhere. Tracers looped low overhead, like ropes of light, flickery and soft. You were so low in the water you couldn't see the land or your own ships behind you. You were wet and cold and tired and if you slipped you could drown; your legs turned to lead and ice but if you stopped you died and if you went on you died. You tried to keep your people together, keep them moving, keep them believing. But all around you, men just disappeared until it seemed you were alone on the watery surface of the planet and the Japs were a nation hell-bent on one sole thing: killing you.

Earl blinked away a shudder, took another pure gulp of this here Jim Beam, as it was called. Fine stuff. He looked at his watch. He had a trip upcoming on the Atchison, Topeka and the Santa Fe, but where it would take him and why, he couldn't remember.

Iwo, in the bunker. That he would never forget.

He killed his way along Charlie-Dog. His flamethrower people hadn't made it. The captain was hit. There was no cover, because you couldn't dig into the ash; it just caved in on you. He jumped into a nest, hosed it with his tommy. The bullets flew and bit into the Japs. It blew them up, tore them apart. Earl had blood on his face, Jap blood. But he kept going, nest to nest, shooting up the subsidiary positions until he'd finally killed his way to the main blockhouse.

It was secured from within. On top of that he had no weapon, as the tommy had become so fouled with ash and blood it had given up. He could hear the Nambus working from the other side of the block-house.

He raced back to the nest he'd just cleared, threw a Jap aside and pulled three grenades off his belt. The Jap things, you banged them to arm them. He grabbed them, ran to the metal blockhouse door, banged them hard and dumped them. He was back dragging the Nambu out from under more dead Japs when the triple concussion came.

The next part was hard to remember, but also hard to forget. He was in the blockhouse. Give this to the Japs, goddamn were they soldiers. They fought to the end, pouring fire out off Charlie-Dog, killing every moving thing they saw. They would die to kill: that was their code. Earl jumped from room to room, or rather chamber to chamber, for the place had a low, dark insect-nest quality to it, and it stunk: shit, blood, food, fear, sweat, old socks, rot, rice. He jumped into a chamber and hosed it down. But he didn't know the Nambu was loaded up with tracers.

When he fired in the smoky darkness, the blue-white tracers tore through all, struck hard surfaces and bounced and bounced again, crazed and jagged. Each squirt on the trigger unleashed a kind of neon structure of pure light, blue-gray, flickery, flung out to embrace the Japs, far more power with the careening bullets than he'd have thought possible. It was like making lightning.

He raced from chamber to chamber, pausing to change magazines on the hot thing in his hands. Odd gun: the mag locked in top, not on the bottom where it would make some sense. It was no BAR; only guys who dreamed up samurai swords and kamikaze planes and human-wave attacks would have cooked up such a silly, junky thing. It even looked slant-eyed. But it worked, always.

In the last room, they waited for him with the predator's eerie calm-ness. They were out of ammo. He didn't care. They didn't care. What happened they expected, as did he. They faced him; one had a sword out and high, but no room to maneuver in what amounted to a sewer tunnel, illuminated by a gun slit. He sprayed them with light and they danced as their own 6.5s tore through them. When they were down, he changed magazines, sprayed them again, unleashing the lightning. Then he threw the hot little machine gun away.

Earl looked at what he had wrought: a massacre. It was too easy. The Japs were committed elsewhere, their eardrums blown out by the shelling, and the gunfire, their sense of duty absolute. He merely exe-cuted them in a sleet of fiery light. He heard a moan from the last chamber and thought: one is alive. But then he heard a clank, mean-ing that a grenade had been primed, so out he spilled, maybe a tenth of a second before the detonation which shredded the last of the wounded.

He returned to the surface, clambering for breath. Men from his platoon had made it up Charlie-Dog now that the blockhouse guns were silenced but if they spoke to him, he didn't hear, for his ears too were temporarily ruined by the ringing.

"Burn it out," he screamed.

One of the flamethrower teams disinfected the blockhouse with a cleansing two-thousand-degree ray of pure heat; the radiance drove them all back.

The captain was saying, Goddamn he never saw nothing like it, ex-cept the captain was from something called Yale and so what he said in that odd little-girl voice of his was "I don't believe I have ever seen a more splendid example of field-expedient aggression." Or something like that.

Earl and his bottle took one more dance. It hit him again, and drove the thoughts out of his head, but then the thoughts came back again.

What was bothersome was the faces. They were vanishing. In one melancholy afternoon in the hospital on Guam after the bad wound on Iwo, he'd done the arithmetic, learned its savage truth.

He had been a sergeant in the Second Marines, then a platoon sergeant also in the Second, and the company gunny sergeant in the Second. When the new Fifth Marine Division was organized in September 1944, he'd been assigned to its 28th Regiment and promoted to first sergeant of Able Company. He had a total of 418 young Marines under him and had been directly responsible to three lieutenants, a captain and finally a major. Of those, 229 had been killed outright. The rest had been wounded, including himself, seven times, three times savagely. None of the officers survived. Of his NCO friends with whom he served at the Marine Detachment in Panama on December 7, 1941, he was the only survivor. Of the company professionals, including officers, from that day, he was the only survivor. Of his first platoon in the Second Marines, on Guadalcanal, he was one of ten survivors; of his company that went into the water off Tarawa, 232 men, he was one of thirty-three survivors; of his company of 216 men that hit the black-ash beach at Iwo, he was one of 111 survivors, but he had no idea how many of them had been wounded seriously. On Tinian and Saipan the numbers were a little better, but only by the standards of the Pacific war.

He knew he should not be alive, not by any law of math, and that the medals he had been awarded were much more for the brute violation of the numbers than for any kind of heroism. Manila John Basilone, the bravest man he ever knew, won the Medal of Honor on a ridge on the 'Canal, stopping a Jap attack with a .30 water-cooled and a fighting spirit and nothing else; he made a bond tour, became a celebrity, married a pretty gal, and was blown to pieces in the black ash of Iwo that first day.

Across from the bar Earl saw himself in a mirror, his eyes black as the black in floodwaters as they rise and there's no high ground left. His cheeks were drawn, and his gray lips muttered madly. He swallowed, blinked, and opened his eyes to see himself again. He saw an empty man, a man so tired and lost he hardly was worth the oxygen he consumed, or the bourbon he drank.

He felt so unworthy.

You ain't no damned good, his father's voice reached him, and he was in agreement with the old man.

I ain't no damned good. Any one of those men was better than me. Why in hell ain't I with them?

Earl took another whack on the bourbon, finished it, looked at his watch. His vision was so blurry he couldn't read it, but given the amount of alcohol he'd drunk, he'd probably missed the train back to Fort Smith, and there'd be all kinds of hell to pay.

He stood up uncertainly, and walked across the bar, and found the men's room. He went in, pulled the door shut, locked the door, took a leak, took out his .45 and thumbed back the hammer.

At no time in the war did he feel as disconsolate as he did now. It wasn't right that he was alive and so many others were dead, and that he had a medal in his pocket that certified him as a HE-RO and they had nothing but white crosses on islands no one would ever visit and would soon forget.

He put the pistol to his temple, felt its pressure, circular. His finger touched the trigger, then pressed it.

The gun didn't fire.

It shivered as it snapped, the small vibration of a hammer falling on a firing pin that leaped forward to strike nothingness. He looked at it, then slipped the slide back a notch, saw that the chamber was empty. He removed the magazine, and found six .45 cartridges, but someone had very carefully taken out the mag and ejected the chambered shell, then replaced the mag. He *knew* he'd loaded it that morning.

Did she do it? She didn't know nothing about guns. Who did it? Maybe he forgot to chamber it? What the hell was going on?

He reloaded, this time threw the slide to fill the chamber and cock it, ease the hammer back to its seating.

He stuffed the gun back in his belt, drew his tunic tight, and unlocked the door.

The lobby of the Carlton Hotel was bright and full of swirling beauty. The light seemed to dance, as if the walls were made of glass. Maybe the VJ Day party was still going on. It was full of pretty young women and their swains, all of them so excited about television and jet planes they could hardly stand it.

Earl slipped through the revelers; everyone was in a tuxedo or a formal gown and gay young things rushed this way and that, hungry for tomorrow to get here.

The boys all were shaven and looked soft; he knew he shouldn't hate them, but he did, and he let that hatred bore through his blur and he felt he needed another drink. Not a fifth of bourbon, but just something to make the pain in his head go away, like a whiskey sour or a gin and tonic or a mint julep. He glanced at his Hamilton and discovered to his relief that he hadn't missed the train; it wasn't yet 7:00. He had time for—

"Sergeant Swagger?"

He turned.

Two men stood beside him. One was a handsome, polished charmer, with a gloss of black hair and movie star teeth, somewhere in his thirties. The other was much older, a gloomy bag of a man, with a sad leathery face and a slow way of moving. He had long arms that his suit only partially disguised and the most gigantic hands Earl had ever seen on a man. His fedora was pushed back carelessly, and his white shirt was gray and spotted. But his eyes were so wary and quick they made Earl think of Howlin' Mad Smith's, or some other old, combat-hard Marine. Earl saw a strap across his chest, under the tie, that indicated the presence of a shoulder holster and from the strain it showed, he knew it carried a big gun.

"Sergeant Swagger," said the first, in tones that Earl then related to his native state, "we've been waiting here for you. Your wife is upstairs packing. She said you'd be along directly."

"What is all this, sir?" said Earl.

"Sergeant Swagger, we've come to discuss a job."

"A job? I got a job. I work in a goddamned sawmill."

"No, a job in law enforcement."

"Who the hell are you?"

"My name is Fred C. Becker and a week ago I won a special election as prosecuting attorney for Garland County, Arkansas."

"Hot Springs?" said Earl. "Now what would you want with me?"

"Hot Springs is the wildest town in America. We have gamblers, we have gunmen, we have whores, we have more crooks than you can shake a stick at and many of them are wearing uniforms and carrying guns. All run by New York mobsters. Well, sir, I'm going to clean up Sodom and Gomorrah and I'm looking for a good man. Everyone I talk to says you're the best."

CHAPTER

3

The city's tallest skyscraper was a spire of art deco, byzantine, glamorous, bespeaking the decadent pleasures of an empire. And from the apartment on the top floor, the empire was ruled.

"It's very New York, eh? I mean, really, one must agree. It's *very* New York," our proud host said to his number-one guest.

"You can say that again," said the guest.

They were quite a pair. One, with the English accent, was in his mid-fifties, five foot ten, solid beef, with a handsome swarthy face. That was our host. He wore an elegantly fitted white dinner jacket, with a rose cummerbund. It fit him like a coating of thick cream poured by a delighted milkmaid. A carnation sparkled in his lapel. His hair was slicked back, and he smoked a cigarette in a holder. He wore a dapper little mustache, just a smudge of one, to suggest not merely masculinity but a certain savoir faire in affairs of business and, as well, the heart. In his other hand, he held a thin-stemmed martini glass. Onyx cuff links gleamed from his cuffs.

"Me," said the other, "now I'm not saying nothing against this, you understand. It's beautiful. It's very beautiful. But I'm a homier guy. I got a place that's what they call Tudor. It looks like a king from your country could have lived there."

"Yes, old man. I know the style. Quite appropriate, I would say. It's actually named for a king's family."

"Yeah," said the guest, "that's me all the way. A real fucking king." He smiled, showing a blast of white teeth.

He was ruddier. He glowed with animal vitality. He wore expertly fitted clothes too, but of a sportier nature, a creamy linen sport coat over a crisp blue oxford shirt, open at the collar. He wore mohair slacks and dazzlingly white bucks. An ascot, a little burst of burgundy silk, completed the ensemble, and in his strong fingers, he clutched a fine Cubano.

"But this is okay," he said again. "It's real swank." He was shorter, more muscular, tanner, more athletic. He had big hands, wide shoulders, a linebacker's pug body. His eyes were especially vivid, as he gobbled the room up. He was not stupid, but he was not really smart either.

"Do you know who did it?" asked his host.

"Did it?"

"The decor. You hire a decorator. You just don't do it yourself. One could never come close."

"Oh," said the sport. "Yeah, a decorator."

"Donald Deskey. The same fellow who did the interiors at Radio City Music Hall. Hence, the wood, the high gloss, the art moderne, the streamline. Why, Cole Porter would be comfortable here."

He gestured with his cigarette holder, and his apartment gleamed before him, cherrywood walls dusky in the glow of muted golden lighting from torchères and sconces, black-lacquered furniture supported by struts of gleaming metal that could have been pried off the *20th Century Limited*. Silk-brocaded drapes billowed in the breeze from the terrace door, and outside the lights of the city sparkled, infinitely tempting.

In the corner of the cherrywood cathedral, a small band played, and a Negro singer with marcelled hair crooned into a microphone. It was up-tempo, smooth as silk, very seductive, about the glories of Route 66 that you'd encounter on the way to Califor-ni-ay. Next to them, another Negro served drinks, martinis mostly, but the odd bourbon or Scotch, to a fast, glamorous crowd. The movie star Dick Powell was there, a craggily handsome head mounted upon a spindly body, a man who beamed beauty and good feeling, and his truly beautiful wife, a woman so unusually comely that in any normal room she would stop traffic. But not this room. Powell's screen girlfriend June Allyson stood off to a side, a small woman, almost perfectly configured but seeming more like a kewpie doll, with her fetching freckles and her spray of blond hair and her crinkly blue eyes.

The other specimens were not so perfect. One was the writer John P. Marquand, surrounded by some admiring fans, all of them exquisitely turned out. Another was the football star Bob Waterford, a gigantically muscular man with a thick mane of hair. He was so big he looked as though he could play without pads. Walter Winchell was expected later. Mickey Rooney was also rumored to be planning an appearance, although with the Mick, one could never be too sure. The Mick burned legendarily hard at both ends of the candle, and he kept to his own schedule. That was the Mick. Then there were the usual assorted politicos, gambling figures and their well-turned-out, even high-bred women.

But the center of attention was another beautiful woman. Her shoulders, pale in the golden light, yielded to the hint of breasts so soft and pillowy that an army could find comfort there, and were cupped as if for display by the precision of her gown, just at the crucial point, where there was but a gossamer of material between her nipples and the rest of the world. She had almost no waist at all, a tiny, insect's thing. Her ample hips were rounded and her buttocks especially firm. The red taffeta evening gown she wore showed all this off, but it was cut to reveal a hint of her shapely legs, made muscular and taut by the extreme rake of her high heels. Her face, however, was the main attraction: it was smart, but not intellectual, say rather cunning. Her features were delicate, except for that vulgar, big, luscious mouth. Her eyes were blue, her skin so pale and creamy it made everyone ache and her hair genuine auburn, like fire from a forbidden dream, a rapture of hair.

"Hi, babe," called the Sporty Guest from across the room, for she was with him.

She ignored him and continued to jiggle ever so seductively to the music, as if in a dreamworld of rhythm. Her dance partner smiled nervously at the boyfriend and Our Host. He was a small, pale boy, weirdly beautiful, not really a good dancer and not really dancing with the woman at all, but merely validating her performance by removing it from the arena of sheer vanity. He had thin blond hair; his name was Alan Ladd, and he was in pictures too.

"I better watch her," said the sport to our host, "she may end up shtupping that pretty boy. You never know with her."

"Don't worry about Alan," said Our Host, who knew such things. "It's not, as one would say, on Alan's dance card, eh, old man? No, worry instead about the blackies. They are highly sexualized. Believe me, I know. I once owned a club in Harlem. They like to give the white women some juju-weed, and when they're all dazed, give them the African man-root, all twelve inches of it. Once the white ones taste that pleasure, they're ruined for white men. I've seen it happen."

"Nah," said the sport. "Virginia's a bitch but she knows if she fucks a *schvartzer* I'll kick her ass all the way back to Alabama."

Our Host aspired to British sophistication in all things, and made a slight face at this vulgarity. But, unfazed and in his own mind rather heroic, he kept on.

"Ben," he said. "Ben, I must show you something."

He took his younger compere through the party, nodding politically at this one and that one, touching a hand, giving a kiss, pausing for an introduction, well aware of the mysterious glamour he possessed, and led his guest to an alcove.

"Uh, I don't get it," said Ben.

"It's a painting."

"I understand that it's a painting. Why is it all square and brown? It looks like Newark with a tree."

"I assure you, Ben, that our friend Monsieur Braque has never seen Newark."

"You couldn't tell that from the painting. Looks like he was *born* there."

"Ben, try to *feel* it. He's saying something. Use your imagination. As I say, one must *feel* it."

Ben's handsome face knitted up as if in concentration, but he appeared to feel nothing. The painting, entitled *Houses at L'Estaque,* depicted a cityscape in muted brown, the dwellings twisted askew to the right, a crude tree stuck in the left foreground but the laws of perspective broken savagely. When Our Host looked at it, he did feel something: the money he'd spent to obtain it.

"It's the finest work of early Cubism in this hemisphere," he said. "Painted in 1908. Note the geometric severity, the lack of a central vanishing point. It predates Picasso, whom it influenced. It cost me $75,000."

"Wow," said Ben. "You must be doing okay."

"I'm telling you, Ben, this *is* the business to be in. You cannot lose. It's all here and the rule of numbers says over the long haul each day is a profitable day, each year a profitable year. It just goes on and on and on, and nobody has to get killed or blown up and sent for a swim with the fishies of the East River."

"Maybe so," said Ben.

"Come, come, look out from the terrace. At night, it is so impressive."

"Sure," said Ben.

Our host snapped his fingers and instantly black men appeared, one with a new martini and the other with a long, thick Cuban cigar, already trimmed, and a gold lighter.

"Light it, sir?"

"No, Ralph, I have told you that you don't hold the lighter right. I have to light it myself if I want it done correctly."

The Negroes disappeared silently, and the two men slipped between the curtains and out into the sultry night.

Pigeons cooed.

"The birds. Still with the birds, eh, Owney?" said Ben.

"I got to like them during Prohibition. A pigeon will never rat you out, let me tell you, old man."

The pigeons, immaculately kept in a rack of cages against one wall, cooed and shifted in the dark.

Owney downed his martini with a single gulp, set the glass on a table, and went over to the cages. He opened one, reached in and took out one bird, which he held close to his face, as he stroked its sleek head with his chin.

"Such a darling," he said. "Such a baby girl. So sweet. Yes, such a baby girl."

Then he put the pigeon back in the cage, plucked the cigar out of his pocket, and expertly lit it, scorching the shaft first, then rolling the end through the flame, then finally drawing the smoke through the thing fully, letting it bloom and swell, sensing each nuance of taste, finally expelling a blast of heavy gray smoke, which the breeze took and distributed over midtown.

"Now come, look," he said, escorting the younger man to the edge of the terrace.

The two stood. Behind came the tinkle of the jazz, the sounds of laughter, the clink of glasses and ice.

Before them curved a great white way.

Lights beamed upward, filling the sky with illumination. Along the broad way, crowds hustled and milled, too far to be made out from this altitude, but in their masses recognizable, a great, slithering sea of humanity. The traffic had slowed to a stop, and cops worked desperately to unsnarl it. Beeps and honks rose with the exhaust and the occasional squeal of tires. Along the great street, it seemed the whole world had come to gawk at the drama of the place, and the crowd seemed an organism its own self, rushing for one or another of the available pleasures.

"Really, it's a good place," Owney said. "It works, it hums, everybody's happy. It's a machine."

"Owney," said Ben, "you've done a great job here. Everybody says so. Owney Maddox, he runs a great town. No other town runs like Owney's town. Everybody's happy in Owney's town, there's plenty of dough in Owney's town. Owney, he's the goddamn king."

"I'm very proud of what I've built," said Owney Maddox, of his town, which was Hot Springs, Arkansas, and of the grand boulevard of casinos, nightclubs, whorehouses and bathhouses that lined it, Central Avenue, which curved beneath his penthouse on the sixteenth and highest floor of the Medical Arts Building.

"Yeah, a fellow could learn a goddamn thing or two," said his guest, Benjamin "Bugsy" Siegel, of Los Angeles, California, and the organized crime confederation that had yet to be named by its investigators but was known by its members, in the year 1946, simply as Our Thing—to those of them that were Sicilian, "Cosa Nostra."

CHAPTER

4

The bar of the Carlton was one of those rooms that made Earl immediately uneasy. It was full of shapes that had no place in nature, mainly circular ones—round, inscribed mirrors, a round cocktail bar, round little tables, rounded chairs with bold striping. It was the kind of a bar you'd expect on a rocket ship to the moon or Mars.

It mi-IGHT as we-ELL be spa-RING

some pretty boy sang over the radio, getting a strange upward twist into words where no such thing could logically be expected. Everyone was young, exuberant, excited, full of life. Atop the prow that lay behind the bar, stocked with enough bottles to besot a division, a young goddess and her pet fawn pranced. She was sculpturally frozen in Bakelite, the struts of her ribs showing, the struts of the fawn's ribs, all of it gleamy, steamy and wet, from the spray of water, somehow rigged to float across her tiny, perky breasts.

"Hey, look at that," said the older man. "Don't that beat a World's Fair in St. Louie?"

Earl hardly glanced at the thing. It seemed wrong. The sculpture was naked. He was drunk. The world was young. He was old.

The three scooted to the last table in a line, nestled into the corner, under a mirror clouded with inscribed images of grapes, dogs and women. It was very strange. Nothing like this on Iwo.

A girl came; Becker took a martini, the old man a soda water and Earl his regular poison, the Jim Beam he'd grown so fond of.

"You don't drink, sir?" he asked the older man.

"No more," said the fellow. "No more."

"Anyhow," said Becker, returning to business, "I just won a special election that we got mandated because we proved that the poll tax was unjustly administered by the city administration. We being myself and twelve other young men, all of us veterans with overseas duty and a sense of mission. As of next Tuesday, I become the prosecuting attorney of Garland County. But of the twelve, I was the only one to win. So until the next election, in the late fall, let me tell you where that leaves me. Out on a limb. Way, way out."

Earl appraised him. He was so handsome a man, so confident. In fact, he was oddly mated with the sad-sack old teetotaler with the watchful eyes and the big hands. Who were they? What did they want?

"So I'm in a tough situation," Becker continued. "I'm getting death threats, my wife is being shadowed, it's getting ugly down there. Hot Springs. Not a happy place. Totally corrupt. It's run by an old gasbag mayor and a judge, but you can forget about them. The real power is a New York mobster named Owney Maddox who's got big-money boys behind him. They own everything, they have a piece of all the pies."

"I still don't see where Earl Swagger fits in."

"Well, what I'm getting at, Sergeant, is that Owney Maddox doesn't want anybody messing with his empire. But that's what I'm sworn to do."

"You must think I'd be a bodyguard," Earl said. "But I ain't no bodyguard. Wouldn't know the first thing about that line of work."

"No, Sergeant, that's not it. In order to survive, I have to attack. If I'm on the defensive it all goes away. We have a chance, a window in time, in which we can take Hot Springs back. They're complacent now, they don't fear me because the rest of the slate lost. What can one man do, they think. If we move aggressively, we can do it. We have to blitz them now."

"I ain't no reformer."

"But you know Hot Springs. Your daddy was killed there in 1942 while you were off fighting the Japanese."

"You been lookin' into me?" Earl said narrowly. He wasn't sure he liked this at all. But then this man was the law, after all, by formal election.

"We made some inquiries," said the old man.

"Well, then you learned it wasn't Hot Springs. It was a hill town way outside of Hot Springs, closer to his home territory. Mount Ida, it was called. And I wasn't fighting the Japs yet. I was on a train with two thousand other suckers pulling cross-country to begin the boat ride out to the 'Canal. And I don't know Hot Springs. My daddy would never take us. It was eighty miles to the east, over bad roads. And it was the devil's town. My daddy was a Baptist down to his toes, hellfire and damnation. If I'd gone to Hot Springs, he'd a-whipped me till I was dead."

"Yes, well," said Becker, running hard into Earl's stubbornness, which on some accounts just took him over, for no good reason.

Earl took another hit on the bourbon, just a taste, because he didn't want his brain more scrambled. But he just didn't get a good feeling about Becker. He glanced at his Hamilton. It was getting near to 7:30. Soon he had to go. Where were these fellows taking him?

He looked at the silent old man next to Becker. What was familiar about him?

"Well, Sergeant—"

But Earl stared at the old man, and then blurted, "Excuse me, sir, I don't know if I caught your name."

"Parker," said the old man. "D. A. Parker."

And that too had a ring somehow.

"You wouldn't be related to—nah."

"Who?"

"You wouldn't be related to that FBI agent that shot it out with all them Johnnies in the '30s. Baby Face Nelson, John Dillinger, Ma Barker, Bonnie and Clyde. Went gun-to-gun with the bad boys of the Depression. Famous, for a while. An American hero."

"I ain't related to that D. A. Parker one damned bit," said the old man. "I *am* him."

"D. A. Parker!"

"Yes, that's me. I'm not with the Bureau no more. And, no, I never shot it out with Johnny Dillinger, though I come close once or twice. I had nothing to do with Bonnie and Clyde. Them was Texas Rangers operating on the fly in Louisiana that caught up with that set of bad apples and did a day's worth of fine work. I tracked Ma and her boy Freddie to Floriday, but I don't think it was my burst that sent Ma to her grave. We believe she killed her own self. I did put eleven rounds into Freddie, and that finished his hash forever. And I did run into the Baby Face twice. We exchanged shots. I still carry not only a .45 bullet that he put into my leg, but the .45 he put it in there with."

He leaned forward, letting his coat slide open. Earl looked and saw a stag-gripped .45, with a bigger set of sights welded into the slide. The gun hung close to D.A.'s body in a complicated leather shoulder holster and harness, well worn. It was even dangerously cocked, sure sign of a real *pistolero.*

"Anyhow, Swagger," said Becker, trying to regain control of the conversation, "what we're going to do is raid."

"Raid?"

"That's it. I'm setting up a special unit. It's young, unmarried or widowed officers from outside of Arkansas, because I can't have them being tainted by the state's corruption, or having their families hunted. This unit will report only to me, and it won't be part of any police force, it won't be set up within a chain of command or anything. We will hit casinos, whorehouses, sports books, anyplace the mob is running, high-class or low. We will be very well armed. We will squeeze them. That's the point: to squeeze them until they feel it and have to shut down."

Becker spoke as if he were quoting a speech, and Earl knew right away that only a part of what the young man planned was for the citizens of Hot Springs. It would be especially for one particular citizen of Hot Springs, namely Fred Becker.

"Sounds like you'll need a lot of firepower," said Earl.

"We do," said D.A. "I have managed to horse-trade for six 1928 Thompsons. Three BARs. Some carbines. And, since I spent the last four years working for Colt, I talked a deal up so we get a deal on eighteen brand-new National Match .45s. Plus we have over fifty thousand rounds of ammunition stored down at the Red River Army Depot, where we'll train for a while. Twelve men, myself, and the only thing we lack is a sergeant."

"I see," said Earl.

"We need a trainer," said Becker.

"I'm too old, Earl," said D.A. "I been thinking about this for a lot of years. I've been on raids not only in the FBI but in the Oklahoma City Police Department before then. I been in twenty-eight gunfights and been shot four times. I've killed eighteen men. So what I know, I learned the hard way: it's my opinion that when it comes to gun work, the American policeman ain't got a chance, because he ain't well enough trained. So what I mean to do is put together a professional, well-trained raid team. Lots of teamwork, total backup, rehearsal, preparation, train, train, train. I include the FBI, especially now, when all the old gunfighters have been booted out. When the Baby Face went down, he took two fine young FBI agents with him, because they weren't well enough trained to deal with someone as violent and crazy-goddamn-bull-goose-brave as him. Lord, I wish I'd been there that day. They put seventeen bullets into him and he kept coming and killed them both. He was a piece of work. So I want this unit trained, goddamn it, trained to the eyebrows. But I need someone who can ramrod 'em. I get to be the Old Man. I get to be wise and calm. But I need a 100 percent kick-ass piece of gristle and guts to whip their asses into shape, to beat the lessons into them. I need someone who ain't afraid of being hated, because being hated is part of the job. I need someone who's faced armed men and shot 'em dead. I need a goddamned 100 percent hero. Now, do you see what this has to do with Earl Swagger?"

Earl nodded slightly.

"Earl," said D.A., "you was born for this job like no man on earth."

"So it seems," said Earl, looking around at all the bright young gay things sipping champagne, dancing the jitterbug, laughing brightly, squeezing flesh, and thinking, *Goddamn, I am home again.*

CHAPTER

5

West Virginia flowed by; or maybe it was Ohio. It was hard to tell at night, and the train rattled along forcefully. Earl sat in the private compartment watching America pass in the darkness, feeling the throb of the rails on the track. His head ached, but for the first time, after a day of heroic drinking, he felt as if he were more or less sober.

The private compartment was a last kindness from his country for one of its heroes. No lumpy seats for the Medal of Honor winner, no sitting upright, unable to sleep because the metal in the ribs still hurt and his back ached. But he wasn't drinking.

Junie slept in the lower berth. He could hear her breathing steadily. But he just sat in the leather seat before the little round table, feeling the rhythms and flowing onward toward what would be his new destiny. Then she stirred.

"Earl?"

"I thought you were asleep, honey. You should sleep some."

"I can't sleep when you can't sleep, Earl. Are you all right?"

"Yes ma'am. I'm fine."

"Earl, you were drinking, weren't you? I could smell it on you."

"I stopped for drinks while I was walking, yes. I was celebrating. I was happy. I met the president. I was at the White House. I got the big medal. I got my picture taken. Won't have many days like that."

"Earl, the medal. It was in the pocket of your uniform slacks. The ribbon got all wrinkled. I put it back in the jewelry case. You should take care of it. Someday you will give it to a son."

"Well, honey, if I ever have a son, I don't think I'll say to him, 'See what a big man your father was.' So I think if I ever have a son, I'll just let him grow up without me telling him how great I was, since I never felt great one damn day in my life."

"Earl, you are so angry these days."

"I will put it aside, I swear to you, Junie. I know this ain't been easy for you. I know I have become different than the man you married."

"That Earl was handsome and proud and he looked so beautiful in his uniform. He looked like a movie star. All the girls loved him. I fell so hard in love with him, Lord, I didn't think I'd live till sunrise. Then he asked me to dance with him. But this Earl is more human than that one. This Earl is more man, more real man. He does his work, even though he hates it, and he never yells at anyone. He's a real man, and he's there every night, and some letter won't come telling me he got killed."

"Sweetie, you are some peach. You are the best."

He leaned over in the dark and gave her a kiss.

She touched him, in a way that let him know that tonight would be a very good night for some intimacy. But he sat back.

"I have to tell you something first."

"Earl, I don't like that tone. What is it? Is it those two men who came to see you?"

"Yes, it is."

"That showboaty fellow in the nice clothes? And that sad old man. I didn't like the showboaty fellow."

"I didn't really like him either, but there you have it. Becker is his name, and he'll be important someday. He's actually an elected official, a politician. Them two fellows offered me a job."

"Did you take it?"

"It means some more money. And it means I won't get my fingers chopped off by the band saw. They'll be paying me a hundred a week. That's more than $5,000 a year before taxes. There's a life insurance plan too, plus medical benefits from the state of Arkansas, so there won't be no worrying about having enough money for a doc. They even gave me a clothing allowance. I'm supposed to buy some suits."

"But it's dangerous."

"Why would you say that?"

"I can tell it from your voice."

"Well, it could be dangerous. It probably won't be. Mainly it's training."

"Training?"

"Some boys. I'll be working with young police officers, training them in firearms usage, fire and movement, generalized tactics, maybe some judo, that sort of thing."

"Earl!"

"Yes ma'am?"

"Earl, you'll be training them for war."

"Well, not exactly, honey. It's nothing like a war. It's for raiding gambling places. This fellow is the new prosecuting attorney down in Garland."

"Hot Springs!"

"Hot Springs. Yes. He's going to try and clean up the town."

"We're moving to Hot Springs?"

Well, damn him if he didn't just let it sit there for a while. He let her enjoy it: the idea of moving out of the vets village at Camp Chaffee, maybe getting a place with a real floor instead of wood slats that were always dirty, and that had walls that went straight up to a ceiling, and didn't arch inward or rattle and leak when it rained. The refrigerator would be big, so she wouldn't have to shop every day. The shower would be indoors; there'd even be a tub. The stove would be gas.

"Maybe so," he finally said. "Maybe in a bit. We'd get a nice house, out of town, away from the commotion. It can get plenty hectic in that place."

"I'm not coming, am I, Earl?"

"No ma'am. Not at first. I have it worked out, though. You'll be fine. The paycheck will come straight to you. You can put a certain part of it in a state bank account, and I'll write checks from that for my spending money. You'll get a list of the benefits, and it won't be no time before we can move."

Junie didn't say anything. She stirred, seemed to roll over and face the bunk atop her, and when she finally settled she seemed further away.

"See, it won't work out, having you down there," he said. "Not at first. I'm going to be in Texas for a while, where we're going to train these kids, then we move up to Garland. But I ain't even going on the raids. I'm more the trainer and the sergeant. I have to ride herd on the younger fellows, just like in the Corps, that's all. And there's a security issue, or so they say, but, you know, it's just being careful."

"I can tell in your voice. You'll go on the raids. It's your nature."

"That's not the plan. They don't want a big fancy hero type like me getting shot."

"That may not be the plan, but you have a nature, and you will obey it. It's to lead other men in battle and help them and prevent them from getting hurt. That is your nature."

"They didn't say a thing about that. The reason we don't want the women down there is just some precautions. It's very corrupt in Hot Springs. Has been for years. All the cops are crooked, the newspapers are crooked, the courts and the judges are crooked."

"I heard they have gangsters there, and whores. That's where Al Capone went and Alvin Karpis and Ma Barker went to relax and take hot baths. They have guns and gangsters. It's where your father got killed."

"My father died in Mount Ida, and he could have died anywhere on earth where there's men who rob other men, which is everywhere on earth. He didn't have nothing to do with Hot Springs. All that other stuff, you can't believe a lick of it. It's old hillbilly boys with shotguns."

"Oh, Earl, you're such a bad liar. You're going off to a war, because the war is what you know best and what you love best. And you're going to leave me up in Fort Smith with no way to get in contact with you and I'll just have to wait and see if somebody doesn't come up with a telegram and say, Oh, Mrs. Swagger, the state of Arkansas is so sorry, but your husband, Earl, is dead. But it's okay, because he was a hero, and this here's another nice piece of plated gold for your trouble."

"Junie, I swear to you nothing will happen to me. And even if it does, well, hell, you got $5,000 and you're still the most beautiful gal in Fort Smith and you don't have to stay in the hut, you could probably find an apartment by that time, when this housing mess is all cleared up. It'll all get better, I swear to you."

"And who raises your son?"

"My— I don't have a son."

"No, maybe it's a daughter. But whatever it is, it sure is getting big in my stomach."

"Jesus," said Earl.

"I wasn't going to tell you until after the ceremony, because I wanted the ceremony to be all for you. But then you went off and you didn't show up all afternoon."

"I'm sorry, sweetie. I never would have guessed."

"What do you think happens? You can't grab me four times a week without getting a baby out of it."

"I thought you liked it when I grabbed you."

"I *love* it. You didn't ever hear me saying no, did you?"

"No ma'am, guess not."

"But it doesn't make a difference, does it?"

"I promised them. I said yes. It's more money. It's a better life."

"Think about your boy, Earl."

But Earl could not. Who'd bring a kid into a world where men fry each other with flamethrowers, machine-gun each other or go at it hand-to-hand, with bayonets and entrenching tools? And now this atom bomb thing: turn the earth into Hiroshimas everydamnwhere. He looked at her, indistinct in the dark, and felt her distance. He thought of the tiny being nestled in her stomach and the thought terrified him. He never asked to be a daddy, he didn't think he was man enough for it.

He was scared. He had a sudden urge, almost overwhelming, to do what he'd never done in the Pacific: to turn, to run, to flee, to leave it all behind him.

He saw his own melancholy childhood, that weary cavalcade of fear and pain. He didn't want that for his boy.

"I— I don't know what to say, Junie. I never thought about no boy or girl before. I just never figured on it."

He had another feeling, one he felt so often: that he was once again failing someone who loved him.

He wished desperately he had a gift for her, something that would make it all right, some little thing.

And then he thought of it.

"I will make you one promise," he said. "It's the only one. I will quit the drinking."

CHAPTER

6

The kid was hot. The kid was smoking. His strawberry-blond hair fell across his pug face, a cigarette dangled insolently from his lips, and he brought the dice, cupped into his left hand, to his mouth.

"Oh, baby," he said. "Jimmy Hicks, Captain Hicks, Captain Jimmy Hicks, Jimmy Hicks, Sister Hicks, Baby Hicks, Sixie from Dixie, sexy pixie, Jimmy Hicks, Baby Hicks, Mamma Hicks, oh, baby, baby, baby, you do what Daddy says, you sweet, sweet baby six!"

A near religious ecstasy came across his face as he began to slowly rotate his tightly clutched fist, and sweat shone brightly on the spray of freckles on his forehead. His eyeballs cranked upward, his lids snapped shut, but maybe it wasn't out of faith, only irritation from the Lucky Strike smoke that rose from his butt.

"Go, sweetie, go, *go!*" said his girlfriend, who hovered over his shoulder. She looked about ten years older than he, had tits of solid, dense flesh, and her low-cut dress squeezed them out at you for all to see. Her lips were red, ruby red, her earrings diamond, her necklace a loop of diamond sparkle, her hair platinum. She touched the boy's shoulder for good luck.

With a spasm he let fly.

The dice bounded crazily across the table and Earl thought of a Jap Betty he had once seen, weirdly cartwheeling before it went in. The Betty had settled with a final splash and disappeared; the dice merely stopped rattling. He looked back at the kid, who was now bent forward, his eyes wide with hope.

"*Goddamn!*" the boy screamed in horror, for the cubes read three and four, not the two and four or the three and three or the five and one he needed, and that was the unlucky seven and he was out.

"Too bad, sir," said the croupier with blank professional respect, and with a rake, scooped up what the kid had riding, a pile of loose twenties and fifties and hundreds that probably amounted to Earl's new and best yearly salary.

The kid smiled, and pulled a wad of bills from his pocket thick as Dempsey's fist.

"He crapped out," Earl said to D.A., who stood next to him in the crowded upstairs room of the Ohio Club, watching the action. "And he's still smiling. How's a punk kid like that get so much dough to throw around? And how's he get a doll off a calendar?"

"There's plenty more where that came from," said D.A. "You don't go to the pictures much, do you, Earl?"

"No, sir. Been sort of busy."

"Well, that kid is named Mickey Rooney. He's a big actor. He always plays real homespun, small-town boys. He looks fourteen, but he's twenty-six, been married twice, and he blows about ten thousand a night whenever he comes to town. I hear the hookers call him Mr. Hey-kids-let's-put-on-a-show!"

Earl shook his head in disgust.

"That's America, Earl," said D.A. "That's what y'all was fightin' for."

"Let's get out of here," Earl finally said.

"Sure. But just look around, take it all in. Next time you see this place, you may be carrying a tommy gun."

The club was dark and jammed. Gambling was king here on the upstairs floor, and the odor of the cigarettes and the blue density of the smoke in the air were palpable and impenetrable. It smelled like the sulfur in the air at Iwo and the place had a sort of frenzy to it like a beach zeroed by the Japs, where the casualties and supplies have begun to pile up, but nobody has yet figured out how to move inland. And the noise level was about the same.

At one end of the room a roulette wheel spun, siphoning money out of the pockets of the suckers. A dozen high-stakes poker games were taking place under low lights. In every nook and cranny was a slot and at each slot a pilgrim stood, pouring out worship in the form of nickels and dimes and silver dollars, begging for God's mercy. But craps was the big game at the Ohio, and at even more tables the swells bet their luck against the tumble of the cubes and piles of cash floated around the green felt like icebergs. Meanwhile, some Negro group diddled out hot bebop licks, crazed piano riffs, the sound of a sax or a clarinet or some sad instrument telling a tale of lost fortunes, love and hope.

Earl shook his head again. Jesus Christ, he thought.

"We got to keep moving, Earl," said the old man. "They don't like baggage in a joint like this. You play or you leave."

As they moved downstairs, they passed through the crowded bar. Five girls tended it, hustling this way and that to stay with the demand. Behind them, in the elaborate mahogany structure, ranks of dark bottles promised an exciting form of numbness.

"You want a drink, Earl?"

"Nah," said Earl. "I gave that shit up."

Earl wore a new blue pinstripe three-piece suit and a brown fedora low over his eyes. He had a yellow tie on, and a nice shiny pair of brown brogues. He felt like he was wrapped in bandages but he looked like $50 worth of new goods, which is what he was.

"Probably a good thing," said D.A. "I won sixteen gunfights drunk, but, goddamn, there came a time when I was drinking so much I was afraid I'd wake up in Hong Kong with a busted nose, a beard, a tattoo and a brand-new Chinese family to support."

"Happened to more than a few Marines I knew," Earl said.

They walked out onto the street. Before them, on the other side of Central like seven luxury liners tied up in dockage, the town's seven main attractions—bathhouses—blazed against the night, and even now were crowded with people seeking the miracle power of the waters, which emerged from the unseen mountain behind them at a steady, dependable, mineral-rich 141 degrees.

People had been coming to this little valley for centuries and so the city had acquired an odd clientele: it was for those in need. If you needed health and freedom from the cricks of arthritis or the rampages of the syph you came to Hot Springs and soaked for hours in the steamy liquid, which if nothing else numbed the pain and cleaned out your dark crevices. When you got out, you felt like a prune. Better? Well, possibly. At least you felt different. But as the years passed, the city grew to offer the fulfillment of other needs, all of them elemental, and its clientele by the year 1946 was not merely the old and the infirm but the young and the very firm: there was no human need that could not be satisfied in Hot Springs in a single evening, from sexual to financial to criminal to redemptive.

The city the hot spigots nurtured was spread along the curve of a now-buried creek, the one side buttressed by the bathhouses, the other by the town's commercial strip, which was a hurdy-gurdy boardwalk: oyster houses, restaurants, shooting galleries, nightclubs, casinos, sports books and of course whorehouses. The street was a broad boulevard, and lit so well it appeared to be a kind of limited daylight. Only the mountain, which the U.S. government owned, was invisible, but every other damn thing was there to see.

"It's like Shanghai in '36," said Earl, "except the whores' eyes ain't slanty."

From their vantage point—across Central, standing on the sidewalk before the Fordyce Bath House and looking up and down the street, which ran between the mountains and seemed to be guarded at the north end by a gigantic gateway consisting of the vast Arlington Hotel on one side and the much taller Medical Arts Building on the other—it seemed gigantic. The lights rolled away to either horizon, a mile of sin and hustle. Yet that was only Hot Springs' most visible self. From the main thoroughfare, other roads curved up into the hills, and each block had a whorehouse and a casino and a sports book, sometimes more than one each. Out Malvern, the color turned black, for in Hot Springs sin knew no racial barriers, and the action got even smokier and steamier out there, toward the Pythian Hotel and Baths, the only place in town where the Negroes who actually provided the labor for the place could sample the burning waters.

"Boy, I don't see how Becker is going to close this place down with just twelve of us," Earl said. "It would take a division."

"Well, here's the drill," said the old man. "There's maybe five hundred sports books in this town, and they're the heart of the operation. Everything feeds off of them. But of them, there's one that's called the Central Book, and all the other books feed off it. It's got all the phone wires and all the race data comes pouring into it; the geniuses in it chalk the odds, and call around town to the other book so that the bets can be laid right up to post time. Then they tab the results, and get them out, and the traffic goes on. It's a great business; the house edge is two percent and the house wins, win or lose. But its problem is it's vulnerable to a wire shutdown. It all depends on how fast they get info from the outside. That's the lifeline. See, here's the deal—if we can shut down that main book, man, we hurt 'em. We *nail* 'em."

"Do we know where it is?"

"Of course not. Lots of folks do, but they ain't gonna be telling us. What we're going to do is hit a variety of places, close 'em down, wreck the machinery, and turn the prisoners over to the cops. The cops won't hold 'em but a day, but the key is wrecking the machinery. You pull those slots off the wall, and you'll see that some of them have been tagged ten or twenty times for destruction by the Hot Springs PD. Somehow, it never gets done. So we smash the slots, wreck the gaming tables, confiscate the money and the slips, and look for financial records or anything that will tell us where the Central Book is. See, it's simple. It's like the war. We take out Jap headquarters and we win."

They were drifting north up Central, and in most of the second- and third-floor windows of the buildings that lined its gaudy west side, girls hung out and called.

"Hey, sugah pie. Hey, you come on up, and we'll teach you a thing or two."

"Come on, baby. Here's where it's so sweet you gonna melt, honey."

"We got the best gals up here, sweetie. We got the prime."

"Care to get laid, Earl?" said the old man.

"Nah. I'll get a dose for sure. Plus my wife has gone and gotten herself pregnant, so I don't need no complications."

"Pregnant? When's it due?"

"Hmm. Truth is, I don't know. She's been that way for a while, only I didn't notice."

"Earl, if I'd a known you had a pregnant wife, maybe I wouldn't have signed you up. This could be scratchy work."

"Don't you worry about it, old man. It's what I do best."

"Shouldn't you be happier? I had a kid, and even though he died young, I never regretted it. Those were happy times. Anyhow, you're going to be a daddy. That's supposed to be a time of joy for every man."

"Ah," said Earl grumpily.

"You'll figure it out, Earl. Believe me, you will."

They moseyed along, past the bathhouses on the right and the casinos and the whorehouses on the left. In time, the bathhouses gave way to a nice little park, where the city fathers had laid out flower beds and trees and the like. It was so pretty, and behind it rose the mountain which presented Hot Springs with its thermal liquids and turned it into a town like no other.

The sidewalk was crowded, for in Hot Springs nobody stood still. The two undercover men slid through knots of the desperate who'd come to Hot Springs out of the belief its vapors could cure them and knots of the rich, who'd come to Hot Springs out of belief in fun. The former were shabby, scrawny and chalky; they looked half dead already, and they were invisible to the pleasure seekers, who were always sleek and in suits or gowns, with straw hats or veiled hats, usually pink and full, usually hearty and hungry and looking forward to the night's fun. Now and then an HSPD black-and-white would prowl the streets, with a couple of slovenly semicomatose officers looking out, watching the crowd for pickpockets or strong-arm boys.

"We should tell them cops there's gambling going on here," said D.A.

"Why, they'd be shocked," Earl said.

At last they came to a magnificent structure maybe four blocks north of the Ohio Club, literally in the shadow of the Medical Arts Building and the gigantic Arlington Hotel, with its tiers of brightly lit rooms. But as magnificent as the Arlington was, it could not compete with the elegance of the place across the street.

It was the Southern Club. Black marble porticos held up by marble columns announced its palatial ambitions; the whole thing was polished to gleam in the dark like something out of a Hollywood movie set in Baghdad. Inside the foyer, a chandelier glittered, sending slices of illumination into the street; the whole place was emblazoned with lights. Limousines pulled up slowly, letting out their moneyed passengers, and the tuxedo was the order of dress for the men, while the women, usually heavily jeweled, wore diaphanous white gowns that clung to their bodies.

"This is where the high rollers go," said D.A. "This is Owney's masterpiece. Man, the money he makes in there."

"What does he think he is, a king or one of them Egyptian fellows who had a tomb the size of a mountain?"

"Something like that," said D.A. "He's got two casinos in there, three parlors for high-stakes poker, and a lounge where he gets the top stars to come in and perform. I think it's Perry Como this week. He even had Bing Crosby one week. Oh, it's the nicest place between here and St. Louis and here and New Orleans. It's a peach of a place. There ain't no place like it anywhere."

"He's doing well, ain't he?" said Earl, watching the place carefully, as if laying plans for a night attack.

"Let's camp here for a bit and see what we can eyeball."

They found a bench on their side of Central, and watched the show progress, as the slow train of limos each dropped off a matched set of swells. It seemed to be some kind of swell convention. Even Earl in his new blue suit felt underdressed.

"Now let me tell you a little story about where the Southern comes from. In 1940, a bridge washes out above Little Rock, over the Arkansas. So the payroll for the big bauxite operation at the Hattie Fletcher Pit that comes down from Chicago won't be rolling that way, that once. Instead, Alcoa ships the money to Tulsa, and from Tulsa to the nearest railhead, which is Hot Springs. One shipment only, while they're shoring up that bridge over the Arkansas. These payrolls is special, down here in the South—see, in 1940, nobody has checking accounts, so it's got to be all cash money. Over $400,000.

"Anyhow, she rolls into the train yard here at Hot Springs late one Friday night, and fast as you can say Jack Sprat, five very tough cookies hit the train in the yard. They know which car is the mail car and everything. They blow the lock with some kind of specially built bomb device, and climb in. One of the guards pulls a gun, and they shoot 'em all down. Tommy guns, four men shot to death in a second. There's four large vaults in the mail car and they know which one to blow open with nitro; they're out and gone with the payroll in less than three minutes. Of course the HSPD can't get its cars over here for love nor money; by the time the State Police get a team in it's practically the next morning, and even when the FBI joins up, whoever done it is long gone. Of course they throw up roadblocks, and roust local law enforcement in three states, and put bulletins on the radio and round up all the known armed robbers and shooters in those same three states. But that job was too slick for any local hoods. I don't think Johnny Dillinger himself could have done such a thing, and of course the manhunt don't turn up a damned thing. They just got away as slick as you can imagine. A Marine like you ought to admire it, Earl: it was a commando raid."

"They had to have inside info," said Earl.

"Clearly they did. Now here's the point: two weeks later, Owney Maddox buys the old Congress Hotel, tears it down, and begins to build on this here Southern Club. Where's he get the money? From outside sources? I don't think so; anyhow, Becker can't find no business records and the deed is entirely in Owney's name. Maybe he's tired of sharing with the big boys, maybe he don't want to be tied to them, maybe he sees an opportunity to take the town over lock, stock and barrel. Of course nobody can prove a thing, but there's four widows and a bunch of orphans who got nothing for the deaths of their husbands, except maybe a nice letter from the railroad. And Owney got the Southern Club."

"I hate the kind who pays others to do the killing."

"Well, well, well," said D.A., checking his watch. "Yep, right on time. Back from a nice steak at Coy's. Yes, sir, there's the man himself."

Earl watched as the darkest, fanciest car he'd ever seen pulled down the line of limos. A Negro in livery came out with a whistle, and stopped traffic, so that the car could slide in without having to wait in line.

"It's a bulletproofed '38 Cadillac," said D.A. "It's the biggest in Arkansas. Probably this side of Chicago."

The car was $7,170 worth of black streamline, with its teardrop fenders and its gleaming silvery grille and the white circles of its tires. It was the Fleetwood Town Car Series 75, absolute top of the Caddy line, its V-16 engine displacing 346 cubic inches, its dark sleekness and rakish hood ornament suggesting a hunger to get into the future. The car slid directly to the place of honor, and immediately two more liveried black men rushed out to open the door for Mr. Maddox.

"Just in time for Perry Como," said D.A.

Owney got out, stretched magnificently, sucked in a breath of smoke from his cigarette holder, and ran his other hand over his slicked-back hair. He wore a creamy dinner jacket.

"He don't look so tough," said Earl. "He looks kind of fancy."

"He's British, did you know that? Or sort of British. He came to this country when he was thirteen, and now he puts on airs and calls everybody Old Man and My Dear Chap and Ronald Colman shit like that. But it's all a con. He was running a street gang on the East Side when he was fifteen. He's got a dozen or so kills. He's a tough little monkey, let me tell you."

Hard to match that description with what Earl thought was a toff, a glossy little fellow who paid too much attention to the way he dressed.

Owney leaned over gallantly, put in his hand, and took a long, silvery limb from a lady, and bent to escort her out of the car. She bobbed, then popped up in clear view.

"Now there's a dame," said Earl. "That is a dame."

"That is, that surely is," said D.A. "Now ain't that the goddamndest thing? I know that one and I bet I know our next guest."

The woman stepped sideways, smiling, filling the night with the dazzle of her lips. She was all dessert. She was what all the gals wanted to be, but never could quite make it, and what all the guys wanted to sleep with. Her hair was an auburn cascade, soft as music.

"What's her story?" asked Earl.

"Her name is Virginia Hill. She's a mob gal. They love her in Chicago, where she was special pals with some of the wops that run that town. They call her the Flamingo, she's so long and beautiful. But again, don't let the looks fool you. She's a tough piece of work from the steel towns of 'Bama. She came up the hard way, through the houses. She's a hooker, or used to be one, and she's been around the life a long time. She's twenty-eight going on fifty-eight. And now, the last player. Now, ain't this interesting."

Yes, it was. The third person out of the car was toasty brown, like some sort of football athlete or other kind of ballplayer. He wasn't in a tux at all, but some kind of tan linen, double-breasted, with a yellow handkerchief and a pair of white shoes on. His shirt was storm blue and he wore a white fedora. A cigar was clutched between his teeth, and even from across the street the tautness of his jaws suggested great strength. He radiated something, maybe toughness, maybe self-love, maybe confidence, but some other thing, well off the normal human broadcasting spectrum.

"Who's the punk?" asked Earl.

"That's Benjamin Siegel. Better known as Bugsy, but not to his face. He's a handsome nutcase from the East Side of New York, very connected to the top guys. He was sent out to L.A. a couple of years before the war, where he's been running the rackets and hanging out with movie stars. But it's very damned interesting. What the hell is he doing here, visiting with Owney Maddox? What are them two birds cooking up, I wonder? Bugsy didn't come here to soak his ass in the vapors, I guarantee you."

The three celebrities exchanged an intimate little laugh and pretended to ignore the gawkers around them, those who felt the power of their charisma. Abreast, they walked up the steps and into the nightclub.

Earl watched them disappear. He squirmed on the bench, feeling a little dispirited. It seemed so wrong, somehow: all those boys dead in the shithole reefs of the Pacific, for "America"; and here was America, a place where gangsters in tuxedos had the best women and the swankiest clubs and lived the life of maharajahs. All that dying, all that bleeding: Owney Maddox. Bugsy Siegel.

"Man," he allowed, "they dress too pretty. Would be a pleasure to git them all dirty, wouldn't it?"

"That's our job," said the old man. "You and me, son. Don't believe they allow no tuxedoes in jail."

CHAPTER

7

Virginia was in a foul mood, not in itself an unusual occurrence, but this morning she was well beyond her usual bounds of anger.

"When are they going to get here?" she demanded.

"I called them. They will get here as fast as they can," said Ben, staring at his favorite thing on earth, his own roughly handsome face in the mirror, as he tried to get his bow tie just right. It was a red number, with little blue symbols of something or other on it. He'd got it at Sulka's, the last time he was in London with the Countess.

"Well, they better shake their asses," Virginia said.

"They" were the squad of bellboys necessary to move the Virginia and Ben show from the Apollo Suite at the Arlington to a limousine to the Missouri-Pacific station for the 4:15, which would take them to St. Louis, where they would transfer to the *Super Chief* on its way back to Los Angeles. So many men were required because wherever Virginia went, she went in style, involving at least ten pieces of alligator luggage. Ben also traveled in alligator and in style, but he disciplined himself to a mere eight cases.

So eighteen suitcases were stacked in the living room of the Apollo Suite, awaiting removal. But Virginia hated to wait. Waiting was not for the Flamingo. It was for the other 99.999999 percent of the world. She decided she needed a cigarette. She walked out onto the terrace and the blinding Arkansas sun hit her. Her sunglasses were already packed. For some reason the sun against her face infuriated her more.

She stepped back into the room, nerves uncalmed by the cigarette. She didn't like to smoke indoors because the smoke clung to her clothes. She was in the mood for a fight.

"This place is a goddamn dump," she said. "Why did we come here? You said I'd meet picture people."

"Sweetie, you did meet picture people. You met Alan Ladd, Dick Powell and June Allyson."

"You idiot," she said. "They ain't *picture people*. They are *Hot Springs people*. Don't you understand the difference?"

"Alan Ladd is big in pictures!" protested Ben.

"Yeah, but his wife manages him and she watches him like a hawk. And she ain't about to help a li'l ol' thang like me! I felt her staring at me! She would have ripped my eyes out, except that if she'd tried, I'd have belted her in the puss so hard she'd see stars for a fucking year. And that Dick Powell, he's like Mr. Bob who ran the company store. Just a big ole politician, slapping the gravy on every goddamn thing! I know his type; big on talk, nothing on getting it done. He'll smile pretty as how-de-do, but he ain't one bit interested in me! I want to meet Cary Grant or John Wayne. I want to meet Mr. Cooper or Mr. Bogart! These are little people. You can't get nowheres in L.A. with little people."

Ben sighed. When Virginia lit up like this, there was no stopping her, short of an uppercut to the jaw, which he had delivered a few times, but she was wearing him down. You can only hit a gal so many times. He wished he had the guts to dump her, but in bed, when the mood was on her, she was such a tigress, so much better than anyone, he knew it was impossible.

"Well, I'm down here on business," he said. "I have a lot to learn from Owney. He has ideas."

"That creep. He's about as British as my Uncle Clytell."

"Sweetie, we'll be back in L.A. in a couple of days. I'll buy you a new mink. We'll throw a big party. Stars will come. But let me tell you! This has been very profitable for me. It's going to get better and better out there. You watch and see where the next ten years take us. We will be so big—"

"You been saying that for six months and you're still the bughouse creep they sent to L.A. to get outta their hair and I still don't have a speaking part! Did you call your lawyer?"

"Well, honey, I—"

"*You did not!* You are still married to that bag Estelle! You're still Mr. Krakow! Mr. Krakow, would you like some eggs with your bacon and let's take the station wagon to Bloomingdale's, dear, they're having a sale! You ain't moved one step closer to no divorce. You bughouse kike, *I knew you'd lie! You liar! You goddamn liar!*"

She turned, and snatched a $200 lamp off a mahogany end table, lifted it and turned toward him. She advanced, nostrils flaring, eyes lit with pure craziness.

But then his own sweet craziness skyrocketed out of control.

"*Don't call me bughouse!*" Ben shouted back. Nothing got him ticked faster than that. A white-hot flash of lightning zagged through his brain, taking all thought and reason from him. He stood, balled his fist and began to stalk his adversary, who approached savagely.

But a knock on the door signaled the arrival of the help, and with a snort, Virginia set the lamp down, opened the door and headed toward the elevator.

Virginia stared stonily at Hot Springs as it drifted by through the Caddy's window. In the broad daylight, it was just another crappy burg, like Toledo or Paducah.

"Virginia," asked Owney, "did you take one of our famous baths? Very soothing."

"I ain't letting no nigger scrub me with a steel-wool mitt while my hairdo melts and my toes wrinkle up like raisins," Virginia said.

"Ah, I see. Well, yes, there is that," Owney replied.

Ben shot him a little look. It said, She's in one of "those" moods.

Owney nodded, cleared his throat, and directed his gaze back to Ben.

"It's a humming joint," said Ben. "You really got something going here."

"So I do. It's called the future."

Ben nodded; it was clear that Owney saw himself not merely as a professional but as some sort of elder wise man, with rare and keen insights. That's why a lot of New York people regarded him as a yakker and didn't miss his pontifications and fake Englishisms a bit. But Ben was curious and had his own ideas.

"The future?"

"Yes. Do you see it yet, Ben? Can you feel it? It's like that Braque hanging in my apartment. You have to *feel* it. If you feel it, its meanings are profound."

Ben's placid face invited Owney onward, and also suggested that Ben was stupid and needed educating, neither of which was true.

"The future. Ben, the wire is dead. The war killed it. It accelerated communications exponentially, old man. We used to control the wire because we controlled the communications. We were *organized*. We could get the race and sports data around the country in a flash, and no other organization, including the U.S. government, was capable of competing. Information is power. Information is wealth. But the war comes along and finally the government understands how important information is to running a global enterprise, and finally they begin to fund research. Once the genie is out of the bottle, there's no putting him back. The next few years will amaze you, Ben. This television? Huge. Person-to-person calling? Instantaneous, without operators or trunk stations. Super adding machines, to make the most arcane calculations the property of the common man. So our great advantage is gone, and with it the source of our wealth and power. We must change! Change or die! They couldn't see that in New York, but believe me, it is coming. Great change. One must ride it, not fear it, but be able to play it, don't you see?"

Ben nodded sagely. Once in 1940 with the Countess he had stayed at Mussolini's summer retreat and heard that bombastic baldy talk in a similar vein. The future! Tomorrow! Fundamental change!

What did it get him, but an upside-down ride on a meat hook at the end of a piano wire after the gunners got done stitching him, and old lady peasants spitting on his fat carcass?

"Yeah, yeah, I see," said Ben innocently.

"Ben, the future is in casinos. That is where the great wealth will come. A city of casinos, a city we own and operate. That is what I'm trying to build here, slowly and surely, with the long-term goal of making gambling—gaming, we'll call it—legal in Arkansas. It's like a license to mint money. People will come in the millions. They can wander the trails in the afternoons, eat food that's cheap, see the shows—Perry Como and Bing Crosby are just a start—and that night enter a magic world and feel the thrill and the excitement that's formerly been felt only by high rollers and aristocratic scoundrels. They'll pay! They'll pay dearly! Ultimately we will become just another American corporation, like Sinclair Oil or Motorola or RCA. Ultimately, we will *be* America!"

"Talk, talk, talk!" said Virginia. "You chumps, a Chicago mechanic could clip you and you wouldn't even see it coming. It ain't going to change, Owney. Them old bastards, they got too much riding on the way they do things. They'll kill you before they let you change the fucking rules, without batting an eyelash."

They were talking so furiously none of them noticed the black '38 Ford with two glum detectives following them a few car lengths back.

. . .

The train lay like a fat yellow snake, huge and wide and imposing. Its diesel streamline seemed to yearn for a horizon, a plain to cross, a river to vault, a mountain to climb. The engine had a rocket ship's sensible sleekness, and a small cab twenty feet off terra firma. It issued noises and mysterious grumblings and was attended by a fleet of worshipful keepers. Conductors and other factotums prowled the platform, examining documents, controlling the flow into and off the thing. The crowds rushed by.

Amid them, but indifferent, and smoking gigantic cigars, the two lords stood in their magnificent clothes, waiting imperially. It would take time for the boys to get the luggage into the compartment and now Owney and Ben were contemplating history.

"This is where that train was jacked, isn't it?" asked Ben.

"It is indeed, old man."

"Nineteen forty-one?"

"Nineteen forty."

"What was the take?"

"I believe over four hundred thousand in cash. The Alcoa payroll for the Hattie Fletcher bauxite pit. In Bauxite."

"In Bauxite?"

"Yes, old man. They named the town after its only product, which is bauxite. The bauxite of Bauxite rules the world, that is, when applied to aluminum by some alchemical process I couldn't possibly understand, and then built into lightweight ships, planes and guns. We won the war with aluminum. The miracle metal. The metal of the future."

"Damn, sure is a lot of the future here in Hot Springs! It was at this station?"

"Not in the station, per se. It was the mail car, and the train was over in the freight docks. You can't see it from here, but this is really a yard. There are several other tracks, controlled by the tower, and warehouses on the other side. You'll see when you get aboard."

"The crew? They've never been caught?"

"Never. They must have been out-of-towners. No local thief could operate at that level of perfection."

"I heard they were Detroit boys, usually work for the Purples. Some done some time with Johnny D back in the wild times. Good people with guns. I heard Johnny Spanish himself."

"I thought he was dead."

"Nobody will ever kill Johnny Spanish. He's the best gun guy in America."

"Well, if you say so. I thought *I* was the best gun guy in America. I could tell you some *fabulous* adventures I had back in New York before the Great War!"

Both men laughed. Ben took a mighty suck on his cigar, a very fine Havana, and looked around in the late afternoon sunlight. It suddenly occurred to him: where was Virginia?

"Where's Virginia?" he asked, instantly coming alert from his torpor.

"Why, she was here a second ago," said Owney.

"She was pesky this morning. She can get real pesky sometimes," he said, soothing his panic as he eyed the crowd. At last he saw her. She had wandered down the platform to get a cigarette while the boys loaded the bags. But—who was she talking to? He could make out a figure, someone strange, someone he didn't know, but hard to see through the crowds. But then the crowds parted magically, and he saw her companion. A tall, tough-looking gent in a blue suit with a fedora pulled low over his eyes and the look of command and experience to him. Ben smelled cop, and a split second later that little flare of rage fired off in his mind.

"Goddamn her!" he exploded, his face white with fury, his temples pulsating, and he began to stride manfully toward his woman.

They spent the morning examining gambling joints from the hundreds in the town, from the smallest, dingiest sports books in the Negro areas out Malvern to some of the more prosaic slot halls on the west side out Ouachita to the elaborate Taj Mahals of Central Avenue. Any one of them could be the Central Book, but how would they know? None of the eight or so they eyeballed, entered, dropped a few bucks' worth of quarters into, seemed remarkable in any way. Then they stopped at a Greek's and had a couple of hamburgers and coffee.

"Is this what cops do?" asked Earl. "They just drive around and look at stuff?"

"Pretty much," said D.A., taking a bite. "But when the shit happens, it happens fast. Just like in the war."

"Okay, Mr. Parker. I believe you."

"Earl, before this is all over, you'll look back on these early days with some nostalgia. This is about as good as it gets."

Earl nodded, and went back to his burger.

Finally, D.A. went off, dropped a nickel and made a call. He came back with a smile on his wrinkled, tanned prune of a face.

"This snitch I got at the Arlington, one of the bellboys, he says Bugsy and the babe are moving out today and the boys are going upstairs to get their luggage and load it up for them. Let's go to the hotel and see if we can't pick 'em up."

Earl threw down his cup of coffee, left some change at the counter and the two of them went out and got in the Ford.

When they got to the Arlington and parked above it on Central, with the grand entrance in easy view, it didn't take long to pick up the caravan. The limo, which looked like it was thirty feet long, led the way out of the hotel's grand entrance. It was followed by a pickup, full of luggage and black men. And behind that, a third car, a Dodge, where six of Owney's minor gunmen and gofers—they were all from a hillbilly family called Grumley—sat dully, pretending to provide security.

From a few car lengths back, Earl and D.A. followed, taking it nice and easy, and kept contact as the folks in the big limo talked on and on. Earl could see that Bugsy and Owney did most of the chatting. The woman just looked out the window, her features frozen in place. The cavalcade made its way through the heavy traffic up Central, and a traffic cop overrode the light to let it pass, while D.A. and Earl cooled their heels behind the red. By the time they got to the station, the black men had the luggage off the truck and loaded onto a couple of hand carts and were hauling it toward the big yellow train.

"Is that the Atchison, Topeka and the Santa Fe?" asked Earl, as D.A. pulled into a space on Market Street.

"No, Earl, that is not. That is the Missouri-Pacific 4:15 for St.

Louis, the first step on the trip back to L.A. Now let's get out and mosey over there and see what there is to see. Probably nothing, but for now I am sick of casing books in Niggertown."

"I roger that," said Earl.

The two split up, and drifted through the gathering crowd as the time of departure approached. Earl lit a cigarette, found a pillar to lean against far down the platform and commenced to smoke and watch. In time, he spotted the two gangsters talking animatedly near the station house, each smoking a gigantic cigar. The two fellows seemed to be having a good enough time. Other than that, nothing much was happening, though more and more people were boarding the train and the conductors seemed a little more frenzied. He glanced at his Hamilton, saw that it was just about 4:00 P.M. The all-aboard would come very soon. His leg hurt a little, as did his left wrist. He flexed his left hand, opening and shutting it, and shifted his weight, trying to keep his mind off of it. He wasn't used to wearing a tie all day, either, and it was getting on his nerves, but he wasn't about to loosen his, even in this heat, until D.A. did the same. He was thinking about a nice hot shower back in his cabin at the Best Tourist Court.

Suddenly someone stood before him, and he cursed himself for his lack of awareness. It was the woman. Her hair was red, and pinned up under a yellow beret. She stood on white, strapped heels in a yellow traveling suit cut right at the knee that showed off more leg than was healthy for anybody. She was staring at him intently, her eyes dark.

"Say, handsome," she said, "did you use your last match to light that butt or would you have one or two others left in the box?"

Nothing shy about this one. And, she smelled great too. Her accent was sugar-dipped, like a fritter hot on a cool Southern morning, and he placed it as either from Georgia or Alabam.

"I might have another one here, ma'am," he said. "Let me just dig through my gear and see."

He stood, pulled the matchbox out from his inside pocket. He deftly opened it, took out a match, and struck it and cupped. He had large hands that protected the fragile flame from any gust of breeze. She came close, cupping his hands in hers, and drew his flame to her Chesterfield.

"There you go," he said.

"Thanks, I needed that." She stood back, inhaled deeply, then exhaled a zephyr of smoke.

"Do I know you?" he asked. "Ain't you in the pictures?"

"Been in a couple, doll," she replied. "But you had to look quick. It's a crappy business unless you know big guys and I just happen to know the wrong big guys. The big guys I know scare the hell out of everybody else. You wouldn't know any big guys, would you, handsome?"

"No ma'am," said Earl, smiling. "I know a couple of generals, that's all."

"Oh, a soldier boy. I thought you might be a cop."

"I used to be a Marine."

"Bet you killed a tubful of Japs."

"Well, ma'am, you just never could tell. It was so fast and smoky."

"My chump boyfriend stayed in L.A. running a sports wire. He's a real hero, the louse. He drags me all the way to this craphole town to meet picture people and they're all small potatoes. It took me ten years to get out of towns like this, and here I am, back again."

"You from Georgia, ma'am?"

"Alabama. Bessemer, the steel town. If you haven't been there, you ain't missed much, sugar. I—"

Earl had the peripheral impression of flailing, of something hot and wild suddenly swarming upon him, animal-like, so fast it was stunning.

"What the fuck is going on?"

It was Bugsy Siegel, his nostrils flaring, his eyes livid with rage. Two flecks of gray gunk congealed in the corners of his mouth. His body radiated pure aggression and his eyes were nasty little pinpricks.

He grabbed the woman, roughly, by the elbow and gave her a powerful yank. The strength of it snapped her neck. He squeezed her arm hard until his knuckles were white.

"What the fuck is this all about, Virginia?" he demanded.

"Christ, Ben, I just got a light from this poor guy," she said as she pulled her arm free.

"Sir," said Earl, "there wasn't nothing going on here."

"Shut up, cowboy. When I talk to you, that's when you talk to me."

He turned back to Virginia. "You fucking slut, I ought to smack you in the face. Get to the train. Go on, get your goddamn ass out of here!" He gave her a shove toward the train, and turned after her.

But then he thought better of it, and turned back to Earl. His hot eyes looked Earl up and down.

Earl gazed back.

"What are you looking at, bumpkin?"

"I ain't looking at nothing, sir."

"You fucking dog, I ought to beat the shit out of you right here. I ought to smash you into the pavement, you little nobody. You nothing. You piece of fucking crap." His anger fueled the color of his language.

"Ben, leave the poor guy alone, I started talking to—"

"Shut up, bitch. Get her to the train, goddammit," he barked at two of Owney's Grumleys who'd shown up in support. Earl saw Owney himself with two others back a few steps and around them a cone of onlookers had formed. It was dead quiet.

"Do you know who I am?" Ben said.

"Ben, get ahold of yourself," said Owney.

"He's just a guy on a platform," the woman yelled, pulling away from the two goons.

But now the focus of Ben's rage was entirely upon Earl, who just stood there with a passive look on his face.

"Do you know who I am?" Siegel screamed again.

"No sir," said Earl.

"Well, if you did, you fucking putz, you would be shitting bricks in your pants. You would be stinking up this joint. You do not want to fuck with me. You don't even want to be in the same state as me, do you understand that, you country fuckhead?"

"Yes sir," said Earl. "I only lit the lady's cigarette."

"Well, you thank your fucking lucky stars I didn't decide to wipe your ass on the railway tracks, you got that, Tex? Do you get that?"

"Yes sir," said Earl.

Bugsy leaned close. "I killed seventeen men," he said. "How many you killed, you pitiful farmer?"

"Ah, I'd say somewhere between 300 and 350," said Earl.

Bugsy looked at him.

"And see," Earl explained further, "here's the funny thing, the boys I killed, they was trying to kill me. They had machine guns and tanks and rifles. The boys you killed was sitting in the park or in the back seat of a car, thinking about the ball game." Then he smiled a little.

At first Bugsy was stunned. No one had ever talked to him this way, particularly not in the face of one of his rampages. And then it struck him that this hick wasn't scared a lick. The guy smiled at Bugsy and—fuck him, fuck him, FUCK HIM!—actually winked.

Bugsy threw his punch with his right. It wasn't a roundhouse, for he was a skilled fighter and knew that roundhouses were easily blocked. It was an upward jab, with the full force of his body behind it, and his reflexes were fast, his strength considerable and his coordination brilliant, all driven by his mottled fury. He meant to punch the cowboy right below the eye and cave in the left side of his face.

He threw the punch and for quite a while—say somewhere between .005 and .006 second—felt the soaring pleasure that triumph in battle always unleashed in him, the imposition of his will on an unruly world, his ego, his beauty, his cunning, all in full expression. He knew important people! He hung out with movie stars! He fucked a countess, he fucked Wendy Barrie, he fucked hundreds of the world's most beautiful starlets! He was Bugsy, the Bugman, Bughouse, friend of Meyer and Lucky, he counted in this world.

Then it all vanished. With a speed that he could never have imagined, the cowboy got a very strong hand inside his wrist to turn the blow, not so much block it, and with his other hand himself strike.

Bugsy was not a coward. He had been in many street fights, and he'd won most of them. He was indefatigable in battle when he had a stake in the outcome, and his rage usually sealed him off from the sensation of pain until hours later. He had been hit many times. But the blow he absorbed took all that away from him. It was a short right-hand punch that traveled perhaps ten inches but it had a considerable education in mayhem behind it, and it struck him squarely below the heart, actually cracking three ribs. It was a hammer, a piston, a jet plane's thrust, an atom bomb. It sucked the spirit from him. The shock was red, then black, and his legs went, and he slipped to the platform, making death-rattle sounds, feeling bile or blood pour from his nostrils to destroy his bow tie. He urped and his lunch came up. He convulsed, drew his legs up to his chest to make the hurt go away, sucked desperately for oxygen and felt something he had not felt in years, if ever: *fear.*

His antagonist was kneeling.

"You know what?" he said. "I only hit you half as hard as I know how. If I see you in this town again, I'll hit you so hard it'll knock your guts out of your skin. Now you get on this train and you go far, far away. Don't come back, no more, no how, not ever."

He stood and looked Owney square in the eye.

"You or any of your boys want to try me, Mr. Maddox, you go right ahead."

Owney and his crew of Grumleys took a step back.

"I didn't think so," said Earl, smiled, winked at the pretty lady and slipped away.

CHAPTER

8

After he regained his voice and his legs, but not his color, Bugsy turned his rage on Owney, demanding to know who the vanished cowboy was. Owney admitted he didn't know at all. As the crew of Owney's Grumley boys led him to the Pullman car and as he nursed the wretched pain in his side, Bugsy passed out what could only be an edict, with the full power of his associates back east behind it: You find out who that guy is. You find out where he lives, who he hangs with, what he does. You mark him well. But do not touch him. I will touch him. Touching him, that's for me, do you understand?

Owney nodded.

Virginia said, "Sugar, you're going to touch him with what now, a howitzer? An atom bomb? A jet?" She threw back her hair, flushed and victorious, and laughed powerfully, a laugh that emerged from a diaphragm as if coated in boiled Alabama sap and grits. "Honey," she said, "you ain't got the guts to face that kind of how-de-do again, let me tell you. Ha! He got you so good! You should have seen the look on your face when he poked you! You poor ol' thing, you done got the white beat off you!"

"Virginia, shut up," said Bugsy. "You were the cause of all this."

"So how was I supposed to know he was Jack Dempsey? Anyhow, you were the idiot that swung on him. Couldn't you see he was a tough guy? He looked tough. He stood tough. He talked tough. And, honey, he sure as hell hit tough!"

"Do you want a doctor, old man?" Owney asked. "We could delay the train."

"And let these hicks laugh at me some more? Let some hick saw-bones pick at me? No thank you. Owney, you said you ran a smooth town. You said we'd all be safe here, you owned things, things ran great in Owney's town. And this happens. Some ringer. He had to be a pro boxer. I never saw no guy's hands move that fast, and I never got hit so fucking hard in my life. So maybe this ain't such a safe town and maybe you ain't doing such a good job."

With that he limped bravely up the steps of the Missouri-Pacific and was taken to his Pullman stateroom by a covey of Negro porters.

Virginia followed, but she turned for a last whisper to the befuddled Owney.

"You tell that cowboy to watch out. The goddamn Bugman holds grudges. And tell that sugar boy if he ever comes to L.A. to look me up!"

Shortly, the train pulled out of the station, and Owney hoped that he was forever finished with Benjamin "Bugsy" Siegel, who had come for a "vacation and a bath" at the urging of Meyer Lansky and Frank Costello, who were big in New York.

"All right," he said when the train pulled out, addressing Grumleys present and elsewhere, "now you know what's going on. Find out who that guy is and find out fast. But don't touch him! Something's going on and I have to know what the fuck it is."

He was troubled: change was coming, he knew, and to ride it out he had to keep things running smoothly down here. Hot Springs had to be a smooth little empire, where nothing went wrong, where boys from all the mobs could come and have their fun, and mix and get together, without problems from the law. That's what he was selling. That was his product. Everything he had was tied up in that. If he lost that, it meant he lost everything.

"Mr. Maddox, he's long gone," said Flem Grumley, one of Pap Grumley's sons and the eldest of these Grumleys. "He just melted so fast into the crowd, we didn't get a fix on him. Who'd have thought a guy would have the balls to paste Bugsy Siegel in the ribs?"

"Find him" was all Owney could think to say.

They drove away from the station in silence. Earl stared glumly into the far distance. His hand hurt a bit. He figured it would be bruised up some in the morning.

"Tell you what," said D.A. finally, "I never saw one man hit another so hard. You must have boxed."

"Some" was all Earl said.

"Pro?"

"No sir."

"Earl, you're not helping me here. Where? When? How?"

"'Thirty-six, '37 and '38. I was the Pacific Fleet Champ, middleweight. Fought a tough Polak for that third championship on a deck of the old battlewagon *Arizona* in Manila Bay."

"You are so fast, Earl. You have the fastest hands I ever saw, faster even than the Baby Face's. You must have worked that speed bag hard over the years."

"Burned a few speed bags out, yes sir, I surely did."

"Earl, you are a piece of work."

"I'm all right," he said. "But I made a mistake, didn't I?"

"Yes, you did, Earl."

"I should have let him hit me?"

"Yes, you should have."

"I think I know that," said Earl, aware somehow that he had failed. He turned it over in his mind to see what the old man was getting at.

"Do you see why, Earl?"

"Yes sir, I do," said Earl. "I let my pride get in the way. I let that little nothing in a railroad station get too big in my head."

"Yes, you did, Earl."

"I see now what I should have done. I should have let him hit me. I should have let him smack me to the ground and feel like a big shot. I should have begged him not to hit me no more. Then he'd think I'se scared of him. Then he'd think he owned me. And if it was ever important, and he came at me again, he'd sail in king of the world, and I'd have nailed him to the barn door so bad he wouldn't never git down."

"That is right, Earl. You are learning. But there's one other thing, Earl. You threw caution to the wind. That was an armed, highly unstable professional criminal, surrounded by his pals, all of them armed. You are unarmed. If you'd have hit him again, you'd probably be a dead man and no jury in Garland County would have convicted your killers, not with Owney's influence on Bugsy's side. So it was a chance not worth taking."

"I'm not too worried about myself," Earl said.

"No true hero really is. But the heroics are over, Earl. It's time for teamwork, operating from strength, careful, professional intelligence, preparation, discipline. Discipline, Earl. You can teach these young policemen we have coming in discipline, I know. But you have to also show it, Earl, embody it. Do you understand?"

"Yes sir."

"It's not a pretty nor a right thing for me to address a hero of the nation in such a way, but I have to tell you the truth."

"You go ahead and tell me the truth, sir."

"That's good, Earl. That's a very good start."

They drove on in silence for a bit.

"Now they know there's a new fellow or two in town," Earl finally said.

"Yes, Earl, they do."

"And that would be why we are not heading back to the cabins?"

"That is it, exactly."

They were driving out Malvern through the Negro section, and now and then the old man eyed the rearview mirror. On the streets, the Negro whorehouses and beer joints were beginning to heat up for a long night's wailing. Mammas hung from the window, smoking, yelling things; on the streets, pimps tried to induce those of either race or any race to come in for a beer or some other kind of action. Now and then a Negro casino, usually smaller and more pitifully turned out than the ones for the white people, could be glimpsed, but mostly it was just black folks, sitting, watching, wondering.

"Tell me, Earl, what was in your room?"

"Some underclothes for a change, some underclothes drying in the tub. Some socks. Two new shirts. A razor, Burma-Shave. A toothbrush, and Colgate's. A pack of cigarettes or two."

"Any books, documents, anything like that? Anything to identify yourself?"

"No sir."

"That's good. Can you live with the loss of that stuff?"

"Yes, I can."

"That's good, because if I don't miss my guess, starting now them boys are going to turn that town upside down looking for the Joe Louis that poleaxed their special visitor. I paid for the cabins through next Monday; if we check out today or make a big folderol about packing and leaving in a hurry, that's a dead giveaway as to who we are. It's best now just to fade quietly. They'll check everywhere for boys who've left suddenly, left in a lurch, left without paying up. So if we don't do anything to draw attention to ourselves, we'll keep them in the dark a little longer."

"Yes sir," said Earl. "I guess I'm a little sorry."

"Earl, in this work, sorry don't matter. Sure is better than sorry. Remember: the mind is the weapon. Think with the mind, not the fast hands."

Owney's Grumleys turned the town pretty much upside down. He had a gang of former bootleg security boys and did all the heavy hitting he found necessary. There were a bunch of Grumleys, all related, including several Lutes, more than a few Bills, and not less than three and possibly as many as seven Slidells, as well as a Vern and a Steve. The Slidell Grumleys were by repute the worst and they had to be kept apart, for they would turn on each other murderously, given half a chance.

A Grumley visited every hotel, tourist court and campground to examine, sometimes sweetly, sometimes not so sweetly, the registration books. Another Grumley or two—usually a Bill and a Lute—traveled the whorehouse circuit. Madams and girls were questioned, and a few sexual adventures were worked in on the sly by this or that Grumley, but such was to be expected. Grumleys were Grumleys, after all. And still another couple of Grumleys checked the bathhouses. Other Grumleys tracked down numbers runners and wire mechanics and instructed them to keep their eyes open double wide. Owney even had some of his Negro boys—these were most definitely not Grumleys—wander the black districts asking questions, because you never could tell: times were changing and where it was once impossible to think of white people hiding among, much less associating with, Negro people, who knew the strangeness of the wonderful modern year 1946? Even the police were brought in on the case, but Owney expected little and got little from them.

In the end, all the efforts turned up nothing. No sign of the cowboy could be unearthed. Owney was troubled.

He sat late at night on his terrace, above the flow of the traffic and the crowds sixteen stories below on Central Avenue, in the soft Arkansas night. He had a martini and a cigarette in its holder in an ashtray on the glass table before him. Beyond the terrace, he could see the tall bank of lighted windows that signified the Arlington Hotel was full of suckers with bulging pockets waiting to make their contributions to Owney's fortune; to the right of that rose Hot Springs Mountain with its twenty-seven spigots of steamy water for soothing souls and curing the clap.

He held a pigeon in his hands—a smooth, loving bird, its purple irises alive with life, its warmth radiating through to his own heart, its breast a source of cooing and purring. The bird was a soft delight.

He tried to sort out his problems and none of them seemed particularly difficult in the isolate, but together, simultaneously, they felt like a sudden strange pressure. He had been hunted by Mad Dog Coll, he had shot it out with Hudson Dusters, he had felt the squeeze of Tom

Dewey, he had done time in New York's toughest slammers, so none of this should have really mattered.

But it did. Maybe he was growing old.

Owney petted his bird's sleek head and made an interesting discovery. He had crushed the life out of it when he was considering what afflicted him. It was silently dead.

He threw it in a wastebasket, gulped the martini and headed inside.

PART TWO

Day Heat

August 1946

9

On the first morning, Earl took the group of young policemen out to the calisthenics field in the center of a city of deserted barracks miles inside the wire fence of the Red River Army Depot. The Texas sun beat down mercilessly. They were all in shorts and gym shoes. He ran them. And ran them. And ran them. Nobody dropped out. But nobody could keep up with him either. He sang them Marine cadences to keep them in step.

> I DON'T KNOW BUT I BEEN TOLD
> ESKIMO PUSSY IS MIGHTY COLD
> SOUND OFF
> ONE-TWO
> SOUND OFF
> THREE-FOUR

There were twelve of them, young men of good repute and skills. In his long travels in the gardens of the law, D.A. had made the acquaintanceship of many a police chief. He had, upon getting this commission, called a batch of them, asked for outstanding young policemen who looked forward to great careers and might want to volunteer for temporary duty in a unit that would specialize in the most scientifically up-to-date raiding skills as led by an old FBI legend. The state of Arkansas would pay; the departments would simply hold jobs open until the volunteers returned from their duties with a snootful of new experience, which they could in turn teach their colleagues, thus enriching everybody. D.A.'s reputation guaranteed the turnout.

The boys varied in age from twenty to twenty-six, unformed youths with blank faces and hair that tumbled into their eyes. Several looked a lot like that Mickey Rooney fellow Earl had seen in Hot Springs but they lacked Mickey's worldliness. They were earnest kids, like so many young Marines he'd seen live and die.

After six miles, he let them cool in the field, wiping the sweat from their brows, wringing out their shirts, breathing heavily to overcome their oxygen deficit. He himself was barely breathing hard.

"You boys done all right," he said, and paused, "for civilians."

They groaned.

But then came the next ploy. He knew he had to take their fears, their doubts, their sense of individuality away from them and make them some kind of a team fast. It had taken twelve hard weeks at Parris Island in 1930, though during the war they reduced it to six. But there was a trick he'd picked up, and damn near every platoon he'd served in or led had the same thing running, so he thought it would work here.

He named them.

"You," he said, "which one is you?"

He had the gift of looming. His eyes looked hard into you and he seemed to expand, somehow, until he filled the horizon. This young man shrank from him, from his intensity, his masculinity, his sergeantness.

"Ah, Short, sir. Walter F.," said the boy, dark-haired and intense, but otherwise unmarked by the world at twenty.

"Short, I'll bet you one thing. I bet you been called 'Shorty' your whole life. Ain't that the truth?"

"Yes sir."

"And I bet you hated it."

"Yes sir."

"Hmmmm." Earl made a show of scrunching up his eyes as if he were thinking of something.

"You been to France, Short?"

"No sir."

"Well, from now on and just because I say so, your name is 'Frenchy.' Frenchy Short. How's that suit you?"

"Uh, well—"

"Good. Glad you like it. All right, ever damn body, y'all say 'HI FRENCHY' real loud."

"HI FRENCHY" came the roar.

"You're now a Frenchy, Short. Got that?"

"I—"

And he moved to the next one, a tall, gangly kid with a towhead and freckles, whose body looked a little long for him.

"You?"

"Henderson, sir. C. D. Henderson, Tulsa, Oklahoma."

"See, you're already a problem, Henderson. Our boss, his name is D.A. So we can't have too many initials or we'll get 'em all tangled up. What's the C stand for?"

"Carl."

"Carl? Don't like that a bit."

"Don't much like it myself, sir."

"Hmmm. Tell you what. Let's tag an O on the end of it. But not an S. That would make you a Carlo. Not a Carlos, but a Carlo. Carlo Henderson. Do you like it?"

"Well, I—"

"Boys, say Hello to Carlo."

"HELLO CARLO!"

In that way, he named them all, and acquired a Slim who was chunky, a Stretch who was short, a Nick who cut himself shaving, a Terry who read *Terry and the Pirates*, a smallish Bear, a largish Peanut, a phlegmatic Sparky. Running short on inspiration, he concluded the ceremony with a Jimmy to be called James and a Billy Bob to be called Bob Billy and finally a Jefferson to be called not Jeff but Eff.

"So everything you was, it don't exist no more. What exists is who

you are now and what you have to do and how Mr. D. A. Parker himself, the heroic federal agent who shot it out with Baby Face Nelson
and put the Barker Gang in the ground, will train you. You are very
lucky to learn from a great man. There ain't many legends around no
more and he is the authentic thing. You meet him tomorrow and you
will grow from his wisdom. Any questions?"

There were probably lots of questions, but nobody had the guts to
ask them.

For a legend, D.A. cut a strange figure when at last he revealed himself
to the men, this time at one of the old post's far-flung shooting ranges.
If they expected someone as taut and tough as jut-jawed, bull-necked,
rumble-voiced Earl, what they got was a largish old man in a lumpy
suit, beaten-to-hell boots and a fedora that looked as if it had been
pulled by a tractor through the fields of Oklahoma, who seemed to do
a lot of spitting.

It was after the morning run and the boys had changed back into the
outfits they'd wear on the street—that is, into suits and ties, and damn
the heat.

The old man didn't give any orders at all and didn't mean to command by force but by wisdom. His first move was to invite the boys to
sit. Then he noted that it was hot, and since it was hot he suggested
they take their coats off. When the coats came off, he walked among
them, and looked at their sidearms, mainly modern Smith or Colt revolvers in .38 Special, worn in shoulder holsters, as befits a plain-
clothesman. One of them even had an old Bisley in .44-40.

"That's a powerful piece of work, young man."

"Yes sir. My grandfather wore it when he was sheriff of Chickasaw
County before the Great War."

"I see. Well, it loads a mite slow for our purposes. Don't get me
wrong. A Colt single-action's a fine gun. So's a Smith double. But this
here's 1946 and it's modern times. So we're going to learn how to get
ready for modern times."

"Yes sir," said the boy. "That is why I came here."

"Good boy. Now, I suppose y'all are good shots. Why, I'd bet all of
you shot expert on qualification. Let's see how many did. Hands up."

Twelve hands came up, unwavering with the confidence of the young and sure.

"All of them. See that, Earl? They're all experts."

Earl, standing to one side with his arms folded and his face glowering in the best sergeant's stare, nodded.

"Yes sir. Been known to use a Smith myself," D.A. said. He threw back his coat and revealed what it had not hidden that effectively: his own Smith .38/44 Heavy Duty, with white stag grips, worn on an elaborately carved Mexican holster off a second belt beneath his trousers belt.

"Yes sir, a fine gun. Now tell me, who can do this?"

He reached in his pocket, pulled out a silver dollar. He turned and lofted the coin into the air. It rose, seemed to pause, then fell. His hand a blur, the old man drew and fired in a motion so swift and sudden it seemed to have no place in time. The ping from the coin, and the speed with which it jerked out of its fall and sailed thirty feet further out signified a hit.

"You," he pointed to the youngest of the boys. "Can you go get that for the old man?"

"Yes sir," said the boy, the one Earl had nicknamed Frenchy yesterday.

Short retrieved the piece.

"Hold her up," said D.A.

The young officer held up the coin, which was distended ever so slightly by the power of the .38 slug punching through its center. The Texas sunlight showed through it.

The boys murmured in appreciation.

"See," said D.A., "y'all think that was pretty neat, huh? Truth is, it's a miss. Because I hit dead center. Usually when I do that trick for the kids, I like to hit closer to the edge, so when they wear it on a thong around the neck, it'll hang straighter. How many of you could do such a thing?"

No hands came up.

"Mr. Earl, you think you could?" asked the old man.

Earl was a very good shot, but he knew that was beyond his skills.

"No sir," he said.

"In fact," said D.A., "there ain't but four or five men in the world who could do that regularly. A Texas Ranger or two. An old buddy of mine named Ed McGivern, a trick shooter. Maybe a *pistolero* in Idaho named Elmer Keith. See, what I got, what them boys I named got, you don't got. That is, a special gift. A trick of the brain, that lets me solve deflection problems and coordinate the answer between my hand and eye in a split second. That's all. It's just a gift."

He turned to them.

"I show it to you because I want you to see it, and forget about it. I'm a lucky man. I'm a very lucky man. You ain't. You're ordinary. You can't do that. Nobody in the FBI could do that. So what I mean to teach you is how an ordinary man can survive a gunfight, not how a man like me can. You've seen fast and fancy shooting; now forget it. Fast and fancy don't get it done: sure and right gets it done. And take them revolvers back to your lockers and lock them up. You won't be using them no more and you won't be shooting with one hand and you won't be trusting your reflexes. This here is the tool of our trade."

He took off his coat, and showed the .45 auto he had hanging under his left armpit in its elaborate leather harness.

"We use the .45 auto. We carry it cocked and locked. We draw with one hand, clasp the other hand to the gun and grip hard, we concentrate on the sights, we lock our elbows until we're nothing but triangles. We got a triangle of arms between ourself and the gun and a triangle of legs between ourself and the ground. The triangle is nature's only stable form. We're crouching a little because that's what our body wants to do when we get scared. We aren't relying on the ability of our mind to do fancy calculations under extreme pressure and we ain't counting on our fingers to do fancy maneuvers when all's they want to do is clutch up. Every goddamn thing we do is sure and simple and plain. Our motions are simple and pure. Most of all: front sight, front sight, front sight. That's the drill. If you see the front sight you'll win and survive, if you don't, you'll die.

"Did I hear a laugh? Do I hear snickers? Sure I do. A man shoots with one hand, you're telling me. All the bull's-eye and police shooting games are set up for one hand. Them old cowboys used one hand and in the movies the stars all use one hand. You don't *want* to use two hands, 'cause that's how a girl shoots. You're a big strong he-man. You don't need two hands.

"Well, that there's the kind of thinking that gets you killed."

He withdrew another silver dollar from his pocket, turned and lofted it high. The automatic was a blur as it locked into a triangle at the end of both his arms and from the blur there sprang the flash-bang of report; the coin was hit and blasted three times as far back as the previous dollar. Again, Short retrieved it. He held it up. It was no souvenir. It was mangled beyond recognition.

"You see, boys. You can do it just as fast two-handed as one."

They worked with standard Army .45s without ammunition for the first day. Draw—from a Lawrence steer hide fast-draw holster on the belt right at the point of the hip—aim, dry-fire. Then cock, relock and reholster. That was D.A.'s system, the .45 carried cocked and locked, so that when you drew it, your thumb flew to the safety as the gun came up on target, and smushed it down even as the other hand locked around the grip and you bent to it, lowering your head and raising the gun until you saw the tiny nub of front sight and the blur of the black silhouette before you.

Snap!

"You gotta do it right slow before you can do it right fast," he would say. "Ready now, again, ready, DRAW . . . AIM . . . FIRE."

A dozen clicks rose against the North Texas wind.

"Now, again," said the old man. "And think about that trigger pull. Control. Straight back. That trigger stroke has got to be smooth, regular and perfect."

On and on it went, until fingers began to get bloody. Even Earl pulled his share of draws and snaps, aware that he among them all could not complain, could not stop. But there were so many troubling things about it.

Finally a hand went up.

"Sir, are you sure about this? I could draw and shoot much faster with my Official Police. I don't like losing my Official Police."

"Any other questions?"

There was silence, but then one hand came up. Then another. And a third.

"The sights are so much tinier than my Smith. I can't pick them up."

"I heard automatics jammed much more than wheelies. It makes me nervous."

"I think I'd feel better carrying at the half-cock, and thumb-cocking as I drew, like I did with my old single-action."

Mumbles came and went.

And even Earl had his doubts. He didn't like walking about with a pistol on safe. To shoot he had to hit that little bitty safety, and under pressure, that might be tough. He didn't like the idea of pointing a gun at somebody set on killing him and getting nothing out of the effort.

"Earl, how 'bout you?"

"Mr. D.A., you're the boss."

"See, men, that's Earl. That's a good Marine to the last, supporting his old man no matter how crazy. But Earl, if I wasn't the boss, what would you say? Come on, now, Earl, tell these boys the truth."

"Well, sir," said Earl, "under those circumstances I'd say I'se a bit worried about carrying that automatic with the safety on. You got to hit that safety to shoot fast and I know in the islands, we many times had to shoot fast or die. No guns in battle are carried with the safeties on. There may not be time to get them off."

"A very good point, Earl. They're all very good points. Which is why today we make the change. You have to understand what don't work as compared to what do work. Let's head back to the indoors."

The unit trooped back to the explosives disassembly building, which had been appropriated as a classroom. There, against one wall, was a shipping box of cardboard, maybe two feet by two feet, swaddled in tape and labels. Earl looked at the label and saw that it was from something called Griffin & Howe, in New York, and searched his memory for some familiarity with the place, but came up with no answer, though the words had a tone he knew from somewhere.

"Coupla you boys, load this up to the table," commanded D.A. and two of the officers did so, by their effort proving that the box contained a considerable amount of steel.

"Earl, would you please open the box for me."

Earl took out his Case pocketknife and sawed his way through the cardboard and staples and tape. When he got it open, he saw that it contained a nest of smaller boxes from Colt's, of Hartford, Connecticut, each about eight inches by six inches, and beside the Colt's logo, it said National Match Government Model.

"Now, I worked for Colt's for a number of years, so I got a deal on these guns. Then I had 'em shipped to Griffin & Howe, a custom gunsmithy in New York. Earl, take one out, please, and show it around."

Earl pulled one box out, pried the lid off it. Inside, a Colt government model gleamed blackly at him, but he saw immediately that the cardbord of the box was slightly mutilated in one spot, where it meant to hold the pistol snugly, as if something larger than spec had been pushing at the box. He pulled the pistol out.

"See what you got?" D.A. asked. "You tell 'em, Earl."

"The sights are much bigger," Earl noted right away. Indeed, the target pistol's adjustable sights had been replaced with a bigger fixed version, a big flat piece with a cut milled squarely into the center; at the front end, instead of that little nubby thing, there was a big, square, wide blade.

"Oversized rear, Patridge front sights. What else, Earl?"

Earl gripped the pistol and his hand slid up tight to nest it deep and his thumb naturally went to the thumb-safety, which had been enlarged into a neat little shelf with the soldered addition of a plate. His whole thumbprint rested squarely on it. No way he was going to miss that thing.

"Now dry-fire it," the old man said.

Obediently, Earl pointed in a safe direction, thumbed back the hammer, pressed the safety up for on. When he plunged it down with his thumb, the thumb met just two ounces or so of resistance, then snapped downward with a positive break. Earl pulled the trigger, which broke at a clean four pounds, without creep or wobble.

"That is a fighting handgun," said the old man. "The best there is. Completely safe to carry cocked and locked. Its ramp polished and smoothed so that it will feed like a kitten licking milk. A trigger job to make it crisp to shoot. A fast, seven-round reload in two seconds or less. A big-ass .45, the most man-stoppingest cartridge there is, unless you want to carry a .357 Magnum, which would take you two years to master, if that fast. And finally, the shortest, surest trigger stroke in the world. Gents, that's the gun you'll carry, it's the gun you'll shoot, it's the gun you'll live with. It's the gun you'll clean twice a day. It's the gun that'll win your fights for you if you treat it well. I should tell you it was all thought out by a genius. Not me, not by a long shot. But that's what the Baby Face did to his .45s. He was a killer and some say even crazy, but he had more pure smarts about guns of any man since old John Browning himself."

Draw, aim and fire.

Draw, aim and fire.

Two hands, the safety coming off from the thumb's plunge as the second hand came to embrace the first in its grip, the rise of the front sight to the target.

"You don't got to line it up," said the old man. "What you're looking for is a quick index. You have to know that the gun is in line; you don't got to take the time to place the front sight directly between the blades of the rear sights. You got to flash-index on the front sight. You see that front sight come on target and you shoot."

Draw, aim and fire.

Draw, aim and fire.

Earl was surprised how well it worked, once you got the hang of it. It helped that his hands were so fast and strong to begin with, and that he'd fired so many shots in anger and so shots in practice meant nothing. But clearly, he had some degree of exceptional talent: the pistol came out sure, it came up and BANG it went off, almost always leaving a hole in the center of the target.

"Forget the head, forget the heart," counseled the old man. "Aim where he's fattest, and shoot till he goes down. Center hit. Clip him dead center. If he don't go down, if he's still coming, shoot him through the pelvis and break his hipbone. That'll anchor him. Some of these bigger boys take a basketful of shooting before they go down.

That's why you have to shoot fast and straight and a lot. Usually, the man who shoots the most walks away."

D.A. watched with eyes so shrewd and narrow they missed nothing. This boy, that boy, this boy again, that one again: little flaws in technique, a tendency to flinch, a lack of concentration, a finger placed inconsistently on the trigger, a need to jerk, or, worst of all, an inability to do the boring work of repetition that alone would beat these ideas into the minds. But D.A. was patient, and kind, and never nasty.

"Short, you are very good, very fast, I must say," he said to the young Pennsylvanian, who, to be sure, was the best of the youngsters, a very quick study.

Short was fast too. Not as fast as Earl or the old man—in time, the old man believed *nobody* would be faster than Earl—but fast. He got it right the first time and kept it right.

Henderson, from Oklahoma, was a bit more awkward. Tall and blond, with arms too long and hands too big, he was all elbows and excess motion. He didn't have the gift for it that Short and some of the others did. But Lord, he worked. He got up early to practice dry-firing and he stayed up late practicing dry-firing.

"You are a worker, son," said D.A.

"Yes sir," said Henderson. "That's what my people taught me." He drew against phantom felons until his fingers were bloody.

"Now this," said Earl, a few days later, "this is the real McCoy."

He held in his hands the .45 caliber Thompson M1928 submachine gun, with its finned barrel, its Cutts compensator, its vertical foregrip, its finely machined Lyman adjustable sight.

Five other such guns lay on the table, sleek and oily.

"Mr. D.A. got a deal with the Maine State Police, which is why these guns all say Maine State Police. This will be our primary entry weapon, not merely for its firepower, but more than anything for its psychological effect. You find yourself on the other side of a gun like this, the thought goes, you don't wanna fight no more. Didn't work with the Japs but it should work with these here Hot Springs hillbillies."

The men looked at the weapon, which he held aloft.

"It's a recoil-powered, open-bolt full automatic weapon. That open-bolt business is important, because it means it can only be fired with the bolt back. You forget to cock it, you are S.O.L. If it don't have a magazine in it, it can't fire, unless you have done stuck a cartridge with your fingers up in the chamber, then cocked it, and I ain't never heard of no man doing that but it's my theory that if there's a way to screw up, some recruit will find it, no matter how well hidden. Don't never put a shell into the chamber because everybody will think it's empty and that's how training accidents happen. You'll have plenty of chance to bleed up in Hot Springs, no need to do it here.

"Now, this evening, I'll teach you how to break it down, how to clean it, how to reassemble it. You will clean it and reassemble it each time you fire it, and the reason for that is the same as the one I gave you earlier: you want to treat it well so it will treat you well. Now, how many men know how to shoot this gun?"

A few hands went up, mainly from the older men who'd joined the unit from State Police agencies.

But so did Frenchy's.

"Frenchy Short, do tell. Well, young man, you come on up here. Where'd you learn to shoot the tommy?"

Frenchy came up.

"My mother knew the police chief of our town. She arranged for me to shoot all the guns for my fifteenth birthday."

"A birthday present. Damn, ain't that something. Come on, Frenchy, show the boys."

So Frenchy went to the firing line, inserted a stick magazine and leaned into the gun.

The Colt Police Silhouette target loomed twenty-five yards downrange, the shape of a man with his wrist planted on his hip.

"Get ready, boys!" Earl said and Frenchy found a good position, and pulled the trigger. Nothing happened. Then he remembered the actuator up top, drew it back with an oily slide of lubricated metal, reacquired the shooting position, and pulled the trigger. Nothing happened.

"Shit!" he said.

"Safety," said Earl.

Frenchy fiddled, eventually turned some lever.

Again he brought the gun to his shoulder.

One shot rang out. The magazine fell to the ground.

"Shit!"

"Now, see, Frenchy here thought he already knew. He didn't wait to learn. He already knew and he wanted to show off. You don't show off at this work, 'cause it'll get you killed. Got that? This is about teamwork, not hey-look-at-me. Also"—he winked at Frenchy—"when you load the mag, you gotta slap the bottom to make sure the mag lock has clicked in. Sometimes it don't lock up all the way but the spring tension holds the mag in place, and you think it's time to be-bop. But it don't bebop, it only bops, once. Frenchy didn't know that, the mag kicked loose. So what does he now say to Baby Face Nelson who is walking toward him with a sawed-off? *Slap* that mag hard, *hear* it lock in."

Earl locked the magazine in, gave it a stiff smack with his palm, then drew back the actuator, then spun and shouldered it.

"Plug your ears, boys, but open your eyes. I'm using tracers so's you can watch the flight of the bullets."

He leaned into the gun with a perfect FBI firing position and fired half a magazine and even though his left wrist was stiff with ancient pain, he gripped the foregrip tightly, pulling it in. That was the whole key to the thing. The gun shuddered, the bolt cycled, the empties flew in a spray, the gun muzzle stayed flat though blossoming with blast and flash and spirals of gas, the racket was awesome as the bullets sped off so fastfastfast it seemed like one continuous roar. It was so bright that no flash could be seen but the chemical traces in the tail end of the bullets still igniting, trailing for a split second the incandescence of the round's trajectory. It was there and not-there at once, the illusion of il-lumination in the form of a line of simple whiteness, almost electrical, straighter than any rule could draw; the line traced from the muzzle to the target without a waver to it. Twenty-five yards downrange Earl's gun gnawed a raggedy hole in the center of the silhouette.

"Great, huh? Well, guess what, that's all wrong. Never fire more than three-round bursts. In the movies they wail away like that, but that's because right behind the camera they got a bohunk with a case of .45 blanks ready to scoot out and reload when the camera's off and the star's taking his Camel break. You will carry all your ammo, and you don't want to use it up for nothing, and unless you are a genius, every goddamn shot after the third is going into the trees. I happen to be a genius. Maybe Frenchy is too. But no other birds here appear to be. *This* is how we do it."

He turned again, brought the gun into play and tapped out three short three-round bursts. Each burst scored the head of the target, each leaked its flicker of flame. By the end, there was no head, only shredded tatters of cardboard.

They worked with Thompsons in the afternoon and the .45s in the morning for several days. They worked hard, and some got the swing of it faster than others, but by the end, each of them was edging toward some kind of proficiency. The tracers, an old FBI training trick, made it easier for a buddy to read the trajectory of the rounds and advise you when the muzzle roamed, throwing bullets to no particular destination. But Earl warned them only to use the tracers in training, never in battle, because first of all they were a dead giveaway to your position and secondly the trace was incendiary and if fired into dry wood buildings or sage or other undergrowth or dead leaves or whatever, would light up a fire. No problem on an island like Iwo, but not good in a city like Hot Springs, where most of the casinos were old wooden structures.

On the fifth day, Earl introduced them to the BAR.

"Now this here gun is a real Jap-killer. It fires big .30 government cartridges at about twenty-three hundred feet per second and they will tear up anything they hit. If you got a boy behind soft cover, this will punch through and get him. Against cars or light trucks, this here thing is The Answer. Twenty-round clips, effective range out to one thousand yards, gas-operated, man-portable, but no lightweight. About sixteen pounds. They usually come with bipods for support, but the first thing that happens is the bipod is junked. These guns already got their bipods junked. Each squad in the Marines or the infantry had one of these guns; they were the base of fire, set up to cover all squad maneuvers and offer long-range suppressive fire.

"We will use these guns sparingly. They will fire through three walls and kill someone across the street going to the bathroom. But you should know them, anyhow, in case we come up against some real desperadoes, who are hunkered in good and solid and want to shoot it out to the last man. That's when the BAR comes into play. It ain't a John Wayne gun. You don't spray with it like you see in the movies. It's got too much power for that."

But the boys found it much easier to shoot than the Thompsons, for the reason that it was heavier, and its weight absorbed the recoil better and because the longer .30 governments were much easier to load in the magazines than the stubby .45s for the Thompson. They'd shoot it at the hundred-yard range, and quickly became proficient at clustering five-round bursts center mass on the silhouettes.

Half days were spent on weapons they'd be least likely to use, the Winchester 97 shotguns and the M-1 carbines. And then they took Sunday off, and most went into Texarkana for a movie or some other form of relaxation while Earl and D.A. plotted the schedule. Everybody knew what was coming next.

The fun part.

CHAPTER

10

Owney never held his meetings at the same place twice. It was a habit from the old days. You didn't want to fall into a pattern, because a pattern would get you killed. If you have a Mad Dog Coll hunting you, you learn the elementary lessons of evasion, and you never forget them.

Thus most of the higher-ranking Grumleys, the bigger casino managers, the head bookmakers, the wire manager, his lawyer, F. Garry Hurst, the men who ran the men who ran the numbers runners, and so forth and so on, were used to being banged all over town when Owney convened them.

They never knew when the call would come and what travel it would demand. So today's mandate was usual in the sense that it was no more unusual than any other mandate. He called the meeting for the bathhouse called the Fordyce, on Central, which had been temporarily closed for the occasion.

They sat naked, swaddled in sheets, under an ornate glass roof, multitinted and floral. It was somehow like sitting *in* flowers. It was daytime, as befit business. Sunlight streamed through the window above, incandescent and weirdly lit by the hyacinth-tinted glass. Each had bathed in the 141-degree water until each had felt like a raisin. Then each had been subjected to a needle-pointed shower that ripped open their pores. Now they sat in a steam room, looking like Roman senators in togas, except that the vapors swept this way and that. Outside, Grumleys patrolled to make certain no interlopers or accidental eavesdroppers were in the vicinity. A couple of Grumley gals even moved into the women's bath area, so as to make sure no ladies lurked there.

The meeting was businesslike, though the Owney on display here was not the cosmopolitan Owney the host, anxious to put on a display of savoir faire for an important out-of-towner, complete to a version of a British accent derived more from an actor than from actual memory. In the privacy of his own sanctum, where his power was absolute and his prestige unchallenged, Owney devolved to the tones of the East Side of Manhattan, where he had been nurtured from the age of thirteen through the age of forty-three.

"Nothin'," he said again, chewing on an unlit cigar, another Havana. "You got fuckin' nothin'?"

"Not a dang thing," said Flem Grumley, the senior Grumley since Pap Grumley's clap had kicked in a month ago, declaring that seasoned operative hors de combat. Flem, hardened in the bootlegging wars of the '20s, spoke a brew of Arkansas diction so dense it took years of concentration to master its intricacies. "We's run the town up, we's run it down. These damned old boys done slipped the noose. Damnedest goddamndangdest thang."

Owney chewed this over a bit, shredding his cigar even further.

"Only," said Flem, "only a bit later cousin Slidell, that being Will's boy Slidell, not Jud's nor Bob's, nor—"

"Yeah, yeah," said Owney, to halt the list of Slidell Grumley fathers.

"Uh, yes sir, that Slidell, he done checked back at the Best out Oua-chita. Seems a feller rented two cabins fer a week. Older feller, sad-like. A younger feller jined him, tough-like, so it goes."

"There were two of them, then?" Owney remarked.

"Wal, sir, maybe. Manager says them boys stopped showing up mid-week. Never came back. Will's Slidell got the key, checked out each cabin. Wasn't nary much-like. Extry underwear, toothbrushes and powder, a Little Rock newspaper. No guns or nothing. Them boys travel light, even if they's the ones, even if they's wasn't.'"

"I don't fuckin' like this shit one bit," Owney said aloud. "If they was nobodies, they fucking wouldn't have thought it to be a big deal. They mighta left town, but not before checking out. These guys, they *knew* I'd be looking for them. That fuckin' cowboy who hit Siegel, he *knew* me. He looked at me and said"—and here he lapsed into a pass-ably convincing imitation of the rumbly vessel that was Earl's sulfur-scorched voice—"'How 'bout it, Mr. Maddox, you or any of your boys want a taste'? He fucking *knew* me. How's he know me? I don't know him. How the fuck he know me?"

Owney gazed off into the vapors as if fascinated by this new prob-lem. That guy had the best hands he'd ever seen.

"That fucking guy, he could hit. I managed a boxer for a few years. Big lug couldn't hit shit. But I know the fight game, and that boy was a hitter!"

"Could they be New York guys? Or Chicago guys?"

"They could be Chicago guys," Owney said. "Bugsy was a New York guy and he sure as shit din't know them. I'd a heard if they was New York. Man, he hit that yid hard!"

"Cops?" someone thought to ask.

"Did you check the cops?" Owney asked Flem Grumley.

"Did, yes sir. Chief says it warn't none of his boys. He ain't hired no new boys. He even called a friend he has in the Little Rock FBI and it ain't no federal thing. No revenooers or nothing like that. Believe me, I know revenooers and these damn boys weren't revenooers. No revenooer ever could hit like that."

"Could they work for the new prosecuting attorney?" somebody asked. "We don't got any sources into what Becker is running."

Flem had an answer: "That boy is so scared since Rufus throwed that dead dog on his lawn he ain't been seen in town! He don't hardly even go to his office!"

There was much laughter.

And that was pretty much it: the rest was old business—a new Chinese laundry near Oaklawn was behind in his payments and would have to be instructed to keep up-to-date; the Jax brewery in New Orleans had delivered too much beer but a Grumley had convinced the driver of the truck not to report it; the wheel at the Horseshoe was running wobbly and cutting into the joint odds, though it could be repaired—but thought had to be put into replacing it; the betting season at Hialeah was just getting started and Owney ought to consider putting a new man or two into the Central Book as the wire would run very hot when Hialeah was up and steaming.

But after the meeting was over, the manager of the Golden Sun, a house near the Oaklawn Racetrack, pulled Owney over.

"I heard something, Owney."

"And what's that, Jock?"

"Ah, maybe it's nothing, but you should know anyhow."

"So, spill."

"My brother-in-law runs a craps game in an after-hour joint for Mickey Cohen in L.A. He used to work on that gambling boat they had beyond the twelve-mile-limit."

"Yeah?"

"Yeah, and times are tough since they closed that ship. But Mickey told my brother-in-law that good things are set up."

Owney listened intently. Mickey Cohen was Bugsy's right-hand man.

"What's he mean?"

"He says there'd be jobs for all the old guys, the real pro table crews."

"So? Is Bugsy going to try and get the ship thing going again?"

"No, Owney. It's bigger than that. Evidently, he's bought a big chunk of desert over the Nevada state line. Gambling's legal in Nevada. Nobody goes there, but it's legal."

"I still don't—"

"He's thinking big. He's going to build a place. A big place. He's got some New York money bankrolling it. It's supposed to be secret. But he's going to build a gambling city in the desert. He's going to build a Hot Springs in the desert. Me, I think it's shit. Who's going to go to a fucking desert to gamble?"

But Owney immediately understood the nature of Bugsy's visit, and saw the threat to his own future. That was Bugsy's game, then. There could only be one Hot Springs. It would be here in Arkansas, where it belonged; or it would be in Nevada, in the fucking desert, where yid punk Bugsy wanted it.

It wouldn't be in two places.

Someone was going to have to die.

CHAPTER
11

D.A. had worked it out very carefully in his mind. He broke the team down into two-man fire teams, and put three of them into each squad, one designated the front-entry team and the other the rear-entry team.

Now it was time to do it, with unloaded weapons but all other gear as it would be, including the heavy vests that everybody hated.

Of course the young Carlo Henderson found himself united with the even younger Frenchy Short, who was full of opinions too important to be kept to himself, which was one reason nobody else would come near Frenchy.

"See," he said, "I would use the shotguns and the carbines. This isn't the '20s. The Thompsons were developed for trench warfare. For spraying. You spray a room, you got—"

"You wasn't ever instructed to spray nothing," said the stolid Carlo. "Mr. Earl told us: three-shot bursts."

"Yeah, well, some of these hicks from the sticks, they'll go nuts if somebody starts shooting at 'em. They'll spray anything that moves. They'll turn one of these casinos into a Swiss cheese house."

"You'd best just do what you're told."

"Ah," said Frenchy. "You're one of them. You probably love all this shit. You probably love that big Mr. Earl throwing his weight around like he's some kind of God or John Wayne or something."

"He seems okay. I heard he was a big war hero."

"Yeah, what'd it get him? Pretend sergeant in Hot Springs, Arkansas, busting down casino doors. Shit. He couldn't do better off a big medal than *that?*"

"What're you even here for if all this is so much crap?"

"Ah—"

"Well?"

"You won't tell anybody?"

"Of course not. You're my buddy. I have to cover for you."

"I got kicked out of Princeton. Boy, was my old man red-assed! He's a big-deal judge, so he got me a job in the police department. What I really want to do is get to the FBI. But not without a college degree, no sir. But if I do well as a cop—"

"Why'd you get kicked out?"

"It's a long story," said Frenchy, and his eyes grew hard and tough with a zealot's fire. "It was another crap deal, believe me. I got blamed for something I absolutely *did not do!* Anyhow, if I can get into the FBI, I can maybe then get into the OSS. You know what that is?"

"The what?"

"The what! Henderson, you're even dumber than you look. It's the Office of Strategic Services. The spies. Man, I would be so good at that! You work in foreign countries and I have a gift for languages and accents. These guys all believe I'm from some Passel O'Toads, Georgia! Anyhow, in OSS you pull shit all the time. In the war they blew up trains and assassinated Nazi generals and cut wires and eavesdropped on diplomats. My uncle did it."

"Well," said Henderson, "you'd best forget about all that and just focus on what we're going to be doing in a few minutes."

"Okay, but I get the Thompson, okay?"

"I thought you didn't like the Thompson."

"I didn't say I didn't like it. I said it was wrong for this kind of work. But I get to carry the Thompson."

"Fine. I'll go first."

"No, I'll go first. Come on, I'm much faster than you, I shoot better than you, I'm quick, I'm smart, I'm—"

"You can't *both* go first and carry the Thompson. That's agin the rules."

"The rules!" cursed Frenchy, as if he'd run up against this one before. "The goddamned rules! Well, fuck the rules!"

The address was Building 3-3-2, in a sea of deserted barracks that spilled across the hardscrabble Texas plain. It looked no different than any other barrack, just a decaying tan building, its paint peeling, its wood drying out, a few of its shingles flapping in the ever-present wind.

That was the target. The twelve officers took up positions in a barracks three doors down, made a preliminary recon, studied their objective, and drew up plans. Stretch, the oldest at twenty-six, a Highway Patrolman from Oregon, was nominally in charge, and he was steady and wise, and knew the wisdom in keeping it simple. It seemed so easy, if only everybody would listen and cooperate.

But almost immediately Frenchy began to undercut him. Frenchy knew better. Frenchy figured it out. Frenchy, charming, loquacious, willful, kept saying, "I'm the best shot, I ought to go first. Really, why not let the best shot go first?"

"Short, can you give somebody else a turn?"

"I'm just saying, the best way is to utilize your best people up front. I'm a very good shot. Nobody has shot as well as I have. Isn't that right? Correct me if I'm wrong. So I ought to be the first-entry guy."

He had very little shame, and no quit in him at all. Finally, to shut him up and get on with the planning, Stretch gave Frenchy the okay to be first man on the rear-entry team, with his partner.

That said, other assignments handed out, and the men suited up, sliding on the heavy armored plates over their suit coats, then donning their fedoras. They got into three cars—two old Highway Patrol Fords, painted all black, and a DeSoto that had once belonged to the State Liquor Control Board—and drove through the deserted streets of the barrack city until they came at 3-3-2 from different angles.

"All teams," said Stretch, into his walkie-talkie and consulting his watch, "deploy *now!*"

The cars halted. The men rushed out. Immediately one fell down, jamming his Thompson muzzle into the Texas loam, filling its compensator with muck. Another, as he ran to the door, banged his knee severely on the swinging steel of the vest, which was really more a sandwich board of heavy metal; he went down, painfully out of action.

But Frenchy, in the lead from the rear car, made it to the door first and fastest. He carried the tommy gun. Carlo, less graceful and more ungainly in his armor, struggled behind.

Frenchy kicked the door.

It didn't budge.

"Shit!" he said.

"Goddammit, you're supposed to wait for me!" Carlo said, arriving, followed by the last four men on the team.

"The fucking door is jammed."

Frenchy kicked it again. It didn't move.

"We ought to—"

But Frenchy couldn't wait. He threw off his heavy armor, smashed in a window, climbed into the frame and dove through it, rolling in the darkness. He stood up.

"Prosecuting Attorney's Office," he screamed. "This is a raid! Hands up!"

"Wait for me, goddammit," huffed poor Henderson, still on the other side of the door.

Frenchy heard them banging. It never occurred to him to unlock it. He did not wait for anybody. He headed down a hall in what was surprising darkness, feeling liberated in the absence of the twenty pounds of armor. The hall led to a wider room, and he raced in, pointing his empty tommy gun at menacing forms which proved to be old desks and tables and chairs. At once the room filled with smoke. The smoke billowed and unfurled, completely disorienting him. He coughed, ran further into the room, all alone, and stepped into a wider space, where the smoke was thinner. All around him things seemed to crash. Before him, he saw shapes. Without thinking about it, he dropped to one knee, put the tommy gun sights on them, and pulled the trigger. The gun's bolt flew forward with a powerful whack.

He recocked, knowing in reality he'd just mowed a few people down, and suddenly a figure appeared before him.

WHACK! he fired again, and a second later noted the surprised face of Carlo Henderson, whom he had just killed. He lurched to the left to a stairwell, kicked it open and raced up it.

"Short!"

He turned. Earl stood behind him, .45 leveled straight at his face for a perfect head shot, and snapped the trigger.

Then Earl said, "Congratulations, Short. You killed three of your own team members, you killed your partner, and you got yourself killed too. Just think of what you could have done if you'd have gotten to the second floor!"

D.A. gathered the young men in the dirt road out front of 3-3-2, invited the fellows to shed the body armor, stack the guns, take off the hats and coats and loosen the ties and light 'em up if they had 'em. It was blazing hot and most of the men had sweated through their clothes. They were a pretty sad-looking bunch: dampened and dejected.

"Now fellows," he said, "I'd be lying if I told you you did a good job. Frankly a bagful of coons locked in a cellar with ten pounds of raw meat might have behaved better. Basically what I saw was a series of mistakes compounding mistakes. I don't know what happened to your communications. Front-entry team at least hung together; too bad you got wiped out by the rear-entry team. Now, as I told you, the deal is simultaneous entrance. That's the trick. You have to be coming from two directions at once with overwhelming force. They have to understand that there is no possibility of victory and that resistance is futile.

"I will admit that we threw you some ringers. Mr. Earl popped a smoke grenade just to confuse the issue. I would say it confused you plenty. Would anyone disagree with me? The back door was locked. Did anybody think to look above the doorjamb? That's where the key was. Instead, at that point, rear-entry team just fell apart. Did rear-entry team walkie-talkie front-entry team? Nah. I was monitoring the radios upstairs. You were out of contact, and when you're out of contact, all kinds of hob can play. Finally, fellows, you can't let yourself get too excited. We had an unfortunate experience where one team member became separated, and got extremely aggressive with his weapon. He was supposed to be in support, but he rushed ahead, brought fire on the other team, then shot his partner, then rushed up a stairwell without securing the zone behind him and got shot by Mr. Earl. Fellows, you have to stay calm. If you let your emotions get the best of you, you become dangerous to your team members. This is about teamwork, fellows, remember. Teamwork, communications, good shooting skills, controlled aggression, sound tactics. That's the core of the art. You got anything, Earl?"

"Only this. I learned this one the hard way. The fight is going to be what it wants to be. You got to be ready to go with it, follow it where it goes, and deal with it. Remember: Always cheat, always win."

Fire and movement.

It was the most necessary training and the most dangerous.

"I saved this for last," said D.A., "because you have to work on your gun-handling skills and your self-discipline before you can even think about such a thing. This is the one where if you screw up, you kill a buddy or a bystander."

The course, as D.A. designed it, was set up in a tempo office building that administered the ranges back when the depot was turning out men for war. Now it was scheduled for destruction when the government's budget would allow it. It could be shot up to everybody's content and all walls but the front one were declared shootable. That gave the men a 270-degree shooting arc.

"You move through in two-man teams, just like on a real raid. The man on the right takes the targets on the right. The man on the left the targets on the left. Short, controlled bursts. Remember, trust your buddy. And, for God's sake, *stay together!*"

That was Earl. He would walk behind each team as they ran the course, as a safety measure.

The guys waited their turns as each two-man team ran the course. Inside the house, they could hear the quick stutters of the tommy guns and the bark of the .45s as each team popped its targets. One by one the teams emerged intact, joyous, and Earl would call up another team.

Finally, it was Frenchy and Carlo's turn.

"Okay, guys, you just take her easy. Short, you listening today?"

"Yes sir."

"Good. Okay, who's on the big gun?"

The two hadn't discussed this. They looked at each other.

"Henderson, you're bigger. You run the big gun. Short, you're a damned good pistol man. You work your .45. Remember, controlled speed, make sure of your targets, keep relating to your partner. Know where he is at all times, and nobody has to get hurt."

"Gotcha," said Frenchy.

The two young officers locked and loaded their weapons under Earl's supervision, then bent and got into the heavy armored vests.

"All right," he said, "muzzles level, we're shoulder to shoulder, we're not rushing, we're all eyes looking for targets. You shoot the black targets. You don't shoot the targets with white Xs on them. That would be civilians. Henderson, remember, three-shot bursts on that thing, dead center. You, Short, you're responsible for the left-hand sector. Henderson, you take the right. Don't hold the gun too tightly. Okay, fellas, I'm right here for you. All set?"

Both youngsters nodded.

"Let's do her good," said Earl.

Frenchy kicked the door, which yielded quickly. They entered, walked in tandem down a long corridor. At a certain point Earl flicked on a wall switch and two targets stood before them. Frenchy, his pistol out, was fastfastfast, putting two shots into the chest of his. A split second later Henderson's three-shot burst tore the heart out of the target on the right.

"Good, good," said Earl. "Now keep moving, don't bunch up, don't stop to admire yourself, keep your eyes moving."

They came to a corner. Frenchy jumped across the hall, his gun locked in the triangle of his arms and supported by the triangle of his legs as he hunted for targets. Carlo came next, dropping into a good kneeling shooting position. Two targets were before them, and Earl felt the boys tense as they raised their weapons, but then relax; the targets were Xed.

"Clear," sang Frenchy.

"Clear," came the answer.

"Good decision," said Earl. "Keep it up."

They moved on to a stairwell.

"Remember the last time?" Earl asked.

That was a hint. Frenchy jumped into the stairwell, covering the back zone, while Carlo fell to the far wall, orienting his Thompson up the stairs. Both saw their targets immediately. Frenchy's .45 rang twice as he pumped two shots into the silhouette from two feet away and Carlo fired a seven- or eight-shot burst, ripping up two silhouettes at the top of the stairs.

"Clear."

"Clear."

The gun smoke heaved and drifted in the smallish space. A litter of spent shells lay underfoot.

"Good work," said Earl.

Frenchy quickly dropped his magazine, inserted another.

"Great, Short. Nobody else has reloaded and some of 'em have run dry upstairs. Good thinking, son."

Frenchy actually smiled.

The team crept up the stairs.

They did another explosive turn as they emerged from the stairwell to confront yet another empty hallway. Down it lurked a series of doors.

"Got to clear them rooms," said Earl.

One by one, the team moved into the rooms. It was tense, close work: they'd kick in a door, scan the room, and find targets that could be shot or targets that couldn't. The gunfire was rapid and accurate, and neither of them made a mistake. No innocents were shot, no bad guys survived.

Finally, there was one room left, the last one.

The two gave each other a look. Frenchy nodded, took a deep breath and kicked the door open, spilling into the room to find targets on the left. One step behind plunged Carlo, who saw three silhouettes behind a table and raised the tommy, found the front sight and pulled the—

Frenchy had a moment of confusion when he felt he should not be moving, but an immense feeling of freedom and speed hit him. It was his armored vest; the strap had popped and the vest slipped sideways, the sudden shift of its weight taking his control from him. The second strap then broke, and the vest fell in two separate pieces to the floor, but Frenchy was too far gone and felt himself sprawling forward as his feet scrabbled for leverage, but instead slipped further on empty cartridge cases.

It was all so unreal. Time almost stopped. The noise of the Thompson became huge and blocked out all other things. He smelled gun smoke, felt heat, even as he fell. He lurched toward the flash and had an instant of horror as he knew, knew absolutely that he would die, for he would in the next instant fall before the path of the bullets and Carlo would not expect him and that would be that.

Shit! he thought, as he plunged toward his death in the stream of .45s.

Yet somehow he hit the ground untouched, stars shot off in his head, and then someone heavy fell upon him and there were muffled grunts.

"Jesus Christ!" Carlo was saying.

"Y'all okay?" asked Earl.

Earl was among them in the tangle on the floor. He disengaged and got up. "Y'all okay? You fine?"

"Gosh darn it!" said Carlo.

"Short, you hit?"

"Ah, no, I— What happened?"

"I almost killed you is what happened," said Carlo, his voice aquiver with trembling. "You fell into my line of fire, I couldn't stop, I—"

"It's okay, it's okay," said Earl. "Just get ahold of yourselves."

"What the heck happened to you? Why were you way out there?"

"The vest broke and I fell forward and my feet slipped on some shells."

"You are a lucky little son of a gun, Short. Mr. Earl, he grabbed the gun maybe a tenth of a second before it would have cut you up. He went through me and he grabbed the gun!"

"Jesus," said Frenchy. A wave of fear hit him.

"Okay, you fellows all right?" said Earl.

"Jesus," said Frenchy again, and vomited.

"Well, see, that's what a close shave'll do to you. Come on now, you're both okay, let's get up and get out of here."

"You saved my—"

"Yeah, yeah, and I saved myself three weeks of paperwork too. Come on, boys, let's get our asses in gear. No need to get crazy about this. Only, Short: next time, check the straps. Do a maintenance check each time you go on a raid. Got that?"

"I never—"

"It's the 'never' that gets you killed, Short."

But then he winked, and Frenchy felt a little better.

There was no officers' club for Earl and D.A. to go to that night, and since neither man drank anymore, it was perhaps a good thing. But D.A. invited Earl out to dinner, and so they found a bar-b-que joint in Texarkana, near the railway station, and set to have some ribs and fries, and many a cold Coke.

The food was good, the place was dark and coolish, and somebody put some Negro jump blues on the Rockola, and that thing was banging out a bebopping rhythm that took both their minds away from where they were. Afterward, the two men smoked and finished a last Coke, but Earl knew enough to know he was being prepared for something. And he had a surprise of his own he'd been planning to lay on D.A. sooner or later, and this looked to be as good a time as any.

"Well, Earl, you've done a fine job. I'm sure you're the best sergeant the Marine Corps ever turned out. You got them whipped into some kind of shape right fast."

"Well, sir," said Earl, "the boys are coming along all right. Wish we had another two months to train 'em. But they're solid, obedient young men, they work hard, they listen and maybe they'll do okay."

"Who worries you?"

"Oh, that Short kid, of course. Something in that one I just don't trust. He wants to do so well he may make a bad judgment somewhere along the line. I will say, he learns fast and he's a good pistol hand. But you never can tell about boys until the lead starts flying."

"I agree with you about Short. Only Yankee in the bunch and he sounds more Southern than any man born down upon the Swanee River."

"I noticed that too. Don't know where it comes from. Any South in him?"

"Not a lick. He told me he had a gift for soaking up dialects. Maybe he don't even notice that he's doing it."

"Maybe. I never saw nothing like it in fifteen years in the Marines."

"Anyhow, I'm asking you because I got some news."

"Figured you did."

"Mr. Becker is getting very restless. He's under a lot of pressure with anonymous phone threats and such-like and townspeople wondering when the hell he's going to do something other than go to his office and close the door without talking to nobody. And his wife is followed by Grumley boys everywhere she goes. We got to deal with that. We got to move, and soon. Are we ready?"

"Well, you're never ready. But we are ready on one condition."

"I think I know what this is, Earl," said the old man gravely.

"So did my wife. She said it was my nature."

"She knows you, Earl. And I know you too, even though I first laid eyes on you three weeks or so ago. You're the goddamned hero. How you made it through that war I'll never know."

"Anyhow, I have to go. The boys have made a connection to me, and they'll be frightened if I ain't there."

"They'll get over it."

"Mr. Parker, I have to be there. You know it and I know it. They need a steady hand, and you've got too much to do setting the raids up with Becker and then dealing with the police and the press afterward."

"Earl, if you get hit, I'd never forgive myself."

"And if one of those kids got hit while I'se sitting somewhere sucking on a Coca-Cola, I'd never forgive myself."

"Earl, you are a hard man to be the boss of, I will say that."

"I know what's right. Plus, no goddamn hillbilly with a shotgun is going to get the best of me."

"Earl, never underestimate your enemy. You should know that from the war. Owney Maddox was called 'Killer' back in New York. According to the New York District Attorney's Office, he killed over twenty men in his time. Once this shit starts happening, he's going to bring in some mobsters who've pulled triggers before. Don't kid yourself, Earl. These will be tough boys. Get ready for 'em."

"Then you'll let me go?"

"Shit, Earl, you have to go. That is as clear to me as the nose on my face. But I want you to go home and talk to your wife first. Hear me? You tell her like a man. So she knows. And you tell her you love her and that things will be okay. And you listen to that pup in her belly. Look, here's twenty-five bucks, you take her out to a nice dinner at Fort Smith's finest restaurant."

"Ain't no fine restaurants in Fort Smith."

"Then hire a cook."

"Yes sir."

"And you meet us Tuesday in Hot Springs."

"Tuesday?"

"Here it is, Earl. Our first warrant. We hit the Horseshoe at 10:00 P.M. Tuesday night. We're going to start the ball rolling with a big one."

CHAPTER

12

He got back late Friday night; the vets village was quiet and it took him some time to find his own hut. The low, corrugated shapes had such a sameness to them that most of the women had tried to pretty them up with flower beds and bushes, maybe a trellis or something silly like that. But they were still essentially tubes half buried in the earth, passing as housing. Eventually, he got himself oriented—fellow could wander for hours in the sameness of the place, all the little streets just like all the other little streets—and found 5th Street, where he lived in No. 17. He knocked and there was no answer. She must be sleeping. He opened the door because nobody bothered to lock up.

He heard her in what passed for the bedroom; it was really just a jerry-built wall that didn't reach the arched tin roof. She breathed steadily, deeply, as if for two. He didn't want to startle her, so he stayed out of that room and instead remained in the large one.

He moved one small lamp so that the bulb would not shine into the bedroom, and turned it on, looking about as he undressed. It was a fairly squalid experience. The furniture was all used, the tin walls overcurving as if boring in, to crush the life out of all possibility here. She'd worked hard to cheer the place up inside as well as out, to disguise its essential governmentness, by painting and hanging pictures and curtains and what-not. But the effort was doomed, overwhelmed by the odor of the aluminum that encapsulated them and the feel of the give in the wooden slats that made up the floor.

The plumbing was primitive, the stove and icebox small, the place drafty. It was no place to bring up a kid.

He went to the kitchen—rather to the corner where the kitchen appliances were located—and opened the icebox, hoping to find some milk or something or maybe another Coca-Cola. But she had not known he was coming and there was nothing. But then a rogue impulse fired off and he opened a certain cabinet and there indeed, as he remembered, was a half-full bottle of Boone County bourbon.

It took a lot of Earl not to drink it. He was not in the mood to say no to bourbon, because the long pull up the western edge of Arkansas on 71 essentially took him through home ground. The road, two lanes of wandering macadam, crawled through Polk County, where his daddy had been the sheriff and a big, important man. Near midnight, the drive took Earl through Blue Eye, the county seat, nestled in the trackless Ouachitas. He hadn't seen it in years. The main street ran west of the train tracks, lined with little buildings. He'd had no impulse to detour to see what had been his father's office and was still the county sheriff's office; nor had he had an impulse to detour out Arkansas 8 to Board Camp, where the farm that he had inherited as the last surviving Swagger lay fallow. He had faced it once, when he was immediately out of the Corps, and that had been enough.

Ghosts seemed to scamper through the night. Was it Halloween? No, the ghosts were memories, some happy, some sad, really just bright pictures in his mind of this day and that in his boyhood, of parades and hikes and hunting trips—his father was an ardent, excellent hunter and one wall of the house was alive with his trophies—and all the things that filled a boy's life in the 1920s in rural America. But he always sensed his father's giganticism, his father's weight and bulk and gravity, the fear that other man paid in homage to Charles Swagger, sheriff of Polk County.

He tried not to think of his father, but he could no more forbid his mind from doing that than he could forbid it from ordering his lungs to breathe. A great father-heaviness came over him, and he could see a spell of brooding setting in, where his father would be the only thing in his mind and would still, all these years later, have the capacity to dominate everything.

His father was a sharp-dressed man, always in black suits and white linen shirts from the Sears, Roebuck catalogue. His black string ties were always perfect and he labored over them each morning to get them so. Daddy's face was grave and lined and brooked no disobedience. He knew right from wrong as the Baptist Bible stated it. He carried a Colt Peacemaker on his right side, a leather truncheon in his back pocket and he rattled with keys and other important objects when he walked. He carried a Jesus gun also, a .32 rimfire Smith & Wesson stuffed up his left cuff and held there by a sleeve garter. It had saved his life in 1923 in a shoot-out with desperadoes; he'd killed all three of them and been a great hero.

Charles Swagger also had the capacity to loom. It was in part his size but more his rigidity. He stood for things, stood straight and tall for them, and represented in a certain way America. To defy him was to defy America and he was quick to deal with disobedience. People loved him or feared him, but no matter what, they acknowledged him. He was a powerful man who ruled his small kingdom efficiently. He knew all the doctors and ministers and lawyers; of course he knew the mayor and the county board, and the prominent property owners. He knew all of them and they all knew him and could trust him. He kept the peace everywhere except in his own home, and from his own aggressions.

Charles didn't drink every night, just every third night. He was a bourbon drinker, and he drank for one reason, which was to feel himself the man he knew everybody thought him to be and to banish the fears that must have cut at him. Thus, drunk, he became even mightier and more heroic and more unbending. His righteousness in all things grew to be a force of nature. His doubts vanished and his happy confidence soared. He retold the story of the day and how he had solved all the problems and what he had told the many people who had to be put in their places. But when he looked about and saw how little his family had given a man of his nobility and family lines, it troubled him deeply. He corrected his wife's many mistakes and pointed out that her people were really nothing compared to his. He pointed out the flaws in his sons and sometimes—more often as he got older—he disciplined his eldest with a razor strop or a belt. That boy was such a disappointment. That boy was such a nothing, a nobody. You would think a great man like Charles Swagger would have a great son, but no, he only had poor Earl and his even more pathetic younger brother, Bobby Lee, who still wet the bed. He instructed his eldest in his insignificance, as if the boy were incapable of understanding it himself, though the boy understood it very well.

"He has no talent," Charles would scream at his wife. "He has no talent. He needs to find a trade, but he's too lazy for a trade! He's nothing, and he'll never be anything, and I'll beat the fear of God into him if it's the last thing I ever do."

Thus, alone in his hut, that boy, grown to be a man, felt again the temptation of the bottle. Inside the bottle might be damnation and cowardice, but it was also escape from the looming of the father. It beckoned him mightily. It offered a form of salvation, a music of pleasure, the sense of being blurred and softened, where all things seemed possible. But you always woke up the next morning with the taste of an alley in your mouth and the hazy memory of having said things that shouldn't be said or having heard things that shouldn't be heard.

Earl opened the bottle and poured the bourbon out. He didn't feel any better at all, but at least he had not fallen off the wagon. He went back over to the couch and lay there in the dark, listening to his wife breathe for two, and eventually he fell off to his own shallow and troubled sleep.

. . .

The next morning she was happy. He was there, it took so little to please her. He listened to her account of the doctor's reports and she asked him to touch her stomach and feel the thing inside move.

"Doctor says he's coming along just fine," said Junie.

"Well, damn," said Earl. "That's really great."

"Have you picked a name yet?" Junie wanted to know.

No. He hadn't. Hadn't even thought of it. He realized she probably presumed he was as occupied with the baby as she was. But he wasn't. He was pretending he cared. The thing inside her scared him. He had no feeling for it except fear.

"I don't know," he said, "maybe we should name him after your father."

"My father was an idiot. And that's when he was sober," she added, and laughed.

"Well, my father was a bastard. And that's when *he* was sober." And they both laughed.

"You should name him after your brother."

"Hmmm," said Earl. His brother. Why'd she have to bring that up? "Well, maybe," he said. "We have plenty of time to figure it out. Maybe we should start fresh. Pick a movie star's name. Name him Humphrey or John or Cornell or Joseph or something."

"Maybe it'll be a girl," she said. "Then we could name her after your mama."

"Oh," he said, "maybe we just ought to make it a new start. It ain't got nothing to do with the past, sweetie."

Junie was showing now. Her face was plumped up, but still the damndest thing he'd ever seen. She was packing weight on her shoulders and, of course, through the middle.

"Honey, I don't know nothing about names. You name the baby. You're carrying the critter, you get to name it, fair enough?"

"Well, Earl, you should take part too."

"I just don't know," he said, too fiercely. Then he said, "I'm damned sorry. I didn't mean to bark at nothing. You getting the money all right? You okay in that job? You don't have no problems, do you, sweetie? Hell, you know what an ornery old bastard I can be."

She forced a smile, and it seemed to be all forgotten but he knew it wouldn't be.

That night he took her into the dining room at the Ward Hotel on Garrison Street, the nicest place to eat in all of Fort Smith.

He looked very handsome. He wore his suit so well, and he was tanned and polite and seemed happy in some odd way, in no way he had been since the war. It warmed her to see him so happy.

"Well," she said, "it does seem like we've come up in the world. You have a car. We get to go out at a fine place like this."

"That's right," he said. "We're on our way. You know, you could probably rent a place in town. You could get out of that vets village. They're going to be building new housing everywhere."

"Well, it seems so silly. Why move now, then move again when we have to go into Hot Springs? I assume I'm coming to Hot Springs sometime."

"Well, yes, that's the plan, I guess."

But a vagueness came across his face. That was Earl's horror: his distance. Sometimes he was just not there, she thought, as if something came and took his mind from him, and gave it over to memories of the war or something else. Sometimes she felt like she was in the *Iliad,* married to a Greek warrior, a powerful man but one who'd shed too much blood and come too close to dying too many times, a man somehow leeched by death. There was a phrase for it that she'd heard in her girlhood, and now it came back to her: "Black as the earl of death." Hill people talked that way, and her father, a doctor, sometimes took her on his trips into the Missouri hollows and she heard the way the folks talked: black as the earl of death. That was her Earl, somehow, and somehow, she knew, she had to save him from it.

The waiter came and offered to fetch cocktails. Earl took a Coca-Cola instead, though he encouraged Junie to go ahead, and she ordered something called a mimosa, which turned out to be orange juice with champagne in it.

"Now where'd you hear about that?"

"I read about it in the *Redbook* magazine."

"It seems very big-city."

"It's from Los Angeles. It's very popular out there. They say California is turning into the land of opportunity now that the war is over."

"Well, maybe we should move out there when all this is over." But the vagueness came to his face again, as if he had some unpleasant association with California.

"I could never leave my mother," she said hastily. "And with the baby coming—"

"I didn't mean it, really. I wouldn't know what to do in Los Angeles. Hell, I hardly know what to do in Hot Springs."

"Oh, Earl."

They ordered roast chicken and roast beef and had an extremely nice dinner. It was wonderful to see him in a civilized place, and to be in such a nice room which was filled with other well-dressed people. The waiters wore tuxedos, a man played the piano, it was all formal and pleasant.

"Now, honey," he finally said.

A shadow crossed her face, a darkening. She knew that tone: it meant something horrible was coming.

"What is it, Earl? I knew there was something."

"Well, it's just a little something."

"Is it about the job?"

"Yes ma'am."

"Well, so tell me."

"Oh, it's nothing. Mr. Parker though, he thought I should come up here and take you on a nice date and everything. He's a fine man. I hope to introduce you to him sometime, if it works out. He's as fine as any officer I had in the Corps, including Chesty Puller. He cares about the job, but he cares about his people too, and that's very rare."

"Earl? What is it?"

"Well, honey, you remember those raids I said I was never going on? Into the casinos and the book joints? Now these young men we have, they've worked damned hard and they've really become very good in the small amount of time. But two weeks. Hell, it takes two years to become a good Marine. Anyhow, these boys, they . . ."

He trailed off helplessly, because he couldn't quite find the words.

"They what?"

"Oh, they just don't quite know enough."

"Enough for what?"

"Enough to do it by themselves."

"I don't—"

"So I said to Mr. Parker, I said I should go along. At first. Just to make sure. Just to watch. That's all. I wanted to tell you. I had told you I was just going to train them. Now I'm going with them. That's all. I wanted to tell you straight up."

She looked at him.

"There'll be guns and shooting? These raids will be violent?"

"Probably not."

She saw this clearly. "No. That is the nature of the work. You are dealing with criminals who are armed and don't want to accept your will. So it is the nature of the experience that there will be violence."

"We know how to handle the violence. If there is any. That is what this training has been about. Plus, we wear heavy bulletproof vests."

She was silent.

Then she said, "But what does that do for me and the child I carry? Suppose you die? Then—"

"I ain't going to die. These are old men with rusty shotguns who—"

"They are gangsters with machine guns. I read the newspapers. I read *The Saturday Evening Post*. I know what's going on. Suppose you get killed. I'm to raise our child alone? He's never to know his father? And for what? To save a city that's soaked in filth and corruption for a hundred years? Suppose you die. Suppose they win? Suppose it's all for nothing? What am I supposed to say to this boy? Your daddy died to stop fools from throwing their money away on little white cubes? He didn't die to save his country or his family or anything he cared about, but just to stop fools from gambling. And if you close down Hot Springs, the same fools will only go some other place. You can't end sin, Earl. You can only protect yourself and your family from it."

"Yes ma'am. But now I have given my word, and I have boys depending on me. And, the truth is, I am happy. For the first time since the war, I am a happy man. I am doing some good. It ain't much, but it's what I got. I can help them boys."

"Earl, you are such a fool. You are a brave, handsome, noble man, but you are a fool. Thank you, though, for telling me."

"Would you like some dessert?"

"No. I want you to go home and hold me and make love to me, so that if you die I can have a memory of it and when I tell our son about it, I will have a smile on my face."

"Yes ma'am," he said. It was as if he'd just heard the best order he'd ever gotten in his life.

CHAPTER

13

Hard-boiled eggs (two), dry toast, fresh orange juice. Then he went over accounts for three hours and made a number of phone calls. For lunch he went to Coy's and had a fillet. On a whim, he stopped at Larry's Oyster Bar on Central and had a dozen fresh plump ones from Louisiana, with a couple of cold Jaxes. He went back and took a nice nap. At 3:00 a girl from Maxine's came over and he had his usual good time. At 4:00 he met Judge LeGrand at the club and they got in a quick nine holes. He shot a 52, best of the week. He was catching on to this damned game. At 6:00 he went to the Fordyce and took a bath, a steam session and a rub-down. At 7:00 he had dinner at the Roman Table restaurant with Dr. James, the head of surgery at the hospital, and Mr. Clinton, who owned the Buick agency; both were on the board of the country club, the hospital, and Kiwanis and the Good Fellows. At 9:00 he went to the Southern, caught some of Xavier Cugat's act, which he had seen a dozen times before, checked with his floor managers, his pit bosses and his talent manager to make certain that Mr. Cugat and his boys were being well taken care of. At 11:00 he walked back to the Medical Arts Building, took the elevator up, got into a dressing gown, and had a martini on the patio, while reading that morning's *New York Mirror,* just delivered from Little Rock. That Winchell! What a bastard he could be.

Owney took a moment before bed and stood at the balcony. He had come a long way. He was unusual in his profession in that he had just a sliver of an inner life. He wasn't pure appetite. He knew he existed; he knew he thought.

Today had been such a good day, such a perfect day, yet such a typical day that he took a little pleasure in it all: how hard he had fought, how tough it had been, and how beautifully it had worked out. So many of them died, like the Dutchman, spouting gibberish as the life ebbed out of him, or Mad Dog, splattered with tommy gun fire in a phone booth, or Kid Twist, who went for a swim in midair after volunteering to rat the boys out; or went crazy, like Capone, down there in his mansion in Florida, a complete lunatic by reports, so hopelessly insane on the corrosiveness of his dose that nobody would even bother to visit him. He remembered Capone, the plump sensualist with a Roman emperor's stubby fingers and a phalanx of legionnaires to guard him everywhere, taking the Apollo Suite at the Arlington because it had two entrances, or, as Alphonse would think of it, two exits. A tommy gun legendarily leaned in a corner, in case Al or a lieutenant had a sudden problem that only a hundred .45s could solve.

"Al, it's safe here. That's the point: it's smooth, it's safe, you can come down here by train and enjoy yourself. A man in your position, Al, he should relax a little."

Al just regarded him suspiciously, the paranoia beginning to rot his mind, turning his eyes into dark little peepholes. He didn't say much, but he got laid at least three times a day. Al was reputed to have an organ bigger than Dillinger's. Pussy was the only thing he really cared about and pussy, in the end, had destroyed him. He was afraid of the needles so he came to Hot Springs, under the belief the waters could cure him. They couldn't, of course. They could only stay the course of the disease a bit. All his soaking in 141 degrees had earned Scarface but a few extra hours of sanity in the end.

Owney finished his martini, turned to check that his pigeons had been fed, saw that they had, and started in, when he was surprised by Ralph, his Negro manservant.

"Sir. Mr. Grumley is here."

"Flem?"

"No sir. The other Grumley. The one they call Pap. He's out of his sickbed."

This alerted Owney that indeed something was up.

He walked into the foyer of his apartment, to find the ghost-white old Pap Grumley supported by two lesser cousins or sons or something.

"What is it, Pap?" asked Owney.

"A Grumley done been kilt," said the old legger, a flinty bastard who'd fought the law for close to six decades and was said to carry over a dozen bullets in his hide.

"Who? Revenuers?"

"It's worse, Mr. Maddox."

"What do you mean?"

"Your place done been raided."

Owney could make no sense of this. One or two of his places were raided a year, but by appointment only. It usually took a meeting at least a week in advance to set up a raid. The police had to be told which casino or whorehouse to raid and when to do it, the municipal judge had to know not to get that drunk that night so he could parole the arrestees without undue delay, the casino had to be warned so that nobody would be surprised and nothing stupid would happen, the Little Rock newspapers had to be alerted so they could send photographers, and the mayor had to be informed so that he could be properly dressed for those photographs. Usually, it occurred when some politician in Little Rock made a speech in the statehouse about vice.

"I don't—"

"They come in hard and fast, with lots of guns and wearing them bulletproof vests. And one of 'em shot a Grumley. It was Jed's boy, Garnet, the slow-wit. He died on the spot. We got him over at the morgue and we was—"

"Who raided?"

"They said they was working for the prosecuting attorney."

"Becker?"

"Yes sir. That Becker, he was there. There's about ten, twelve of 'em, with lots of guns. They come in hard and fast and one of 'em shot Garnet dead when Garnet pulled his shotgun. Mr. Maddox, you got to let us know when there's going to be a raid. What am I supposed to say to Jed and Amy?"

"Where did this happen?"

"At the Horseshoe. Just a hour ago. Then they chopped up all the tables and the wheels with axes and machine-gunned the slots."

"What?"

"Yes sir. They turned them machine guns loose on over thirty slots. Shot the hell out of 'em too, they did. Coins all over the goddamned place. Nickels by the bucketful."

"They were working for Becker?"

"Yes sir. He was there, like I say. But the boss was some big tough-looking stranger. He was a piece of work. He shot Garnet. They say nobody never saw no man's hands move faster. He drew and shot that poor boy dead in about a half a second. Nailed him plug in the tick-tocker. Garnet was gone to the next world before he even begun to topple."

The cowboy! The cowboy was back!

By the time he got there, reporters and photographers were already on the scene. They flooded over to Owney, who was always known for his colorful ways with the language, those little Britishisms that sold papers. There were even some boys from Little Rock in attendance.

But Owney was in no mood for quips. He waved them away, then called a Grumley over.

"Get the film. We don't want to let this out until we know what's happening. And send 'em home. And tell 'em not to write stories until we get it figured out."

"Well, sir," said the Grumley, "there's already a press release out."

He handed it over to Owney.

HOT SPRINGS, August 3, 1946, it was datelined.

Officers from the Garland County Prosecuting Attorney's Office today raided and closed a gambling casino in West Hot Springs, destroying 35 slot machines and much illegal gaming equipment.

The raid, at the Horseshoe, 2345 Ouachita also confiscated nearly $32,000 in illegal gambling revenues.

"This marks the first of our initiatives to rid Hot Springs of illegal gambling," said Prosecuting Attorney Fred C. Becker, who led the raid.

"We mean to put the gangsters and the card sharks on notice," said Mr. Becker. "There's no longer a free lunch in Hot Springs. The laws will be enforced and they will be enforced until gambling and its vices have been driven out of our city."

Operating on a tip that illegal activities were under way . . .

Owney scoffed as he discarded the sheet: maybe the thirty-foot-high neon sign on the roof of the Horseshoe that said 30 SLOTS—INSTANT PAYOUT! was the tip-off.

"Who the fuck does he think he is?" Owney asked the Grumley, who had no answer.

"Where's my lawyer?" asked Owney and in short order F. Garry Hurst was produced.

"Is this legal?" Owney demanded. "I mean how can they just fuckin' blow down the doors and start blasting?"

"Well, Owney, it appears that it is. Becker is operating on a very tiny technicality. Because Hot Springs Mountain is a government reserve, any illegal activities within the county that are subject to affecting it can be construed to come under injunction. So any federal judge can issue warrants, and they don't necessarily have to be served by federal officers. He can deputize local authorities. Becker's got a federal judge in Malvern in his pocket. There's your problem right there."

"Damn!" said Owney. He knew right away that clipping a federal judge would not be a good idea, just as clipping a prosecuting attorney wouldn't, either.

"Can you reach him?"

"He's eighty-two years old and nearly blind. I don't think money, whores or dope would do the trick. Maybe if you snuck up behind him and said boo."

"Shit," said Owney.

"It's a pretty smart con," said Hurst. "I don't see how you can bring legal action against the federal government, and through that technicality Becker is essentially operating as a federal law enforcement officer. He's got the protection of the United States government, even if the United States government has no idea who he is."

"Okay, find out all you can. I have to know what the hell is going on. And I have to know soon."

Owney headed inside, where Jack McGaffery, the Horseshoe's manager, waited for him.

"Mr. Maddox, we never had a chance. They was just on us too fast. Poor Garnet, that boy never hurt a fly, and they blowed him out of his socks like a Jap in a hole."

But Owney was less interested in the fate of Garnet than he was in the fate of the Horseshoe. What he saw was an admirably efficient job of ruination accomplished quickly. The roulette wheels and the craps tables could be replaced quickly enough, although a roulette wheel was a delicate instrument and had to be adjusted precisely. But the slots were the worst part.

Usually, the slots were simply hauled away to a police warehouse, stored a few weeks, then quietly reinstalled. Some of them had dozens of TO BE DESTROYED BY HSPD stickers on their backsides.

But this time, someone had walked along the line of machines and fired three or four tommy gun bullets into each. The heavy .45s had penetrated into the spinning guts of the mechanical bandits and blown them to oblivion. The Watlings looked like dead soldiers in a morgue, their glossy fronts cracked or shattered, their adornments of glass spider-webbed, their stout chests punctured, their freight of coins spewed across the floor. Reels full of lemons and cherries and bananas lay helter-skelter on the floor, along with springs and gears and levers. They were old Watling Rol-a-tops from before the war, though well maintained, gleaming and well bugged and tighter than a spinster's snatch, ever profitable. The Rol-a-tops, though, were the proletarians of the gambling universe. More obscenely, a Pace's Race, the most profitable of the devices, was included in the carnage. It was a brilliantly engineered mock track where tiny silhouettes of horses, encased in mahogany under glass, ran in slots against each other, and by the genius mechanics of the thing, the constantly changing odds whirled around a tote board, the odds themselves playing the horses. Its glass shattered, its elegant wood casing broken, its tin horses bent and mangled, the thing lay on its side, all magic having been beaten out of it.

Owney shook his head sadly.

"We kept people out," said Jack. "All the coins are still there. Them boys didn't get no coins, that's for sure."

"But they got $35,000?"

"Sir, more like $43,800 and odd dollars."

"Shit," said Owney. "And all the records."

"Yes sir. But wasn't airy much in them sheets."

Of course not. Owney wasn't foolish enough to keep sensitive documents in casinos.

"But sir," said Jack. "Here's something I don't understand."

He pointed at the walls. Every ten or twelve feet, someone had whacked a hole with an ax. Owney followed the gouges, which circled the main room of the casino, continued up the stairs to Jack's looted office, and followed a track into both the gals' and the men's rest rooms.

Looking at the destruction in the women's room, he said finally, "Who did this?"

"Well, it was an old guy. There was an old guy who came in after all the ruckus was done. He had a hatchet and he went around chopping holes in the wall while the younger boys chewed up the tables and gunned the slots."

"What'd he look like?"

"Like I say, Mr. Maddox, old man. Face like a bag of prunes. Big old man. Sad-like. He looked like he seen his kids drownded in a flood. Didn't say much. But he was some sort of boss. Meanwhile, the tough guy supervised the cracking of the tables, and outside, Becker and his clerk handed out them news releases, answered some questions, posed for pictures. Then they all up and went. Nobody made no arrests."

"Hmmmm," said Owney. He had been caught flat-footed, and someone smart somewhere was behind it. That old man chopping at the walls. He was clearly someone who knew what he was doing. He had a sense of the one place Owney was vulnerable. You could raid on places in Hot Springs for years, and as soon as you closed one joint down, another would spring up, sustained by the river of money that was track betting. But the old man was looking for the wiring that would indicate the secret presence of the Central Book, where the phones poured their torrents of racing data, and Owney knew if he found it, he could dry Owney out in a fortnight.

Goddamn the wire! He was trying to get out of that business but he was still tied to it, it was still his lifeline, and he was still vulnerable to its predation.

One thing was for sure: next time he'd be ready.

"Jack, get Pap in here."

When the old man came, Owney went to the point.

"I want 'em all armed now. Nothing goes easy anymore. They'll never have it as soft as they had it tonight. If they want a war, we'll give 'em a goddamned war. They got guns? We'll get bigger guns. Tell the Grumleys, they will get back for what was done to them tonight."

"Wooo-ooooooooo-doggies!" yelped the haggard old sinner, and danced a mad little jig there in the ruined casino.

CHAPTER

14

By three separate cars, the raid team arrived at the courtyard of the Best Tourist Court at around 9:30 P.M. The neon of the Best was spectacular: it washed the night in the fires of cold gas, in odd colors like magenta and fuchsia and rose around each cabin. It looked like a frozen explosion.

In this strange illumination, the men loaded magazines quietly, slipped into their bulletproof vests, checked the safeties, locked back actuators, tried to stay loose and cool and not get too excited. But it was hard.

Across the street they could see the looming shape of the old ice house, and next to it, the Horseshoe itself, somewhat rickety and wooden like most of the casinos built in the 1920s, with its blazing neon sign thirty feet high atop the roof: 30 SLOTS—INSTANT PAYOUT! and the double green neon horseshoes at each end of the sign.

"Hard to miss," said D.A.

"It's not like a secret or nothing," said one of the boys, possibly Eff—for Jefferson—up from the Georgia Highway Patrol. A designated tommy gunner, he was loading .45s into a stick magazine.

Earl was alive in ways he hadn't been alive for a year. He felt his eyeballs extra-sharp, he tasted the flavor of the air, his nerve endings were radar stations reading every rogue movement in the night sky. He walked around, checking, examining, giving this boy or that the odd nod or pat of encouragement.

Becker pulled in, with a clerk. He seemed especially nervous. He walked among the men smiling dryly, but he kept running his tongue over his gray lips. All he could think to say was "Very good, very good, very good."

Finally he approached the two leaders.

"I like it. They look sharp," he said.

"It ought to go okay," said the old man.

"You, Earl, you agree?"

"Mr. Parker's got it laid out real nice, sir," said Earl.

"Okay. When it's clear, you send a boy out. At that moment I'll call HSPD and announce a raid in progress and request backup. Then I'll call the newspaper boys. I did alert the Little Rock boys to have a photog in the area. But that's okay, that's secure. Got it?"

"Yes sir," said D.A., but suddenly Earl didn't like it. Okay, Owney owned the local rags, but how safe were these Little Rock people? He pulled D.A. aside.

"I'm going to go in early," he said.

D.A. looked at him.

"You'll be right in the line of fire for twelve nervous kids."

"Yeah, but in case somebody in there gets a little crazed or has been tipped off, I might be able to cock him good and save a life or two. This'll probably be the only raid we can get away with that."

"I don't like it, Earl," D.A. said. "It's not how we planned it. It could confuse them."

"I'll be all right," said Earl. "It could save some lives."

"It could cost some lives too," said D.A.

"Look at it this way," said Earl. "We'll never get a chance to pull this trick off again. They'll be waiting for it in all the other places. We might as well do it while we can."

D.A. looked at him sharply, seemed about to say something, but then reconsidered; it was true he did not want a killing on the first raid, for he believed that would turn the whole enterprise inevitably toward ruination.

"Wear your vest," he cautioned, but even as he said it, he knew it was impossible: the vests were large and bulky and looked like umpire's chestpads, and everybody hated them. If Earl walked in with a vest on, it would be a dead giveaway.

"You know I can't."

"Yeah, well, take this."

He handed over a well-used police sap, a black leather strap with a pouch at the end where a half pound of buckshot had been secreted.

"Bet you busted some head with this old thing," said Earl with a smile.

"More'n I care to remember."

Earl looked at his Hamilton in the pink light and shadow. It was 9:45. Between the tourist court and the casino, Ouachita Avenue buzzed with cars.

"I'm sending in three teams in the front and two in the back," said D.A. "I'll move the rear teams in first. I'll run them teams around the ice house, and they'll rally in its eaves, on that southwest corner. At 9:59, they'll move single file down to the rear entrance. We have sledges. At ten, they hit the door, just as the three front-entry teams go through the foyer and fan out through the building. Luckily it's a simple building, without a lot of blind spots or tiny rooms."

Earl nodded.

"That's good," he said. "But maybe instead of going around the ice house, you ought to move 'em around the other side of the casino, sir."

D.A. looked at him.

"Why?" he said.

"It's nothing. But the manager's office seems to be upstairs on that same corner. Maybe he's up there, the window's open, and he hears scuffling in the alley, or somebody drops a mag or bangs into a garbage can. Maybe it ticks something off in him, he takes out a gun, he heads downstairs. The rear-entry team runs into him with a gun out on the stairway. Bang, bang, somebody's hurt bad. See what I'm saying, sir? I think you'd do best to run 'em around that other side of the building."

"Earl, is there anything you don't know?"

"What to name my kid. How to balance a checkbook. Which way the wind blows."

"You are a smart bastard. All right."

Earl checked his .45, making sure once again that the safety was still on, and, from the heft, that indeed the piece was stoked with seven cartridges. He touched the three mags he had tucked into his belt on the back side. He touched his sap.

Then he went among the boys.

"Listen up, kids," he said.

They stopped fiddling with their tommy guns and drew around him.

"Slight change in plan. I'm going to go on and be in there. I have a favor to ask. Please do not shoot me. You especially, Short. Got that?"

There was some nervous laughter.

"Okay, I'll be in the main room, at the bar. Mark me. If I move fast, it's because I've seen someone with a gun or a club. I say again and now hear this: Do not shoot old Mr. Earl."

Again, the dry laughter of young men.

"You are broken down into your teams, you have your staging assignments and your route assignments. And remember. The fight's going to be what it wants to be, not what you want it to be. You stay sharp," and he moved away from them and disappeared.

Frenchy was annoyed. The last man on the last team. He was backup on the rear-entry team, the third fire team. That made him sixth man through the door. It did get him a tommy gun, however. He felt it wrapped under his coat as he crossed Ouachita, huge, oily and power-

ful. He waited for the cars to part, then dashed across, as the others
had done, one man at a time, the tommy gun secured up under his suit
coat, the heavy armored vest rocking against him as he ran. No car
lights shone on him; nobody from the Horseshoe saw him, or could be
expected to.

He ran to the Horseshoe's northwest corner, then threaded back
alongside the west wall of the casino. Inside he could hear the steady
clang of the slots, the calls of the pit bosses and the more generalized
hubbub of a reasonably crowded place.

He slid along the edge of the building, ducking the wash of lights
that shone from the shuttered windows. His eyes craned the parking
lot to his right for movement, but there was none at all. Five men had
passed this way before him, and at last he joined them, in a little cluster at the southwest corner of the big, square old building.

"Six in," he said.

"Time check," said Slim, who as the second-most-senior man of the
unit was running the rear entry team. Slim was a heavyset, quiet fellow
from Oregon, a State Trooper out there. He was one of three actual
gunfight veterans on the team.

"2150," said his number two, Bear.

"Okay, let's hold here," Slim said, trying to control his breathing.
"We'll move to the door at 2158."

They hunched, tensing, feeling the sultry weight of the air. It was all
going so fast. Getting across the street and reassembling at the rallying
point seemed much simpler than it was supposed to be. No screwups
at all.

"One last time, let's go over assignments. I'm one; when the door
goes, I pile through it first, with my .45, covering the right side of the
rear hall, turning right, moving into the main room and covering the
right again."

Two, three and four ran through their assignments, droning on about
turns to left or right and sectors to cover with pistol or tommy gun.

"I'm five," said Henderson finally. "I go down the hall, past the
casino, turn right, take the stairs up to the manager's office, which I
cover. Securing that, I work the men's and women's rooms."

"I'm six," said Frenchy. "I grab the blonde, I fuck her fast, then I spray the room with lead, killing everybody, including you guys. Then I light up a smoke and wait for the newspaper boys and my Hollywood contract."

"All right, Frenchy," said Slim. "Cut the shit. This ain't no joke."

"All right, all right," said Frenchy. "I'm six. I support five up the rear stairs with the tommy, covering the left-hand side of the stairwell. I cover him in the manager's office, and then we check the two rest rooms. I hope there's a babe on the pot in the lady's."

"Cornhole," someone muttered.

"Now what's the last thing we heard?" asked Slim. "What should be freshest in our minds?"

There was stupefied silence.

"Damn, you guys already forgot! Mr. Earl is going to be in there. He'll be at the bar. So you guys especially, three and four, you make sure you do not cover him. No accidents. Got that?"

Taking the silence as assent, he then said, "Time check?"

"Uh, 2157."

"Shit, we're late. Okay guys, single file, follow me. You ready with that sledge, Eff?"

"Yes I am."

"Let's move out."

They scooted down the rear of the building and came to rest in the lee of the door. The alley was dark. All was silent.

"On the tommies, safeties off."

Silently, the men found the safeties of their weapons and disengaged them, while three edged around with his sledge, getting ready to give the door a stout whack just above the handle.

Slim looked at his watch. The second had ticked around, until it reached straight up.

"Do it," he said.

Earl stepped into a well-lighted space. It wasn't nearly as crowded as the Ohio had been that night. A big guy eyed him as he walked through the doorway, clearly a muscleman or some kind of enforcer, but he was so close to the door he felt the palooka would have no chance to react when the fellows spilled through in a few minutes.

He moved on into the big room, which was simply the majority of the building. It was just a space to house the sucker-swindling machinery, decorated along horse-racing lines, with jerseys and crops and helmets and horseshoes festooning the walls. The lights were bright, the smoke heavy, and the slots were set against the walls where a number of weary pilgrims fed them coins to what appeared to be very little financial gain on their part. In the center of the room a couple of tables offered blackjack, there was a poker game going on but without much energy and a roulette wheel ticked off its reds and blacks as it spun to the amusement of another sparse crowd. But the main action was craps, where the players were louder and more excitable.

"Eighter, eighter, eighter from Decatur."

"No, no, Benny Blue's coming up, here comes the big Reno, I can feel it in my bones."

Perhaps because it was built around dynamic movement, this game seemed to draw the most passion. Its players crowded round, and gave their all to the drama.

"Yoleven, yoleven, yoleven!"

Earl slid to the bar and ordered a beer, which was delivered by a plug-ugly without much sentimentality.

"First one's on the house, long as it ain't the last one."

"Oh, it's going to be a long night, trust me, brother," said Earl, taking a sip of the brew.

He measured the bartender, who looked like a tough cracker and thought he might have to cool him out. When the man's attention was on other customers, Earl snuck a peek down and under the bar, where he saw, among the bottles and napkins, a sawed-off pool cue, and a sawed-off 12-gauge pumpgun. The weapons were hung under the bar right next to the cash register. At 2159, Earl thought he'd mosey down and set up there.

Meanwhile, he scanned the crowd, looking for security types. So far only two: the big guy at the door and the barkeep. Maybe there was another someplace but he sure didn't see him.

Smoke heaved and drifted in the bright room. He picked up his beer and moved on down to the cash register, until he was parked just above the cached weapons. The hand on the clock on the wall said ten o'clock, straight up.

Three's sledge hit the door, rebounded once. He caught it and being a strong young Georgia vice detective, swung again, to the sound of wood shattering and ripping. A blade of light fell into the alley as the door was blasted from its hinges and fell wretchedly to one side.

The men scrambled in.

There was a sense of craziness to it, as they stumbled over each other and no one could quite get his limbs moving fast enough. Their eyes bugged as the hormones of aggression flooded through their bodies. They rushed along, bringing the guns to bear, looking hungrily for targets to kill.

Slim was shouting *"Hands up! Hands up! This is a raid!"* and others took up the call, *"Raid! Raid! Raid!"*

Frenchy had but a glimpse of the first two teams as they fanned out and dispersed into the casino's main room. But he churned along in the wake of Carlo Henderson, his partner, who was strangely animated to grace by all the excitement and moved ahead purposefully, quickly found the right-hand stairwell, and began to assault the stairs, screaming *"Raid! Raid! Hands up!"*

Frenchy was with him when a man appeared at the top of the stairs. Frenchy knew in a second he'd shoot if Carlo weren't in the way, but he couldn't fire and he sat back waiting for Carlo's shots to ring out. But Carlo didn't shoot.

"Hands up! Get those hands up and you won't get hurt!" he screamed, thrusting his .45 in his two hands before him, aimed straight at the heart of the figure, who threw his hands skyward and went to his knees.

Carlo was next to him like some kind of sudden athlete, spun him, leaned him against the wall, spread him and searched him. A Colt .32 pocket model came out and was tossed down the stairwell.

"You stay put!" Carlo demanded, reached up, gracefully snagged the guy in one half a pair of cuffs, wound him quickly around and clipped

the other wrist and sat him down with a thump. He was wearing a white tuxedo and Frenchy bet he'd be the manager.

Perhaps that's why when the two men kicked open the casino manager's office and scanned it quickly for threats, they found nothing.

"Clear!"

"Clear on my side!" replied Frenchy.

Next they did the washrooms. A fairly drunk guy was propped against the urinal; Frenchy gave him a nudge and he fell backward, spraying pee in a wide arc, but the two young policemen, though encumbered in vests and with weapons, were so horrified of the prospect of being splashed, they leapt back and missed the dousing. Frenchy felt a flare of rage, and stepped forward to club the drunk with his tommy gun butt, but Carlo interceded and brought him under control. The drunk lay in his own piss, screaming, "Don't hurt me, don't hurt me!"

"You stay here till we come get you," Carlo screamed. Then he turned to Frenchy. "Come on, goddammit!"

They ducked next into the ladies'. It was clear, except for a closet, which they tried and found locked.

"Smash it?" asked Frenchy.

Carlo pulled really hard. It wouldn't open.

"Yeah," he said. "You smash it open since you want to hit something. I'm going to take that drunk and the guy in the tux downstairs before they run away."

He disappeared.

Frenchy had a weird need to spray the door with the Thompson. Nah, he knew that would be wrong.

Instead, he beat at it until the jamb gave, and pulled it open. Nothing inside except a wash bucket and a mop.

He heard a thump or something coming from outside. He ducked out, searched, saw nothing. He looked into the casino manager's office and it appeared empty.

He thought nothing of it and downstairs he could hear the loud voice of D. A. Parker, "Now, ladies and gentlemen, you just stand clear, we are from the Prosecuting Attorney's Office and don't mean no harm to any citizens. You just relax and you'll be able to go home in a bit."

. . .

There was a quiet moment when the world seemed to hang suspended. Then it exploded.

Earl sat calmly as the doorway burst open and the first man through swung his .45 like a scythe and neatly clipped the security man at the door. Great anticipation, great reaction. Earl watched the hand with the gun invert, then flash outward toward the stunned piece of beefcake, heard the odd, meaty sound as the gun made contact with the face, and watched as the enforcer dropped into a puddle. Other raiders spilled into the room, fanned out, and took over the room.

It was good. He was proud. No one was out of control, no one was gesturing crazily or screaming. They simply asserted command. They were professional, and Stretch, who was doing the shouting, had an authoritative voice untarnished by fear or doubt.

"Hands up! Hands up! Show us hands!"

Hands went up; people froze. Even the croupiers and the pit bosses froze with the sudden, overwhelming display of force.

That is, except for the bartender.

Earl knew his man. The bartender reacted with his guts instead of his brain, and, alone among them, he spun and grabbed reflexively for a weapon under the bar.

Earl probably could have broken his arm with the sap. Instead, he thumped him lightly and perfectly, intercepting the plunging limb and striking it at the nearly fleshless bone along the arm's top.

"Ah!" the bartender groaned, driven to his feet by the agony of the blow that had turned the whole left-hand side of his body numb. He sat back, clasping the bruise to him and in pure animal terror recoiled and tried to go tiny and harmless.

"You be a good boy!" Earl warned.

Earl turned back and saw that the situation was now in complete control. Nobody else moved.

"You okay, Mr. Earl?" asked Slim.

"B'lieve I'm fine," Earl said, taking his badge out of his pocket and pinning it to his lapel.

"You were one inch from catching a tommy gun burst in the guts," one of the raiders said to the bartender, who still groaned at the pain.

Earl leaned around the bar, plucked out the pool cue and threw it across the floor. Then he pulled out the sawed-off pump, pointed it down, and jacked the pump hard, ejecting six twelve-gauge shells. He dumped the empty thing on the bar, its pump locked back to expose the unfilled chamber.

D.A. was there next.

"Now, ladies and gentlemen, you just stand clear. We are from the Prosecuting Attorney's Office and don't mean you any harm. You just relax and you'll be able to go on home in a minute."

"Can we keep our winnings?"

"Anything on your person you may keep. Sorry, but anything on the tables will be confiscated by the Prosecuting Attorney's Office."

There was some grumbling, but as the guns came down and the hands came down, everybody seemed to be making the best of it.

In another second Carlo Henderson appeared with a squawking guy in a white tux, hands cuffed behind him.

"Who the hell are you? What the hell is going on? I am Jack Mc-Gaffery, manager of the Horseshoe, and Owney Maddox is going to be plenty jacked at this."

"Reckon he will be, sir. Are you aware there are illegal gaming devices on the property?"

"Naw, do tell? Never noticed a thing, there, Sheriff. By God, Owney Maddox will have your *ass* for this. You ask these folks. He won't—"

"Well, sir," said D.A., "you tell Owney Maddox if he wants to make an appointment with Mr. Becker, to go right ahead. Meanwhile, soon's we get these folks out of here, we're going to destroy the illegal—"

"*Destroy!* Jesus Christ, man, you must be *crazy!* Owney will hunt you to your last day on earth!"

"Don't think you get it yet, McGaffery. He ain't hunting us, we're hunting him. We're the new boys in town and by God, he will wish we'd never come. All right, fellows, let's get it done!"

They began to herd the citizens out the front doors, while a few other raiders moved the casino staff to one side. Earl stood watching and noted that Frenchy finally arrived from upstairs with his Thompson gun. He hadn't shot anyone yet; that was good.

"All right," Earl commanded. "Peanut, you bring the cars up close and we'll get the axes out and go to town. Y'all, you just sit down over there, and watch what we do so you can give Owney Maddox a good report. Mr. Becker will be here soon. We'll see if you're gonna be arrested or not. I want—"

Earl had a thought before him which was something like "I want you to pay close attention to what a thorough job we do, because we're going to do a lot more thorough jobs before we're done," which was meant for the casino staff as a note of intimidation for Owney Maddox and the Grumley boys. That way he'd know he had some problems and he'd get serious about them.

But that thought never got out.

Instead, from the corner of his eye, he saw something move that shouldn't move at all. It was a shape, a form, a shadow, and no clear outline was visible, for it seemed to emerge from the back entrance in a flash of a second. Earl only recognized that it was a human form and that a hard, cold thing that rose at an angle above it was the double barrels of a shotgun.

Earl could not command himself to draw and fire. No man could move that fast from the rational part of his brain. He simply swept aside the coat, drawing the gun, his thumb flying to and pushing off the safety, his other hand clasping the grip and cradling the first hand, his elbows flying and then locking, almost as if he'd willed it rather than done it, and in the next billionth of a second the pistol reported loudly, kicked against his tight double-handed grip and ejected a spent brass shell.

In the close room the noise was tremendous. It bounced off walls and its vibrations sprang dust from rafters and countertops. It unleashed energy from everywhere, as citizens dove for cover, raiders dropped and pivoted, aiming their weapons off the cue from Earl, and even D.A. got his gun out fast and into play. Only Frenchy stood rooted in place, for Earl's bullet had passed within a foot or so of him before it plowed into the center chest of what appeared to be a vacant, doughy-faced young man in an ill-fitting Sunday-go-to-meeting suit.

His eyes locked on Earl's as the shotgun fell from his hand, and implored him for mercy. The request was too late, for it wouldn't have mattered if Earl fired again or not. The young man went down like a sack of spring apples falling off a wagon, hitting the floor with the crack of bones and teeth breaking; his blood began to pump from his heart across the floor in a spreading satin puddle.

Everybody was yelling and diving and moving at once, but Earl knew it was over. He'd seen the front sight on the chest at the moment he'd fired.

"Goddamn, Mr. Earl," somebody said.

"That damn boy!" said McGaffery. "He didn't have the sense of a mule. You didn't have to kill him, though."

"Maybe he ain't dead," said a raider.

"He's dead," said D.A., holstering his automatic. "When Earl shoots, he don't miss. Good shot, Earl. You boys see that? That's how it's done."

Earl himself felt nothing. He'd killed so many times before, and not only yellow men. He'd killed white men in Nicaragua in 1933, with the same kind of gun that Frenchy carried.

But he felt it in his heart right away, the difference: that was war. This was—well, what was it?

"You killed a Grumley," said the bartender, still holding his bruised wrist. "Now you got the Grumleys on you. Them boys don't forget a thing. Not never. The Grumleys will mark you and dog you the rest of your days, mister."

"I been dogged before, mister" was all Earl said; then he turned to the raiders and said, "Okay, let's get going. You got some busting up to do. Come on."

But he didn't like the killing either. It wasn't a good sign, Grumleys or no Grumleys.

CHAPTER

15

Owney knew the most important thing about his situation was to pretend he had no situation.

Thus, though Hot Springs' insular, gossipy little business, gambling and criminal communities were literally aflame with speculation about the raid, and the *Little Rock Courier-Herald* and the *Democrat* had run pieces, it was important for him to suggest that nothing was really amiss. He got up, dressed dapperly—an ascot!—and went for a stroll down Central, saying hello in his best Ronald Colman voice to all those he knew, and he knew many people. He was especially British today, even wearing a Norfolk jacket and flannels, with a dapper tweed hat.

"Cheerio," he said wherever he went. "Be good sports. Keep the old upper lip stiff. Tut tut and ho ho, as we say in Jolly Olde."

He attended a luncheon for the hospital board and dropped in at the Democratic Ladies' Club, where he made a donation of $1,000 toward the clubhouse redecorating project slated for that fall. He met Raymond Clinton, the Buick agency owner, and had a long discussion about the new Buicks. They were beauts! He said he was thinking about retiring his prewar limo. It was time to be modern and American. It was the '40s. The Nazis and the Japs were whipped! We had the atom bomb!

But even as he was going about his public business, he was relaying orders through runners to various of his employees, directing a search, putting pressure on the police, sending out scouting parties, setting up surveillance at Becker's office in City Hall and convening a meeting.

The meeting was scheduled for 5:30 P.M., in the kitchen at the brand-new Signore Giuseppe's Tomato Pie Paradise, where Pap Grumley and several ranking Grumleys, F. Garry Hurst, Jack McGaffery and others showed up as ordered. Everybody gathered just outside the meat locker, where about a thousand sausages hung in bunches and strings. The smell of mozzarella and tomato paste floated through the air.

"No siree, Mr. Maddox," said Pap. "My boys, they been up, they been down. These coyotes have vanished. Don't know where they done gone to ground, but it ain't in no goddamn hotel nor no tourist camp. Maybe they's camping deep in the hills. Shit, my boys couldn't find a thing. We may have to go to the hounds to git on these crackers.

Know where I can git me a troop of prize blue ticks if it comes to that. Them dogs could smell out a pea in a pea patch the size of Kansas. One particular pea, that is."

He spat a gob of a fluid so horrifyingly yellowed that even Owney didn't want to think about it. It landed in the sink with a plop.

"You got boys coming in?" Owney, the high baron of New York's East Side, asked in his native diction.

"Yes sir. Got boys from Yell County. The Yell County Grumleys make the Garland County Grumleys look tame. They're so mean they drink piss for breakfast."

Owney turned to Jack McGaffery.

"And you? You made the fuckin' calls I told you?"

"Yes sir. We can get gun boys from Kansas City and St. Paul inside a week if we need 'em. It ain't a question of guns. We can put guns on the street. Hell, there's only a dozen or so of them."

"Yeah, but we gotta find the fuckers first."

He turned to Hurst.

"What do you make of it?"

"Whoever thought this out, thought it out well," said the lawyer. "These boys were well armed and well trained. But more to the point, whoever is planning this thing has thought long and hard about what he is attacking."

"Garry, what the fuck are you tawkin' about?" said Owney.

"Consider. He—whomsoever *he* may be—has certainly made a careful study of Hot Springs from a sociological point of view. He understands, either empirically or instinctively, that all municipal institutions have been, to some degree or other, penetrated and are controlled by yourself. So he sets up what appears to be a roving unit. It stays nowhere. It has no local ties, no roots, no families. It can't be reported on. It can't be spied on. It can't be betrayed from within. It permits no photographs, its members do not linger or speak to the press, it simply strikes and vanishes. It's brilliant. It's even almost legal."

"Agh!" Owney groaned. "I smell old cop. I smell a cop so old he knows all the tricks. You ain't pulling no flannel over this old putz's eyes."

He looked back at Jack.

"The cowboy was the fast one. The rest were punks. But you said a old man was in command. That's what you said."

"He was. But I only heard the name Earl. 'Earl, that was a great shot,' the old man said to the fast cowboy after he clipped Garnet. But no other names were used. The old one was in charge but the cowboy was like the sarge or something."

"Okay," Owney said. "They will hit us again, the bastards. You can count on it. They are looking for the Central Book, because they know when they get that, they got us. Meanwhile, we will be hunting them. We got people eyeballing Becker. We follow Becker, he'll be in contact with them, and somehow, he'll lead us to them."

"Yes sir," said Flem Grumley, "'ceptin' that Becker never showed at his office this morning, and when we sent some boys by his house, it was empty. He moved his family out. He's gone underground too."

"He'll turn up. He's got speeches to make, he's got interviews to give. He wants to be governor and he wants to ride this thing into that big fuckin' job. He's just another hustler. He don't scare me. That god-damn cowboy, he scares me. But I've been hunted before."

"Pray tell, by whom, Owney?" asked Garry.

"Ever hear of Mad Dog Coll?"

"Yes."

"Yeah, well, Mad Dog, he comes gunning for me. He steals my best man, fuckin' Jimmy Lupton, and holds him for ransom. I got to pay fuckin' fifty long to get Jimmy back. He was a pisser and a half, that fuckin' kid. Balls? Balls like fuckin' steel fists. Crazy but gigantic balls. So you know what the lesson is?"

"No sir."

"Bo Weinberg catches him in a phone booth with the chopper. The chopper chops that mick fuck to shit. Don't matter how big his fuckin' balls are. The chopper don't care. So here's the lesson: everybody dies. Every-fuckin'-body dies."

After the meeting, Owney went to his car. He checked his watch to discover that it was five o'clock, 6:00 New York time. He told his driver where to go.

The driver left Signore Giuseppe's, drove down to Central, turned up it, then up Malvern Avenue and drove through the nigger part of town, past the Pythian Hotel and Baths, past cribs and joints and houses, then turned toward U.S. 65, the big Little Rock road over by Malvern, but didn't drive much farther. Instead, he stopped at a gas station along the edge of Lake Catherine.

Owney got out, looked about to make certain he was not followed. Then he went into the gas station, a skunky old Texaco that looked little changed since the early 1920s, when it was built. The attendant, an old geezer whose name should have been Zeke or Lum or Jethro nodded, and departed, after hanging out a sign in the window that said CLOSED. Owney checked his watch again, went to the cooler, took out a nickel bottle of Coca-Cola, pried off the cap and drank it down in a gulp. He took out a cigarette, inserted it into his holder, lit it with a Tiffany's lighter that had cost over $200, and took a puff.

The cigarette was half down when the phone rang.

Owney went to it.

"Yeah?"

"I have a person-to-person long-distance call for a Mr. Brown from a Mr. Smith in New York City."

"This is Brown."

"Thank you, sir. I'll make the connection."

"Thanks, honey."

There were some clickings and the rasp of interference, but a voice came on eventually.

"Owney?"

"Yeah. That you, Sid?"

"Yeah."

"So what the fuck, Sid? What the fuck is going on?"

"Owney, I tell ya. Nothing."

"I got a boy busting my balls down here. Some hick ex-soldier prosecutor who thinks he's Tom Fuckin' Dewey."

"Not good."

"No, it ain't. But I can take care of it. What I'm worried about is that fucker Bughouse Siegel. Frank and Albert and Mr. Lansky all like the little fuck. Is he behind my trouble down here? Is he trying to muscle me out of the business? It might do him some good."

"Owney, like you said, I asked some questions. What I hear is he is just pissing money away into a big hole in the ground out in some desert. That hot-number babe he's got with him, you know, she ain't too happy. She's been talking to people about what an asshole he is. She has friends. She has a lot of friends and he leaves her alone in Hollywood to go out to the desert and piss some more money into a hole. Only I hear that broad ain't ever alone. She still has the hotsies for Joey Adonis, among others."

"So the Bughouse has that to worry about before he worries about my little action down here?"

"That's what I hear. But Owney, I have to tell you the big guys do like him. They sent him out there. He has their ear. I'd look out for him. He thinks big."

"Yeah, he thinks big, with my thoughts. I gave him his whole idea. He thinks he can fuckin' build a Hot Springs in the desert. There's nothing there but sand. Here, we got nature, we got mountains, we got lakes, we got—"

"Yeah, but in that state, gambling's legal, so you don't get raided. Remember that. That's a big plus."

"We're not *supposed* to get raided here."

"So you said. Owney, the guys, they always say, That Owney, he runs a smooth town. That's why they like to go there. The baths, some dames, some gambling, no problem, no hassles with the law. That's what they like. As long as you provide that for them, you will have no problems."

"Yeah."

"Owney. Best thing you can do is forget about Bugsy, and keep that town running smooth. That's your insurance policy."

"Yeah," said Owney. "Thanks, Sid."

It was on the way back that he had his big thought.

"Back home, sir?"

"No, no. Take me to the newspaper office. And then call Pap Grumley. Tell him to find Garnet Grumley's mother. Or someone who looks just like her."

CHAPTER

16

"So tell me what happened up there, Henderson," Earl asked Carlo.

"I guess I screwed up. I thought I had it covered. I thought we done a good job."

Earl nodded.

The raiders were headquartered in the pumping station of the Remmel Hydroelectric Dam, which blocked the Ouachita River and had thereby created Lake Catherine, and lay between Magnet and Hot Springs, on Route 65, not far at all from the Texaco station where Owney had gotten his call from New York. The pumping station, which was administered by the TVA and run out of Malvern, not Hot Springs, was a large brick building at the end of three miles of dirt road off U.S. 65; though most of its innards were taken up with turbines turning and producing electricity for Hot Springs, the upper floors had surprising space and provided room for fourteen cots, as well as hot showers and indoor plumbing. It was better than most places Earl had slept during the war. D.A. had thought all this out very carefully.

"Tell me what happened."

"Well sir, we done our best. I am truly ashamed it wasn't good enough. But we got up there fast, we nabbed that bird McGaffery on the steps, there was a goddamned pissing drunk in the men's room, and we run him downstairs too, and we checked all the closets."

"So Garnet Grumley could not have been up there?"

"I don't think so," said Carlo. "But if I missed him, then I missed him."

"He was not up there," said Frenchy. "Mr. Earl, we went all through that place. I even beat the lock off the closet door in the ladies'."

"See," said Earl, "I do not particularly care for having to shoot a boy dead, who was after all only doing his job and as it turned out had forgotten to load his shotgun. Either of you killed anyone?"

Both men shook their head no.

"I *swear* to you, Mr. Earl, that fellow did not come from up there," said Frenchy. "He must have snuck in from the outside. Or maybe he came up from the cellar."

"Wasn't no cellar," said Carlo. "And we'd have seen him in the alley if he'd been lurking up there. Mr. Swagger, I do believe it was my fault and I am very sorry it happened. It wasn't Frenchy's. I was number one on our fire team, so the job was mine, and I muffed it. If you give me a next time, I will sure try hard to do a better job."

"Jesus, Henderson," said Frenchy. "He wasn't up there. It's not your fault, it's not my fault. It just goddamned happened is all and everybody is lucky it was him that got killed, and not one of us."

Earl pushed something across the table at them.

It was the *Hot Springs New Era,* the city's afternoon paper.

FARMBOY SLAIN IN COP "RAID"
Locals decry "Nazi" tactics
"He was a good boy," Mom says.

"Christ," said Frenchy.

Carlo read:

Raiders from the Prosecuting Attorney's Office shot and killed a local man while invading a local nightclub.

The incident occurred at the Horseshoe Club, on Ouachita Avenue in West Hot Springs, late last night.

Dead was Garnet Grumley, 22, of Hot Springs, shot by a raider as he wandered in from the upstairs bathroom.

"Garnet was a good boy," said his mother, Viola Grumley, of eastern Garland County. "He did all his chores and milked his special cow, Billie. I wonder what he was doing in that downtown club. But I wonder why they had to shoot such a harmless, God-fearing boy."

Fred C. Becker, Garland County Prosecuting Attorney, refused to talk to *New Era* reporters.

In a news release his office provided, he claimed that officers shot in self-defense while on a raid aimed at local gamblers.

See *New Era* Editorial, Page 7.

"Boy, I'll bet that one's rich."

"Oh, it is," said Earl.

The two young men flipped pages.

New Jayhawkers?

In the era preceding the Civil War it was common for night riders to terrorize Arkansans in the name of a just cause, which was more a license to hate. Town burnings, robberies, lynchings and other malicious acts were the order of the day. History remembers these brigands as Jayhawkers and under that same name it consigns them to evil.

Well, a new plague of Jayhawkers is upon us. Unlike their predecessors they don't ride horses and carry shotguns; no, they ride in modern automobiles and carry machine guns.

And, like their brethren from a century ago, they hide behind a supposedly "just" cause, the elimination of gambling influence and corruption from our beautiful little city. But, as before, this is a clear case of the cure being worse—far worse—than the disease.

"Ouch," said Carlo.

"Newspaper morons," said Frenchy.

"Well, they do leave out the fact that the late Garnet spent fourteen months in the state penitentiary for assault and that he had a juvenile record that goes back to before the war," said Earl. "And D.A. says that Viola is no more his mama than you are, Short. He's an orphan Grumley, raised at the toe of a boot in the mountains, and pretty much your legger attack dog, and little else. So if a man had to die, better it was him than you or me."

"Yes sir," said Carlo.

"Okay, let me tell you two birds something. You are the youngest, but that don't bother me. You are probably also the smartest I got. I don't hold that smart boys ain't no good in combat, as some old sergeants do. But I do know your smart boy is easily distracted, and naturally doubtful, and has a kind of sense of superiority to all and sundry. So let me tell you, that if you want to stay in this outfit, you put all that aside. You put those smart-boy brains on the shelves and you commit to doing what you're told and doing it well and thoroughly. Elsewise, you're on your way back to where you come from, and you can tell your buddies there you were a bust as a raider."

"Yes sir," said Carlo.

"Now rack up some sleep. We're going again tonight."

CHAPTER

17

The Derby was filled that night. At one of the booths, the young, leonine Burt Lancaster held court like a gangster king, surrounded by cronies and babes, his teeth so white they filled the air with radiance.

In another, the young genius Orson Welles sat with his beautiful wife, eating immense amounts of food, an actual second dinner, and downing three bottles of champagne. Rita Hayworth just watched him sullenly as he uttered the words that were to become his signature: "More mashed potatoes, please."

Mickey was there, of course, though without his wife. He was with a chorine who had even larger breasts than his wife. He was smoking Luckies and drinking White Russians and looking for producers to shmooze, because he could feel himself, in his dreams at least, slipping ever so slightly.

Bogie was there, with a little nobody named Bill something or other, a Mississippi-born screenwriter who was lost in the rewrites of Ray Chandler's *The Big Sleep*. Bogie called him "Kid," got him good and drunk, and kept trying to get him to understand that it really didn't matter if anybody figured out who did it.

And Virginia was there, with her swain Benjamin "Bugsy" Siegel, and Ben's best Hollywood friend, Georgie Raft.

"Will you look at that," said Ben. "Errol Flynn. Man, he don't look good."

"He's all washed up, I hear," said Georgie, drunkenly. "Warner's may drop him. Look at him."

Errol Flynn was even drunker than Georgie Raft and his once beautiful face had begin to show ruination. It was a mask of beauty turning inexorably into a burlap sack hung on a fencepost.

"Yeah, well, they didn't pick your contract up either, Georgie," said Virginia.

"I bought my way out of my contract," said Georgie. "I gave Jack a check for $10,000 and walked out of his office a free man."

"I heard he would have paid *you* the ten long to take a hike," said Virginia.

"Can it, Virginia," said Ben.

Raft stared moodily into his drink. For a tough guy, he had an amazingly delicate little face, a nose as perfectly upturned as any pixie's.

"It ain't been easy on him," consoled his best friend from the old neighborhood, where they'd specialized in heisting apple carts.

"Why don't you beat up a casting director, Ben? That is, if you could find one you could take. Maybe you could make Georgie big again."

"I don't know what's the matter with this bitch," Ben explained to Georgie. "Ever since we got back from the South, she's been acting funny toward me."

He looked at her. But goddamn, she was still the female animal in all her surly glory, tonight with a huge wave of auburn cream for hair, meaty big-gal shoulders and breasts scrunched together to form a black slot in the ample flesh into which a man could tumble and lose his soul forever.

"Yeah," she said, "maybe it has something to do with all the times you fly out to the fucking desert and watch Del Webb pour Mr. Lansky's money into a big hole in the ground."

Another row was starting.

"Kids, kids, kids," consoled Georgie. "Let's enjoy ourselves. We have a great table at the Brown Derby in a room filled with movie stars. People would kill to get what we have. Let's enjoy. Garçon, another Scotch, please."

The three friends each retreated briefly to his or her libation, tried to settle down and collect themselves, then returned to conviviality.

"Virginia, it's a big thing I got going. You'll see. The big guys all believe in it. It'll be bigger than Hot Springs."

"Hot Springs is supposed to be in Hot Springs, not in a desert. Owney Maddox is supposed to run Hot Springs. That's the way it's supposed to be, Ben. You ought to know that."

Ben allowed himself a snicker.

"You think Owney's so high and mighty? You think nobody would stand against Owney? Well, let me tell you something, Owney's got some troubles you wouldn't want."

"Owney's okay," said Georgie. "He knew some people and helped me get started out here."

"Owney's finished," said Ben. "He just don't know it yet."

"Owney's a creep but he can take care of himself," Virginia argued, then took another sip of her third screwdriver. She could outdrink any man in Hollywood except for Flynn. "He pretends to be a British snob but he's an East Side gutter rat, just like you two pretty boys."

"Virginia, Owney's got troubles and the big guys know it. I heard about it all the way out here. He's got some crusader raiding his joints and he doesn't know how to get the guy. His grab on that town is shaky and once it slips, you just watch everybody walk away from him. It happened to him in New York, it'll happen to him in Hot Springs. He lost the Cotton Club, he'll lose the Southern. You just watch. He'll end up dead or with nothing, which is the same thing."

"And would you be the guy to take it from him?"

"I don't want nothing in Hot Springs. But I don't want Hot Springs being Our Town either. We need a new town, and I mean to build one in the desert. You just watch me, goddammit."

"Ben, the only thing you've built so far is a hole in the ground for somebody else's money."

"Virginia, you are so rude."

"Don't you love me for it, sugar?"

"No, I love you for them tits, that ass, and the thing you do with your mouth. You must be the only white girl in the world who does that thing."

"You'd be surprised, honey."

"Hello, darling. Your bosom is magnificent."

This was from Errol Flynn, an old pal of Virginia's from some weekend or other. Flynn leaned into their booth, his famous hand-some face radiating a leer so intense it could melt a vault door.

"Hit the road, you limey puke," said Ben.

"Hi, Georgie," said Errol, ignoring Ben. "Tough luck about War-ner's. They'll drop me next."

"I got some deals working. I'll be okay. Errol, how're you doing?"

"Well, there's always vodka."

"Errol," said Virginia, "just don't doodle any more fifteen-year-olds. Jerry Geisler might not get you out of it next time."

"In like Flynn, old girl. Oh, Benjamin, didn't see you there, old fel-low. Still looking for buried treasure? There's a very good map to it in *Captain Blood.*"

"You Aussie bastard."

The reference was to one of Ben's more regrettable adventures. With a former lover who billed herself a countess by way of some for-gotten marriage to an actual Italian count, he had rented a yacht and gone to an island off the coast in search of pirate's treasure. It had been quite the joke in Los Angeles in the social season of 1941.

"Don't pick on Ben," said Virginia. "He has big plans. He does know where the treasure is buried and it is in a desert, only it ain't on an island."

"Virginia, you bitch."

"Tut tut, old man," said Errol, moving on to another table.

"You shoulda smashed him," said Georgie. "He can be an asshole. You understand, I can't take him on because he still has Jack Warner's ear, and he might talk against me. I might get another shot at Warner's, so I don't want to do nothing now."

"You're dreaming," said Virginia. "You couldn't smack him because you're afraid of him. He's pretty tough, they say. And genius here couldn't smack him because he can't smack anybody without puking all over his clothes."

"Virginia, leave it alone."

"Did he tell you that story, Georgie? He tries to strong-arm this cowboy in Hot Springs and the guy hits him so hard he can't sit up straight for a week and a half. And I had to listen to him all that time, whinin' like a baby."

"I'll fix that guy."

"Yeah, you'll fix him. You and some army. Ben, why don't we go back right now? Fix him this week. Get it out of the way?"

Ben's eyes clouded and his face tightened.

"I got business to take care of first."

"He's spooked by this guy. So he'll hire goons to clip him, because he don't have the guts to do it man on man."

"I will fix that guy," Bugsy swore. "I will fix him after I fix Owney and after I fix Hot Springs. Forget Hot Springs. Its time is over. The future is in the desert, goddammit, and I will lead the way."

CHAPTER 18

The Belmont lay close to the Oaklawn Racetrack, just south of Hot Springs. If the Horseshoe was your run-of-the-mill joint, with a hundred duplicates on almost any street in town, the Belmont was a step up the food chain. It offered the fancier gamblers a sense of class without quite demanding of them the tuxedoed glamour—with its Xavier Cugats and its Perry Comos—that a place like the Southern Club might. The entertainment tended to be regional, usually a piano combo that played light jazz. It sold cocktails at the bar, not shots, not champagne. Its machines were the sleeker Pace Chrome Comet, which looked as if it could get up and fly, the hottest thing from the year 1939, as its reels spun bells and apples and bananas and oranges this way and that. These machines weren't as tight as the older models, which meant that once or twice a night a line of bells would pop up and pilgrim would be rewarded with a silver cascade of nickels. The house payoff was a modest 39 percent.

It stood in the same hollow as the now deserted racetrack, under a low piney ridge, and it had been done up in the style of the antebellum South, to resemble a wooden plantation house with fake columns and white trim that a Scarlett O'Hara might have designed. A valet crew parked cars; the overhanging elms gave it hushed and muted elegance.

Rather than enter the gates and move into the parking lot, in plain sight of the valets, D.A. elected to infiltrate from the empty racetrack. The three cars discharged their men on the far side, and there the raiders loaded magazines, checked weapons, put on vests and went over their plans for the last time. Becker was already there, this time with two men on his staff and a clerk-driver.

D.A., Earl and Becker hunched undercover in a racetrack portico, examining a diagram of the Belmont with a flashlight.

"Since this is a bigger, more complicated structure," said D.A., "I'd rather have muscle up front. I'd send ten men through the front door and side door—a six-man team and a four-man team—and I'd bolt that kitchen door and leave two men out back to cover it. That way, you got all your force up front and you get it into play."

"I don't want any shooting," said Becker suddenly. "I don't want anyone else getting hurt."

There was a quiet moment.

Then D.A. said, "Well, sir, then I guess we better gather the boys up and take 'em home. I ain't sending men into a dangerous situation with the idea they can't defend themselves."

"No, no," said Becker. "They *can* defend themselves. I just want 'em to *think* before they shoot."

"If they think before they shoot," said Earl, "they may die before they shoot."

"We train 'em to shoot instinctively. They've been trained hard. There won't be no mistakes."

"Like the Horseshoe?" Becker said.

"That weren't no mistake, sir," said the old man. "That was a completely justified legal shooting during the commission of a bonded officer's official duty, and we ought to thank the man who done it, for it probably saved some lives."

Becker seemed to vacillate, almost biting his lower lip like a child.

"It just played bad in the papers, that's what I mean. I have more photogs from Little Rock here," he finally said. "We need the Little Rock papers behind us. They'll get the state behind us. The Hot Springs papers don't matter. But you can't screw up in front of Little Rock reporters. Okay?"

Both officers nodded, and Earl was thinking: This bird wants everything. He wants us to raid without killing and he doesn't want the action to get out of control. He's worried more about the press than the young men who are going in tonight. You can't control this work like that.

"We'll brief the boys," said D.A.

"Excellent. I'll meet up with the photographers." Becker looked at his watch: it was 9:35 P.M.

"Ten P.M., as usual?"

"We can't set up that fast," said D.A. "Make it 10:30."

"I told the photographers to meet me across the street at 9:45. Dammit, they'll get bored."

"Ten-fifteen then, if we hurry."

"That's good," said Becker. He walked back to his car and his clerk drove him away.

"He's shaky," said Earl. "I don't like that."

"I don't like it neither."

They beckoned the raiders over, and briefly went over the plan.

Earl finally said, "You, Henderson and Short, you'll be the cover team."

He could feel Frenchy's eagerness seem to melt in the dark.

"Want you to slip up and jimmy the kitchen door with a crowbar or something, so nobody can get out. If somebody does get out, he's wanting to get out bad, so you cuff him and cover him closely. Okay?"

"Yeah," said Henderson.

"Remember, be cool, calm, collected. Y'all been doing good. I'll go in after the entry team, but you be listening to Slim, he's the boss. I'm just along for support."

"Yes sir."

The unit moved around the racetrack single file. They could see the Belmont twinkling through the trees and hear the jazz streaming out of it, almost with a clink of cocktail glasses and the late-night odor of cigarettes to it.

"We'll go through the trees up high, on the ridge; then we'll file down and around the building. The entry team will go around front. There's people out there, so you have to control them right away."

But Earl drew D.A. aside.

"That ridge is a little steep," he whispered. "With these vests and the Thompsons, coming down in the dark could be tricky. Somebody could fall, we could get an accidental discharge. See, I'd keep 'em down here and just slip behind the line of sight from the front here on the right. Rally at the corner. Send the teams around, set up, and move fast, real fast."

D.A. looked at him for just a second, and a peculiar light came into his eyes, invisible in the night.

How does he know? he thought.

But then he saw the wisdom in Earl's counsel.

"Yeah, that's good, Earl."

Earl told the team of the new plan.

"You're on safety now. Team leaders, when you get there at the rallying point, you remember to tell your tommy-gunners to go off safety. If they have to shoot, something better come out when they pull the triggers besides cussing. Got that?"

Whispers came in assent.

"Henderson, you got that crowbar?"

"No sir," said Henderson, "but I do have a length of chain and a padlock."

"Good. You all straight?"

"Yes sir."

"You're also in support. If it gets wild, your job is to come in through the back. Got that?"

"Yes sir."

"Short, you got that?"

No answer.

"Short!"

"Yeah, yeah. I'm all set."

"Okay," said Earl. "Let's do it."

Frenchy and Carlo separated from the congregation of raiders. They slithered around the back of the plantation house, keeping low, under the view from the windows. They scuttled alongside the foundation, at last coming to the kitchen door. It was closed already, but the windows on either side were open, and a steamy light and a sense of urgent bustle poured out of each. They could hear Negro men talking among themselves.

Henderson slipped forward, looped the chain around the door handle, pulled it tight, looped it against the doorjamb, and clamped the lock shut. It would hold tight enough to prevent an exit, unless somebody really leaned into it.

The two men crept out to the perimeter of trees and set up in a defensive position about thirty yards in back of the house.

"You better give me the Thompson," said Carlo.

"Not a chance," said Frenchy. "You're fine."

"I can't hit anything at this range with a .45."

"Yeah, well, I have the Thompson and I'm keeping it. Get that straight right now. We wouldn't be in shit squad if you hadn't screwed up. So you don't deserve the Thompson."

"I screwed up? You screwed up! You didn't do a last check, or you would have found that hillbilly."

"I did do that last check. He wasn't up there. That's what you should have said to Earl, not this 'I'm so sorry' crap. If you act guilty, the facts don't matter. You are guilty."

"You should have checked."

"I did check. So here we are, dumped out back so we don't fuck up again."

"Somebody has to do this job."

"Nobody has to do this job. We all should be going in."

Frenchy was really getting steamed. Something about Earl really had him angry. Earl this, Earl that, God Earl, King Earl, Earl the leader of the pack! It was beginning to wear on him.

"What's so special about Earl?" he blurted.

"Earl's a hero and you're lucky to be here to learn from him," was all Carlo could think to say. "Now shut up and pay attention. We should be doing our jobs, not yakking about this stuff like old ladies."

Of course Becker's change in schedule had thrown the whole thing off. They weren't in position until 10:10, and in the darkness it took about four minutes to get organized into the proper squads and fire team, all trying to do it silently while crouching in the bushes under the windows. Fortunately, there was no perimeter security, no patrolling guards, no dogs, for if there had been, surely the whispering, bickering raiders would have been easily spotted.

Finally, with just thirty seconds to go, Earl got them straightened out, and the side-entry squad peeled off to beeline to the side door, which stood unguarded.

Earl looked at his watch.

"Okay," he said, "I'm going to go out and get the valets out of the way."

"You be careful," Slim said.

"*You* be careful," Earl said. "You're going in. I'm just going to roust some teenagers."

Earl stood, slipped out of his vest, which again would blow his cover, and rounded the corner.

He walked up the walk where three kids about eighteen or so lounged smoking under a neon sign that announced VALET. They wore absurd costumes that he could tell from their posture they despised.

"Hi, fellas," he said.

The boys looked up, caught short. Where the hell did this bird come from? But he was so chipper and bodacious the way he strode manfully up the flagstones to them.

"Uh—" the oldest began.

"See, fellas, I'm from the Prosecuting Attorney's Office." He pulled open his suit coat to show the badge pinned over his left breast. "Now we have something just about to happen here, and I don't want none of you boys getting hurt, so why not just step aside a bit, and turn and face the wall, maybe rest your hands up agin it."

"Are we under arrest?"

"Not unless you robbed a bank. Robbed any banks?"

"No sir."

"Ain't that swell."

"I better call Mr. Swenson," said one of the boys, reaching for a phone mounted on the wall.

Earl's fast hands beat him to the destination. He grabbed the phone, and with a snap popped the cord that ran to the receiver. "I don't think that would be a good idea," he said merrily. "Mr. Swenson's going to find out we're here soon enough, believe me."

Using the authority of his body language, he herded them along the front of the casino until they were a good twenty yards from their positions.

"You wouldn't have no guns, would you?"

"No sir," came a reply.

"'Cause I don't want to have to hurt nobody. You just rest up agin the building for a few minutes while this thing happens and everything will be just fine."

Earl turned a bit, and gave a whistle and watched as the raid began.

"There's the signal. Safeties off. Let's do it," said Slim.

He led his five men around the corner of the building to the front door. The door was open and a security officer, talking to a woman just inside the entrance, looked up in surprise. Terry, Slim's number-two man, clubbed him with the compensator on the end of his Thompson muzzle, opening a vicious wound in the side of his face, and he went down. The woman screamed but the raiders rushed past her like McNamara's band and began to fan out into the casino, their guns much in evidence, their fedoras low over their eyes, their square vests like sandwich boards across their bodies.

"Hands up! Hands up! This is a raid!"

The side-door team hit its entry point with the same velocity and urgency. The doors didn't need sledges but merely stout kicks. The men poured in and fanned out on the other side of the room. A team raced upstairs, clearing rooms, finding only gamblers and staff members, but no resistance.

It was over in seconds.

"Y'all go home now," Earl said to the valets. "This place is closed. You find other jobs tomorrow, hear?"

Earl walked in, his badge pinned to his lapel, and seconds later D.A. pulled up in a car.

It had gone exactly as planned: the overwhelming show of force, the speed of deployment, the cleverness of the raiders as they separated gamblers from workers, the pure professionalism of it.

"Clear upstairs," came the call.

"Clear in the kitchen," came another call.

"Now ladies and gentlemen," said D.A., "this here's a raid on an illegal gambling facility by the Prosecuting Attorney's Office. You will be checked and released if there are no outstanding warrants on you. You may keep any winnings you have on your person. We'll have you out of here in no time, if you cooperate with us. And my advice is: if you like to gamble, try Havana, Cuba, because that's where you're going to have to go."

Mr. Swenson, the manager of the place, was brought between two raiders, cursing and spitting. A rotund man, with slicked-back hair and a summer tuxedo, he wore a red carnation in his lapel. Earl plucked it out and inserted it into his mouth, shutting him up.

"When we want to talk to you," he said, "we will tell you. Otherwise you suck on that flower like a lollipop and watch us tear this joint up so you can tell Owney Maddox he's finished in this town."

Then they heard the machine gun fire.

"There they go," said Carlo.

But from the rear, behind the trees thirty yards out, the two young officers saw nothing. They heard glass breaking, doors being shattered and other signals of men moving aggressively against an objective. It was over very quickly.

"That's it?" said Frenchy.

"I guess," said Carlo.

"Well, let's get in there."

But Carlo wasn't sure. He realized now he had no clear post-raid instructions.

"I think we ought to hang here till we're released."

"Come on, it's over. You can tell it's over. I don't want to miss the party."

"There's going to be plenty of party. Let's just sit here a bit longer."

"Shit, sit here in the dark, while everybody else is having a great time? Come on, this is stupid. Who died and left *you* in charge? That's where we're needed, not sitting out here like a couple of Boy Scouts."

Carlo let it simmer. Rather than argue with his partner, he just hunkered yet more solidly against the weight of the tree, saying nothing, moving not a muscle or a twitch, signifying the conversation was over.

"Look," said Frenchy, "we were put out here to cover this back entrance. Nobody's coming out this back entrance. So we're just wasting our time."

Finally, it seemed he was right. There was no more bustle from the kitchen and no evidence of movement or escape from the door.

"All right," Carlo finally said, "let's go."

They got up.

"Put that safety on," said Carlo. "I don't want you roaming around with a live gun."

"Safety's already *on*," said Frenchy, though of course it wasn't, nor did he have any intention of putting it on, not till the party was over.

The two young men walked to the kitchen door, feeling the bulk of the would-be plantation house loom over them. Carlo bent, unlocked the padlock, coiled the chain, and opened the door, stepping in.

Frenchy followed him and—

Whoa, there.

He caught a peripheral of movement from his left, spun, and saw a second figure leap silently from the window, collect himself, join his partner and start to head off.

Frenchy dashed at them, intercepting them halfway to the trees.

"Hold it!" he screamed. *"Hands up!"*

He braced them from thirty feet with the Thompson, his finger dangerously caressing its trigger, which strained ever so gently against the pad of his fingertip.

But neither man seemed particularly challenged by the heavy gun aimed at him.

"Hey, hey, watch it, kid, them things is dangerous."

The other laughed.

"He's more gun than man, I'd say." They separated slightly.

"Don't move!" barked Frenchy.

"We're not moving? Are we moving? I don't see us moving. Do you see us moving?"

"I'm not moving," said the other. "If a lawman tells me not to move, I'm not moving, no sir."

"Hands! Show me hands!"

But neither man raised his hands.

They were two tough-looking customers in suits with hats drawn down across their eyes, mid- to late thirties, both handsome in a rough way. They were utterly calm. The one on the right was even smiling a little bit. The signals they were putting out utterly confounded him.

"Look, kid, why don't you put that gun down and go inside before somebody gets hurt," said one. "You don't want to do nothing stupid now, do you? Something that you'd regret your whole life? I mean hell, this is just a penny-ante gambling bust that ain't supposed to happen and it's all going to be straightened out in—"

Frenchy fired. The gun shuddered, heaved, flashed, spit smoke and flung a line of empties off to the right, pounding against his shoulder. Three-round burst? No siree bob. He hosed them, blowing them backward like tenpins split by a bowler's strike, and they tumbled to the earth in a tangle of floating dust and gun smoke.

"I don't do stupid things, asshole," he said.

Then he fired another burst, to make sure they stayed down.

Carlo, halfway through the kitchen, got there first. He found Frenchy standing thirty-odd feet from the bodies, screaming hysterically.

"Asshole! Assholes! You fucking *pricks!*"

A tendril of smoke curled out of the compensator of the tommy and a litter of brass shells lay at his feet. The stench of gun smoke filled the air.

"What happened?"

"Fuckin' guys made a move. I got 'em. Goddamn, did I get 'em. Got 'em *both,* goddammit!"

"You okay?"

Clearly he wasn't. His eyes were as wide as lamps and his face was drawn into a mask of near-hysteria. He sucked at the air mightily. He seemed to stagger, then dropped to one knee.

"What the hell happened?" yelled Earl, arriving in a second.

Frenchy was silent.

"He nabbed these two guys making a getaway. He braced them, they drew and he dropped them. Looks like he clipped them both."

Earl walked over to the bodies as D.A. arrived. Two other raiders showed up, and then Becker, alone.

"What the hell is going on, for God's sake? I have two Little Rock photographers and two reporters out front, and they want to know what the hell happened."

"The officer dropped two runaways," said D.A. "They drew on him? Isn't that right, son?"

But Frenchy was silent.

Earl kneeled, put a hand out to each throat to feel for a pulse, but purely as an obligation. Each pulse was still. The two men lay on their backs. Frenchy had shot very well. Dust and smoke still floated in the air, and the blood continued to ooze from a network of wounds, absorbed by the material of the suits, so that each man was queerly damp, a sponge for excess blood. One's eyes were open blankly. The other's face was in repose. A hat was trapped under one head but the other hat lay a few feet away. The wounds were mostly in the torso and gut; both faces were unmarked.

"They drew on you, right?" asked D.A.

Frenchy was silent.

Earl heard the question and did the next bit of very dirty work. He pulled the sodden suit coats away from the bodies and checked for weapons. No shoulder holsters, no hip holsters, no guns jammed in belts, no guns in pockets, no guns in ankle holsters, no guns in suit pockets.

Earl rolled one over slightly, and gingerly withdrew a wallet. It contained what looked to be about $2,000 in cash and a driver's license in the name of William P. Allgood, from Tulsa, Oklahoma. A business card identified Mr. Allgood as an oil equipment leasing agent.

"Shit," said Earl, turning to the next body. That was a Phillip Hensler, also of Tulsa, a salesman for Phillips Oil.

He walked back.

"They wasn't armed," he said.

"Shit," said D.A.

"Oh, Christ," said Becker. "He killed two unarmed men? Jesus Christ, and I've got reporters here? Oh, Jesus Christ, you said they were trained, this wouldn't happen! Oh, Christ!"

"It's worse. One's a goddamn oil salesman, one leases drilling equipment. Both from Tulsa."

"Oh, shit," said D.A.

By this time, the Hot Springs police had arrived, and out in the lot, the gumballs flashed red in the night. A heavyset detective came around the corner with two uniforms.

"Mr. Becker? What the hell is going on?"

"One of my investigators shot two fleeing men," said Becker. "Naturally, we'll want a full investigation."

"Shit," said the cop.

"Y'all get on out of here until we're done," said Earl.

"Hey, buddy, I'm Captain Gilmartin and I—"

"I don't give a fuck who you are," said Earl, ramming his chest square against the fat man's gut, "I got six tommy guns that say you get the fuck off my operation till I let you on it, and if you don't like that, then there's some woods over there and whyn't you and I go discuss this a little further?" He fixed his mankiller's glare against the cop and watched the man melt and fall back.

"Take it easy, Earl," said D.A. "The police can control the crowd and look at the bodies when we're gone."

Earl nodded.

But someone else came up to the mute Becker, one of his assistants.

"Fred, the press guys are really getting difficult. I can't hardly contain 'em. They want to come back here and see what we bagged."

"Shit," said Becker. Then he turned to D.A.

"So you tell me what to do. You *promised* me this wouldn't happen. Now we got a situation where we've killed two innocent men. Unarmed men."

"Well, we don't know nothing about 'em yet," D.A. said.

Earl was so disgusted with Becker's panic that he turned and walked away, over to where Frenchy knelt in the grass with Henderson more or less holding him. He knelt too.

"You saw them make a move?" he asked.

"He ain't talked yet," said Henderson.

"Short. *Short!* Look at me! Snap out of it, goddammit. You saw them make a move?"

"I swear to Christ they did," Frenchy said, swallowing.

"They ain't armed."

"I know they were going to try something. I saw his hand move."

"Why would his hand move? It had nothing to move toward."

"I— I—"

"Did you panic, Short? Did you just squeeze down on 'em because you was scared?"

"No sir. They made a move."

"Son, I want to help you. Ain't nobody here going to do it. That Becker, he'll throw you to the wolves if it makes him the youngest governor in the state of Arkansas."

"I— I know they moved. They were trying something."

"Is there any evidence? Did they say anything? I mean, give us something to work with. Why did you fire?"

"I don't know."

"Did you see anything, Henderson?"

Carlo swallowed. He decided not to mention Frenchy's cursing the dead bodies, his state of lost anger.

"He was just standing there with the smoking gun. They were dead. That's all."

"Shit," said Earl.

But someone was standing over him.

Peanut, the biggest man in the unit, a former detective from Atlanta, loomed over them.

"Whaddaya want, Peanut?"

"Well sir," said Peanut, "I may be wrong, but I don't think I am."

"What?"

"Them boys. The boys Short bushwhacked."

"Yeah?"

"I looked 'em over real careful."

"They're a couple of salesmen from Tulsa."

"No sir. B'lieve one's Tommy Malloy, out of Kansas City, and the other's Walter Budowsky, called Wally Bud. Bank robbers."

"Bank robbers?"

"Malloy's number one on the FBI's most wanted list. Wally Bud is only number seven. But that's who it is, killed deader'n stumps over there."

"Jesus Christ," said Frenchy. "I'm a hero!"

CHAPTER

19

Cleveland was on the phone. Owney didn't want to take it and you never could be too sure about the security of the phones, even if Mel Parsons, who ran Bell Telephone in Hot Springs, maintained that no one could eavesdrop without his knowledge.

Still, Owney knew he had to take the call.

He had a martini, and a Cubano. He sat in his office in the Southern. One of the chorus girls kneaded the back of his neck with long, soothing fingers. Jack McGaffery and Merle Swenson—neither with a club to manage—sat earnestly on the davenport. F. Garry Hurst smoked a cigar and looked out the window. Pap and Flem Grumley were also in attendance, though as muscle slightly exiled to a further circle.

"Hello, Owney Maddox here."

"Cut the English shit, Owney. I ain't one of your stooges."

"Victor? Victor, is that you?"

"You know it is, Owney. What the hell is going on down there? My people tell me some cops knocked off Tommy Malloy and Wally Bud. I'm supposed to tell Mr. Fabrizzio that? Mr. Fabrizzio liked Tommy very much. He knew his dad back in the '20s when his dad legged rum across Superior for him."

"It's nothing. I got some pricks who—"

"Owney, Jesus Christ, this is serious shit. There are people unhappy all over the goddamn place. Tommy was down there because you said he'd be all right. Send your boys down, you said; I run the town, the town welcomes visitors. What the fuck, now I got two dead guys?"

"I'm having some trouble with a local fuckin' prosecutor. It ain't a big thing."

"Oh, yeah? It was pretty fucking big to Tommy Malloy. He's fucking dead, if I recall."

"I got some kind of rogue cop unit. These guys, they're like another mob: they just open fire and to hell with anything else. It's like the Mad Dog is runnin' them. I will take care of it. Mr. Fabrizzio and his associates have nothing to worry about. It's safe for Cleveland, it's safe for Chicago, it's safe for New York. Ask Ben Siegel, he was just down here. He saw the town. Ask him."

"Owney, it was Bugsy *called* Mr. Fabrizzio. That's why I'm on the phone right now."

"That kike fuck," said Owney.

Now it was official. Bugsy was talking against him. That was tantamount to a declaration of war, for it meant that Bugsy was lobbying for permission from the commission to move against him. Whatever was going on with goddamned Becker, it was helping Bugsy no end.

"Look, Vic, we go way back. You know me to be a man of my word. I'm fuckin' dealing with this. I will take care of it. A week, maybe two, that's all, then we're back exactly doing what we've been doing since '32."

"Bugsy says, once he gets his joint up and running, that's the kind of shit would never happen. He guarantees it. Gambling's legal out there."

"Yeah, but it's a fucking desert. It's full of scorpions and lizards and snakes. Great fun. I can see what you'd be telling Mr. Fabrizzio after a snake bit him onna ass!"

"Well, you got a point there, Owney. Just get it taken care of. And this is advice from a friend. Imagine what your enemies are saying."

Owney hung up, only to get a new call. It was from the lobby, saying that Mayor Leo O'Donovan and Judge LeGrand were here, they had to see him.

"Send them up."

This was troubling. By time-honored fiat, meetings with Hot Springs officials were conducted on the sly, never in observable public spots, particularly a casino. This meant that the two men, who more or less administered the town under his benevolent guidance, were seriously spooked.

He turned to the girl, whose face was pretty but vacant.

"Honey, you go now. You come visit Owney later tonight."

She smiled a bright, fake smile, so intense that he thought he might already have had her. Maybe he had. He couldn't remember.

In any case, as she ducked out, the two town officials ducked in, and didn't even notice Pap and Flem Grumley, who under normal circumstances they would have avoided like a disease. After all, the Grumleys *were* a disease.

Owney offered them a drink, a cigar, and an earnest demeanor.

"Owney," said Leo O'Donovan, His Honor, a watery-eyed old hack who like to parade around the town in his cabriolet behind horses named Bourbon and Water, "I'll come to the point. People are unsettled with this kind of violence. Suddenly, the town is turning into Chicago in the '20s."

"I'm working like hell to locate these characters! What do you think I been doing, Leo, sitting on my hands? You think it's fuckin' good for me when two boys get clipped on my own fuckin' territory? Next thing, we won't be getting the Xavier Cugats and the Perry Comos and the Dinah Shores down here, and then we're screwed."

"Jeez, Owney," said Leo, dumbfounded. "I thought you were *British.*"

Under the intense pressure of his situation, he had slipped and let his New York persona show in front of people not in the inner circle.

"Well," he said, somewhat archly, "when one finds oneself in a gangster movie, one must act the gangster, no? No, Garry?"

F. Garry Hurst said, "Absolutely, old toff. Mr. Maddox sometimes *pretends* to be an East Side gangster for the amusement of his staff."

Pap chimed in with, "He's a proper English gent, the finest in these here parts, Mr. Mayor."

The mayor looked at Pap as if he'd just been addressed by a large hunk of dogshit, sniffed and turned back to Owney.

"You have to do something, Owney. The town is coming to a stop."

"Oh, I hardly think that's quite the case, Leo. The girls are still doing their mattress-backed duties, the alcohol is still flowing, the horse wire still thrums with electric information, the fools still bet the horses, the wheel and the dice, Xavier continues to wow them, and Dinah is scheduled for next week. I've just replaced my old Watlings here at the Southern with brand-new Mills Black Cherries, the very latest thing. Fresh from the factory in Chicago, seventy-five of them, the most beautiful machine you've ever seen. I've got the best room in the country. So you see, we really haven't been affected a bit. We've lost two houses out of eighty-five, and less than $100,000, plus around sixty-five slots. It's nothing. It's a trice, a trifle, a gossamer butterfly wing."

The two officials were hardly consoled.

"Owney," said Judge LeGrand, "the mayor is onto something. Like FDR said, the main thing we have to fear is fear its own black-assed self. If people lose their confidence in the town, Hot Springs goes away. It disappears. It turns into Malvern or Russellville or some other bleak little nowhere burg. Like many cities of fabled corruption, it is sustained merely by the illusion of vice and pleasure, which is to say, the illusion of security that such human weaknesses ain't only tolerated, they are encouraged. If that image is damaged, it all goes away."

The judge spoke a harsh truth.

Publicly Owney could only say, "I swear to you both, we will work on this issue."

Privately a million thoughts poured through his head.

"What I'm saying," the judge continued, "is that this problem had better be dealt with quickly. I think for our business interests, what we need is a show of force, a stand, a victory."

"Judge, old man, your sagacity is unmatched. And I say in a response hardly as eloquent but equally as heartfelt: I will take care of this. As I said, we are working on it. For your part, I expect the following: business as usual. The same payments in the same pickups. You enforce discipline with yours so I do not have to enforce it with mine. That is clear?"

"It is," said Leo. "We'll do our part."

"We are all taking the right steps," said Owney, to signify that the meeting was over.

The two men left.

"Any bright guys got any bright ideas?" he asked. "Or do I have to fire you mutts and bring in some heavy fuckin' hitters from Cleveland or Detroit or KC?"

"Now, sir," said Pap, "ain't no damned call to be talking to a Grumley like that. You know us Grumleys go to the goddamn wall fer you every damn time you need us, Mr. Maddox. That's God's honest truth."

He hitched up his pants, stiff with indignity, and launched a gob of something blackish toward the spittoon, which it rattled perfectly.

"Telephones," said Flem.

"What?" said Owney.

"Goddamn telephones. If'n them boys is hiding in secret, and if we follow Mr. Becker but don't never see him leavin' town, and he's there every goddamned time, he's got to be reaching them boys by telephone. You know the boss of the phone company. So whyn't we tap into his lines, and listen to his calls. That way we get to know where they gonna be striking next. And we'd dadgum be waiting for 'em. Radio intelligence, like. We done it to the Krauts in Italy, toward the end of the war. Intercepted their messages, sure as shit."

"You know, Owney, that's very good," said F. Garry. "That's quite good, actually. I'm sure Mel Parsons could provide technical guidance. After all, he's an investor too, isn't he?"

"Yes, he is. Goddamn, that *is* good. Pap, you raised a fuckin' genius."

"I knowed about what happened in Italy in '45," said Flem proudly. "That's whar they court-martialed me."

"They court-martialed you?"

"Yes sir. The second time. Now, the third time they . . ."

It was D.A.'s idea but it was Earl who figured out how to make it work.

He called Carlo Henderson the next morning.

"Henderson," he said, "how'd you like to go on a little trip?"

"Uh. Well, sir—"

"No big deal. Just a little lookie-see party."

"Sure."

"You got a straw hat?"

"Here?"

"Yeah?"

"No sir."

"How 'bout some overalls, a denim shirt, some clodhopper boots?"

"Mr. Earl, I'm from Tulsa, not the sticks. I went to college. I'm not a farmer."

"Well, son, that's fine, because guess what's in this bag?"

He handed over a paper sack, much crumpled, weighing in at around five pounds.

"Uh . . . overalls, a denim shirt, some clodhopper boots and a straw hat?"

"Exactly. Now I want you all dressed up like Clyde the Farmer. I'm going to have one of these federal dam workers drive you downtown. Here's what I want. You just mosey around the block City Hall is on, where Mr. Becker's office is. And the blocks a couple each way."

"Yes?"

"Here's what you're looking for. A phone company truck and man. Parked somewhere in that vicinity, working probably on a pole, but maybe under the street or at some kind of junction box. Now the thing is, you can't let him see you watching him. But if you see him, you watch him close, see, because I think you'll see he ain't really working. He's actually playing at work. But he's got earphones and a rig set up to the pole knobs or some such, don't know what it'd be. But he's really listening. He'd be all dialed into calls coming out of Mr. Becker's office."

"But we don't get calls from Mr. Becker's office."

They got pouches delivered by a fake postman, with the information for that night's raid encoded, a system put together by D.A. with the express intention to avoid a wiretap.

"That's right. We don't. You know it and I know it. Mr. Becker knows it and we both know D. A. Parker knows it, because he thought it up. But *they* don't know it. We could let him tap his butt off, but Mr. D.A. came up with an idea to turn their little game against them. This one could turn into some real damn fun and I don't know about you, Henderson, but goddammit, I could use me some fun."

CHAPTER
20

GANGSTERS SLAIN IN HOT SPRINGS read the headline in the Little Rock *Arkansas Democrat* two days after the raid.

**Prosecuting Attorney's Raiders
Send Two "Most Wanted"
to County Morgue**

Hot Springs—Officers from the Prosecuting Attorney's Office shot and killed two highly dangerous wanted men in a nighttime raid on an illegal gambling establishment here tonight.

The shootings occurred at the Belmont Club, on Oakland Boulevard in South Hot Springs, at approximately 10:30 P.M.

Dead were Thomas "Tommy" Malloy, 34, of Cleveland, Ohio, a bank robber who was listed as No. 1 on the FBI's most wanted list, and Walter "Wally Bud" Budowsky, 31, also of Cleveland. Budowsky was No. 7 on the list.

Both men were pronounced dead at the site.

Malloy, a career criminal since his teens, was wanted on several charges of armed robbery, including the July 5, 1945, robbery of a Dayton, Ohio, bank and trust that left two officers dead and two more wounded. That crime catapulted him to No. 1 on the FBI's list, but he is wanted in connection with at least 12 other charges, including a kidnapping, two counts of assault with attempt to kill and several more counts of fleeing across interstate lines to avoid prosecution.

Budowsky is also suspected in taking part in the Dayton job, as well as several other crimes. Both men served time in the Ohio State Penitentiary.

The editorial was even better.

Becker: A Man of His Word

It seems that when Garland County Prosecuting Attorney Fred C. Becker gives his word, that word is as good as gold.

Elected in a controversial election just last month, Becker has moved aggressively against organized crime interests in Arkansas' shameful bordello town 35 miles to the south, raiding two casinos in the past week. Long a haven for gamblers, gunmen and ladies of the night, Hot Springs is becoming downright dangerous for such folk, owing to Becker's crusade.

At the same time, it's becoming a place of pride for citizens who obey the law, worship God and go to church on Sunday.

Becker is to be commended for his efforts and maybe Arkansas would do well to think about hitching its wagon to his star in the 1948 gubernatorial race. If he can clean up Hot Springs, a Herculean labor if ever there was one, then who knows how far he can go?

This was a good day for Becker. The *Arkansas Democrat* was the only paper with a reputation outside the state; it could get him noticed nationally. Who cared what the Garland county rags screeched about or their demands for indictments against the raiders; they had no circulation outside the county, no influence on party politics, no reach to the state's bosses, no connections to the national press.

Already that seemed to be happening. He was onto something. The winds of change were in the air; the tired old men who'd run the country while the boys were off fighting had to step aside now, and whoever saw that first and seized that opportunity would go the furthest. If he became governor in 1948, he would be the youngest governor in the history of Arkansas, one of the youngest governors in the United States. The sky was the limit; who knew where that could take him, particularly if the radio networks began picking up on it.

Already *Life* was sending a man down, and that meant *Time* would follow and probably *Time*'s imitator, *News-Week*. Those magazines were read in Washington, where it really counted. Maybe . . . Senator Becker. Maybe . . . even bigger.

So after his morning news conference—a love celebration, really, in which the Little Rock boys pulled rank on the snippier Hot Springs bumpkins and asked flattering, softball questions—he went back to his office to luxuriate in his success. As a matter of fact, he wasn't an aggressive prosecutor so much as an ambitious politician. There were a number of routine matters before him—moves to prosecute traffic offenders, county statute violators, petty criminals in the Negro section—but all of them could wait.

Instead, he loaded up the bowl of his English briarwood with a fine mild Moroccan tobacco, lit it up, and enjoyed the sweetness and the density of the smoke and the pure pleasure: he concentrated on enjoying the moment, and more than a few minutes passed in this state of high bliss before a knock came at the door.

It was Willis O'Doyle, his number-one clerk, who had ambitions of accompanying his chief as far as his chief could go. O'Doyle had a communiqué from D.A., an out-of-schedule communication unusual in and of itself.

It said, when decoded, "Please call us at 2:00 P.M. tomorrow and order us to raid Mary Jane's, in the Negro section out Malvern Avenue. This will pay very big dividends."

Hmmm, he thought. What the hell is this about?

Earl came to them that very morning.

"All right, fellas," he said. "You want to gather 'round?"

The raiders, sleeping on cots, spent lazy days when they weren't actually scheduled to hit some place. Earl had plans to keep them in shape with various dry-fire exercises but it seemed so pointless because there was so little room in the pumphouse station and they couldn't work outside, because of fear of discovery. So he let them sleep, stay clean, clean their weapons and otherwise occupy themselves until the word came on the target that night.

This was his first urgent gathering since they'd swung into operation.

"We have an opportunity," he said. "In the service, the CO'd just give the order and I'd draw up a plan and that would be that. But this ain't the service, and it's your butts on the line, so I figure you ought to have some say-so in what we do next. Fair enough?"

The men nodded or murmured assent, even the still-sleepy Frenchy Short, now something of a hero for his victory over the two gangsters.

"Y'all know what radio intelligence is?"

"Fred Allen?" somebody said.

"No. *Gangbusters!*"

There was some laughter.

"Not quite," said Earl. "It's what you can do when you break the other guy's code. Or it's what you can do when you know the other guy's broken your code, only he don't know you know. Well, we now got us a chance to play a little radio game, 'cept that it's a telephone game.

"Mr. D.A. knows all the tricks, and he figured Owney's boys would be trying like hell to find us. He figured they'd even try and tap Mr. Becker's phone lines. That's why we don't use telephone lines. Well, goddamned if Carlo Henderson didn't go downtown yesterday dressed like a farmer, and goddamn if he didn't find a telephone crew set up at a junction box where all the prosecuting attorney's lines are shunted through to the big Bell office. So they are listening. Here's a coupla things we could do.

"First, we could just mark it, and make certain we never gave up nothing on the phone. See, that would keep them guessing, and it would cause them to spread out their resources, because mind my words, what they want to do is ambush us.

"Now here's another thing we could do: we could pass out phony information. We could say, See, we're going to Joe's Club. So they'd set up to get us at Joe's Club, only we'd hit Bill's Club. That way we'd be sure to have a raid without no problems. We could probably do that two, three times. Then they'd catch on, and that game'd be over.

"But there's one last thing we could do. We could pass out the information that we were going to hit Joe's Club. So you can bet they would load up at Joe's Club. They'd love to hit us and hurt us and kill some of us. They'd love to humiliate Mr. Becker and send us home in shame. But here's the wrinkle. We know that they know. So instead of them hitting us, we lure them in, and then we hit them. They think they got us marked, all the time we're marking them. We counter-ambush and we smoke 'em good. See? Their best shot is blasted, the power and the prestige of Owney Maddox and his hillbilly gunmen is made to look pathetic. We found a place on Malvern that'd work right fine. Called Mary Jane's."

"Hell," said Bob Billy, one of the most aggressive raiders, a Highway Patrolman from Mississippi, "I say we go and kick some fellers upside the head."

Cheers and laughter and agreement rose.

Earl let it die down.

"Okay," he said. "That's fine and good, but understand where you're going. You're going into the fire. Sometimes you can't control what happens in there. Blood will be shed, blood in this room. Know that going in. If it's more than you bargained for, it's okay. But I want a vote, and I want it secret, so nobody feels pressure. I want it written down. A simple no or yes. Because we can't make this work if we don't believe in it."

It was unanimous.

CHAPTER 21

"He's finished," said the Countess.

"But suppose he isn't?" Ben said.

"He's finished. I know he's finished."

"But suppose he isn't? He's a tricky bastard, slippery and smart. He gets out of it somehow. And he hears I been talking against him. And he gets to thinking about it. And he hears about the desert and the building I'm doing and the plans I got. And he reads the writing on the wall. He knows that even though I'm in a different state two fucking thousand miles away, he and I are at cross purposes."

"Don't get paranoid, darling."

"What's paranoid?"

"The idea that everyone is out to get you."

"Everyone *is* out to get me."

"But not yet. Because you are smarter and quicker and you see these things so much sooner."

They lounged by the pool of the Beverly Hills Country Club, beside a diamond of emerald-blue water patrolled by the legends of the movie business, their wives, their children, their managers, their assistants, their bodyguards. The Countess wore a white latex suit à la Esther Williams; her legs were tan, her bust was full, her toenails were red.

Bugsy wore a tight red suit that showed off his extremely athletic body, his ripply muscles, his big hands, his larger-than-life penis. He too was tan, and his hair gleamed with oil, the sun picking it up and glinting off it fabulously. He looked like a movie star, he wore movie star sunglasses and he sipped a movie star's drink, a piña colada, from a tall glass.

Virginia was on one of her trips back east, to visit certain aging relatives or so it was said. He actually wasn't too clear on where she was, but it helped to have her gone, as she could be a pain in the ass. She'd been really annoying of late.

The Countess, by contrast, was a more comforting person. Her name was Dorothy Dendice Taylor DiFassio, the last moniker making her an authentic countess, though the count had long since been abandoned. She was one of Ben's earliest Southern California lovers and she had connections to Italy through her title, and the two of them had some crazed adventures together.

"That is why I need a backup plan and I need it now."

"You'll come up with something."

"I have to be ready. He's now involved with this goddamn crusader. Everybody's talking about it. He got two Cleveland boys clipped on him and right now his name is mud in every syndicate spot in the country. He is so weak now he can hardly keep it going. But I know him. He'll come up with something, he'll get out of it, you'll see."

"You give him too much credit, darling. Look, there's a cute one!"

She pointed at a pool boy. These creatures came from all over America to become movie stars. Most failed but some actually got as far as pool boy. They modeled their bodies and their blond locks around the club, hoping to catch a producer's eye. The one she noticed, though, was beefier than most and not blond at all, but rather dark-haired.

"You, boy," she called.

"Christ, Dorothy," said Bugsy, "are you going to fuck him right here?"

"Possibly. But it would hurt my chances for a table at El Morocco. Boy, come here."

The lad obliged.

"What's your name?" she asked.

"Roy, ma'am," he responded.

"Roy, eh? How wonderful. Roy, I think I'd like a whiskey sour with a lemon twist. Do you think you can remember that?"

"Yes ma'am."

He lumbered off.

"That one's going to be a big star some day," she said. "He's got a certain *je ne sais quoi.*"

"I'll say," Bugsy said. "The way he was staring at my dick shows what a future he's got in this fruit town!"

"Ben, you are so crude. I don't think he's homo."

"The handsome ones are all homo. Anyhow, back to *my* problems."

"Oh, that's right, darling," said Dorothy, "I forgot. Yours are the *real* problems. The rest of us are simply bedeviled by petty annoyances."

"Well, Dorothy, I do not think Roy the Pool Boy is going to pull out a chopper and clip you right here. I am at risk and I've got to deal with this problem."

"Do you want him killed?"

"Ah—difficult. I'd have to get permission. It'd have to go through channels. And everything's so spread out these days. It used to be a few blocks of Brooklyn, now it's everywhere, from coast to coast. Getting things okayed can be tough and time-consuming."

"So what you really want is him eliminated, but not necessarily killed."

"That would be right, yeah. If I could get him sent up for five years or so, he'd have nothing when he got out."

"Hmmm. What are his weaknesses? His vanities?"

Ben thought hard. He remembered the beautiful art deco apartment overlooking the city, the phony English accent, the liveried staff, the sense of elegance.

"He wants to be a British gentleman. He wants to be cultivated. He wants to be like the real Gary Cooper, not the real Cary Grant. He likes furniture, art, food. He wants to be a king. He's tryin' to be bigger than who he is. He's tryin' to forget where he came from and what made him."

"I see," said the Countess. "Quite common, actually. And exactly why I treasure you so dearly: you are what you are to the maximum. There's no hypocrisy in you. Not a lick of it."

"I guess that's a compliment."

"It is. Oh, hello, what's this?"

It was Roy the tall Pool Boy. He held a whiskey sour on a silver platter and he offered it to madame.

She opened her alligator purse and removed a $50 bill.

"For you, darling," she said.

"Thank you, ma'am," he said, bowing a little so that he could get a better look at Bugsy's dick stuffed in his tight bathing suit.

Then he went away.

"A look like that could get him killed in a lotta places on the East Side," said Ben.

"And he is what he is," she said. "Anyway, art? Art? You said art? He collects art."

"Yes."

"Hmmmm," she said. "You know, collecting is a disease. And even the most rational and intelligent of men can lose their way when they see something they must have. This should be looked into, darling. This has possibilities."

CHAPTER

22

"Guns?" asked Owney.

"Yes sir," said Pap. "Not just the six-shootin' guns we carry during the day. Guns."

"Traceable? I wouldn't—"

"No sir. 'Bout fifteen or sixteen years ago, when it was a time of road bandits and generalized desperado work, it was Grumleys what run houses of safety in the mountains. We had boys from all over. I'se a younger man then, and we Grumleys, we took 'em in, and fed 'em and mended 'em. The laws knew to stay far from where the Grumleys had their places in the mountains. So I seen them all, sir, that I did. Why, sir, was as close to him then as I am to you now. Johnny, such a handsome boy. Reminded me of a feller from the movies. Lord Jesus, he was a handsome boy. Beaming, you might say. Filled the room. A laugher, a fine jester. And just as polite and respectful to our Grumley womenfolk as a fine Mississippi gentleman, he was, he was indeed. Oh, it was a sad day when that boy went down."

"Johnny?"

"Johnny Dillinger. The most famous man in America. And that other smiler, the one from the Cookson Hills acrost the line in the territory? He rusticated some time out with the Grumleys too. The newspapers called him Pretty Boy, but I never heard no one call him but Charlie, and even Charles most ofttimes. Charlie was a good 'un, too. Big-handed boy. Big strong farm hands, Charlie had. Charlie was one of the best natural shots I ever seen. He could shoot the Thompson sub gun one-handed, and I mean really smart and fine-like. Would take the stock off. Shoot it one-handed, like a pistol. And Ma. Ma and her boys comes through a time or two. Knew Clyde Barrow and that Bonnie Parker gal too. They was just li'l ole kids. Scrawny as the day was long. Like kitty cats, them two, rolling on the floor. Never could figger on why the laws had to shoot them so many times. Seen the car they was driving. It was put on display up in Little Rock. Took the Grumleys to show 'em what the laws could do if they'd the chance. Them laws, they must have put a thousand bullets into that car, till it looked like a god-damned piece of cheese."

"And you got guns? Enough for this job?"

"Enough for any job, sir. Your Thompson sub guns, five of 'em. Drums. And, sir, we have something else."

"Ah," said Owney, fascinated as always by the old reprobate's unlikely language, part Elizabethan border reiver's, part hillbilly's. They sat in the office of a warehouse near the tracks, where Owney's empire received its supplies and from which point it made its distributions; Owney had declared it to be his headquarters for this operation. Grumleys in overalls with the hangdog look of mean boys about to go off to do some killing work hung around.

"What might that be, Pap?"

"Why, sir, it be what they call a Maxim gun. The Devil's Paintbrush. It's from the First Great War. The Germans used it. It's got belt after belt of bullets, and we've never used it. My father, Fletcher, got it in a deal with a Mexican feller who come to Hot Springs in 1919 for to buy some women to take back to Tijuana. Wanted white gals. Thought he'd make a fortune for his generalissimo. Well, we got this gentleman's Maxim gun, but he never got any white gals. Wouldn't sell no white gal to a Mexican."

A Maxim gun! Now that was some power.

"We'll set it up on the second floor," Pap explained. "When them boys come to call, we'll let them come in and up the stairs. Then my cousin Lem's boy Nathan will open up with the Maxim. Nathan is the hardest Grumley. He served fifteen years of a life sentence, and prison taught him savage ways. Nathan is the best Grumley killer. Onct, he shot a clown. Never figgered out why. I ast him once. He didn't say nothing. I guess he just don't like clowns. He's a Murfreesboro Grumley, and they grow Grumleys hard down there."

"I thought it was the Yell County Grumleys that were so hard."

"Yell County Grumleys *are* hard, naturally. But you take a naturally hard Grumley and you toughen him up in a bad joint, and what you got is something to make your blood curdle. That Mr. Becker would beshat his drawers if he but knew what awaited."

"It's a shame he won't be along. We hear he arrives afterward, always."

"He won't arrive afterward this time. There won't be no afterward," said Pap. "They'll only be blood on the floor and silence."

"That I believe," said Owney, looking at the dance of black madness in the old man's glittering eyes.

"Mr. Maddox," said Flem Grumley, arriving from some mission. "We just heard. My cousin Newt has it from the phone tap at Hobson and Third. They're going to hit Mary Jane's tonight."

"Mary Jane's?" said Owney, unfamiliar with the place.

"It's in Niggertown."

"It's going to be hot in Niggertown tonight," said Pap. "Oooooooooo-eeeee, it's going to be hot. We'll even boil us a cat for luck!"

It was a time of waiting. Earl thought it was like the night before when the big transports wallowed off an island, and you could hear the naval guns pounding all through the night, but in the hold, the boys were in their hammocks, all weapons checked, all blades oiled, all ammo stashed, all gear tight and ready, and they just lay there, smoking most of them, some of them writing letters. There'd always be a few boys shooting craps in the latrines, loudly, to drum away the fears, but for most of the boys it was just a time to wait quietly and pray that God would be watching over them and not assisting Mickey Rooney with his racetrack betting the next day.

In the pumping house, the slow grind of the valves almost sounded like the transport's engines, low and thrumming, and taking you ever onward to whatever lay ahead. It was late in the afternoon. These boys were dressed and ready. The guns were cleaned and loaded, the magazines all full, the surplus walkie-talkies checked out and okayed, the vests lined up and brushed clean. The men were showered and dressed and looked sharp in their suits. They sat on their cots, smoking, talking quietly. One or two read the newspaper or an odd novel.

Earl walked over to Frenchy, who stood by himself in front of a mirror, trying to get a tie tied just right. He could tell from the extravagant energy the kid was investing into the process that it was a way of concentrating on the meaningless, like oversharpening a bayonet or some such. Kids always found something to occupy their minds before, if they had to.

"Short? You okay?"

"Huh?" Short's eyes flew to him, slightly spooked.

"You okay?"

"Fine. I'm fine, Mr. Earl."

"You upset?"

"Upset?"

"About dumping them two bohunks. First time you draw live blood it can spook a fellow. Happened to me in Nicaragua in '32. Took a while to get used to it."

"Oh, that?" said Short. "Those guys? No, see, here's what I was thinking. Wouldn't it be better if I was interviewed by *Life* magazine? I hear they're coming down here. Or maybe it was the *Post*. Or even *Look*. But anyway, me and Mr. Becker. He's the legal hero, I'm the cop hero. We're a team, him and me. I think that would be so much better. See, that way the public would have someone to respect and admire. Me."

Earl gritted his teeth hard.

At 8:20 Earl stopped at a Greek's, got a hamburger and a cup of coffee and read the papers. More about Jayhawkers and who they'd kill next. When would indictments be delivered or did Becker's control over the grand jury give his raiders carte blanche to rob and kill whoever they wanted? Who were these Jayhawkers? How come they never met the press or issued statements? How come the good citizens of Hot Springs didn't know who they were or have any explanation of how they worked?

After eating, he got back in his vehicle and began a long slow turn out Malvern, past the Pythian Hotel and Mary Jane's, and then went onward for another several blocks, just in case.

At Mary Jane's he saw nothing, no commotion or anything. It was just another beer joint/whorehouse with some slots in the bar, like a hundred other Hot Springs places. There was no sense that tonight would be any different than any other night: a few girls sat listlessly in the upstairs windows, but there wasn't enough street traffic yet for them to start their yelling. The downstairs of the place didn't seem very full of men, though later on, of course, it would be different. White boys wouldn't head on down to Niggertown for a piece of chocolate until they were well drunk and had got their courage up. Black men were probably still working their jobs, cleaning out the toilets in the big hotels or running the dirty towels to the big washing machines in the bathhouses or rounding up the garbage.

But Earl got a good glimpse of the place. It was a brick building standing alone on the street, with shabby buildings nearby but not abutting it. Possibly it had once been a store of some sort, before the black people had moved into this part of town and took it over. It had a big front window, shaded, and above there were a bunch of windows that looked down on Malvern. Earl liked the bricks; he'd worry about a wooden building because heavy bullets like those from a BAR would sail clean through and do who knew what damage further down the block.

Earl made three more circuits on his grand trek, making sure he wasn't followed, making sure that nothing was out of order, that no cops had set up. So far it looked like a go.

At 9:20 he dropped a nickel into a downtown phone box and called D.A., who had a network of snitches he'd been working.

"Are we all set?" D.A. asked.

"Yes sir. The boys are ready. I haven't made radio contact with them yet, but that'll happen soon. Any news?"

"One of my snitches told me that around noon, a truck pulled up behind Mary Jane's, and a bunch of white men got out and hustled in."

"They're loading up. They've bitten."

"He said there were eight of them, in overalls. Earl, eight's a bit. They could cause some serious wreckage."

"Yes sir. I think we can still get it done. I don't want to postpone at this point. We have the jump on them."

"All right, Earl. I trust your judgment on this one. I haven't told Becker yet. He's going to be pissed."

"Yes sir. But this was a good plan and it's going to work and the boys wanted to push it. I still think it's going to be a great night for our side."

"Well, Earl, God bless us. Remember, wear your vest. I'll go to Becker at exactly 10:00 P.M. when you hit, and have him order up medical backup and the police to set up a perimeter."

"Yes sir."

Earl hung up.

He drove around a bit, wondering when the streets would fill up. But strangely they never did. A few white men seemed to mosey around the area but that density of the black throngs that was such a fervid feature of Malvern Avenue, that sense of whores and working-men and jive joints and housewives and kids, of them all in it together, riding the same ship toward the same far destiny, that was gone.

Finally, at 9:40 he pulled up a few blocks away, parked and went into a small grocery. A few old black men lounged near the cash register where the proprietor sat.

"Howdy," Earl said. "Looking for a place called Mary Jane's. Y'all know where that is? Heard a fella could have hisself a good old time there."

The men looked at one another, then over to the proprietor, the wisest among them clearly, who at last spoke.

"Suh, I'd take my business out of town tonight. There's a strange feelin' in the air. The wimmens been talkin' 'bout it all afternoon. Git your babies in, they been sayin'. There's gonna be bad-ass troubles over there at Mary Jane's tonight. Gun trouble, the worst kind of trouble there is."

Earl nodded.

"Sir, I think you're speaking the truth."

"You look like a cop, suh," said the old grocer.

"Grandpop, I am," said Earl, "and y'all have picked up on something. Make sure your children are in because it's going to be a loud one, I guarantee you."

"Y'all going to kill any Negroes?"

"Don't aim to, Grandpop. This one's between the white boys."

There was no Mary Jane and there never had been. No one could re-member why the place was called by her name. Its owner was a tall, yellow-skinned black man named Memphis Dogood. Memphis had two long razor cuts on the left side of his face, one of which began on his forehead, opened a hairless gap in his eyebrow, skipped his recessed eye and picked up again, running down his cheek. The other crossed it about an inch above the jawline. One—the long one—was delivered by a gal named Emma Mae in New Orleans in 1933. He couldn't remember how he got the other scar, or which came first.

In Mary Jane's, Memphis made the decisions. He rented the slots, ancient, tarnished machines from before the First War, a couple of old Mills Upright Perfections, a Dewey Floor Wheel or two and even one rattly old Fey Liberty Bell, from the Boss—a Grumley cousin named Willis Burr, far beneath even Pap's notice—and bought his liquor as well from the Boss. He paid 48 percent of everything to the Boss. He skimmed a little, but every time the Boss looked at him with squeezed eyes and jiggled the spit in the pouch of his mouth, mixing it with tobaccy juice for a nice hard splat, as if he were puzzling over the figures, it scared Memphis so he swore he'd never do it no more. But he always did.

Memphis ran a fair joint. The gals might act up but usually Marie-Claire, the octoroon, took care of them. She was his main gal, and she packed a wallop in her left fist. His customers were also usually all right. Some of the younger bloods might act up now and then, on booze or reefer, and he'd once had to thump a boy with a sap so hard the boy never woke up and had to be laid out by the tracks. The polices come by to ask questions, but nothing never came of it. Now and then, a white boy or usually two or four white boys, usually drunk, would show up, on the hunt for some colored pussy, because you wasn't no man till you dipped your pen in ink. They were well treated, for it was always known that if you hurt a white boy there'd be all kinds of hell to pay.

On that day, Memphis Dogood fully expected no surprises. He was vaguely aware that something of a political nature was happening in town but those things usually ran their course on the other side of the line. He had no opinions about vice or gambling or prostitution, except that he hated reformers and knew a few who'd preach all day, work up a sweat, then come on down for some relaxation with his gals, so he knew them to be hypocrites. Even a white minister once came down, and he ended up with two gals, and did each of 'em right fine, or so they claimed.

Memphis, at any rate, was sitting in the small back room behind the bar, with a pimp's .25 lying on the table, counting up money from the night before. He also had a sap and a pearl-handled switchknife out. It was the slow season. Might have to let a gal go. Why didn't the Boss cut down from 48 percent to 38 during the slow season when the ponies weren't running? But the boss never would and only a fool would mention it to him. It was a good way to turn up missing. It was said that the floor of Lake Catherine was full of Negro men who'd asked the Boss a question the Boss didn't like.

The door in the back room opened loudly and he heard the labor of men struggling with weight. He knew somehow from the way they breathed that they were white men.

Was it some batch of Holy Rollers, or maybe Klan boys, drunk and looking for a fight?

He picked up his sap and walked back there, but was met halfway by two men with suitcases. Behind he could see two more struggling with a bunch of canvas-wrapped pieces, and behind that two more. All were wearing overalls and had low mountaineer's hats pulled over their eyes. All wore gunbelts loaded up with cartridges and heavy revolvers, man-killing revolvers. They had nearly fleshless faces and gristly semibeards and had a look he knew and feared: of tough, mean, violent crackers, the sort who thought no Negro was human and made up lynch mobs or whatever, and who fought all them terrible battles against the Union in the great war and were still proud that they had stood for slavery and that the bastard Lincoln hadn't made it out of 1865 alive.

He knew them immediately to be Grumleys, but of a more violent breed than the Grumleys who controlled the Negro section of town.

"Say there," he said, swallowing, "just what is it y'all boys think it is that you're doing?"

"Tell you what, nigger," said the first, "you just go on about your business and don't pay us no nevermind, and you'll do just fine. You hear me, nigger?"

"Yas suh," said Memphis, who, though he acknowledged the might of the white man as a natural condition of the universe beyond the reach of change, did not like being treated so arrogantly in his own place, particularly when he paid the Boss 48 percent every Tuesday, regular as rain.

"See, I don't explain nothing to no nigger. You got that, boy? We are here because we are here and that's all the goddamned hell you got to know. You got that?"

"Yes suh."

"We be upstairs. But I don't want you going nowheres, you know what I am telling you? I and my cousins, we are here until we are done, and I don't want nobody knowing we are here and I don't want no nigger making any business about it, do you understand?"

"I do, suh."

A stronger voice bellowed, "Jape, you stop jawing with that nigger and help us get this goddamned thang upstairs. Have the boy hep too."

"You pitch a hand, now, nigger," said Jape, ordering Memphis to assist with the labor. He went quickly over, as directed, and found himself given a large wooden crate, with rope handles. He lifted it—ugh, sixty, seventy pounds, extremely heavy for its size!—feeling the subtle shift of something dense but also loose in some way, like a liquid, only heavier. He could read a bit, and he saw something stamped on it, first of all a black eagle, its wings outstretched, its head crowned and then words that he didn't understand: *MG/08*, it said, and next to that, in a strange, foreign-looking kind of print, *7.92 X 57 MM MASCHINEKARA-BINER INFANTERIE PATRONEN.*

At 9:45 Earl made a last drive down Malvern for a look-see at Mary Jane's. Again, it was surprisingly empty. A single white man sat at a table to the right, in overalls, with a low-slung hat down over his eyes and a half-full whiskey bottle on the table before him. His fiery glare seemed to drive most people away.

Above, a few gals hung out the sporting house's windows, but they were listless, almost pallid. Earl recognized fear of the paralyzing variety; he'd seen enough of it.

He pulled around the block for a look down the alley. It was deserted. He turned off his headlamps and drove slowly down the alley, pulling up about a hundred feet short of the rear entrance to Mary Jane's, and with binoculars studied the rear of the building.

It was a brick rear with a door that would have to be blown, but no windows overlooked it, so there was no worry of enfilade fire. There was no sign of life along the cobblestones of the alleyway, which shone not from rain but from the liquidation of the moisture in the air against the still warmish bricks. As the night cooled, the slickness would disappear.

Earl picked up his walkie-talkie, snapped it on, and pressed the send button.

"Cars one, two and three, are you there for commo check?"

There was some crackly gibberish, but then cutting through the squawks came the reply.

"Earl, this is car one, we are set."

"Earl, same for car two."

"Earl, I ditto for car three."

"Car one, there's a white boy sitting at a table to the immediate right of the entranceway in the bar. Do you read?"

"Roger."

"'Less I miss my guess, there's your first Grumley boy. So when the initial entry team goes up the way to the door, I want you to leave one man behind at the car with a Thompson and I want that boy zeroed. If he rises from the table with a weapon, he has to go down. Got that?"

"Roger on that, Earl."

"Be careful. Short burst. You ought to be able to bust him with three. Don't let the gun get away from you."

"It won't happen."

"You other two units, you are set. This whole damned thing turns on how fast you git through that back door."

"Yes sir. We are ready."

"Okay, you fellas, you do yourselves proud now, y'hear?"

"Yes sir."

Earl felt like a cigarette. He glanced at his watch. It was 9:57. He flicked a Lucky out, lit it up, took a deep breath and felt good about the thing. What could be done had been done. It was clear there would be some surprises for the Grumley boys.

He slipped out the door of his car, letting it stay ajar, and headed back to the trunk. He popped it. Inside lay his vest and a 1918 A1 Browning Automatic Rifle.

Fuck the vest. He was way down here where there was no shooting. He didn't need the vest.

He took the Browning, slid a twenty-round mag into the well, snapped it in and threw the bolt to seat a round. Then he pulled out a bandolier with ten more magazines for the gun and withdrew four magazines, which he put in his suit coat pockets, two in each for balance. He threw the bandolier back inside and closed the trunk gently.

But he could not help thinking: What is wrong? What have I forgotten? Am I in the right place? How soon will medical aid arrive? Will this work?

But then it settled down to one thing: What is wrong?

The call came from upstairs. It was Nathan Grumley, behind the big German gun, which was mounted on its sled mount just at the head of the stairs, with its belts of ammo all flowing into it.

"Jape, you see anything?"

"Not a goddamned thing 'cept these here fat niggers," Jape called back. He sat alone at a table in the bar. Around him, the slots were unused. The place was practically empty but three boys had bumbled in and he had directed that they stand nonchalantly at the bar. If they didn't want to, he suggested they have a talk with his uncle, at which point he pulled back his jacket which lay crumpled on the chair next to him and revealed the muzzle of his tommy gun. All complied, though one wet up his pants when he saw the gun.

By a clock on the wall Jape could see that it was virtually 10:00. He took another sip on the bourbon, warmed by its strength, finding courage in it. He was a little nervous. The cut-face nigger was behind the bar, looking spooked as shit. Good thing he'd gone behind the bar

and cleaned out the baseball bat, the sawed-off Greener and the old
Civil War saber like his grandpap might well have carried.

Then, precisely at ten, a car pulled up, its lights off. Jape reached
over and slid the Thompson out from under the coat, shucking the
coat to the floor. The gun came over until he held it just under the
table, ever so slightly scuttling his chair back. He could see some
confusion out by the car, but it was dark and he wasn't sure what
to do.

"You niggers stay where you is!" he commanded. "Nathan, I think
they're here, goddammit."

The sound of the big bolt on the German gun being cranked was
Nathan's response.

"We gonna jambalaya some boys!" Jape crooned to the terrified
black men.

"I don't want to die," came a gal's voice from upstairs, high-pitched
and warbly. "Please, sirs, don't you be hurtin' me."

"Shut up, 'ho," came the response.

The raid team broke from the car and headed toward Mary Jane's.

Jape's fingers flew toward the safety of the gun, and pushed it off. By
Jesus, he was ready.

Everything was lovely. Two State Police were bodyguards and there
were a lot of guns in the room, carried by veterans who'd waded ashore
at Anzio and Normandy and suchlike, so at last Fred Becker felt safe
and among friends. He was able to put aside that gnawing tension that
was his closest companion through all this mess.

He was meeting with his group of reformers, all men like himself, at
Coy's Steakhouse, on a hill just beneath Hot Springs Mountain on the
east side of the city. Three national correspondents and a photogra-
pher from *Life* were in the room too.

But the circumstances were only nominally political. The young
men were here to celebrate Fred's success and what it would mean for
them all, as they foresaw their own co-option of the levers of power in
the Democratic party in the next election, and their eventual takeover
of the city on a thrust of righteous indignation. For Fred and his

raiders had given the town hope and loosened the grip of the old power brokers. One could feel it in the air, the sudden burgeoning spring of optimism, the sense that if people only stood up things didn't have to stay as they always did, locked in the hard old patterns of corruption and vice and violence.

All the wives were there. It was a grand evening. It was as if the war had been won, or at least the light at the end of the tunnel glimpsed. Toasts were made, glasses raised, people almost broke into song. It was one of those rare nights of pure bliss.

Then a shadow fell across the table. He looked up to see the long, sad face of D. A. Parker.

"Mr. Becker?"

"Yes?"

"I think you'd best come with me. The boys are working tonight and you're going to be needed down there."

"What? You said—"

"You remember I asked you to make that call yesterday concerning a place on Malvern Avenue. We used that to set up an opportunity that looked very promising," said D.A., hoping to cut off the tirade that accompanied Becker's instruction in any raid plans that masked the prosecuting attorney's deep ambivalence about the use of force and his own physical fear, which was immense.

Fred rose.

"Folks," he said, "honey," acknowledging his wife, "I've got to run. There's work to be done and—"

At that moment came the sound of gunfire. Machine-gun fire. It rattled through the night, a liquefied rip familiar to each man who'd served in a war zone. It could be no other sound. If you've heard it once you know it forever.

Fred's face went bloodless.

"Sounds like the boys are doing fine," said D.A.

CHAPTER

23
What is wrong?

He didn't know. But some weird vibration of distress hummed in his ear. Something somehow was wrong.

Two cars, lights dimmed, pulled down the alley, passing him, coming to rest at the rear of Mary Jane's. Silently, the doors sprang open, and eight members of the rear-entry team got out, cumbersome in their vests with their awkward weapons. Without noise they assembled into a stick as Slim led them to the door, a shotgun out before him and aimed at the knob. Except for a scuffle of feet and the breathing of the men, muted but still insistent, it was quiet.

What is wrong?

Then he knew.

They would know we'd also come in the rear because that's our signature. We go in multiple entrances simultaneously. We swarm in: that's D.A.'s best trick. Therefore, knowing that, they will have to ambush us from the rear.

But how?

There's no room to fire from the building at men this close and there's no sign of men moving in on them. The alley had been entirely deserted this whole time: only Japanese Marines could hide so silently.

Then Earl knew where they'd be.

They'd be down the block. He recalled a truck parked there, on a cross street, a good two hundred feet ahead, and he instantly diverted his gaze down the alley, trying to see through the dark.

Suddenly from the front, the sound of guns firing angrily, long bursts chewing the night apart, bullets blowing into wood and glass.

Then Earl saw movement in the dark. He couldn't make it out clearly: just a sense of movement as one darker shade of blackness moved twenty-five feet and planted itself directly across the alley exit to a cross street half a block down.

He waited, forcing his concentration against the subtly differing shades of blackness.

He thought he saw something squirm and believed it to be a tarpaulin being pulled back to reveal men hunched over the lip of the truck bed, as if settling in to aim.

Earl fired: the BAR chopped through its first magazine in less than two seconds, and far off he saw over the jarring sights the flashes and puffs as his bullets jacked into something metallic, possibly a truck, lifting dust and sparks from it. He slapped a new magazine in fast, and fired another long burst into it, holding the rounds into it, watching them strike and skip off. A shot, then a second, came from the truck bed, and then somehow a gas tank went, lighting up the night in a roiling orange spume and in its concussive force lifting the truck ever so slightly and setting it down. A man in flames with a Thompson gun ran from it, dropped the gun and fell to the alleyway.

Earl looked back to Mary Jane's to see the last of the rear-entry team race into the place.

The car pulled up out front.

They were so tense their breaths came in dry spurts, like rasps scraping over a washbucket.

"Okay," said Stretch, just barely in command, "you know the drill. Let's go. Peanut, you're on the big gun."

"Gotcha," said Peanut, sliding down behind the fender of the car, raising his Thompson as he fingered off the safety, and checked with the same finger to make certain the fire selector was ratcheted toward full auto. His front sight bobbed and weaved but then stabilized and came to rest on the man slouching at the table in the barroom.

The three remaining men, their loads in their hands, charged up the walk to the storefront. It wasn't far, maybe twenty-five feet. They kicked open the door and screamed "*Raid! Raid! Get your hands up!*"

Jape saw the door open, goddamn! and was so excited he thought he'd piss up his pants. He kicked the table away to brace the Thompson against his hip, feeling his hand curve over the huge hundred-round drum to grab the foregrip and hold it tight.

"*Raid! Raid!*" came the shouts, and as he raised the weapon he had the consciousness of glass or something breaking and it was as if he were being mauled by a lion who leaped at him from nowhere, and from that sensation there came the sensation of drowning, sinking, falling, all of it toward fatigue and ultimately sleep in darkness.

The three at the door were not aware that behind them Peanut had fired, bringing down the barroom gunman with one perfectly placed burst. They were themselves unarmed, except for handguns still holstered. What they carried, two apiece, were buckets half filled with screws, stones, pieces of broken glass and scrap wood, and quickly, each lobbed his burden, one then the other, into the bar to the stairway, where the buckets hit, and emptied their contents in a rattle of things scraping and clanking and falling and crashing. It was no substitute for the sound of human feet in a normal world, but in the superheated one of house combat—gunshots now came from behind too, for some odd reason—it was enough to confuse the gunner upstairs, who now fired.

Nathan, the prison-hardened Murfreesboro Grumley behind the weapon, simply kept the butterfly trigger depressed. The gun, mounted on a securely heavy sled tripod, fired for about two minutes, and it poured down such a hail of 8-mm fire that the floor which absorbed it shattered, while broken flooring nails flipped through the air, amid the clouds of other debris that flew. The gun was so terrifying that D.A.'s plan simply fell apart.

The front-entry team retreated hastily to its car and took up cowering positions. The rear-entry team, all eight men including Frenchy and Carlo, collected in a choke point just out of the beaten zone, unable to think, talk, signal or otherwise function intelligently in the rawness and the hugeness of the sound. Courage was beyond the question; it was meaningless in the face of such a volume of fire, and the men looked at each other bug-eyed and confused. They needed a leader and he didn't get there for another thirty seconds, though without his vest and with a BAR.

"*Get back!*" Earl screamed, for he knew that the gunner would soon see he was firing at nothing and would swing fire.

They scuttled backward, and in the next second, the gunner de-ratcheted his gun from the sled tripod, swung it radically to the right and sent another eight hundred rounds through the wall into the hallway where until that second the men had been.

The gunfire atomized the thin plaster and wood wall that separated the stairwell from the hallway. Dust and chips flew; the air filled with poisonous brew.

Earl waited now until he heard a clink.

That meant a belt had run out and he heard crankings and clankings as Nathan attempted to speed-change to a new belt. But instead of racing out, Earl merely scrunched along the now blasted hallway, raised his BAR along the same axis the bullets had just traveled, and fired an entire magazine upward through the shattered wall of Mary Jane's.

He rammed another magazine in, fired it in a flash. Then he slithered around the stairwell and looked upward. He could see nothing in the floating smoke and plaster and wood powder.

An odd noise came to his ears. He tried to identify it but his ears rang so from all the firing that it took a second or two. Then he had it: it was a steady drip . . . drip . . . drip.

Earl looked and saw—blood. It coagulated on the top of the stairway, paused, then dripped down, drop by drop by heavy drop, until a tide overtook the individual drops and began to drain off the top of the stairs in a jagged track.

"Hey, up there," he called. "This don't have to go on. Ain't no lawmen hurt yet nor no citizens. Y'all throw your guns down and come on out."

He thought he heard the scurrying of men, a hushed argument.

As he crouched there, the blood rolled down the steps with more force, and to his left and right raiders came to flank him, setting up good shooting positions.

The silence wore on, but then they heard what sounded like shuffling.

"Get ready," whispered Earl.

They could track the shuffling down the hallway until at last a figure emerged. It was a Negro girl, about twenty, in a slip and a pair of high-heeled shoes. Her face was swollen, her eyes red and huge. She clutched herself with her arms. Her lips trembled. She seemed shaky on her heels.

"You be careful, missy," Earl said. "You come on down and you'll be all right. We don't mean to hurt you or your friends none."

"Sir, I—"

The bullets hit her in the back, blowing her sideways against the wall; she jackknifed, her eyes rolling up, then fell forward off the top stair. She rolled down the stairway, arms and legs flung this way and that, her head bobbing loosely. Earl grabbed her, and held her close, getting her blood all over him. He felt her struggle to rise, watched her eyelashes flutter as if to make a last claim on life, and then she died in his arms. He was holding her hand so tightly he thought he'd break her fingers.

"Hey, you lawmen," came a low Grumley voice. "You come on up and git more of that. We got lots of it up here fer you too. And we got four more nigger gals up here and they ain't gittin' out alive, 'less you go and get our truck."

"Your truck is blown all to shit," Earl called back. "I lit it up my own self and whoever was aboard is burnt crispy. You hurt any more of them gals and I will personally see that you leave here in a pine box. You come out or you'll toast in hell tomorrow morning, that I swear."

He turned to the closest man to him, who happened to be Frenchy.

"You know where my car is?"

"Yes sir," said Frenchy.

Earl took Frenchy's Thompson and spare magazines, unscrewing the stock bolt as he spoke.

"You head on back there and open the trunk and git me some more of them BAR magazines. I'm clean out. You bring 'em to me, 'cause I may need 'em."

"Can I have my gun?" said Frenchy nervously.

"Go on, git the goddamn magazines!" said Earl, pushing him rudely back down the hallway.

He had the bolt out and tossed the stock away. He turned to Stretch.

"I'm going to head up for a lookie see. Y'all stay here."

"Earl, you ain't got no goddamn vest."

"I can't move with the goddamn vest. You hold here but you wait on my signal. You got that?"

"Earl, we ought to wait till—"

"You do what I tell you!" Earl said, his dark, mad eyes boring into the boy, who turned away under the assault.

Bitterly, Frenchy ran by other crouching raiders out into the alley. Twice he was stopped by men who wanted to know what was going on, but he ran onward.

He got to the alley and saw that each end was now blocked by police cars, whose red lights flashed into the night. A light came on him and he pulled his vest aside to show the badge on his chest, and ran ahead, getting to Earl's car.

He opened the trunk, and found a boxful of BAR mags, all loaded.

Suddenly two policemen and some kind of plainclothes detective were there by him.

"What the hell is going on, bud?" asked the detective.

"We may need backup. They have four Negro girls held hostage up-stairs. We killed a batch but there's more."

"Hell, we ain't going in there. Sounds like a goddamned war."

"You go to Becker!" Frenchy said hotly. "He'll tell you to come up and support us."

"I ain't getting no men shot up over nigger whores, bud. You god-damned Jayhawkers started this one, you finish her up. I don't work for no Fred Becker."

"Where is Becker?"

"He's up front posing for photographers and I got a feeling he's pretty goddamned upset over this goddamned battle thing y'all got go-ing in Mary Jane's."

"Yeah, well, fuck you and the mule you rode in on, Zeke," said Frenchy, and then turned and ran with the mags.

He was halfway there when he heard the sound of tommy guns.

. . .

Earl slithered ever so slowly up the staircase, climbing over the debris of screws and what-not. When he reached the halfway point he could see over the edge into the hallway. Spread out and gazing resolutely at the heaven he'd never enter lay a mean-looking old Grumley boy, his eyes black and blank as diamonds. He lay in his own blood and a litter of hundreds of shells. Another boy lay a few feet away, his hands clenched around his belly, which blossomed blood.

Earl pointed the Thompson at him.

"You best show me your hands or I will finish you right here," he said.

"I am so gutshot I am going nowheres, so you go ahead and finish me, you law town bastard," said the man, who turned out to be but a boy of twenty, though his face was clenched in pure adult hatred.

"Lay there then and bleed," said Earl. "It don't make no matter to me."

He slipped up another step, saw that the feed lid on the big German machine gun was still up, meaning it could no longer be fired. He slipped a bit farther forward, grabbed the snakelike curl of ammo belt that lay beneath the gun, and gave it a yank. He held it, then yelled, "Watch out, coming down," and flicked it downward. He signaled with his fingers: three, then he pointed to his handgun.

Obediently, three raiders—Slim, as senior man, Terry and Carlo, who were next in the stick—yielded their Thompsons to others and slid up the steps until they were just below him.

"They must be down at the other end in one of them rooms, but they got them gals. If you have to shoot you use your pistols and you aim carefully, you got that? You shoot at Grumleys, not at motion. They may push the gals out first. Shoot their legs, their pelvises and wait for the girls to break free. Then you go for chest or head. Got that?"

"Earl, they got machine guns!"

"Y'all do what I tell you or I'll get three more birds and you can go wait in the cars."

"Yes sir."

"I'm going acrost the hall. You cover me, you got that?"

"Yes sir."

"You make sure you got your goddamn vests on."

"Yes sir."

"Okay. On the count of three. Ready. Three!"

Earl jumped across the hall, almost slipped in Grumley fluid and empty shell casings, but made it. Just as he ducked into a room, a man at the end of the hall stuck his head out with a tommy gun and blasted a lengthy burst at him, but immediately the three raiders returned fire, driving him back.

"I think I got him," said one.

"I don't know," said another.

Earl, meanwhile, looked around the room. Squashed into the corner and holding on dearly to each other, two more Negro gals cried softly.

"Y'all be quiet now," said Earl. "We're going to get you out, okay?"

One of them nodded.

Earl peeked around the corner and saw nothing. He nodded over to Slim and held out two fingers, cranked his thumb back to indicate he was sending the women over.

Slim nodded.

"Okay," he said, "y'all get over here and get ready to run. I'm going to fire a little bit. They won't be shooting. You just jump over to the stairs and go on down and somebody will take care of you. Don't you pay no mind to the shooting I'm going to do. You got that?"

Both nodded.

Earl stepped out into the hall, and fired half a magazine into the ceiling at the rear of the corridor, watching the bullets tear into the plaster. The two girls dipped across, where they were grabbed by Carlo, who ushered them downstairs.

Frenchy returned to the hallway adjacent to the stairwell, breathing hard. He could see that the action had moved upstairs. He bent over and retrieved Earl's BAR, took one of the magazines, and implanted it. Then he cranked the bolt back.

The thing was heavy, and as he had his pockets jammed with other loaded magazines, he felt quite a burden as he rose. He walked around to where other raiders crouched at the foot of the stairs. He could see three others up there.

"I got Earl's gun reloaded," he said.

"Well, he seems kind of busy just now," said Eff.

"Well, hell, he sent me to get ammo for that gun and so he must need it."

Eff and the others just looked at him.

"Look out," he commanded. "I'm taking it up to him."

Frenchy pushed his way by them and began to edge his way up the steps.

Earl watched the room at the end of the hallway. He heard a motion, like a squirming or shifting, and the next thing he knew a man laid out with a shotgun and fired. He felt the sting of pellet, but fired too, finishing off the magazine. The bullets whacked chunks of plaster off the wall and the Grumley boy slumped and fell amid a white cascade of shattered masonry.

Frenchy started when the gunfire suddenly erupted. At that moment also his foot found a puddle of Grumley blood that had coagulated on the fourth step. Before he knew what was happening, he slid downward, struggled for purchase and fell hard. He clenched as he fell and was aware that he squeezed off a five- or six-shot burst of automatic rifle fire. Men ducked and fell to avoid the shots, and the gun pivoted in his descent, still pumping, and sent a load of bullets through the window, blowing it out in the process.

But then he was down, hard, his ass suddenly hot with pain from the fall.

"Jesus Christ, Short! What the hell are you doing?"

"I fell, goddammit. Is anybody hurt?"

"You are a lucky son of a bitch," someone said. "You didn't clip nobody down here but you're going to have to pay for a new window."

"Fuck it," said Frenchy. He pushed the mag release button so that the half-empty mag fell out, and replaced it with one from his coat pocket. Then he picked himself up, climbed the rest of the way, and bullied his way between the raiders at the top.

"Earl," he shouted, "I have the BAR."

Earl looked at him, shook his head. But then he nodded, and gestured for the boy to come across.

He stepped into the hallway, and fired, issuing suppressing fire that again chewed into the masonry far at the end of the hall.

When Frenchy made it safely across, he pulled him back and took the BAR. Frenchy reached for the Thompson, but Earl threw it across the room onto the bed.

"You leave it be. Stick near me, and when I drop a magazine, you hand me a new one. You got that?"

"Yes sir," said Frenchy.

But Earl was already leaning out the hallway.

"Slim," he said, "y'all be ready over there. I'm going to work my way down the hall. You weave behind me, clear the rooms. I think they's empty. When I get into the room next to the one they're in, I'm going to shoot through the walls. This .30 caliber should kick right through. I'll shoot high but I'll scare the shit out of 'em. They'll a-come running out, and you boys be ready, you got that?"

"Yes sir," said Slim.

"You ready, kid?" he asked Frenchy.

Frenchy gulped.

Earl stepped out, the BAR locked in the assault position, its butt clamped under his arm, its long muzzle pointing down the hall. Like his caddie Frenchy cowered behind, two mags in one hand, one in the other, others stuffed into his suit coat. It seemed almost comic—the man with the vest cowering behind the man without one—but nobody laughed.

As second in the stick, Carlo let Slim dash forward into the first room, duck in and shout "Clear!"

It was his turn. As Earl moved forward, hunched and urgent, and passed the next doorway, he jumped toward it. Ooof! He stumbled, caught himself, and looked down to discover a Grumley toppled over in a pool of his own blood, his fingers latticed around a belly wound that still pulsated. But Carlo could tell in a second he was dead, and flew on.

He kicked open the door, scanned quickly over the sights of the .45 which he had locked before him at the end of his two tightened arms. He pivoted, finding the room empty, checked behind the door, then dashed to a closet, finding only frilly women's clothes.

"Clear!" he yelled.

"Clear!" came another call, as a third raider worked a room behind Earl's staunch advance.

Finally, there was only the one room left, the last room on the right. A dead Grumley lay on this floor too, though Carlo wasn't sure when he'd been hit. He couldn't remember many details of the past three or four minutes.

He crouched in a doorway, on his left knee, his pistol fixed on the last entryway, his wrists braced against the wall. Slim was above him in the same position, only standing, and down the hallway, two or three other raiders had taken up positions in doorways.

Earl yelled to the surviving Grumleys.

"We got y'all covered. You come on out and you won't get hurt."

"Fuck you, lawman," yelled a Grumley from inside. "You come in this room, we're gonna start blasting these here nigger gals and we'll all go to hell for breakfast."

"Don't hurt them gals. They ain't done nothing to you."

"No man tells a Grumley what to do, you bastard. Who the hell you think you are! This is *our* town, it ain't yours. You get out of here or by God there'll be blood in rivers spilt. No Grumley goes down easy, you hear me?"

But Earl wasn't listening. Instead he'd slipped into the room next door, oriented his automatic rifle to the common wall with the room where the last Grumley boys crouched with their hostages. He stitched a burst across the wall, about seven feet high. The old wood and plaster board vaporized under the buzzsaw of .30 caliber bullets. The magazine was done in two seconds. Dust floated heavily in the air.

"Another," he yelled, and Frenchy placed the mag in his hand. He jammed it in and fired it off in another single roaring blast.

Dust blew and floated everywhere, like fog.

Screams came from inside the room.

Suddenly the door blew open and a Negro gal sprawled out, thrown out by two Grumleys to draw fire. But she didn't, for the raiders stayed unexcited and reasonable, and in fact after falling to her knees, she got up and ran down the hallway, screaming "Don't shoot me, oh please, sirs, don't shoot me."

Earl fired another magazine, and it was enough.

They all broke from the room, Grumleys in rage and fleeing prostitutes in panic, figures in the foggy dust only readable by body postures.

In the fog, only gun flashes leapt out. Carlo fired at what had to be a man and brought him down as two or three of the gals ran clear. Above him, Slim found a target and fired, and his man fell backward, his finger jacking the trigger of a Thompson, which whittled a nasty gash in the ceiling. Two more black girls fled by, and a last Grumley came out of the room with a shotgun and three raiders shot him simultaneously and he fell down atop still a third.

Dust heaved. From somewhere women howled. Gunsmoke filled the air.

Earl clicked in a new magazine and slid to the side of the last door, then stepped in.

A last Grumley huddled in the corner, behind the large yellow mass of a woman in a dressing gown who screamed and blubbered but could not escape his iron grip. He had a big revolver jammed into her throat.

"I'll kill this sow!" he screamed. "Throw down your guns or by God I'll kill this—"

But as he spoke, Earl flicked the BAR selector switch to semi-auto, brought the rifle to his shoulder like a marksman and shot him where what little of his head could be seen, just above the left ear, not a killing shot, but the rifle bullet had such velocity it spun him around to the wall. The big woman pulled away and fell to the floor and began to crawl, and before the Grumley could get his gun back into play, Slim and Carlo hammered him several times.

It was finally quiet at Mary Jane's.

"Jesus Christ," said Slim.

"Man," said Carlo. "I never saw nothing like that."

"Everybody okay?" asked Earl.

"Mr. Earl, you're bleeding."

"I picked up some pellet somewhere in there. It ain't a goddamn thing. The boys all right? Frenchy, you okay?"

"Yes sir," Frenchy said heavily.

They quickly checked to discover no casualties.

They moved back into the hallway and looked at what they had wrought. Dead Grumleys lay along the hallway, which itself was a corridor of ruin, as so many shots had torn through wood and plasterboard, and the air remained heavy with gunsmoke and floating dust and grit. Empty cartridges in the hundreds littered the floor. The blood had pooled here and there.

"There, boys," Earl said, "y'all take a good look. That is the world you have entered. Now I want you to form a detail and pick up all the weapons. If them Hot Springs detectives get ahold of the Thompsons, they'll just go back to the bad boys and we'll have to take 'em all over again. If that goddamn machine gun is too heavy to carry, Slim, you find someone who knows about such things and strip the toggle bolt. If nothing else, I want that bolt sunk deep in Lake Catherine, so we don't have to worry about it no more. If you can't find no one, you come to me."

"What if the cops—"

"The cops ain't gonna stand agin you tonight. Nobody's going to stand agin you tonight."

As the men spread out to retrieve the fallen guns, another raider came down the hall to Earl.

"Mr. Parker's downstairs, Earl. He wants to see you."

"Yeah, yeah," said Earl. "I'll get there in a moment. I don't hear no ambulances. It's clear now. Tell 'em to get some ambulances in here in case any of these gals are shot up. I think we saved most of 'em."

They could hear a woman wailing loudly downstairs.

"Mr. Earl, you should know: there's a problem."

"What would that be, son?"

"Some women got shot."

"We lost one, by my count. Them Grumley boys shot her."

"No sir. Not here. Down the block at the Pythian Hotel. Two Negro gals sitting in the parlor. Somehow a burst came through the window and kilt 'em both. The Negro peoples are down there all het up, and the cops may have a riot. Mr. Becker is goddamned upset and there's all these reporters here."

24

The facts were tragic. Mrs. Alva Thomas, forty-seven, of New Albany, Georgia, and Miss Lavern Sevier Carmichael, twenty-three, of New Iberia, Louisiana, had been sitting in the lobby of the Pythian Hotel and Baths when the gunfire down the street had erupted. While most sensible people got down on their stomachs at the sound, the two ladies, in deep religious concentration, declined to do so. God's attention was elsewhere. Each was hit but once. The .30-caliber-model-of-1906 bullets had flown a long way and not lost but a mite of their power when they struck the two women fatally.

The Reverend Tyrone Blandings, of the leading Negro church in Hot Springs, requested a meeting with Mr. Becker. There he was formally apologized to, and told the county would pay for the shipping and funeral expenses of the two bodies, but that the enforcement of the law must be absolute and sometimes in these confrontations between the sinners and the sinless, unaccountable accidents happened. It was God's will. He must have a plan.

Meanwhile, Mayor O'Donovan empaneled a group of elder Hot Springs citizens to investigate the out-of-control Jayhawkers who turned the city into a war zone. If it had been within the purview of his powers, he informed the newspapers, he would have called a grand jury and issued indictments, but unfortunately it was only the prosecuting attorney who had the legal power to convene such an assembly.

The outstanding warrants on seven of the nine Murfreesboro Grumleys were never acknowledged in the Hot Springs newspapers, though the bigger Little Rock papers made certain this evidence reached the public up front.

The dead were listed, all of them Grumleys or Grumley cousins: Nathan Grumley, forty-two; Wayne Grumley, Jr. twenty-one; Jasper "Jape" Grumley, twenty-three; Bowman Peck, twenty-seven; Alvin Grumley, twenty-eight; Jeter Dodge, thirty-two; Duane Grumley, thirty-two; Buddy "Junior" Mims, thirty-three; Dewey Grumley, thirty-seven; Felton Parr, thirty-nine; and one unidentified body, burned beyond all recognition, presumably that of R.K. Pindell, age unknown, gone missing. Of the eleven, Nathan was clearly the most violent, as he had spent twelve years in the penitentiary on a case of second-degree murder and was suspected of a variety of other crimes, including rape, child molestation and dozens of counts of armed robbery as well as being widely suspected of killing a clown. He was also a known contract killer for Jefferson Davis Grumley, known as the "Boss of Pike County," and brother to Elmer "Pap" Grumley, once known as the "Boss of Garland County," though now thought to be retired.

But each of the other Grumleys or Grumley cousins had at least one and some as many as five outstanding warrants lodged against their names, for crimes that went anywhere from breaking and entering to suspicion of murder. So those Murfreesboro Grumleys, most people acknowledged, were not innocents.

The next evening, Mr. Becker gave a speech before the Better Business Bureau of Hot Springs in the Banquet Room of the Arlington Hotel. Giving speeches was a gift of his, as he had that rare ability to project concern and empathy and at the same time heroic will. He bit his lip when he discussed his dilemma in sending his men in against so dangerous a foe as gamblers and wanted men armed with machine guns, but then in the end decided it was worth it, for the law had to be served no matter the cost. The law was what separates us from the apes, after all. And unlike some men, he felt the weight of the deaths of Negroes as heavily as he felt the deaths of white folks; he was sorry that such a thing had occurred, but he assured his listeners it was unavoidable, as part of his commitment to reform. The gambling and corruption that had marked Hot Springs for a century had to be stopped and he would stop it, no matter what it cost him. Most of the men in the room believed that he himself had led the raid, as he frequently referred to "his boys" and the risks they had taken for Hot Springs and for America. He knew the way ahead was tough but he knew it was the right way.

They gave him a standing ovation.

As for the raiders, early the next morning they were informed that Mr. Becker had decided the best thing for them to do would be to go on vacation for a bit. All their weapons were to be secured and they were to drive back to their training headquarters at the Red River Army Depot, and from there commence a week off.

But of course there were two private chats to be gotten out of the way. One took place between Earl and Frenchy and, surprisingly enough, was initiated by Frenchy, in the ramshackle room that served as Earl's operations center in the pumping building.

"I wanted to apologize," he said early. "I fucked up."

"How's that?" said Earl.

"With those two Negro women. I fired those shots. I was racing up the steps, I tripped on a shell, I'd just loaded the BAR. I felt it firing. I—"

"You was in a battle zone, why wouldn't you have had your finger on the trigger? At any time a Grumley might have jumped out at you with a gun."

"I'm still sorry. If only—"

"Don't waste no time on *if onlys*. You can run it through your head a thousand times and if this thing or that thing is different, it all turns out different. But maybe it turns out worse, not better, don't forget that possibility."

"Yes sir," said Frenchy.

"Good," said Earl.

"Thank God," said Frenchy, "that they were only Negroes."

Earl said nothing. But then he thought a second, as Frenchy returned to the bunk area, and said, "Just hold on."

"Yes sir."

"I wish you hadn't said that."

"Mr. Earl? I guess I meant, think of the *problems* we'd have if they'd have been white. That's what I meant."

"No, that ain't what you meant. I know what you meant. You meant, hey, they was only niggers."

Frenchy said nothing, but he seemed to squirm with discomfort.

Then he replied, "They were only Negroes. I would never say nigger because my parents told me it was uncouth, but still, they were only Negroes. And the truth is, some of the boys are wondering why we went to so much trouble and risked so much to save some black prostitutes."

"Okay, you listen here, Short, and you listen good. Third day on Tarawa, third day after that long walk in through the cold water, I got plugged by a Jap sniper. I like to bled out but two boys from the Ammunition Company that we used as litter bearers, they crawled out and got me. Lots of fire going on. Japs everygoddamnwhere, you hear me? They drug me in, they dumped me on their litter and they carried my bleeding ass back to the aid station. Didn't say a word. Negro boys. I'm dead but for them two, and a few hours later one of 'em hisself was drug in, and they laid him next to me, and he died. I watched him die. Damned if his blood weren't the same goddamned color as mine. Bright red, when it come out, then turning sort of blackish. So don't you tell me they're any goddamned different."

He didn't realize by the end he was screaming, but as Frenchy shrank back further and further it became clearer and clearer and he looked up to see everybody else around him staring, all the guys.

"So any other bird got a complaint?"

There was silence.

"You are good, brave boys. You are as good as any Marines. But underneath, your blood is the same color as any Negro's, so when a Negro dies it's a real hard death. Anybody have any goddamned problem with that?"

"No sir," came a comment.

"Then get your asses back to packing up. We have to move back to Texas before we can take some time off."

If Earl seemed to have a particularly brutal edge to his voice, they were all unaware of a reason. But perhaps it had to do with a previous discussion Earl had just concluded with D.A., which developed along different lines.

"Earl," D.A. said, "this smells of so many kinds of bad I don't know where to start."

"Start at the top, finish at the bottom," said Earl.

"The kid who killed them two gals? Becker wants him dumped. He wants his ass gone. He says it's the smart move. It'll quieten the Negroes, it'll show we're responsive to community pressures and that we've got hearts and consciences."

"If that boy goes, I go," said Earl intractably.

"Earl, I—"

"If that boy goes, I go. No other way."

"Earl, Becker and some of his people are beginning to think we are out of control."

"I can't fight no other way, Mr. Parker. Fighting's too goddamned tough as it is to do it while being second-guessed by folks who've never done a lick of it and don't have no stomach for it nohow."

"Earl, in truth, you made some faulty decisions."

"I know I did. But it ain't on the boys, it's on me. If mistakes were made, I made 'em. You'd best fire me, Mr. Parker, and leave them boys alone."

The old man just shook his head.

"Damn," he said, "you are a stubborn man. You don't have some kind of craziness in your head that makes you want to die, to be with your pals in the Pacific? They say that's common. Is that what's going on with you? Is that why you didn't wear the vest?"

"I didn't wear the vest because I had to move fast. The vests ain't no good when you move fast. They're heavy, they're cumbersome, they eat up your energy real fast, and they only stop shotgun and pistol. They wouldn't have stopped that big German machine gun a lick."

"But you keep jumping into the guns."

"It's the only way I know."

"You are a hard piece of work, Earl. But I keep having to say the same goddamned things. You have to wear the damned vest. That's how I want it done. You were to command from outside, not inside. This isn't the Marine Corps. You are a law officer, sworn true, and your job is to follow the instructions of your superior, which is me. Earl, I will not steer you wrong. Don't you trust me?"

"I do trust you. You are a fair and decent man. I have not a doubt about that one."

"But you don't trust Becker."

"Not a goddamned bit."

"He wanted me to fire you too, Earl. I told him if you went, I went. Now you tell me if that Short goes, you go. This don't sound like it's working."

"It's the only way I know, Mr. Parker."

"Call me D.A., goddammit, Earl. Okay, Short gets one more chance, you get one more chance."

And what he didn't say was that he had only one more chance.

"Now I want you to go home. The boys go home for a week, you go home for a week. And get those goddamned pellets plucked out of your hide, so you won't be so disagreeable, do you understand? And see your wife. The poor woman is probably very upset with you."

CHAPTER
25

They got back to the Red River Army Depot, were paid in cash the money owed them, and left early the next morning for Texarkana and from there to all points for a week of pleasure. Some went home, some, whose homes were too far, headed down to the Texas beaches, but a day away by train, some headed for that lush and Frenchy town, New Orleans.

All, that is, but two of them.

Carlo Henderson was tapped by D.A. late that morning, as most of the others had left. He was in no hurry because he was going to catch a late bus out of Texarkana for Tulsa, where he planned to visit his widowed mother. But that was not to be.

"Yes sir?"

"Henderson, Mr. Earl tells me you're doing very well. You've got a lot to be proud of."

Carlo lit up with a smile. Earl, of course, was a God to him, brave and fair but not a man given to much eloquence in his praise.

"I am just trying to do my duty," he allowed.

"That's important, isn't it?"

"Important?"

"Duty, son."

"Yes sir," said the boy. "Yes sir, it is."

"Good, I thought you'd say that," said the old FBI agent. "Now let me ask you this: what do you think of Mr. Earl?"

Carlo was taken aback. He felt his jaw flop open, big enough for flies to fill, and then he swallowed, gulped and blurted out, "He's a hero."

"That he is," agreed the old man. "That he is. You've heard these rumors that Earl won a medal, a big medal, in the Pacific? Well, they're true. Earl was a great Marine out there. Earl killed a lot of the Yamoto race. So any young man who gits to study and learn and benefit from Earl's bravery and leadership ability, he's a lucky young man indeed, wouldn't you say?"

"Yes sir," said Carlo, for he felt that way exactly.

"But you should know something, Henderson," D.A. continued. "Earl's was the very toughest of wars. Five invasions. Wounds. Lots of men lost on hell's far and barren beaches. You get my drift?"

Carlo did not.

"It takes something from a man, all that. You can't go through it and come out the same. It wears a man down and exhausts him. It blunts him. Now, son," continued the old man, "I am a mite worried about something. See if you follow me. You ever hear of this thing called combat fatigue?"

"Yes sir," said Carlo. "Section 8. Cuckoo. You can't do your job no more, even though you ain't been hit. So off you go to the nuthouse."

"Them jitters, they don't always make it so you want to go to hospital. Sometimes they make it so you just want to die and git it over with. It's part of combat fatigue. It's called a death wish. You hear me? Death wish."

The concept sounded somehow familiar to Carlo, but he wasn't sure from where. And he wondered where in hell this was going.

"See, here's what can happen," D.A. explained. "A fellow can be so tired he don't want to go on. But he's got too much guts—they call it internal structure, the doctors do, I have looked it up—to quit. So he decides to kill himself doing his duty. He takes wild chances. He be-haves with incredible bravado. But he's really just trying to git hisself killed. Strange it is, but they say it happens."

"Is that what's going on with Mr. Earl?" Carlo asked.

"I don't know, son. What do you think?"

"I don't know neither, sir. He seems all right, I guess."

"Yes, he does. But dammit, I have told him three times on raids to wear the damned vest and he will not do it. I have told him his job is to stay outside and coordinate, over the walkie-talkies. But again, he's got to be right up front where the guns are. And that last stunt. Why, he walked down that hallway in plain sight, daring them boys to shoot him. What a fool thing to do. He could have laid back and with that BAR just opened fire and finished their hash off."

"He was afraid of hurting them colored girls."

"Never heard of such a thing in all my days."

"Yes sir."

Now that he thought about it, Carlo had to admit it did seem pecu-liar.

"So anyway," said D.A., "I am mighty worried about Earl. I do not want to be a party to his self-destruction. I picked him, I offered him this job in good faith and I expected him to do it in good faith, and not try and get himself killed. Do you understand?"

"I think so, sir."

"Now, there's one other thing as well."

The boy just stared his way.

"You know I respect and appreciate Earl as much as any man on the team?"

"Yes sir."

"And you know I think he's a true American hero, of the type there ain't many like anymore. Mr. Purvis, he was one. Audie Murphy, now there's another. William O. Darby, he was another. But Earl's quite a man, that's what I think."

"I do too, sir," said the boy.

"So I ask myself a question so hard I can hardly put it in words. Which is: Why did he lie?"

"Sir?"

"Why did he lie? Earl told a lie. A flat, cold, indisputable lie and it's got me all bothered, bothered as much as his crazy need to get hisself kilt. I tried to dismiss it but I couldn't. There seemed no point to it, none at all, not even a little one."

"He lied?"

"He did."

"It don't sound like him."

"Not a bit. But he did."

"On what topic?"

"The topic was Hot Springs."

"Hot Springs?"

"I asked him dead-on. Earl, have you ever been in Hot Springs? No sir, he said. 'My Baptist daddy said Hot Springs was fire and damnation. He'd beat our hides off if ever we went to Hot Springs.' That's what he said."

"But you think he has?"

"Shoot, son, it's a pitcherful more than that! At least three times I have planned a certain way, based on my reconnoitering and my experience. And in each damn case, he has at the last second said, Now wait a minute, wouldn't it be better if . . . And each goddamn time his way was better. Better by far."

"Well, I—"

"Better because he knew the terrain or the site of the buildings. The last time was the best. He's in the alley watching the rear entry team, holding it all together on the radio. But suddenly he gets this feeling the team will be ambushed from behind. So he's looking down the alley when they move a truck with gunmen in it down toward Malvern, with an enfilade on the rear to Mary Jane's. How's he know to look there? It's dark as sin, but he knows where to look? How?"

"Ah. Well, I guess—"

"Guess nothing! I asked him straight up and he told me he was just lucky he was looking in the right direction. Bullshit! I swear to you, he goddamned *knew* there was just the slightest incline down that little street, called Guilford, toward Malvern. He *knew* a truck could roll down, no engine involved, just by releasing the emergency brake, and git into shooting position. So that's exactly where he looked and by

God when he saw them boys sliding into position he was ready. He emptied two BAR mags into that truck and up she went like the Fourth of July and three more of Pap Grumley's cousins went to hell. He *knew.*"

The old man seemed astounded, turning this bit of information over and over in his mind. It fascinated him.

"All right," he said, "here's what I want. You take this week and you turn all your detective skill loose on Earl. Earl's background. Earl's past. Who is Earl? Why's he working the way he is? What's going on in his head? What do his ex-Marine pals say? What's his folks say? What's his family doctor say? How was he in Hot Springs? When was he in Hot Springs? Why was he in Hot Springs? What's going on? And you report to me. So I can decide."

"Decide?"

"Decide whether or not to fire Earl. I will not be party to his suicide. It's more than I care to carry around on my shoulders. I will not have him using me to git hisself kilt. Do you understand?"

"I am not a psychologist, sir. I can't make that call."

"Well, dammit, I can't make it neither, not without some help. If I fire Earl, the whole goddamned shebang falls apart, that I know. And I got that bastard Becker to answer to. But if I send him ahead and he gets killed, I got my own self to answer to. Both of them are stern taskmasters."

"Yes sir."

"This is a hard job. Maybe the hardest of all. Harder than walking down that hallway in all that dust and smoke with Grumleys with tommy guns at the other end."

The boy's face knitted in confusion, but then he saw that the old man had all but made up his mind that he would fire Earl. That is, unless he could be talked out of it, on the strength of something that he, Carl Donald Henderson, could dig out. And that was what he was good at, digging, ferreting, going through files, making calls, taking notes, comparing fingerprints, alibis, accounts and stories. So in that sense he could help Earl, he and he alone, and the heaviness of the task that had just been offered him filled him with solemnity.

"I will look into it, sir."

"Good. Here's a file on what I have. It'll git you started. There's people to talk to."

"Yes sir. Where am I going, sir?"

"You'd start in his hometown. It's called Blue Eye, out in Polk County."

At the bus station, Carlo used up all his change calling his mother long distance and telling her he would not be coming in after all, he had another assignment.

Then he went to the Greyhound window, and bought a ticket for Blue Eye, on the 4:30 bus that drove up Route 71 through Fort Smith to Fayetteville, and then he bought some popcorn and a root beer and sat for the longest time, watching the slow crawl of the clock hands, reading a John P. Marquand novel that he couldn't keep track of, and trying not to think about the mysteries of Earl Swagger. The file sat unopened on his lap. He could not bring himself to look at it somehow, any more than he could bring himself to take off his Colt .45, secreted in the fast-draw holster behind his right hip. He was just too used to it.

They called the bus at 4:15 and, ever obedient and respectful of the rules, he was one of the first to board. He sat halfway back, on the right, for it was said that the ride was smoothest there.

And then he saw Frenchy Short.

Yes, it was Frenchy all right, though not in his usual blue serge suit, but dressed far more casually, in denim jeans, a khaki shirt and a straw cowboy's hat, with a carpetbag full of clothes under tow. Was it Frenchy? Yes, it was Frenchy! He almost left his seat to yell a greeting, but then he looked at Frenchy and saw that he too was in line to board a bus.

Then his bus pulled out and Frenchy was gone.

But later, that night, when he got to Blue Eye, he had to ask the driver, "You know that bus that was in the dock next to us at Texarkana?"

The driver just looked at him.

"You know that one? I didn't get a look at it, but where was it headed?"

2162

"That'd be the Little Rock bus," the driver said.

"Oh, the Little Rock bus."

"Yes sir," said the driver. "It heads straight on up 30 through Hope, on up to Little Rock."

"It just goes to Little Rock?" asked Carlo.

"Yep. Well, that's where she finishes. She stops at Hope and Malvern and all them towns. Then she veers over 270 and toward Hot Springs. That's the Hot Springs bus. Most folks take it to Hot Springs, for the track and the gambling. Hot Springs, that's a damned old hot town, you'd best believe it, son."

CHAPTER 26

The aspirin worked well enough on through De Queen but the throbbing began just beyond. He took some more but it didn't seem to help. Particularly, there was a pellet lodged between the layers of muscle on the inside of his left biceps and when it rubbed a certain way it sent a jack of pain through the whole left side of his body, once so bad he had to pull off Route 71 and let it pass. It made him thirsty for a powerful drink of bourbon.

He couldn't stop in Blue Eye because he knew too many folks and too many folks knew him. The next towns up the road offered no promise, small, dying places like Boles and Y City, mere widenings in the road, too small to have a doctor.

Finally, he came to Waldron, in Scott County, a town large enough to support such a thing. Waldron lay in a flatlands between the mountains, essentially a farm town, and it had grown prosperous on the rich loam of Scott. It was large enough to support a Negro district, a servant population to provide comfort to the wealthy white families in the area. Earl drove through it looking for a certain thing and at last found it: Dr. Julius James Peterson, OB-GYN, as the sign said. He parked around back and slunk up the back steps like a man on the run. It was near nine o'clock, but a light shone from within the frame house.

He knocked and after a bit the door opened, though a chain kept it from flying fully wide.

"Yes?" the man said, and there was fear in his voice, as there would be in the voice of any Negro man answering a nighttime knock and finding a large white male on the other side.

"Sir, I need some medical help."

"I'm a baby doctor. I deliver babies. I can't help you. You could go onto Camp Chaffee. There's a dispensary there that's always open if it's an emergency. They wouldn't turn you down. There's a small hospital for white folks in Peverville too, if you want to go that way. I can't let you in here."

"I can't go to them places. I'm by myself. This ain't no raid or night rider thing. I'm a police officer."

Earl got out his wallet and showed both the badge and the identification card, officially stamped with the seal of the great state of Arkansas.

"I can't help you, sir. You are a white person and I am a Negro. That's a chasm that can't be bridged. There are people around here who would do my family great harm if I practiced medicine on a white person. That's just the way it is."

"I guess I ain't like them others. Doc, I need help. I got some pellet riding under my skin, hurts like hell, makes me want a drink bad, and if I start drinking again, I lose everything. I have cash money, no need to make no records. Nobody seen me. I will be quietly gone when you are done. I'm asking a mighty favor, and wouldn't if I didn't have to."

"You say you are not an outlaw?"

"No sir, I am not."

"Are you armed?"

"I am. I'll lock the guns in the trunk of the car."

"Go do that. After I remove the pellet you can't stay here."

"Don't mean to."

"Then disarm and come in."

Earl did as he said he would, then slipped in the door. The doctor took him to a shabbily appointed but very clean examining room. Earl took his shirt off and sat on an examination table that had stirrups of some sort at the end. He didn't like the look of them stirrups.

"I count six in all," he said. "The one in my arm, for some reason it hurts the most."

The doctor, a mild-enough-looking black man of lighter, yellowish complexion and hair that was almost red, looked at the mesh of scars on his body.

"The war?"

"Yes sir. The Pacific."

"Then you know pain and won't go into shock. This will hurt. I don't have anesthetics here."

"Okay. It don't matter. I can get through anything if there's a promise of better on t'other side."

The doctor washed, sterilized a long, sharply pointed probe and began to dig. The first three pellets came out easily enough, though not without pain. The doctor disinfected each wound with alcohol, a flaming sensation if ever there was one, then bandaged each with a gauze patch and a strip of adhesive. The fourth and fifth were deeper and even more painful. But the last one, in the arm, was a bastard. It wouldn't come and it seemed the more the man dug, the further into the muscle it slipped. But Earl didn't move or scream; he closed his eyes, tried to disassociate himself from his hurting, and thought of other places, better times, and his teeth ground together as if they meant to crush each other to dental powder, and then he heard a clink as the last pellet was deposited in a dish.

"You're not from around here?" said the doctor. "No white man would let a black one inflict so much pain on him without the word 'nigger' being spoken at least ten times."

"Funny, never crossed my mind. I grew up in Polk County."

"No, I'd say you grew up in the South Pacific and became more than a man, you became a human being."

"Don't know about that, sir."

"I won't ask you how you got these wounds. I doubt it was a hunting accident. It's not bird season. And I heard tell of a great battle in Hot Springs, but I know you not to be a Grumley sort. So if you carry the badge of the law, I assume you're a good man. I know you're a lucky one: No. 7 birdshot doesn't play so gentle in most cases."

"Been lucky my whole life. What do I owe you?"

"Nothing. It's not a problem. You continue with the aspirin, have another doctor look at it the day after tomorrow. Possibly, he will prescribe penicillin, to fight an infection. But you must go now."

"Sir, I have a hundred dollars. I'm guessing you don't charge poor women who come to you much if anything at all. You ain't no rich doctor, I can tell. So you take this hundred, and it's for them."

"That's a lot of money."

"Hard earned too, by God, but I want you to have it."

He pressed the money on Dr. Peterson, shook his hand, dressed and slipped out the back, in the dark, as he had come.

"Well, ain't we a sight?" he said with a laugh. "You're all swoll up and I am full of holes."

"Earl," she said, "that is not funny a bit."

"No ma'am. I don't suppose it is."

Chastened, he took another sip on his Coca-Cola and then a bite of his hot dog. Under his shirt, his wounds still occasionally stung, particularly the arm, where the doc had dug so deep. They sat at a picnic table in a park in Fort Smith that overlooked the Arkansas River, a meadowy place that rolled down to the water, where the pines sprouted up. There, the black waters rushed thunderously along; there must have been a big rainstorm up north.

But there were no storms here. It was a hot, bright Sunday in August, a year after they dropped the big ones on the Japs, and people frolicked in the shadow of an old courthouse, famous in an earlier century for its public hangings. Adults pushed their babies along the walkways in elaborate strollers; young servicemen from Camp Chaffee spooned with their townie belles. Even Negroes were welcome; it was an afternoon on the Grand Jette, Fort Smith style, complete to points of light in the bright air, and in the green of the pines, and if there weren't monkeys on leashes there were spaniels on them. Everybody was eating Eskimo Pies or hot dogs and thinking about the future and no one looked to the southwest, for in that quadrant of the scene lay the vets' cemetery, newly expanded, hills of rolling white markers that gleamed in the sun so freshly planted were they. One of the state's other war heroes rested there, William O. Darby, the young Ranger major who'd fought the Germans in Italy so hard and then gotten killed by a piece of metal the size of a dime from an artillery shell late in the spring of 1945 while he stood on a hill as an observer. Earl didn't want to go anywhere near that.

"You were in that ruckus all the papers wrote up," she said.

"I was there, yes."

"And that's why you have bandages all over your body."

"I caught some pellet, that's all. It ain't no big thing. Hurt myself shaving worse most mornings."

"Earl, they say that was the most violent gunfight in the history of the state. Fourteen people died."

"Eleven of 'em was bad-boy Grumleys, as low a form as has existed, whose passing is of no note whatsoever. They didn't have to die. They could have surrendered to the law, easy as pie."

"It wasn't their nature."

"No ma'am, guess it wasn't."

He looked at her. Her face had broadened considerably, and her shoulders, legs and arms thickened up a bit. But still and all: a beautiful woman, an angel, full and fair and blond and decent, the very best of America. She licked at her Eskimo Pie, with that special grace that seemed hers alone. She was the only human being on the planet who could eat an Eskimo Pie in the full blaze of afternoon and not spill a drop of it.

Under her breasts, the child seemed eager to come into this world, so forcefully did it thrust itself out and away from its mother. She had worn a red maternity blouse to hide it, but the subterfuge was pointless: that was a lot of baby in there.

"I am so frightened, Earl, that you are going to die for nothing and I will be alone with this child," she said, the last of the ice cream pie gone.

"If it happens, you will get a nice big chunk of insurance money from the state. It'll get the two of you a fine start in a new life. Maybe you'll meet up with a fellow who's around more than I am. And that money is more than my mama got when my old man got hisself bushwhacked back in '42. She got a gold watch, a hundred dollar burial fee, and commenced to drink herself to death in a year. I know you'll do better."

He took another sip on the Coca-Cola. The river wound blackly through the trees, but between here and there, boys threw a ball or sailed planes, girls cradled dolls, moms and dads held hands.

"I am so sorry," he finally said. "I know you didn't sign on for this thing. But I am in it now, and I don't know how to get out of it."

"You could just quit and go back to the sawmill."

"You know I couldn't do that."

"No. You have no quit in you, that's for sure."

"I think I could go to Mr. Parker and see about getting a loan against the money they'll be paying me before this thing is finished. Maybe there's a credit union or something. Also, there's some veterans' rights I got coming I ain't looked into yet. That way I could move you out of that damned Quonset hut in the village and into a nice little place much closer. Say in the towns outside of Little Rock. I'd see you much more often."

"Earl, it seems so ridiculous with the farm."

He sat a long moment, looking again down and across the meadowy grass to the river. Then he said, "I wasn't trying to hide that place from you. It wasn't no secret. I just never got around to telling you about it."

"I wasn't prying. A letter came from the Polk County tax assessors bureau, which had been forwarded by the Marine Corps. It was stamped Open Immediately. I opened it. You owed back taxes on two hundred acres out in Polk, out Route 8. It was past due: $127.50, plus a three dollar penalty. I sent them a check. Then I got to thinking about it and so last week, before all this gun-battle business, I had Mary Blanton drive me out there. We spent the day on the farm."

"It's a nice place, I recollect," he said. "The old man had it up and running pretty tight at one point."

"It's a wonderful place, Earl. The house needs work, mainly paint, but there's a big garden. I counted four bedrooms. The kitchen hasn't been touched in years. It could use some work too. But Earl, there's land. There's farmland which could be leased out, there's a creek, there's a stand of timber where you could hunt and raise your children.

There's meadowland and a corral and a fine barn. Earl, honey, we could be so happy out there. And we own it. We already own it. We could move in tomorrow. I don't have to stay in a sewer pipe and take the bus to work. I could teach in Polk County. When the baby comes, he or she'd have a wonderful place to grow up."

"The week I left the Marine Corps," he said, "when I was driving up to Fort Smith for you, last December? I stopped there and spent some time."

"You don't want to go there, do you, Earl? I can tell from your voice."

"I almost burned it to the ground. That would have felt good. I'd love to see that place go up in flames. It's . . ."

He trailed off.

"It's what, Earl?"

"There's a lot of hurting in that place. It's haunted. You see a pretty little farm and I see the place where my brother died. He hung himself in 1940. I hardly knew the boy. I sure didn't do him no good. His big old brother didn't do a pie's worth of good for him. Like everybody else, I let him down. Nobody did him no good. Nobody stood up for him. In the basement of that house my old man used to beat me and so I suppose he beat Bobby Lee too."

"It wouldn't have to be like that. We'd paint it white, I'd get the garden up and running, you could lease out the fields like your daddy did, it could be a good house, a happy house. It could be a house full of children."

Earl finished his hot dog.

"I don't know. I just ain't sure I could face that place. Let me think her over."

"Earl, I know you have a melancholy in you over your childhood. But you have to think of your child's childhood. Do you want him born into a Quonset hut on a military base? Or on a big, beautiful farm on the most beautiful land in the state?"

"That is not an easy question," he said.

"No, it is not."

"I'd sell the goddamned place if I could. But land is so cheap now, and it's so far out, I'd never find a buyer. When's that goddamned postwar boom going to hit Polk County? Anyhow, I'll think some."

"You'll think *hard* on it?"

"Yes ma'am."

"All right, Earl. I know you'll work it out. I know you'll do the right thing. You always do."

For the next few days, Earl was perfect. There was never a harder-working, more cheerful man, a better husband. He repainted the inside of the Quonset hut apartment a bright yellow, a day's worth of backbreaking labor, but worth it, for the lighter color cheered the place up. He loaded the old sofa up on the roof of his government Dodge and took it to a dump, then went over to the Sears, Roebuck in Fort Smith and bought a new sofa for her, a pretty thing in green stripes. That made the rooms even brighter.

He redug the garden, weeded it, trimmed the hedges. He took her out to dinner, twice. They went for walks. He listened to the baby move and the two of them tried to think up names for it. She wrote long lists and he laughed at Adrian and Phillip, he thought Thomas and Andrew were okay, he liked Timothy and Jeffrey. The problem was, except for Adrian, each of the names had a boy somewhere attached to it, a Marine who'd died or been maimed and was carried out by stretcher bearers screaming for his mama.

But Earl tried not to let any of that show on his face. He tried so hard to be the kind of man he thought she deserved, the kind of man he thought he wasn't. He never told her about the way his father would sneak up on him and whisper something fierce and hurtful in his ear, then steal away, to leave nothing but sunlight and trees blowing in the breeze.

Finally, he drove her to the doctor's office and sat out front during the exam and then the doctor brought him in and spoke to him while she dressed. Earl had seen lots of docs, and this one was no different from any in an aid station, a field hospital or a hospital ship: a grave official type man, with a blur of mustache and eyes that were somehow lightless.

"Mr. Swagger, first of all, the baby and your wife are both doing fine. The health of both seems well within the parameters of what we'd qualify as a normal, healthy term. The baby should be right on time. I'd say first week in October."

"Yes sir, great. That's great news."

"Now I did want to say something to you. There's no cause to be alarmed just yet, but I have noted that the baby is situated a certain way in your wife's uterus. Not abnormal by any means, but at the same time not exactly where we'd expect it to be."

"Yes sir," said Earl gravely. "Does Junie know this?"

"No, she doesn't. I'd prefer her not to know. It would cause anxiety, quite possibly undue. It may not be anything to get alarmed at."

"But it means something. What does it mean, sir?"

"There can be complications. Usually of no consequence. But what happens sometimes in this case is that the child arrives in the wrong presentation. That is, instead of breeching face up, it breeches face down. Then it gets tricky. I want you prepared."

Earl nodded.

"It says in the paperwork you're a state employee. An engineer, a crew foreman?"

"No sir. I work as an investigator for a prosecuting attorney in another county."

"I see. Law enforcement. Is it demanding?"

"Sometimes."

"You were in the war, weren't you?"

"Yes sir. The Pacific."

"Well, then, you've seen some emergency medical situations I'd guess."

"A few, yes sir. I was wounded a few times."

"Good. Then you know what can happen."

"Are you telling me there's a chance my wife could die?"

"A very small one."

"Jesus," he said. "For a damned baby."

"The baby is very important to her, as it would be to any woman. That's part of being a woman, and that's part of what's so wonderful about women. And that's part of the reason I'd prefer her not to know. Sometimes we men have to make the serious decisions."

"Yes sir."

"So what I am saying is that if the complications are grave, I may have to make a choice. I may only be able to save one, the child or the mother. I am assuming the mother would be your choice."

"Ain't no two ways about it. We didn't plan this kid, I ain't settled in this job yet, the timing was all off. And I don't feel much for it. Don't know why, I just don't."

"Many men who came back from a hard war feel the same way. I've heard those words a hundred times. I think it'll change when you hold your child, but to many men who've been in combat, the idea of bringing a new child into a somewhat profane world seems pointless."

Earl thought: You just said a mouthful, Doc.

"Anyhow, here's what's most important. You must be around when the child is born. I don't know what sort of arrangement you and your wife have, with your work so far away, but you absolutely have to be here in case a decision is needed. Do you understand?"

"Sir, I've made my decision."

"Yes, but if the baby comes late at night or when I'm not on call, I might not be here. Any of a dozen things could happen. It's quite common for the delivery to be assisted by the staff resident. That would be a younger doctor, possibly not willing to make the decision that you just made. He might not have the sand to intervene and you could lose them both. So you need to be here. You may have to fight for your wife's life. You may even have to fight your wife for it."

Earl nodded.

"But I can see something on your face," the doctor said.

"Yes sir. The job I'm in, sometimes it gets very complicated and I can't get back. I just don't want to let nobody down."

"Well, Mr. Swagger, you'll just have to decide what's more important to you. You don't want someone else making that decision, do you? No, Mr. Swagger, please, please, try and be here."

"Yes sir," said Earl, feebly, knowing it might not happen that way. "I'll do my best."

CHAPTER

27

Pap Grumley danced a dance of grief and shame. It was a strange mountain dance that somehow connected with people who worshipped the Lord with poisonous snakes or through the speaking of tongues, practices which were part of Grumley life in one way or other.

He was dressed for mourning, all in black, black frock coat, black pants, his black boots, a black hat that could hold twenty gallons, pulled low over his eyes. Eleven coffins filled with Grumleys had been lowered into the ground and words were said over them. All the Grumleys and assorted clans were there, including Pecks, Dodges, Grundys and Pindells. The women and the men were grim in their mourning clothes, their taut mountain faces bleak and severe, their blue eyes gray with pain, their demeanor dignified and stoic, yet hurting massively.

A Grumley preacher said the Lord's words, about how He must have wanted Grumleys in heaven for a peculiar hard job, so He sent for a whole lot of them, to stand by His right hand and help Him spread the Word. But the words he said were not nearly as eloquent as the dance Pap danced.

The spirit moved in him. He tramped in the dust, back and forth, he shivered, he shook, he stamped. The music was unheard by men's ears but came from a part of all the Grumley soul, old mountain music, the whining of a fiddle played by a drunk who'd watched his children die one by one of the pox, and had felt the cold creeping in late at night when blankets were thin and a fiftieth or a sixtieth day of feeding on taters and nothing but had just been finished, with a fifty-first or a sixty-first in view for tomorrow. It was a dance of ancient Scotch-Irish pain and within it lay a racial memory of life on a bleak border and the piping of grief and the wailing of banshees late in the cold night, where a man had to survive on his own for the government belonged to one king or another; it was reiver's music, or plunderer's music, the scream of rural grief, of a way of thinking no city person who didn't fear the harsh Presbyterian God but who had not also run 'shine against the mandates of the Devil City in far-off eastern America, the demon city lodged between Maryland and Virginia, where godless men passed laws meant to take the people's and the Grumleys' freedom and convert it to secret wealth for the castle people, could but feel.

"That man bound to 'splode, look to me," said Memphis Dogood. "He is a hurting old boy."

"He may indeed, old fellow. These Grumley chaps take things like this quite seriously," said Owney.

Owney and Memphis sat in the back of Owney's bulletproof Cadillac, which had wound down the miles between the Medical Arts Building and this far Grumley compound in a trackless forest just north of Mountain Pine.

Had the Grumleys known a Negro man was one witness to the privacy of their ceremony it is altogether possible they would have hanged him or tarred him, for the Book is explicit in its denunciation of the sons of Ham, and they took the Book at its literal truth. That was what was so Grumley about them. But Owney wanted Memphis to behold the festival of grief that attended the burial of the eleven Grumley dead on the theory that it might get Memphis more talkative than he had heretofore been.

So the two of them watched from leather seats in the back of the V-16—Memphis had never seen such a fine car—as the Grumleys, en masse, and Pap, in particular, mourned.

Pap stamped and the dust rose. Pap twitched and the dust rose. Pap did three this way then three that and the dust rose. He danced amid a fog of dust, the dust coating his boots and trousers into a dusky gray. His face too was gray, set hard, his eyes blank or distant. He folded his arms and gripped his elbows and danced and danced the afternoon away. His back was straight, his neck was stiff, his hips never moved. God commanded his legs alone, and had no use for the rest of him, and so deadened what was left until it reached a form of statuary.

"That boy could dance all night," said Memphis.

"And into the morrow," said Owney. "Now Memphis, you are possibly wondering why I brought you out here."

"Am I in trouble, Mr. Maddox? Weren't nothin' I could do, 'splained it to the bossman. Didn't say nothin' to nobody. Them revenooer boys, they knowed you had yo' Grumleys spread all over my place. And they was loaded up for bear. Next thing old Memphis know, the Big War done broke out. Ripped up my place right good."

"I need more. I need the kind of detail a clever man can provide, a shrewd man, who's fooled by nothing in this world. That would certainly be you. A man doesn't last in the brothel profession unless he's a keen judge of character. So you would notice things others might not. Tell me, Memphis, about them. About him."

"You mean they bossman?"

"Yes."

"Suh, I don't mean you no disrespect, but if Grumleys all you got to go agin that boy, then, suh, you be in a peck o' hurt. You be in a tub o' hurt."

"Describe him, please."

"Uh, he mean serious bidness." He scanned his memory for helpful images. "Nigguhs talk about Bumpy in Harlem."

Bumpy Johnson. Owney knew Bumpy well. Bumpy used to sit with his own gunman at a back table in the Cotton Club and even the toughest white mobsters avoided him directly. Yes, he saw the comparison, for Bumpy's every motion and dark, hooded eyes said: If you mess with me, I will kill you.

"Bumpy in Harlem. Yes, I knew him."

"He had that. Whatever Bump had, this boy had it too. Nigguhs can pick that up. A nigguh hafta figger out right quick if a man mean what he say. And this here fella, he surely did. His own dyin' don't mean shit. Don't mean shit."

"We call him the cowboy," said Owney.

"My gal Trina? She say he worked it upstairs so no nigguh gals git shot. All them bullets flyin', he worried about 'hos gittin' shot. Ain't that nuthin'? Ain't no white man like that down here. Hear tell they got some like that up North, but ain't no white man like that down here."

"What do you mean, Memphis?"

"He wouldn't shoot no gals. He shot over they heads. So they don't kill no nigguh gals."

Now this was a new detail that hadn't emerged in Owney's investigations.

The cowboy had something for Negroes? What on earth does that mean?

"And my main gal, Marie-Claire? She say, that ol' Grumley holdin' a gun agin her throat, sayin' he shoot her. Now, suh, you know any white po-lices in America just laugh and say, 'Go'n and shoot that nigguh gal!' Be laughin' all about it! But this here fella, he lif' his rifle, aim careful, and hit that las' Grumley right upside the haid. So Marie-Claire twist away, and them other fellas, they hammer that las' Grumley. Ain't no white cop do that, and nobody know that better than Memphis Dogood, I'm tellin' you right, suh. I gots the scars to prove it."

"You are probably right," said Owney: he knew that in that situation in every city in America the policemen would have simply fired away, killing both the felon and his hostage and therefore accomplishing two objectives: saving themselves any danger, and providing a highly amusing few seconds.

The cowboy loves the Negro people for some reason.

Interesting.

"Well, you've been very helpful, Memphis."

"Thank you, suh," said Memphis Dogood.

"Unfortunately, I can't drive you home."

"Suh?"

"Yes. Can't be seen with you. You know, appearances, all that. Those fellows over there, they'll take care of you."

"Mr. Maddox, them's Grumley boys and—"

"Nothing to worry about, old man. You have my guarantee."

He smiled. The door was opened, and Owney's driver leaned in, put his large hand on Memphis's shoulder, and directed him outward.

Some Grumley boys, young ones, watched, then began to mosey over to Memphis.

CHAPTER

28

Among the many things his colleagues did not know about Walter F. (formerly "Shorty" and now "Frenchy") Short was the following: he was wealthy.

Not rich, not a millionaire, not a playboy, a polo player or a "movie producer," but still he had a private income that would keep him perpetually comfortable to indulge his pathologies, as derived from old family investments in Canadian timber, American pharmaceuticals and railroads and a large interest in a Philadelphia manufacturing company that made, of all things, the little brass ringlets that served as belt notches in the web gear GIs had used in defeating the Axis in the recent war.

So when Frenchy arrived in Hot Springs in overalls, a threadbare khaki shirt, a beat-up coat and a low-slung fedora, a .45 on his belt behind his right hip, his first move would have surprised everyone. It was to go to his apartment.

He kept it in the New Waverly Hotel, and slunk through the lobby, largely unnoticed. He showered, beating off the road dust of the bumpy bus ride. Then he toweled off, and took a nap until later in the evening. Arising, he went to his closet and picked out a nice Brooks Brothers whipcord suit, light for summer, a pair of Weejun loafers, a blue shirt and a red-and-black-striped regimental tie. Under a crisp panama hat, he went out and about the town, a perfectly dressed sporting man whom no one could possibly associate with the grim young posse of Jayhawkers who had so alarmingly shot the town up over the past several weeks.

At first he did what any young man would do in such circumstances. He gambled a little, he had a nice meal, a few drinks, and then he went to one of the finer establishments at the far end of Central, traveling past the Ohio, the Southern, the Arlington and so many other monuments to Hot Springs' principal obsessions, and got himself laid up one side and down another.

That accomplished, he taxied back to the New Waverly and slept for two straight days.

On the third day he made a trip to a surplus store, and made a number of surprising purchases. That afternoon and night, he pleasured and partied again. He made no phone calls, because he had no friends and his family was not particularly interested in where he was or what he was doing, not after the trouble he had caused it; they just wanted him far out of Pennsylvania, for the rest of his life.

On the fourth day, he slept late again, took a light meal in the New Waverly dining room, then repaired to his room. There he opened the paper sack he'd brought from the surplus store the day before, removed his new ensemble and put it on: a new pair of black gym shoes, a black Norwegian sweater and a pair of rugged blue denim work pants. He also had a light tool kit in a brown valise. He slipped out the back of the hotel, and negotiated his way through alleys and lanes and byways, as if he had secretly studied the town's layout on maps (he had) until at last only a fence separated him from his destination.

Someone once said, in discussing the OSS, that aristocrats make the best second-story men and Frenchy was about to prove the wisdom of this judgment. He climbed the fence and moved swiftly to the building, a four-story brick affair. A skeleton crew managed the switchboards, but that bullpen was on the first floor, just off the main entrance. The upper floors were all dark.

Frenchy found a foothold that was a brass hose outlet, and from there made a good athletic move up to a window ledge, used the strength in his wrists and forearms to haul himself up to the roofline of the first-floor rear portico, gave a mighty *oof!* and pulled himself finally to the roof of the portico. He lay there, breathing heavily, imagining himself pulling such a stunt against the German embassy in Lisbon in search of codes or secret agent identities, just like his uncle had done.

But there were no SS men with machine pistols guarding the Hot Springs Bell Telephone office in late August of 1946. They had, as a species, largely vanished from the earth. The only potential opposition for Frenchy was a night watchman who never left his post on the first floor. Why should he? Who on earth would even conceive of breaking into a phone company? What would a thief be after—nickels from the pay phones?

Frenchy was fully prepared with shims and picks to crack the building; after all, at Choate he had famously liberated a biology exam for the first-formers, and made himself a legend among the populace while going blithely unpunished. At Princeton, he had tried the same trick with a physics exam, and gotten caught and expelled (the first time), but getting caught was a function of being ratted out by a bluenose prick who didn't believe in such things.

But—hello, what's this?—instead of having to use his treasury of deviant devices, he found the second-story man's best friend, the unlocked window. In a trice, he was in.

He discovered himself in a darkened office and snapped on his flashlight. He learned instantly that this was the foyer of the personnel office, of no use to him whatsoever. He stepped carefully into the hallway, then taped the door lock so that it wouldn't lock behind him, then left another tiny mark of tape high on the door so he could remember which one it was for his escape plan, and then began to patrol.

He walked down darkened corridors, checking out door titles. BOOKKEEPING. BILL PAYMENT. DIRECTORY PREPARATION. REPAIR ASSIGNMENTS. SALES. And so on and so forth, all the little fiefdoms so necessary for the care and maintenance of a modern monopoly. At last, on the silent third floor, he discovered what he thought he needed: ENGINEERING.

He used a shim to pop the lock, slid adroitly in, and again taped the lock behind him. He sent his flashlight beam bouncing around the room. Only banality was revealed: a number of drafting boards, a number of messy desks, some cheesy, cheery Bell Telephone morale posters on the institutional green walls, the glass cubicle of a supervisor, and finally and most important a horizontal filing cabinet, that is, a wall-length chest of thin, wide drawers, each marked by geographic grid references.

Shit, he said.

Time to get to work, he thought.

Many of his former friends and his family thought that Frenchy was lazy. Exactly the opposite was true; he was capable of very hard work, relentless and focused. His oddity of mind, however, was that it never occurred to him to simply *do* what was required of him; rather he would invest three times more energy and six times more discipline in figuring out how *not* to do it. He was addicted to shortcuts, quick fixes, alternative routes, cutting corners, doing things his own way, no matter what, no matter how much the cost. "Does not follow directions," his kindergarten teacher had written and no keener insight into his personality was ever revealed. It had made for quite a colorful first twenty years on the planet—his was one of those rare, bright but naturally deviated minds. He was cunning, practical, nerveless, self-promoting, rather brave and completely self-possessed at all times, or nearly all times.

So now he applied himself with a concentration that would have astonished his many detractors, who had never been allowed a glimpse of the real Frenchy and who had nicknamed him Shorty. He began at the beginning, and studiously invested close to four hours in running over the diagrams in the drawers which he correctly assumed to be wiring diagrams.

His thinking on this problem was original and far in advance of D.A.'s or Earl's and a prime example of how well, when focused, he could work things out. He reasoned that Owney Maddox's empire was only secondarily an empire of force, violence, debt collection and municipal subversion; primarily, it was an empire of the telephone. Everybody knew this: the racing data had to pour in from the tracks of America, there to be distributed instantaneously to all the minor duchies of the empire, the dozens of nondescript books around town in the back of Greek coffee joints, drugstores, haberdasheries or what have you. The legendary but mysterious Central Book was therefore, as all agreed, the linchpin to the operation. They could only really bring Owney down by taking it out, drying up the info and therefore starving him out in a short while. Earl and D.A. especially knew this.

But Frenchy determined the next step, which is that the Central Book could only be accomplished with phone company collusion. Somewhere, somehow, someone in this building had made secret arrangements for wires to be laid into an otherwise bland building in Hot Springs, and those wires had to be routed somehow so they wouldn't pass through the switchboard that unified the town. A stranger couldn't call an operator and say, "Honey, get me Central Book!" Therefore, somewhere in this building had to be an answer.

He now industriously examined wiring diagrams. He quickly learned that a symbol, a little black diamond, indicated the presence of a phone junction, and suspected that the Central Book would have an unusual concentration of black diamonds. So his eyes searched the schematics for clusters of black diamonds. But the problem wasn't that there weren't any, but that there were too many. It seemed every page had a cluster and sometimes more than one, and often enough he recognized them from the addresses—one, for example, was the Army and Navy Hospital, which made sense, because wounded boys still lingering from the war's effects would be in constant telephone contact with family and loved ones. So what he had to do was hunt for a cluster of black diamonds that had no justification.

This sounds like boring work, and for most it would be. For Frenchy it was pure bliss. It enabled him to forget who he was, what his demons commanded him to do, his paranoia, his fears, his considerable accumulation of resentments, the perpetual nervousness his bravado only partially concealed. He worked swiftly and with great intensity and thoroughness, pausing now and then to write down the address of a diamond cluster he couldn't identify.

On and on he worked, until it was growing light in the eastern sky. He looked at his watch. It was 6:00 A.M., and soon the day shift would come along. He still had five drawers to search, and not enough time to do so.

He determined to come back the next night, and the next too, if need be. Quickly he closed the drawer he was working on, looked to see if he'd left traces of his presence, and noted nothing and stood to rise.

But then he said: what the hell.

He plucked open one of the drawers yet unexamined, and pulled at a pile of diagrams, as if in a blur or a dream. He didn't even look hard at them, but simply let them flutter through his peripheral vision. He saw that somebody had spilled some ink. They'd made a mistake. He passed onward.

But then he thought: there haven't been any other mistakes.

He rifled back, found the page, and Jesus H. Christ Mother Mary of God, there was a concentration of phone lines so intense it looked like a Rorschach ink blot. In it, he saw his future.

He noted the address, and said to himself: Of course!

CHAPTER

29

"No," said Ben, "no, that one has splatters. It didn't have splatters. No splatters."

"What did it have, darling? You have to help me, you cute little boo-boo," said the Countess.

"You two birds," said Virginia, "you actually think this shit is fun! My feet hurt. We been walking for ten years."

"Virginia, I told you not to wear them really high heels."

"But she looks gorgeous, darling," said the Countess. "She's more edible than any of these paintings, and I love the shade of her pretty pink toenails."

"Dorothy, you're the one they should call Bugsy. You're as screwy as they come."

The threesome stood in the modern wing of the Los Angeles County Museum before a bewildering display of the very latest in decadent art. The painting immediately before them looked like Hiroshima in a paint factory, an explosion of pigment flung demonically across a canvas until every square inch of it absorbed some of the fury of the blast.

"That guy has problems," observed Bugsy.

"He's a bastard. A Spanish prick who collaborated with the Nazis and beats all his women. But he's the most famous artist in the world. He gets a lot of pussy."

Ben leaned forward to read the name.

"Never heard of him," he said. "He ought to take drawing lessons."

"You never heard of him! You never heard of nothing didn't have a dame or a ten-spot attached," said Virginia, bored. Dammit! The spaghetti strap of her right shoe kept slipping off her foot and coming to nestle in the groove of her little toe. There, it rubbed that poor painted soldier raw. She kept having to bend over to readjust it. She did so one more time, and heard boyfriend Ben say to his best friend Dorothy the Countess from directly behind her, "Now *that's* art!"

"You dirty-minded Jew-boy," she said. "Ben, you are so low. You come to look at pictures and you end up doing close-ups on my ass!"

"He's just a boy," said the Countess. "Virginia, what can you expect? That's why we love him so."

"Yeah, Dorothy, but you don't have to uck-fay him no more. I still do."

The Countess laughed. Her raffish friends filled her with glee. They were certainly more amusing than the dullards she'd grown up with in Dutchess County.

"Anyhow, dear: no splatters?"

"None. Not a one. I'm telling you, it looked like Newark with a tree."

"Newark?"

"I been to that town," said Virginia. "It's New York without Broadway. It's just the Bronx forever. Wops and guns. I wouldn't go back on a bet."

"Newark meaning? What was its quality of Newarkness?"

"Square, dark, dirty, crowded, brown. I don't know why I thought of Newark."

"Oh, it's so obvious. In that little rat brain of yours, darling, New York is still glamorous and adventurous. But if you subtract the neon and the glamour, you're left with nothing but masses of grimy buildings. Voilà: Newark."

"I wish I could remember the fucking name. He told me the name. It just went right out of my head. Virginia, you remember the name? Oh, no, that's right, you were rubbing your tits against Alan Ladd."

"I don't think he noticed. He'd never get me a part in a picture. His wifey wouldn't let him."

"Our attentions are wandering again, are they not?" said Dorothy. "Let us recommit them to the object at hand."

"It may not matter, anyhow," said Bugsy. "He's smack in the middle of a fucking war down there. Eleven of his boys got blown out of their boots in some nigger cathouse thing. Everybody's talking he's going down."

"That cowboy may get him," said Virginia. "Dorothy, did our hero ever tell you how he straightened this cowboy out at the train station in Hot Springs? Guy lights my cigarette, so Benny pulls his tough-guy act on him. But the cowboy ain't buying it. So Ben gives him a poke. Only it don't land, and the cowboy hits Ben so hard it almost makes him bald. Ben cry-babied for a month and a half and I notice he ain't been back to Hot Springs. He ain't going back until somebody takes care of the cowboy."

"Virginia, he hits me harder every time you tell that story," said Ben. "It's her favorite story. She's been telling it all over town. I got New York guys calling me and asking me if I settled up with the cowboy, for Christ's sakes."

"But you haven't. See, Dorothy, he really does fear the cowboy."

"He knew how to throw a punch, I'll tell you that," said Bugsy, remembering the hammerblow to his midsection. "But I'll tell you what else. When I finally get a line on his ass, he will be—hey, hey! There it is! It was like that," he said excitedly. "Virginia, wasn't that it?"

He pointed to a dense, enigmatic work, darkish and lacquered.

Dorothy didn't have to examine the label. She knew a Braque anywhere.

30

Earl's daddy? they said. Earl's daddy was a great man.

It wasn't like it was now, they said. Back then the law meant something and the law meant Earl's daddy, Charles.

Things are wild now, but they wasn't when Earl's daddy was around. Earl's daddy kept the law. Nobody done busted the law when Earl's daddy was around.

Earl's daddy was a *great* man.

Even if Earl won a big medal killing Japs, he wasn't the man his daddy was. Now that man was a great man.

I don't know nobody who'd stand against Earl's daddy.

You know, Earl's daddy was a big hero in the Great War. He killed a mess of Germans.

It was nearly unanimous. In Blue Eye, Arkansas, the one-horse town that was the seat of Polk County, the station stop for western Arkansas on the Kansas City, Texas & Gulf run to New Orleans, and a place where the weary traveler could get a cold Coca-Cola off of Route 71, Earl's daddy still cast a big and a bold shadow. You could ask about Earl in a grocery store and in a barbershop or at the police station and what you heard about wasn't Earl at all, but Earl's daddy. He was such a great man, it was said, that his own sons were overwhelmed by him. One ran away and t'other kilt hisself at fifteen. That was a sad, sad day, but Earl's daddy kept going, because he was a man who did his duty and knowed what his duty was. Hell, in the '20s, he killed three bank robbers. And many's the big-city boy or the uppity nigger who thought he could put one over on Earl's daddy and ended up with a knot on his head the size of a pie plate, for Earl's daddy brooked no nonsense, had fast hands, the lawman's will and a leather birdshot sap that seemed never far from his right hand.

Carlo went to the cemetery. There was the big monument that read CHARLES F. SWAGGER, CAPT. AEF 1918 SHERIFF 1920, 1891–1942 and "Duty Above All" in marble bas relief on a pedestal atop which stood the sculpture of a patriotic American eagle, its wings unfurled to the sky, its talons taut and gripping. The wife was nowhere to be found, nor was the younger son.

"Now that one," said a Negro caretaker who noticed the young man, "that one, he was a stern fellow. He didn't take no guff, no sir. He put the fear of God in everydamnbody."

"He was a great man, I hear," said Carlo.

The old man laughed, showing few teeth and pink gums. "Oh, he surely was," he said, "a very *damn* great man!" He toddled off, chortling.

Carl went to the newspaper office, and looked up in the bound volumes the story of the tragic day of Charles's death. Wasn't much. Evidently old Charles had been coming back from his monthly Baptist prayer weekend at Caddo Gap, driving through Mount Ida late, and he saw the door open behind Ferrell Turner's Liquors. He parked his car and got out his flashlight and went to investigate, even if he was in Montgomery County and not Polk. He was close to Polk, just a few miles, he saw what could have been a crime and he went to investigate.

One shot was fired by a burglar and down the old hero went. Probably some damned kids with a stolen gun and some hooch, looking for more hooch before they went off to war. Simple, stupid, tragic; they found him the next day and buried him two days later. It was a shame Earl's daddy had to die so pitifully. Both his boys was gone then, his wife was a drunkard and nobody from the family showed up when that great man was put to rest, but most of the rest of the county was there, great men and small, rich men and poor, man, woman and child, for in some way Earl's daddy had affected them all.

Carlo spoke to the new sheriff, a veteran named Beaumont Piney who'd been training for North Africa when Earl's daddy had gotten killed, and to the mayor and to other politicians, deputies and municipal employees and never got much beyond the recognition of Charles's greatness. But finally, on the third day, and a pointless interview with the county attorney, he heard a voice on his way out coming from down the hall.

"Goddammit, Betty, right here, I said 'Fifteenth,' but you just typed 15-h without no damn *t!* You have to type the goddamn thing over. Can't you be more careful, goddammit!"

The woman sniveled and wept and then the screamer stopped screaming and Carlo heard, "I'm sorry, it ain't nothing, I got to watch my damn temper, please, Betty, I didn't mean nothing, it don't matter."

And the secretary said, "But Mr. Vincent, my name is Ruth, not Betty. And I've worked here three whole weeks."

"Oh," said the man. "My last secretary was named Betty."

"No sir," Ruth said, "she was named Phyllis. Don't make a difference, though. Both Betty *and* Phyllis quit."

"Now don't you quit, Ruth. I don't mean no harm. I just yell too damn much. Here, now, I have an idea. Why don't you take this afternoon off?"

"Well, sir—"

"No, no, I insist. I yelled, you got upset, you got to take a nice afternoon off."

There was some shuffling, but in a second a woman came out, her hat on, her eyes reddened and swollen, and a formidably large, sheltering bear of a man led her out as if he were taking his infirm mother to see the doctor.

The couple walked by Carlo without noticing, and as they went, Carlo finally saw the name on the door of the now empty office: SAMUEL C. VINCENT, ASSISTANT PROSECUTING ATTORNEY.

He walked in and waited in the outer office and waiting room.

In a minute or so, the large man returned, his eyes black with intensity. His hair was a thatch that had never seen a comb and grew in every direction and he wore frameless specs that blew his dark eyes up like camera lenses. He was fleshy, not soft but large and strong. His suit fit like it'd been bought off the rack by someone who knew nothing about suits and it was covered with flecks of burnt ash.

"Who the hell are you, sonny?" he demanded, fixing the young man with a glare.

"Sir, my name is C. D. Henderson. I'm an investigator with the Garland County Prosecuting Attorney's Office," he said. He got out his badge and offered it to the man, whose eyes flashed that way, then back to his face, where they lit square and angrily.

"What the hell problems they got in Garland County bring 'em over here to Polk? Your Fred Becker has enough fun gittin' his picture in the paper all the damn time, what's he need over here? He going to start raiding in Polk now? B'lieve the colored folk run some illegal bingo in their church on Saturday night. That'd be a good raid. Hell, he'd get lots of ink out of that one!"

Carlo let the squall blow past, tried to look as bland as possible.

"Sir," he said, "this isn't anything about that. Mr. Becker don't even know I'm here. I'm here at the request of my supervisor, Mr. D. A. Parker."

"Parker! The old gunfighter! Yeah, he's the kind of boy you'd want if you'd be going to bang down doors and shoot places up! You don't look like no gunfighter to me, son. Do you shave yet?"

"Onct a week, sir."

"You was probably in the war, though. You was probably a general in the war?"

"No sir. Spent two months in Florida in the Air Corps, till they realized I didn't see colors too well. That's why I'm a policeman."

"Well, come on in, but let me warn you, I hope you ain't no fool, because I am not the sort who can stay civil in the presence of fools. You're not a fool, are you?"

"Hope not, sir."

"Good."

The assistant prosecuting attorney led him into the office, which was not merely a mess but already half afog with pipe smoke. A deer head hung off the wall, but possibly it had died of asphyxiation, not a rifle bullet. In one corner well-thumbed legal volumes lay behind a glass case. The rest was documents, case folders, police reports, everywhere. Literally: everywhere.

"Let me tell you it ain't easy running a county when your prosecutor is a political hack like ours," said Mr. Vincent. "May have to run for the goddamn job myself one of these damned days. Now, sit down, tell me what you're investigating and why you came all the way out to the West." He began to fiddle with a pipe, clearly feeling the room wasn't smoky enough.

"Well, sir, I'm looking into the background of a man born and raised here in Polk County. You may know him."

"Earl. You'd be the johnny asking about Earl. Thought so." He got the pipe fired up, and belched a smokestack's worth of gassy unpleasantness into the air, which hung and seethed. The young man's eyes immediately began to water.

"Let me tell you something, sonny. If Earl's involved in that ruckus over in Hot Springs, it'd be a damned shame. Not after what Earl gone through. I'd hate to see Earl die to make Fred C. Becker the youngest governor in the nation. That would be as pure a crime as any Owney Maddox ever perpetrated. Is he on that raid team?"

"Sir, that is confidential information. No one knows who is on that raid team."

The older man fulminated a little. "No finer man was ever born in these here parts than Earl. He went off to war and won the Medal of Honor. Did you know that?"

"I knew he won a big medal."

"He did. He fought all over the Pacific. He's as foursquare as they come. If you're investigating him, you'd better have a goddamned good reason, or I'll throw you out of my office on your bony young ass myself."

"Sir, he ain't be investigated for no crime. No sir."

"What, then?"

"Well sir, as Mr. Parker explained it to me there's something called a 'death wish.'"

"A what?"

"A death wish. Some men for some reason, they *want* to die."

"Craziest goddamn thing I ever heard of."

Carlo nodded. Then he said, "But I see from them diplomas you went to Princeton University, out east. Hear that's a pretty good school. Did me some reading on what Dr. Freud said about death wishes. I'd bet you'd have run across it too, in your time educating."

Sam Vincent stared hard at the young man.

"Say, I'll bet you think you don't miss a trick, do you?"

"Miss 'em all the time, sir. But I'd bet a dollar against a cup of coffee that someone who went to Princeton and Yale Law School and wants to be elected a prosecuting attorney himself real soon-like, I'd bet he knows more about a death wish than most."

"Well, all right then. I have heard of such a thing. I will say Earl has a melancholy streak to him. Would that be a death wish? Don't know. I do know his daddy encouraged discipline and obedience with both his boys, and wouldn't brook no messy feelings or nothing. They were raised to do the job and see it through, and Earl certainly proved out. But they were both boys for holding things in and maybe that's what D. A. Parker sees as sadness unto death in Earl."

"Yes sir."

"Do you know Earl?"

"Yes sir."

"What do you think of Earl?"

"I—I think he's the bravest man ever lived," said Carlo. "I seen him do some things no man should have the grit to pull." He thought of Earl advancing through the dust with the BAR, daring the Grumleys to come out and shoot at him, letting his people get behind cover in the doorways. He thought of Earl taking that shot on a Grumley to save the Negro gal's life.

"Nobody wants nothing bad to happen to Earl," said Sam.

"Yes sir."

"Is that all?"

"Well. One of the things Mr. Parker wanted me to look into is this: Was Earl ever in Hot Springs? It seems he knows it damned well."

"Never. Never, never, never. Old Baptist Charles thought Hot Springs was hell and blasphemy. He'd have beat the hide off his boy if he'd have caught him in that sewer."

"I see."

"Earl has a gift for terrain. All the Swaggers do. They have natural feelings for land, they're fine hunters and trackers and they have an uncommon gift for shooting. They are born men of the gun. Charles Swagger was a wonderful hunter, got a buck every damned year. Tracked the county up and down, and always came home with game. A wonderful shot. The finest natural shot I ever saw, and I've hunted with some fine shots. Don't know where it comes from, but all them boys could shoot. Earl's daddy was a hero in a war too, and he shot it out with three desperadoes in a Main Street bank in the '20s, and sent them to hell in pine boxes. So if Earl seems to know things, it's just his gift, that's all."

"I see. Let me ask about one last thing. Earl's brother. He had a brother, named Bobby Lee. He hung himself, I believe, back in 1940. You probably hadn't gone off to fight in 1940. Maybe you were here for that."

Sam Vincent's eyes scrunched up and even behind the glasses, Carlo could make out something there.

"What you want to dig all that up for? Poor Bobby Lee. It ain't got nothing to do with anything. That's long over and done."

"I see."

"Hell, Earl was somewhere in the Marines then. It don't mean much."

"You knew Earl?"

"I knowed 'em both. Earl was two years ahead of me at high school and Bobby Lee was ten younger. I was the prosecutor that handled Bobby Lee's death. I was there when they cut him down. I wrote the report. You want to see it?"

"I suppose."

"Betty!" Sam called.

"Her name is Ruth and you gave her the day off."

"Goddamn her. Don't think she'll work out neither. You wait here."

The older man left and Carl sat there, suffocating, as the fog in the air wore him down. He felt a headache beginning and he heard Sam banging drawers and cursing mightily.

Finally, Sam came back.

"There, there it is."

He handed over the file, and Carlo read what was inside. It turned out to be straightforward enough: on October 5, 1940, the fire department was called by Mrs. Swagger and a truck got out to the place fast. The firemen found her crying in the barn at the feet of her son, who had hanged himself with a rope from a crossbeam. Sam arrived and directed that the body be taken down. The sheriff was located and he arrived from a far patrol and took over. Sam made the necessary interviews as brief as possible and supervised as the boy's body was taken to the morgue. The boy was buried without ceremony a day later and the sheriff never talked about it again. The county judge ruled death by suicide.

"No autopsy?" Carlo asked.

"What?" said Sam.

"Didn't y'all do an autopsy?"

"Son, it was open and shut."

"Well sir, I learned my policing in Tulsa under a chief detective inspector named O'Neill and if I'd have closed on a suicide without an autopsy, he'd have—"

"Henderson, you're like all the kids today. You think every damn

thing is a crime. It's my job to represent the state in these tragic in-
stances and believe me there wasn't nothing in that circumstance
worth an autopsy. I wasn't no greenhorn neither. I'd been assistant
prosecuting attorney since 1935. I'd seen a lifetime's worth of squalor
and misery and pain and lost life. So I made a judgment."

"But it was irregular?"

"You are a persistent son of a bitch, ain't you?"

"I take great pride in my investigative work, sir. I believe I have a
calling at it."

"Okay. You believe in law and order?"

"Of course I do. More than anything."

"Now you listen to me. Law and order. Law *and* order, you understand? That's a easy one. But let me ask you. Do you believe in law *or*
order? That one ain't so easy."

Carlo drew a blank. He wished he were smarter and could play ball
with this sly dog.

"Seems to me they are the same," he finally allowed.

"Maybe mostly. But maybe not. And if you've got to choose, what
do you choose?"

"I don't see how there can be one 'thout the other."

"Sometimes you got to give up on law to save order. Sometimes order is more important than law. By that I mean, sometimes you learn
something that might hurt order. It might hurt the way people think
on things. They have to trust the man with the badge. He's got to be a
paragon, a moral certainty to them. If he has weaknesses, and those
weaknesses become public knowledge, well, my God, who knows
where it might lead. To doubt, then chaos, then anarchy. The edifice is
only as strong as its weakest buttress. So sometimes you make a call:
you don't deal with something. You let it pass, you shave a corner, you
do this, you do that. Because the idea of the lawman as a man of honor
and virtue and courage and decency is much more important than
that lawman himself. You understand?"

Carlo did, of course. He now knew what the old bastard was getting
at. He himself knew cops who were drunks or cheats or liars or cowards. But if you made a moral cause of it, and by that cause held the
larger issue of the police up to ridicule, you only weakened the struc-

ture that supported the community or, even larger, the nation. So a police officer or a prosecutor had to use a certain discretion: there was a time to act, and a time to look away, and that was the heart of it.

"You've been a great help, Mr. Vincent," Carlo said, rising. "I can see the people in this county are well represented."

"Don't be in no hurry, Henderson. You ain't done learning for today. You and me, we got a place to go. You want to learn a thing or two? Then by God so you will. Get your hat and let's go."

The police station was in the same City Hall building but without direct hallway access, for arcane architectural reasons. It was actually outside, so they walked around the corner through small-town America to its entrance. At least half a dozen people said, "Howdy, Mr. Sam," and tipped a hat, and Sam tipped his in return. The trees were in full leaf, so the sun wasn't so hot and a cool wind blew across them.

"Stop and look," Sam said as they stood atop the stairs that led to the station. "What do you see?"

"A small town. Pretty little place."

"Where and how most people live, right?"

"Yes sir."

"It's all stable and clean and everything's right in the world, isn't it?"

"Yes sir."

"It's order. And that's what you and I, we work to defend, right?"

"Right."

"We defend the good folks from the bad. From the monsters, right?"

"Yes sir."

"We defend order. But what happens, Henderson, when you got yourself a situation where the good folk *is* the monster?"

Carlo said nothing.

"Then you got yourself a fine kettle of fish, that's what you got," said Sam. "And you and I, son, we got to clean it up. It's really the most important thing we do. You see what I'm driving at?"

"Yes sir."

They walked in, past the duty sergeant's desk with a wave, back into the day room and the detective squad room—more waves—then past the lockup and the little alcove where there was a vending machine for Coca-Cola and another one for candy bars, down a dim corridor, until finally they reached a room marked EVIDENCE.

Sam had the key. Inside, he found a light, and Carlo saw what was merely a storeroom, boxes and boxes on shelves, the detritus of old crimes and forgotten betrayals. A few guns, shotguns mostly, rusting away to nothingness on the dark shelves. The shelves were labeled by year and Sam knew exactly where he was going.

They went further into the room, to the year marked 1940 on the shelving. Sam pointed to a box on a high board marked SWAGGER, BOBBY LEE. Carlo had to strain to his tiptoes to get it down, though it was light, being composed of little beyond documents and manila envelopes.

Immediately Carlo saw that the documents were mere photo duplicates of the one he'd already read. But the older man grabbed an envelope, opened it, looked at it, and then handed it over.

"Take a gander," he said, "and learn a thing or two."

And Carlo beheld the horror.

CHAPTER

31

"Them two," said Vince Morella, who managed the Southern.

"Yes, I see."

"Shall I send some boys over?"

"No. Not at all. Send over a bottle of champagne. Very good stuff. The best, in fact."

It was between sets in the grillroom at the Southern, beneath the cavernous horse book and casino upstairs. This week's act: Abbott and Costello.

"You sure, Owney?"

"Very."

"Yes sir."

Vince called his bartender over and whispered instructions. Shortly thereafter, at the bar where two men stood drinking club sodas, the barkeep approached with a bucket full of ice and a green bottle.

"Fellows," he said, "this is your lucky day."

"We already ordered drinks," said the older man.

"You didn't order no *alcoholic* drinks. So the owner wants everybody happy and he sent this over, his compliments. Enjoy."

He worked some magic and with a pop the bottle was pried open, its cork caught in a white linen towel. He poured some frothy bubbly into two iced glasses.

"Bottoms up," he said.

The younger of the men, with tight, ferocious eyes, picked up the glass and poured it back into the bucket.

"I drink what I like," he said.

It was the cowboy and his older partner. Owney recognized them now clearly from the train station, where the cowboy had smashed Ben Siegel. They reeked of aggression as they sat at the bar, especially the cowboy. Strong of frame, erect, his bull neck tense, his dark, short hair bristly. Darkness visible: he had a look of darkness, dark eyes, dark features, a gunman's look.

A space had cleared away around him. Though elsewhere in the room, elegant men in dinner jackets ate dinner with their begowned wives and mistresses, here at the bar it was quiet and tense. The bartender swallowed, smiled pathetically and said, "I don't think Mr. Maddox is going to like that."

"I don't give a shit," said the cowboy, "what Mr. Maddox likes or what he don't like."

The bartender slipped away, reported to Vince, who in turn reported to Owney.

"They's asking for it," said Flem Grumley. "We should give it to 'em."

"Yes, yes, let's shoot up the most beautiful and expensive spot between St. Louis and New Orleans. And while we're at it, let's shoot up my roomful of brand-new Black Cherries, clanking away upstairs and paying the house back 34 percent and buying you and yours clothes, food, cars and your children's medicine. How clever."

He fixed Flem with a glare; Flem melted in confusion.

"They want something, else they wouldn't be here, eh, old man? Let's see what it is."

He inserted a Nat Sherman into his onyx cigarette holder, lit it off a silver Dunhill and stood.

"You boys stay here. I don't need any beef around."

"Yes sir," said Flem, speaking for the phalanx of Grumleys who surrounded Owney ever since the Mary Jane's shoot-out.

He walked over.

"Well, fellows," he said, sitting down at the bar, but facing elegantly outward, "isn't this a little brazen, even for you? I mean, my chaps could polish your apples in about seven seconds flat, eh what?"

Neither of his antagonists said a thing for a bit. But then the cowboy spoke.

"You try something fresh and tomorrow they'll bury ten more Grumleys. And you too, friend. And you won't care whether we made it out or not."

As he spoke, he pivoted slightly to face Owney, and his coat fell open, revealing a .45 in a shoulder holster. The thickness of his belt suggested it supported another .45.

Owney looked him over. He had a little Mad Dog to him, with the glaring eyes and the total absence of fear, regret, doubt or hesitation. But he also had a command to him. He was used to people doing what he said.

"Who are you? Still playing mysterious? We'll find out soon enough. You won't remain anonymous much longer. Somebody'll talk. Somebody always does.'

"You'll be finished by that time. You can read our names in the fishwrap at the penitentiary in Tucker."

"I won't serve time at Tucker. Or Sing Sing. Or anywhere. That's what lawyers are for, old man. They can get a chap out of anything. Now, really, what do you want? Are you measuring this place for a raid? Yes, do come, guns blazing, and kill a doctor or a judge or a politician. That'll do Becker no end of good."

"Listen here, Maddox," said the old man. "We come to talk straight out. You can't scare us, you can't bluff us, you can't stop us. We mean to keep coming at you. The more you squawk, the more killing there's going to be. Why don't you just cash in and get out now. You've got your millions. Move off to Mexico or Switzerland or out to Nevada or someplace."

"Well spoken, old fellow. He's got a bit of the philosopher to him, doesn't he? But you see the analysis is faulty: this isn't about money. We all know that. It's about some other thing. It's about who's the boss."

"We don't care much about that," said the cowboy. "We just mean to run you out of town or bring you down. Them's the only two possibilities."

"A third: you could die."

"It ain't likely," said Earl. "'Less you get some real bad boys."

"A fourth," said Owney. "For the old fellow, a nice retirement contribution. A nice nest egg. Well invested, he could live grandly. As for the cowboy here, he comes to work for me. I've heard the reports. You're a good gunman. They say as good as Johnny Spanish, maybe better. You come work for me."

"I bet you even think that's possible," said the cowboy. "See, here's the thing. You're a bully. You like to push people around. I don't like that, not even a little. In fact, it gets my blood all steamed."

It was amazing, and truly rare. Here was a man who seemed literally fearless. His own death had no meaning to him. Owney could read his essential nihilism in the blackness radiating from his eyes. He had Vincent the Mad Dog's contempt for life and willingness to risk his own anytime for any stake in any fight in any street or alley. Memphis Dogood was right: he didn't fear death. And that made him very dangerous indeed.

"Do you really think you can scare me?" said Owney. "I've fought on the street with guns and knives. I've shot it out with other gangs in the most brutal city on earth. When you've had a crazy black Irish boyo named Mad Dog out for your blood, and you're alive and he's dead, let me tell you, you've done something. And Mad Dog's only one."

"Yakkity-yak's cheap. We talk lead."

"You listen to me, cowboy. Oh, hello Judge LeGrand"—he waved his champagne glass in salute to the politician and issued a wondrous smile at the judge and Mayor O'Donovan, who accompanied him— "and you listen intently. The day after the next raid, a bomb will go off. In the Negro town. It'll kill twenty or thirty Negroes. Everybody will think some night riders did it, or some fellows in hoods. The investigation will be, I think one can safely predict, feckless. But you and I, friend, we'll know: you killed those Negroes. And you'll kill more and more. So I'm afraid you'll have to be the one who leaves town. Or turn the streets red with Negro blood and think about that for the rest of your life, old man. Enjoy your champagne. Cheers."

He rose and walked away.

CHAPTER
32

"Why are you showing me these?" said the doctor, his face pained.

"Well, sir," said Carlo, "I went to the library and I looked up medical journals. I spent three days. Shoot, a lot of it I couldn't even understand. But you wrote a paper published in 1937 called 'Certain Patterns in Excessive Discipline *in Situ Domestico.*' I read it. You seemed to be talking about a similar thing."

"It's the same," said the doctor, who was head of the Department of Pediatrics at the University of Oklahoma, in Norman, in whose office Carlo now sat.

The doctor—his name was David Sanders and he was in his forties, balding, with wire-frame glasses—looked squarely at Carlo.

"That paper didn't do me a bit of good, except that it got me laughed at. A man has a right to beat his children, everybody says so. Spare the rod, spoil the child. To suggest that a child has a right not to be beaten, well, that's radical. I even got some letters accusing me of being a communist."

"Sorry to hear that."

"So I gave it up. It was infinitely depressing and nobody wanted to hear about it. So I gave it up."

Carlo said, "I see you won a Silver Star. It's up there on your wall. So you can't be a coward."

It was, next to degrees and other professional awards, books and photos of fat, smiley babies.

"That was a war. It was different."

"Still, if anybody can help me, maybe you can."

"You want a lot, Officer Henderson." Sanders sighed and looked at the photographs.

There were eight of them. The boy, naked on a morgue slab, from various angles. The rope burn was livid, and his neck was elongated, strangely wrong, clear testament to asphyxiation by hanging. But that was only part of it.

"The welts," said Carlo.

"Yes. This boy has been beaten, many times, with a heavy strap or belt. There's second-degree scar tissue all over his back, buttocks and upper thighs. He's been beaten beyond all sense or reason. Almost daily, certainly weekly, and nobody cared or intervened."

"Was he tortured? Them spots on his chest. Look like cigarette burns to me."

"Oh, I think to his oppressor, the beatings were satisfying enough. The cigarette burns were almost certainly self-inflicted. When I was looking into these matters, I saw a lot of it."

"I don't get it. Why would he do that to himself? Why would he want *more* pain?"

"The victim comes to believe that somehow it's *his* fault. He's the problem. He's no good. He's too weak, stupid, pitiful. If only *he* were gone, it would be all right. So he finds himself guilty and sentences himself to more torture. He finds small, cruel, barely bearable rituals for inflicting the punishment upon himself. He is blaming himself for the crime, not the person who is beating him. It's a fairly predictable pathology. I gather from the elongation of the neck he finally ended it?"

"Yes sir," said Carlo. "This was all back in 1940."

The doctor turned one of the photos over, where the date had been stamped: OCTOBER 4, 1940, POLK COUNTY PROSECUTING ATTOR-NEY'S OFFICE.

"Well, at least the pain stopped."

"Do most of them commit suicide?"

"It's not uncommon, from my preliminary survey. But the rest? Well, go to any prison and ask the right questions and you'll find out. You raise a child in great pain, he comes to believe pain is a normal condition of the universe. He feels it is his right to inflict it. From what little research I did, I saw what looked to be a frightening pattern: that our most violent criminals were beaten savagely as children. They simply were passing the lessons of their childhood on to the rest of the world."

"Who would do that to a boy?"

"Oh, it's usually the father. I see a father who secretly hates himself, who almost certainly has a drinking problem, who quite possibly works in a violent world, who was almost certainly savagely beaten himself. He considers it his right to express his rage at the world for disappointing him in the flesh of his son. But he's really expressing his rage at himself for knowing that he's not the man the world thinks he is, and he's feeling the strain of maintaining the facade. I don't know. I only know he'd be pitiful if he weren't so dangerous."

"Suppose he was a policeman?"

"Again, I'm just speculating. But he'd be a man used to force. He'd believe in force. His job was to use force."

"This one used it a lot. Not just on his sons. The people in his town consider him a damned paragon, a hero."

"Again, not surprising. Almost banal. Who knows why, really. That's the difference between public and private personalities. We consider that what goes on at home, in the privacy of that castle, to be nobody's business."

"Suppose this boy had an older brother. Would he have been beaten too?"

"I don't know. But I don't think this kind of behavior pattern just starts up suddenly, out of nothing. It's ancient, almost omnipresent. My guess is, he'd have been beaten too."

"That boy—the older brother. He left home at sixteen, went and joined the Marines, and never went home again. What would he feel?"

"Mr. Henderson, I'm not a psychologist or a psychiatrist. I have no X-ray vision. This is all speculation."

"No sir. But ain't nobody know this business like you."

"Well, I'd say, this older brother would feel grief and rage and deep survivor's guilt. You'd expect him to be emotionally crippled in some respect. You'd expect him to have an unhealthy view of the universe— he'd believe that at any moment the world was about to shatter and some huge malevolent force would break in and whip him savagely. That would be difficult to live with. He could easily become a monster."

"Could he become a hero? An insane hero who took amazing risks?"

"Well, I hadn't thought of that. But I can see how the war would be the perfect vessel for his rage; it would give him complete freedom. And when he was in battle, he wouldn't be haunted by his past. So other men would be frightened, but he'd be so preoccupied, he'd actually feel very good because his memories were effectively blocked for once. Was he in the war?"

"He won the Medal of Honor on Iwo Jima."

"Very impressive. What happened to the father?"

"He was a law officer who got himself killed. I guess he was a little too used to whacking people in the head, and he whacked one boy who had a gun."

"Sometimes there is justice."

"I never thought I'd say it about a dead police officer, but, yes, sometimes there is justice."

CHAPTER

33

"It's there."

"How do you know?"

"I went, I saw."

"How do you know?"

"If you look at it from the outside, you'll see that there's four windows across the back. But if you go where they have the slots and the gambling stuff, you can only see three windows. There's a kind of dead space to the rear. It *has* to be there."

"You're sure?"

Frenchy, back a day early, sat alone with Earl and D.A., just returned from Hot Springs. It was early on a sunny afternoon; outside it was Texas, and nothing but. The temperature was hotter than hell, the atmosphere drier than a desert, and all the wood seemed about to crack from sheer cussedness. The wailing wind picked up a screen of yellow dust and threw it along in front of it. But the three men, sweaty but still in suits and ties, sat in the Assembly Room and talked it all out.

"Yeah, that's it. Plus, if you go out and follow the phone wires, you'll see that there's an unusual number of poles outside in the alley. Where there should be just one pole, there's two, for all the lines. I know. I checked. It's there. It's at the Ohio Club. It makes sense. It's downtown, he can walk to work, he can keep an eye on it, it's close to everything, it's so heavily used that no one would think you could hide a phone room in it. We never would have found it."

"You found it," Earl said.

"Well, *I* found it, yeah. But I'm a genius. I have a very sly mind. Everybody says so."

The boy smiled unsurely as if he wasn't quite sure that this was going as expected. D. A. Parker and Earl looked at him with hard, level eyes.

"Maybe he's right," said D.A. "We should check it out."

"It's the Ohio Club. The Central Book, I'm telling you. Not in the casino but on the same second floor, in the back. It's obvious. I found it."

He smiled in the way a man who thinks he's really winning some points smiles.

"We'll go up there tomorrow and check it out," D.A. said.

"Yeah," said Earl.

"We can close this thing down early next week," said Frenchy. "We take that place out, Owney's licked. You said so yourself. That's the key. What can he do? He has no other place set up and all the horse books die. They die in a matter of days. So what's he do, spend *his* money to keep the town operating. Or bail out? We all know he'll bail. He's *got* to."

He summed it up admirably.

"There's a problem," said Earl.

"What's that, Earl?" asked D.A. "If he's got it, he's right. And Owney won't be detonating no bombs in Niggertown because once it gets out the phone room's closed down, all his boughten judges and cops are going away from him 'cause they know he won't git enough money to pay them off."

"No, that's not the problem." He looked hard at Frenchy. "Now, you got anything to add?"

"What do you mean?"

"You sniffed this out on your own? All by your lonesome?"

"Yes sir."

Earl looked hard again at the boy.

"You lying to me? Short, are you lying? You could get us all messed up if you're lying."

"Hey," said Frenchy fearlessly, "I know that. No, I'm not lying."

"Earl, what?"

"Goddamn you, Short!" Earl bellowed.

Frenchy recoiled, stung.

"Earl, what—"

"There ain't no windows at all atop the Ohio Club. And there ain't no extra phone poles out back."

"Ah, well—"

"Earl, how do you know?"

"I know. I know, goddammit! I notice stuff like that, and by God, I know that!"

"Ahh, well, maybe, uh—" Frenchy bumbled.

"Short, I'm going to ask you one more goddamn time. Where'd you find this shit out? Where? Are you just making it up?"

"Ah. Well, actually, uh—"

For the first time in his life, Frenchy Short wasn't sure what to say. He had a gift for improvisation under stress, that he knew; it had saved him getting cooked a number of times, though alas, a few times it hadn't. But he was also utterly confused, because this great treasure was the home run that would make him a hero, he was sure, and erase completely the ambiguity of the killing of the two mobsters and the awkwardness of the accidental slaying of the two Negro women. It meant he was the star, the best boy, the success.

"Short, you better tell us," said D.A.

"It just makes sense."

"Actually, it don't make no sense at all."

"*Short!* Goddammit, you tell me!" Earl shouted.

"Okay, okay. What difference does it make?"

"It makes a difference, Short," said D.A.

"I broke in."

"You broke in? To the Ohio Club?"

"No. The phone company."

Frenchy explained his thinking, his night mission, his burglary, his discovery.

"Jesus Christ," said D.A. "Do you know what could have happened to us if you got nabbed by the cops?"

"I wasn't going to get nabbed. It's Hot Springs, Arkansas, for God's sakes, not the U.S. Mint."

"Shit," said D.A.

"What difference does it make? I got it, didn't I? Without a problem. No sweat. And it's right, dammit. It's the breakthrough we needed. Who has to know? Nobody has to know. It doesn't matter. I didn't burglarize anything. I didn't *steal* anything. I just looked through some drawers, that's all. Hell, those drawings might even be in the public domain, for all I know."

"I don't know what difference it makes, but we got to tell Mr. Becker. He will have to know."

"But it's good information. It *is* good, isn't it, Mr. Earl? I mean, it's good combat intelligence."

"It is, Short."

"What will happen to me?"

"I don't know."

"Can't you just say you got an anonymous tip?"

"No. Not anymore. Becker wants more control from now on. I can't order up the raids myself. He has to check off. I have to run this by him. We have to see what he says, all right?"

"Look," argued Frenchy, "now that we *know* what it is, it's just a matter of time until we can find something to support it. Once we find that out, we go to Becker and say that that's the primary evidence. Then we have our cause, we take the joint out, and we're all heroes and we go home happy. It's easy."

"You are a clever little bastard," said Earl.

"I ain't getting into no big lying situation. I will have to run this by Becker. It's his call. If it were my call, who knows, but it's his call, he's the one who has to answer for it, he's the one signing the checks. It may be different now after all that shooting last time out. We just got back from a trip to Hot Springs, looking exactly for this information. But goddammit, Earl, you and I'll git back up there tonight and talk to him. Short, you stay here. Don't you tell nobody. You hear? *Nobody!* Got that?"

"Yes sir," said Frenchy. "But I'm telling you, this can be the big one."

Frenchy spent the day in Texarkana. A movie called *O.S.S.* with Alan Ladd had just come out, and he sat through it twice, though he knew it was phony. It couldn't have been like that in the war. The girl was some new actress he'd never seen, and who wasn't that beautiful, and everyone smoked. But they didn't have the class the OSS people had, Frenchy was sure; his uncle had class, a savoir faire, a mysterious intimation that life was more fun if you cultivated an ironic disposition and could hold your liquor.

When he got back, it was around 6:00. Three of the men had returned already, Bear, Eff and Billy Bob, called Bob Billy for silly reasons, and the four had a kind of hearty how-ya-doin' escapade there, exchanging stories. The three had gone to New Orleans and had a really fine time. When the conversation got around to Frenchy, he got very vague. He just said he'd had a damned good time too.

Then a car pulled in, and it was Earl and Mr. D.A. They welcomed the men back, chatted pointlessly for a while, and finally left. Earl nodded at Frenchy and he joined the two in the office.

They sat. It was darkening, and the old man turned on a lamp that filled the dreary little room with yellow light. Outside a bit of Texas wind moaned.

Finally the old man looked up.

"Here, I got this for you," he said. It was a letter, on the official stationery of the Garland County Prosecuting Attorney's Office. "Mr. Earl had to work like hell to get this. He swore Fred Becker up one side and down the other, and said he'd walk if Sid didn't cough up a letter."

"A letter?" said Frenchy.

"A letter of recommendation. You deserve it," said the old man.

Frenchy looked over at Earl, who just sat there, darkness shading his eyes.

To Whom It May Concern:

Walter F. Short was in the employ of this office as an investigator and warrant-serving officer between July 28 and September 12, 1946. During this time, he performed his duties with exemplary courage and professional commitment. He exhibited a great deal of enterprise in the accomplishment of all tasks given him. He has a great future in law enforcement.

> Fred C. Becker
> Prosecuting Attorney
> Garland County, Arkansas

"It ain't bad," said D.A., "considering at one point this afternoon he wanted to indict you and send you to jail for breaking and entering."

"I don't understand it."

"You been fired, son," said Earl at last.

"I've been fired?"

"Mr. Becker says he's got to allay community fears about us being out-of-control gunmen. He has to tell people that he's taken command of the team, and that the 'bad apples' have been let go. You got the nod as the bad apple. As I say, he wanted to make a public example of you. Earl here got him to see what a bad idea that was."

Frenchy just stared off into space.

"I found the Central Book," he finally said. "Doesn't that count for anything?"

"It counts for not going to prison and walking out of here with a nice letter that'll git you a job anywhere you want. Meanwhile Earl and I have to find some way to justify the raid. We got to do it all legal-like. That's Mr. Becker's order."

"It's not fair," said Frenchy.

"No, it's not."

"It's just politics," said Frenchy.

"Yes, it is."

"You can't let him do this."

"I can't stop him from doing this," said the old man. "I can't stop him from doing anything. He says the governor is leaning on him from above and he's got people in the community leaning on him from be-low."

Frenchy turned to Earl. "You supported this?"

Earl looked him in the eye.

"Sometimes you get a bad officer above you. It ain't supposed to happen, but it's in the cards. So you got to go along until you get an opportunity to make things right. You got to hold the unit together, you got to put up with the shit, you got to keep running the patrols. You got to take some losses. You're the loss, Short."

"Jesus," said Frenchy. "All these guys, from Podunk City and Hick Town U.S.A., and Toad Pond, Oklahoma, and *I'm* the one that gets canned. Jesus Christ, I *fought* for you guys. I *killed* for you guys. It's just not right. Can I at least *see* Becker?"

"Bad decision," said Earl. "He don't like face-to-face things. Figures, I'd say. Anyhow, he don't like that kind of pressure and he could still indict you for B and E, or maybe even if he wanted to for shooting them two boys out back of that casino. Do yourself a favor. Learn from this, get the hell out of town, and go on with the rest of your life. You're young and smart. You won't have no trouble."

"But I—"

"Yeah, I know. But the key thing here is, don't let it get to you. Take it from me, son. Just start over fresh, and don't let this thing haunt you. Me and Mr. D.A., we're sorry. But it's an outfit thing, a politics thing. Learn from this: it's the way the world works."

CHAPTER
34

Pap Grumley's death, of the commingled impact of grief and clap, pretty much finished the Grumleys as a possibility, as far as Owney was concerned. He would keep the Grumleys around to service his empire, to receive and make his payoffs, to lubricate the machine, to bust the odd debtor and the like, but he knew that without Pap's stalwart leadership and heart, the Grumleys were done as a fighting force. Flem would stay as his factotum, but Flem would never be the man Pap was. Flem wasn't a wartime leader, not by a long shot.

So Owney finally made the decision that he'd been toying with all these weeks. He went to his gas station near Lake Catherine and placed his long-distance call to Sid in New York. He spoke to Sid, told him what was required. Sid did the legwork, made the connections, set up the proper channels and finally Owney reached the party he needed to reach. This was a Mr. A, who himself was speaking from a pay phone to avoid the possibility of federal wiretaps.

"Thank you so much for talking with me, Mr. A. I hate to bother you."

"It's nothing. Talk to me, Owney. Tell me what I can do to help you," said Mr. A.

"I got a problem. I got cops like you never saw. These fuckers, they come inta one a my joints with machine guns and shot the shit out of the place. They killed eleven boys of mine. Chicago, the fat Sicilian, that Valentine's Day thing, it wasn't nothing like this. Down here, it's the South, there are no laws."

"Owney, the boys are talking. You know how it is when the boys talk."

"And that shmata Ben Siegel is talking too. Right? I know he is. It's how a yentzer like that operates."

"Owney, no need to run down the other fellow. Ben is out in L.A., doing his job. You leave Ben out of this."

"Yes, Mr. A," said Owney, slightly stung.

"Owney, you have to take care of this. You ran a tidy little place down there and everybody was happy. People went down there for vacation and they were happy. They played the horses, the wheel, the slots, they met some girls, they laughed at Abbott and Costello, they heard Dinah Shore, it was very nice. Now you got bullets flying and people dying everywhere. You can't do business in a climate like that, you can't have no fun. Things don't grow like we all think they should."

"I agree with you totally, Mr. A. Growth. Stability is the fertilizer of growth, which is the destiny of prosperity. What I have here is a franchise on the future. This is what will be, you'll see. Except for these crazy cops."

"Very good, Owney. You still understand, I see. Now, you want we should send some fellas? I could dispatch some very good Jersey people."

"Nah. Not hitters. Hitters ain't got no stomach for this. Hitters take guys out to the marshes and clip 'em with a .32 in the back of the head. It ain't like that down here. It's a fuckin' war. Plus, hitters'd stand out like fuckin' sore thumbs."

"So what do you need?"

"I need soldiers. I mean real hard-ass fucking soldiers, been in some scrapes, shot it out with the fucking cops, ain't afraid of nothing. Like the scary shit, when the lead flies. There are some boys like that."

"Sounds like you want Marines."

"Nah. What I want is armed robbers. I want the best armed robbery crew. They'd be the boys who could run a thing for me. They could plan and wait and spring a trap and shoot the shit out of it. They'd have the discipline, the long-term, wait-through-the-night guts. Okay. You know who I want, Mr. A. I want Johnny Spanish and his crew. They worked for me before. They worked for me in '40."

"Johnny's retired, Owney."

"Johnny owes me. He hit a big fucking score in '40. Biggest caper of his career. I set that job up for him."

"Whyn't you just call him? I could find the number."

"Mr. A, coming from you, it would be better. He's black Irish. You know, I come from England. The Irish, they got a thing about the English."

"Just 'cause you tried to starve them to death."

"Hey, I didn't starve *nobody*. All the time I have these problems with the Irish. That goddamned Vincent the Mad Dog, another black Irish, want to bust my balls. God, was I glad when he got his ass blown to shit."

"All right, Owney. I can make a call. I can ask a favor. But you know, Johnny and his people don't work cheap. Johnny goes first-class. He deserves first-class."

This, of course, was Owney's problem with Johnny. Johnny and his crew—that would be Jack "Ding-Dong" Bell, Red Brown, Vince "the Hat" de Palmo and Herman Kreutzer—took 60 percent of the take, leaving 40 for the local setup guy. This was unprecedented: in all other similar transactions, the armed contract robbers only got 50 percent. But they were the best, if a little aged by now. So if Johnny came down here for a bit of business and there was no up-front promise of a take, Johnny would need a cash down payment and a big backside splash.

"It has to be Johnny," said Owney.

"It's done. He'll be there before the week is over."

"You got to hurry, Mr. A. These guys are one strike from taking over down here."

"Owney, Owney, Owney. Johnny will take care of it all. You can trust Johnny. We'll look out for you, Owney. You can trust your friends."

CHAPTER

35

Junior Turner, the sheriff of Montgomery County, looked at Carlo Henderson with a grimace of the purest dripping scorn. Junior was a big man in his thirties, with a face that looked like old possum hides hung on a nail in a barn somewhere. His fat belly exploded beyond the perimeters of his belt and there were stains of a disagreeable nature on his khaki shirt. He wore a big Smith & Wesson Heavy Duty .38/.44 in a fancy belt, the only fancy thing about him. Then he turned and launched a majestic gob of Brown Mule from his lips. It took off with a disgusting slurping sound, seemed to elongate as it followed the parabola of its arc, a yellowish tracer bullet glistening with mucus, tobacco curds and spit, until it struck dead center into the spittoon with a coppery clang, rocking the vessel on its axis.

"This here's a small town, my friend. We don't much cotton to outsiders stirring up our business."

Mount Ida, a smear on the roadside consisting of a bar, a general store, a Texaco station and a sheriff's office, stood in the trackless Ouachitas, encapsulated almost totally in a wall of green pine forest, about halfway between Blue Eye and the more cosmopolitan pleasures of Hot Springs. It united the two by a sliver of road called 270, mostly dirt, occasionally macadam, all of it lost and lonely through the high dense trees.

"Sir, I am on official business," said Carlo.

"You say. The official bidness of Garland is bidness. So why'n hell's a little old boy like you rutting around in a crime done happened in our county four years back? It was open and shut. If you read the papers, you know ever goddamned thing."

"I am just following up a loose end."

"Now what loose end would that be, son?" asked Junior, casting a yellow-eyed glance around to his two deputies, who guffawed at the sheriff's rude humor.

"I am not at liberty to say, sir," said Carlo, feeling the hostility in the room.

"Well, son, I ain't at liberty to just open my files to any joe what comes passing this way," the sheriff said. "So mebbe you'd best think 'bout moving on down the road."

"Sir, I—"

But he saw that it was useless. Whatever grudge this man had against Garland County and its representatives, it was formidable and unbridgeable. He knew he was out of luck here. He rose and—

"So you tell the Grumleys if they want to check out Montgomery, they can just go on straight to hell," the sheriff said.

"I'm sorry?"

"You tell the Grumley clan Junior Turner of Montgomery says they should go suck the devil's own black goat's milk. I said—"

"You think I'm working for the Grumleys? You think I'm a Grumley?"

"He got that Grumley look," said the one of the deputies, evidently called L.T. "Sort of narrow-eyed, towheaded with a yellow thatch all cut down. Them eyes blue, long of jaw, a rangy, stretchy boy."

"I think I smell a damned Grumley stink on him," said the other deputy. "Though I 'low, Grumleys most usually travel in packs."

"It ain't common to see a Grumley on his lonesome," said Sheriff Turner.

"I killed a Grumley," Carlo said.

"You what?"

"A couple, actually. It was hard to tell. Lots of dust flying around, lots of smoke. Mary Jane's, it was. I see they're now calling it the greatest gunfight in Arkansas history. I fired a lot, I know I hit at least two, and they went down."

"You kilt a Grumley?"

"I know you heard about that raid. That was us. That was me. That's what this is all about. The Grumleys. Putting them out of business for good. Driving 'em back into the hills where they can have sex with their cousins and sisters and be no bother to good folk anymore."

"L.T., you hear that? He kilt a Grumley," said the sheriff.

"He must be one of them boys working for that new young Becker feller," said the deputy.

"I figgered he worked for Owney and Mayor O'Donovan and that

Judge LeGrand and the gambling boys, like all the Grumleys these days. That ain't so?"

"I almost got my butt shot off fighting gamblers with machine guns," said Carlo. "Grumleys all. A Peck and a Dodge too, I believe."

"Grumley cousins," said L.T. "Just as hell-black low-down mean too. Maybe meaner."

"Damnation! Damnation in the high grass! Damnation in July! He's okay! He's goddamned okay," said the sheriff, launching another naval shell of yellowish gunk toward the spittoon, where it banged dead bull's-eye, a rattle that reached the rafters.

"Sheriff's brother was a state liquor agent," said L.T. "That'd be my Uncle Rollo. In '37, some ole boys set his car aflame. He was in it at the time. Burned up like a fritter that fell into the stove hole."

"No man should die the way my brother did," said the sheriff. "Since then, it's been a war 'tween the Turner and the Grumley clan. Which is why ain't no Grumley in Montgomery County."

"I think he's okay, Junior."

"By God, I say, he *is* okay. He's *more'n* okay. He's goddamned fine, is what he be. Son, what's it you want?"

Did Carlo want recollections? The boys provided them. The files, the photos, the physical evidence. It was his for the asking. Did he want to examine the crime scene? Off they went.

In a few hours of cooperation, Carlo learned what was to be learned, which, as Junior said up front, wasn't much. In the crime scene photos, Charles Swagger lay face forward in his automobile, his head cupped against the wheel, his one arm dangling, fingers languid, pointed downward. A black puddle of blood lay on the floor of the Model T, coagulated at his feet. His old six-gun, a Colt's Army from 1904, was in the dust, one of its rounds discharged. Marks in the dust indicated no kind of scuffle. The back door to the warehouse behind Ferrell Turner's liquor store had been pried open, though nothing taken. There really wasn't much to go on, but the final conclusion reached by the Mount Ida detective, one James Fields, seemed to sum it up as well as anything.

"It appears the decedent saw or heard something as he drove through town late. He pulled around back, put his spotlight on the door, and saw some movement. He got out, drew his gun, called, then started forward. He was shot, returned fire once (probably into the air or ground, as no bullet hole was found), then returned to his car as if to drive to the hospital or a doctor's, but passed out. The recovered bullet was a .32 caliber, lodged in his heart. A manhunt and exhaustive search for clues unearthed nothing; the case remains open, though until this officer returns from wartime service it will go on the inactive list."

It was dated January 20, 1943, the day before Jimmy Fields went off to the war he never returned from.

"Ferrell found him the next morning, early," recalled L.T. "Just lying there, like in the photo."

"Nobody heard the shots?"

"No sir. But that don't mean nothing. Sound is tricky this deep in the woods. Ferrell slept about three hundred feet away in his general store but he was a drinking man. He could have slept through anything. Jimmy done a good job. He worked that case hard. If there'd a been anything to find, he'd have found it."

They went to the crime scene, only a couple of hundred feet from the office. There, Carlo stood in the dust behind the liquor store and saw that the warehouse was really more of a shed, secured with a single padlock, which itself could easily be pried loose.

"What's he keep in there?"

"The beer, mostly. It's cool and once a day a truck delivers the ice. It's the only place 'round here that sells cold beer."

"I suppose I could talk to Ferrell."

"Sure, but Ferrell didn't see nothing. But I know you want to be thorough. So, yeah, let's go talk to Ferrell."

That talk was short; Ferrell did know nothing. He'd gone out back early in the morning to open up for the ice delivery and the milk truck and been surprised to find Charles Swagger's old Ford there, old Charles Swagger dead in it. He'd heard no shots.

Carlo asked modern, scientific questions that couldn't be answered by any living man, about bloodstains and trails and fingerprints and footprints and whether there was dust of the kind that was from the ground here found on Charles's boots. Ferrell had no idee; he just called the polices and the boys all come over and Jimmy Fields done took over. The only answers to those questions died with Jimmy in the hedgerow country.

He asked as he had asked everybody: Did you all know Charles?

Charles was a great man, they said. We seen him every damn month on his way to prayer meeting at Caddo Gap.

As the afternoon wore on, poor Carlo began to see his time was wasted and whatever he learned really was of no importance in regard to his original mission, which had nothing whatsoever to do with Charles Swagger, his angers, his violence, his fury, his death, but with Earl Swagger, his melancholy, his courage, his baffling behavior, his possible lie about being in Hot Springs before. It almost made him dizzy. He felt he'd wandered into a madhouse and didn't belong, was learning things best forgotten, that meant nothing except obscure pain in years back, not worth recalling.

At nightfall, he went to say his farewells to Sheriff Junior Turner and thank him for his cooperation. After all, in the end, Junior had done all right by him, once the original misunderstanding was cleared up. But Junior had other ideas. Did he want to come up to the house and eat dinner with all the Turners? Er, no, not really, but Carlo now saw no polite way out of it, and Junior and his boys seemed really to want his company, a rare enough occurrence in his life. So in the end, he meekly said yes, and was hustled off.

And what a dinner. Whatever the Turners did, they ate well. Squirrel stew in a black pool of bubbly gravy, like a tar pit, collard greens, turnips, scrapple, great slabs of bacon all moist with fat, taters by the long ton, in every configuration known to man, chicken-fried steak, big and gnarly and soaked in yet a different variation on the theme of gravy, corn on the cob or shelled and mushed, a mountain of grits slathered in a snowcap of butter, hot apple dumpling, more coffee, hot, black and strong, the attention of flirty little Turner girls, somebody's female brood of cousins or nieces or something (never too clear on exactly who these girls were) and, after dark, corn likker and good storytelling.

It was night. Mosquitoes buzzed around but the Turner boys, all loquacious, were sitting about on the porch, smoking pipes or vile cigars imported from far-off, glamorous Saint Louie, in various postures of lassitude and inebriation. In the piney Ouachitas, crickets yammered and small furry things screeched when they died. Up above, the stars pinwheeled this way and that.

The subject was set by the day's events and it turned out to be the man who was both god and devil to them, who but Charles Swagger, former sheriff of Polk County, a man who walked high and mighty and treated such as them as the scum of the earth.

"He was a proud man," an unidentified Turner said, from the gray darkness of the porch, in a melancholy of recollection, "that you could read on him. But you know what the Book sayeth."

The dark chorus supported this point.

"Yes sir."

"You do, you do."

"That'd be the truth, that would."

"That's what she says. You listen, young feller. Luke's a preacher, he know the Book."

"The Book sayeth, pride goeth before the fall."

"And you know what?" said Junior Turner. "After the fall, it hangeth around too!"

Everybody laughed, including slightly overwhelmed and slightly overstuffed Carlo.

"You saw him often?" he asked, amazed that Charles was so big to them, for after all, this wasn't his county, and his office was forty miles of bad road to the west.

"Ever damn weekend in four," said a Turner. "He'd go on over to that Baptist prayer camp. He been a good Baptist. He been Baptist to the gills. He'd come on through in that old Model T of his, with the big star on it, and he'd stop at Ferrell's store, and have hisself a cold Coca-Cola. You'd see him watching and keeping track."

"He was great at keeping track."

"He stand there in that black suit and he's all glowery-like, you know. Big feller. Big hands, big face, big old arms. Strong as a god-damned blacksmith. Wore the badge of the law. Brooked no nonsense from no man. You'd as soon poke a stick at a bear as you'd rile up Charles Swagger."

"He must have been a worshipful man."

"Well sir," said a Turner, "you could say that. He'd be headed on to-ward Caddo Gap. He'd be going to worship a cribful. That Baptist prayer retreat camp, that'd be at that Caddo Gap."

"Yes, that would, and the old man, that's where he'd head, to do his own kind of worshipfulness."

And they busted out laughing.

The Turners howled into the night! It was like the drunken deities of a fallen Olympus snarfing out a bushel basket of giggles and guffaws at the latest vanity of their pitiful progeny, that tribe of hairy-assed scuf-flers and hustlers known as mankind.

"Oh, he was a prayerful man," somebody said.

"He worshipped all right."

"Pass that jug, Cleveland."

"She's a coming, Baxter."

"I still don't—" started Carlo.

Junior Turner delivered the news: "He did worship. He worshipped at the altar of titty and cooze! He drank the sacred elixir of hooch. He tested God's will and mercy by betting it all on the throw of them little old cubes with the dots! What a great man he was."

"That old boy, he was a inspiration to us all."

Carlo was suddenly confused.

"I don't—"

"He didn't go to no prayer meeting at Caddo Gap. No siree, not a goddamn bit of it. He'd come through here and make a big play of how holy he was, and tell ever damn body about the prayer retreat, then he'd roll on out of town, up Route 27 toward Caddo Gap. But god-damn, then he'd cut through the woods on some old logging road and git back on 27 out near to Hurricane Grove and head on his way to where he's really going. Hot Springs, the Devil's Playpen. One day a month, Charles gathered up a hundred or so dollars from the niggers and white trash he'd beat over the head, told his old wife he's going to talk to Jesus, came through here, then cut over to Hot Springs, where he whored and drank and gambled, same as any man. So high and mighty!"

"Jesus," said Carlo.

"He was a man of sin. Vast sin. He had the clap, he had ten girlfriends in ten different cribs. He never went to the quality places, where he'd might like to chance recognition. Nah, he went to low places, in the Niggertown or up Central beyond the Arlington. He's a reg'lar, all right."

"How do you know?"

"Ask Baxter. Baxter knows."

"I ain't a sinner no more," said Baxter, in the darkness. "The Lord done showed me a path. But in them earlier years, I done some helling. I knowed him 'cause I pumped gas for him so much as a youngster when he stopped for his Coca-Cola. I seen him onct, twicet and then ever damn place, ever damn time. He didn't have no badge on then. He wore a gal on each arm, and the smile of a happy goddamned man. Sometimes the cards smiled, sometimes they didn't, but he kept coming back. He had the best life, I reckon. He was a God-fearing man of civil authority twenty-nine days a month and on the thirtieth day he's a goddamned hellion who got his old pecker in ever kind of hole there was to be had in Hot Springs. Great man! Great man, my black asshole!"

"This is the truth?"

"This is God's honest truth," said Junior Turner. "We all knew it. Not nobody back in his hometown did, but we sure did. So when he got hisself kilt, we figgered it was gambling debts or woman trouble. Whoever done it did a good job of covering it up. But goddamn, he paid the devil his due, that I'll say."

"You didn't investigate?"

"Well, son, I was in combat engineer school at Fort Belvoir, in Virginia that day. My deputies was in—where was you, L.T.?"

"Getting ready for the Aleutians."

"Hell, everybody was some damn place or other. Only Jimmy really was here and by God he'd tried like hell to get in, till finally the standards dropped in '43 and they took him. Jimmy didn't see no percentage in turning the light on Charles Swagger's hunger for flesh and gitting himself involved in what goes on in Hot Springs. Hot Springs, that's a evil town. If Charles went to Hot Springs for pleasure, he knew there'd be a price to pay, and by God, he ended up paying it."

"I see."

"If you want to know who killed him, I'll tell you how to do it."

"Okay," said Carlo.

Junior leaned forward.

"You look for a silver-plated Smith & Wesson .32 bicycle gun. Little thang, .32 rimfire, couldn't weigh more'n ten, twelve ounces. Charles called it his Jesus gun, and he kept it secured up his left sleeve by a sleeve garter. He carried the Colt, a Winchester '95 carbine in .30 government in the car, just like the Texas Rangers love so deeply, but that little gun was his ace in the hole. That was the gun he kilt Travis Warren's little brother Billy with in 19 and 23, during the Blue Eye bank robbery. He shot Travis dead with the Colt, and his cousin Chandler too, but old Billy hit him with a 12-gauge from behind, and knocked him down and bloody with buck. Billy walked up, kicked the Colt across the floor and leaned over to put the shotgun under Charles's chin for a killing shot, and Charles pulled that li'l silver thang and shot that boy slick as a whistle 'tween the eyes. Anyhows, whoever kilt that old man in 1942, he stole that gun. Everyone who knew a thing about Charles knew it was missing. The Colt was there on the ground, you seen it. But the Jesus gun was missing."

Carlo knew it was a bad idea, but he couldn't help from asking.

"Why do they call it a Jesus gun?"

"'Cause when he pulls it on you, you are going to meet Jesus. Billy sure did, at the age of only sixteen."

"Wonder if Billy likes heaven?"

"Bet he do. Plenty of cooze in heaven! All them angel gals in them little gowns. They don't wear no underpants at all."

"Now don't you go talking that way 'bout heaven," warned Baxter. "It could have consequences. There are always consequences. That's the lesson in tonight's sermon."

Eventually, most of the Turners gave up the ghost and retreated to farmhouses or cabins. It suddenly occurred to Carlo that he had no place to stay, he was too drunk to drive and could see no way clear to a happy solution to his problem. But once again Junior Turner came through, and dragged him upstairs to an unused bedroom, where he was told to get his load off and stay the night, Mama Turner would have grits and bacon and hot black coffee in the kitchen beginning at 6:00 and running through 9:00.

Carlo stripped, blew out the candle, pulled a gigantic comforter over his scrawny bones, and his head hit the pillow. He had a brief fantasy about the farmer's daughters, since there'd been so many pretty Turner girls fluttering this way and that, but no knock came to his door, and as a graduate of a Baptist college he wouldn't have known what to do if one did. And then the room whirled about his head one more dizzying time and he was out.

His dreams tossed in his mind, though. Strange stuff, the product of too much white lightning and too much gravy mingled into a combustible fluid. He could make head or tails of none of it, though it disturbed him plenty and once or twice pulled him from sleep. He'd awaken, wonder where the hell he was, then remember, lie back and sail off again to a turbulent snoozeland.

But the third time he awoke, he knew it was for good. He was sweaty and shaking. Was he sick? Was he going to get the heaves or the runs? But his body was fine; it was his heart that was rocketing along at a hundred miles per hour.

He felt a presence in the room. Not a Turner cousin, comely and sweet, but something far worse: a haunt, a ghost, a horror. He reached out as if to touch something, but his fingers clawed at nothingness. The thing was in his head, whatever it could be. What was it rattling about in his subconscious, trying to find a way to poke a hole into his conscious, trying to get itself felt, noticed, paid attention to? Whatever, it was unsettling. He rose, went to the window, saw the Turner yard, bone-gray in the radiant gibbous moonlight, a swing hanging from a tree, a bench close by, where loving daddies could watch their baby sons play, and guard them and look after them, as his had done for him, as most had done for theirs. It was a scene of such domestic bliss and becalmed gentility it soothed him, but the luminous grayness of it suggested a photo negative, something somehow in reverse, and he saw another daddy, Charles the Tyrant, with his immense reservoir of hidden violence, his hatred, his disappointment, his vanity, his egoism, his self-doubt, and he saw him beating a boy child in that ghostly light.

"You ain't no damned good!" he heard the old man scream. "What is wrong with you, boy! You fail at everything! You are such a god-damned disappointment!" *Whack!* the strap across the legs, *whack!* the strap across the back, *whack!* the strap across the buttocks, the thumbs grinding bone bruises into the boy's arms as the larger man pinioned him in endless, suffocating rage.

What happens to such boys? What becomes of them? They become so full of hatred themselves they lash out at the world. They become monsters hell-bent on punishing a world that did nothing to protect them. Or they become so full of pain they don't care if they live or die and off they rush into the machine guns. Or they hang themselves at fifteen, for there is no hope on earth left.

Then at last he saw it.

He tried to push it away but it made such perfect sense now, it unified all the elements, it explained everything now.

How did Earl know so much about Hot Springs?

Because he'd been there.

Why couldn't he tell anyone?

Because he'd been there secretly, tracking someone, setting a trap for someone.

That man was his father.

Earl couldn't be frightened by his father, for by '42 he was a strong Marine sergeant with a couple of boxing titles to his name, and combat in Nicaragua and all over China, not the scrawny, frightened six-teen-year-old who'd fled home in 1930 to escape the father's rages.

But Earl had some last business with his father. He saw how Earl's mind would work. Earl was going to the Pacific and he would probably die. His division had orders to Guadalcanal by that time. He had no expectation of surviving the great crusade in the Pacific, for after Guadalcanal there were another hundred islands, with twisted names, letters in combinations never seen before, an archipelago of violence beckoning, promising nothing but extinction. But he had a powerful debt to pay back to the man who'd beaten him, and worse, the man who'd beaten his younger brother, without Earl there to stop it.

And Earl would know about the Jesus gun, and his father's trick of wearing it in his sleeve, secured by a garter.

In his mind's eye, Carlo saw what he hoped had not happened but whose logic was absolute and powerful: Earl, AWOL from the Corps, tracking his own daddy through the bawdy houses and flesh parlors of Hot Springs in January of 1942, and then at last facing him, facing the monster.

Had Earl been the man who killed his daddy?

It terrified Carlo, more than anything in his life ever had, but he knew he had to find the truth.

CHAPTER

36

It was always about money with Johnny. Johnny expected to be paid very well, very well indeed, and he also insisted on charging Owney a tax for being English. He called it his Potato Famine bonus: $20,000, over and above the agreed-to sum, just because . . . just because all them laddies and lasses had starved in the bogs of County Mayo a hundred years ago.

"Old man," protested Owney, "my people were selling fish and sweeping streets in the slums of the West End at the time. Doubt if they had a ha'penny between them. It was the lord highs what ruined the potato crop and set your people to dying in the river glens."

"Ah," said Johnny, all a-twinkle with blarney, "if you English shop-keeps had the nerve to overthrow them wig-wearing nancy boys and gone and made a proper revolution, mine'd not had to flee to the slums of New York and peck out a new life. We'd all be living in the castle now."

We are living in the castle now, boyo, Owney thought, but didn't express it. You couldn't argue with Johnny, and so the deal was done and Ralph brought Johnny another mint julep. He and Owney sat on Owney's terrace above the rumble of Central late in the afternoon. The cars churned down the broad avenue, the pigeons cooed lovingly.

"I see the mountain's still a fair eyeful," said Johnny, looking beyond the Arlington to North Mountain, which rose in pine-crusted glory across the way, all twenty-one of its springs still blasting out the steamy mineral water, as they had since time immemorial.

"The town has changed in six war years, eh, Johnny?" said Owney.

"In 1940, she was still a Depression town. Now she's modern. Now she's a beaut. She still lights up the night sky, I'll be betting."

"That she does."

"Now, tell me about these boyos who are plaguing you. They sound like the Black and Tans you Brits sent up to raid on us in the '20s."

"You would know, Johnny," said Owney.

"I would indeed. I was in County Mayo and the pubs of west Dublin running with me brothers with the Lewis guns and the Thompsons, hunting and being hunted in them alleyways. I do hate the Black and Tans. Sure but they made the people suffer. They burned, they pillaged, they tortured. Night riders, anonymous, hard to get at, highly secretive, well armed. Sounds about the same, does it not?"

"Well, almost," said Owney. "These boys don't torture. They don't burn. They sure pillage, though. They've cost me close to a hundred grand in lost revenues in two months."

Actually, it was closer to three hundred grand, but Owney knew if he gave the correct number, Johnny would make a lightning calculation and up the agreed-on cost appreciably. That was Johnny; he held all the cards and he loved it.

Johnny's raven hair was brilliantined back and his olive complexion radiated ruddy good health. He was fit, vigorous, handsome as the bloody devil himself, at forty-seven years old. He wore a double-breasted bespoke suit in gray flannel, and bespoke shoes as well. When he smiled, the sky lit up in the pure glowing radiance of it. Everybody loved Johnny. It was hard not to love Johnny. He'd fought in the Great War, the Troubles in Ireland, where he'd learned his dark skills, and since 1925 had worked his violent magic on these shores. Men wanted to drink with him, women to sleep with him. What an odd glitch it was that a man so gifted by God had this one little thing: he liked money that others had earned, in large piles, and if someone or something got in his way, he had not the slightest qualm about touching the trigger of his Thompson and eliminating them with a squirt of death. It never occurred to him to feel remorse. His mind wasn't built that way. He had killed thirty-nine men, most of them officers of the law or bank or plant security, or German soldiers or British troopies but occasionally the bullets flew beyond targets and struck the innocent. It didn't matter to him, not one little bit.

"So tell me, Owney, tell me about these dark lads, and we'll get to getting you your money's worth."

Owney explained details of the shoot-out at Mary Jane's, confessing puzzlement at the victory of the men with the lesser guns over the men with the greater guns.

"See, your problem was your ambush site," said Johnny. "The Maxim's a fine gun, as all hearties found out in the Great War, but she's got to have a wide field of fire and has to be laid just right. Shooting down some stairs don't do a fella no good at all; it minimizes what you've got going for you. I can see you've never planned an ambush against trained men, eh, Owney? Nor had that border reiver scum from the mountains."

"I guess not."

"Your hero fellow kept his cool and understood that the ballistics of his weapon allowed him to shoot through wood. He waited till the belt clinked dry, then he enfiladed the stairwell. From that point you were doomed. As Herman will tell you when he gets here, properly deployed, pound for pound there's not a better gun about than a Browning Automatic Rifle."

"So what are we going to do? I'm running out of time. I've threatened to bomb Niggertown to keep them from raiding, but only the cowboy cares about the niggers. Sooner or later, that threat will lose its meaning and even he will have to go ahead. And if they get the Central Book, the money dries up fast, and I am in a world of trouble."

"That would be the checkmate move, then?"

"Yeah, and we could do everything right and on the last day, they could hit that joint and we'd be fucked. So we have to act fast."

Johnny's face fell into a density of concentration. He thought out loud.

"The chances of bumbling into them in another raid are remote. The chances of jumping them in their home ground are also remote.

Plus, difficult to handle. No, we've got to find a prize so sweet they'll not be able to resist. We've got to lay a trap so deep they won't ever suspect. We've got to find something that makes them unbearably agitated."

"And what would that be?"

Johnny said, "This Becker. You say he likes to get his picture in the paper?"

"He does."

"Then it's got to be something with splash. Something with style. Something that would get the *New York Herald Tribune* out here and *Life* magazine."

"Yes."

"So much glory that Becker will not be able to turn it down."

Owney thought hard. He didn't have a clue.

Johnny looked at him with impatience.

"Come on, goddammit. Use that thinker you got up there. You're like the Brit generals during the war, you can only think about moving straight ahead."

"I just don't—"

But Ralph was suddenly there, hovering.

"Ralph?"

"Mr. Maddox, Vince Morella is here."

"Christ!" said Owney. "What the hell. It can't wait?"

"He's very insistent."

"Jesus Christ!" He turned to Johnny. "Wait a second. These Arkansas boys, they can't get *nothing* straight."

He rose, went into the living room where Vince Morella stood, holding hat in hand nervously.

"What the fuck, Vince. I'm inna middle of an important meeting."

"Sorry, sorry, sorry, Mr. Maddox, but I think you'd want to hear this right away."

"So?"

"I get to the club this morning, go into my office, and there's a guy sitting there. He's already *in*. He says he wants to meet with you."

"Jesus Fucking Christ, I told you—"

"You don't get it. He's one of them."

Owney's eyes narrowed suspiciously.

"He's—"

"He went on all the raids, knows who they are, where they're quartered, how they operate, what they'll do next, how they communicate. He'll give it all to you!"

Owney's eyes narrowed. Now this he finally understood.

"For money, eh. Somebody always sings for the moolah."

"Not for money. That's why he had to see *you*. For something only you can give him. He's a college kid. His name is Frenchy Short."

Night Heat

CHAPTER

37

Both men were grouchy, dirty and cranky. Road dust clung to them in a gritty film. A shower would be so nice, a sleep. This was their third trip to Hot Springs from Texas in as many days, with the bitterness of a bad scene with Becker and the sad scene with Frenchy Short yesterday. And today was a high killer. Above, the sun beat down, a big hole in the sky, turning the sky leaden and the leaves heavy and listless. No wind puffed, no mercy, as if they'd brought some godforsaken Texas weather with them.

Dressed in farmer's overalls with beaten-up fedoras pulled low over their eyes and .45s tucked well out of sight, they sat on the front porch of the Public Bathhouse, that is, the pauper's bathhouse, at least in the shade. Other poor people—genuine poor people—lounged about them, too sick to look anything other than sick, come to Hot Springs for the waters of life, finding only the waters of—well, of water. The Public was the least imposing of the structures on Bathhouse Row, but it looked across the wide boulevard of Central Avenue at the Ohio Club.

It was a thin, two-story building, wedged between two others, the Plaza Building and the Thompson Building; its big feature was a kind of mock-Moorish gilded dome, completely fraudulent, which crowned the upper story, and a dormer of windows bulging out over the first-floor windows. It was in the Ohio that he and the old man had observed Mickey Rooney and his big-busted wife number two throwing away thousands of bucks in the upstairs craps game.

"That's going to be a hard place to bust," said D.A.

"I'd hate to do it at night when it's all jammed up," said Earl. "You got all the traffic and pedestrians, you got all the gamblers upstairs, you got Grumley riffraff with machine guns, you got Hot Springs coppers real close by. It could make Mary Jane's look like just the warm-up."

"Night's out. I don't think that bastard Becker would go for another night raid, especially downtown. Too many folks about."

"I'm thinking about five, before the avenue and the joint fill up. We run some kind of cover operation. Maybe we could get our hands on a fire truck or something. Go steaming in with lights flashing and sirens wailing, be in on them before they figure it out and once we get it, we have the place nailed. Nobody dies. We close down that place, we put the word out among the Negroes to watch real careful for strange white people in their neighborhoods."

The two men sat in silence for a while. Then the old man said, "Let's go get us a Coca-Cola. My whistle could use a bit of wetting."

"Mine too," said Earl.

They walked south along Central, came finally, after oyster bars and whorehouses baking emptily in the noonday sun, the girls still snoozing off a night's worth of mattress-backing, to a Greek place. They went in, sat at the fountain, and got two glasses of Coca-Cola filled with slivers of ice.

"It ain't the how of the raid," said D.A. "It's figuring out the why of it. We have to *justify* it. Short was right on that one."

"Maybe we lay up outside, pick up a runner, and sweat him. When we break him, we hit the place."

"But we got it all set up first? Don't like that. Also, Owney'd track down the runner and kill him and maybe his family as a lesson. I don't like that."

"No, I don't neither. Maybe we find someone who works in the joint who'd testify."

"Who'd that be? He'd become the number one bull's-eye in the town. Sooner or later, we move along. Sooner or later, he'd get it. Some Grumley'd clip him for old timey sake."

"Yeah, that's right. Maybe a Grumley. Find a Grumley to talk. Turn on his kin for a new start."

"But we ain't got no budget to finance a new start. We can't protect 'em. There's nothing we can offer that'll make a Grumley turn. Finally, them Grumleys hate us. We put eleven of 'em in the ground, remember? They might still come looking. It don't matter that Pap up and died hisself off. Flem don't have Pap's grit, but he's just as much a snake."

"We got to find out where they're weakest and attack 'em there."

"Give it to Owney, he knows his business. Ain't no 'weakest.'"

"He is a smart bastard. He's been running things a long time. Goddamn, I hate being this goddamn close and not getting it done."

"We'll get it done, Earl. One way, the other, sooner, later. We'll get it done. That I swear."

They drove back, the long, grueling three-hour pull through southern Arkansas down U.S. 70, through Arkadelphia and Prescott and Hope, making Texarkana by 4:00 and the Red River Army Depot by 5:00.

The boys were sitting outside the barracks, looking disconsolate. There was an Arkansas Highway Patrol truck and three Texas Highway Patrol cars. A group of Highway Patrolmen seemed to be running some kind of operation.

Earl and D.A. walked up.

"What the hell is going on?" Earl said.

"They come to git our guns," said Slim. "Got a piece of paper signed by the Arkansas governor, the Texas governor and a federal judge. Becker signed off on it too."

"Shit," said D.A., pushing past them. "What's all this about? Who's in charge here?"

"You'd be Parker?" said a tall Arkansas Highway Patrol officer. "Parker, I'm Colonel Jenks, commandant of the Arkansas Highway

Patrol. Sorry about this, but at ten this morning, I got a call from the governor's office. I went on over there and he'd evidently just chewed the hell out of poor Fred Becker and got him to issue an order. By eleven the governor's staff had taken it before a judge, and by noon they's on the phone, working out a deal with these here Texas boys. They want us to take charge of your heavy weapons and your vests. Y'all can still carry .45s, but—"

"Sir," Earl said to the commandant, "we try and do this work without a base of fire and we will end up in a pickle for sure. That's something I learned in the war, the hard way."

"I ain't saying what you done is bad. Nobody's had the sand to go face-on with them Hot Springs Grumleys and their out-of-town mobsters till you came along. But the governor's gitting heat from all sorts of folks, and that's how governors work. We serve at his pleasure, so we do what he says. That's the way it be."

"Earl," one of the boys called, "it don't seem right. How can we do this work if we don't go in well heeled?"

"Yeah," another said, "if we run into more Grumley bad boys with big ol' machine guns, what're we supposed to do?"

"You got the best pistol skills in the state," said Earl. "You will prevail. That I know."

But it disturbed him nonetheless.

"Can't we make some disposition so that if we get a big raid and it looks scary we can get our firepower back?" asked D.A.

"Sir," said Jenks, "you'll have to work that out with the governor. I can't settle it at this level. Your Mr. Becker will be the one to make that case."

"Only case he makes is to git his picture in the paper."

"I have to get these guns up to Little Rock tonight, and locked in the armory at State Police headquarters. As I say, it ain't my decision. I just do what I'm ordered to do. That's the way it be."

Now the guns came out: the Thompsons, looking oddly incomplete without magazines, three apiece under the arms of State Troopers. Then the Brownings, so heavy that a man could carry but one. Earl recognized, by a raw cut in the foregrip wood where he'd banged it against the doorjamb, the gun he'd carried as he walked down the hall, keeping up a hail of fire, Frenchy behind him, feeding him the magazines.

"Hate to lose that goddamn BAR," said D.A. "That's what keeps 'em honest."

"It ain't fair," screamed a boy, who turned out surprisingly to be Slim, the oldest and the most salty. "They can't be asking us to continue on these raids without no fire support. That ain't right."

"It ain't right," said D.A. "I'll be talking hard with Becker. We'll get this worked out."

"But we—"

"It's not—"

"We depend on—" came a tumble of voices.

"Shut it off!" Earl bellowed, silencing his own men and shocking the Highway Patrol officers. "Mr. D.A. said he'd work on it. Now just back off and show these boys you're trained professionals who obey your officer." That was his command voice, perfected over hard years on parade grounds and harder years on islands, and it silenced everyone.

"Thanks, son," said Colonel Jenks. "Can see you're a man who knows his stuff. Bet I know which one you'd be."

"Maybe you do, Colonel," said Earl.

"Heard nothing but good things about the ramrod down here. They say he's a heller."

"I do a job if it comes to that."

"Good man," the colonel said, as if marking him for future reference.

A sergeant came to D.A.

"Sir, you'll have to sign the manifest. And what about the carbine?"

D.A. scratched his chicken-track signature on the paper and said, "What carbine?"

"Well sir, in the original manifest you had six Thompsons, three BARs, six Winchester pumps and six M-1 carbines. But you only got five carbines."

"Hmmm?" said D.A. He looked over at Earl. This was a mystery, as the carbines had never been deployed, they'd simply stayed locked up down here in Texas. Earl didn't like the carbine, because its cartridge was so light.

"We never used the carbine," said Earl.

"Well sir, it says you had six, but we only rounded up five."

"I don't have no idea. Any of you men recall losing a carbine?"

"Sir, we ain't touched the carbine since training."

"The carbines was never up in Hot Springs."

"Colonel Jenks, what do you want to do here, sir?" asked the sergeant.

Jenks contemplated the issue for at least a tenth of a second. Then he declared, "Call it a combat loss, write it off, and forget all about it. We don't have to make no big case out of it. It ain't even a machine gun. Now let's get out of here and let these men git going on their training."

CHAPTER

38

It took a day to set up through the auspices of a friend of his who was an FBI agent in Tulsa and knew who to call. Carlo ended up paying for it himself, because he knew there was no budget and that D.A. would never approve. But he had to know.

He had never flown before. The plane was a C-47, though now, as a civilian craft, it had reverted to its prewar identity as a DC-3. It left Tulsa's airfield at 7:30 A.M. and flew for seven hours to Pittsburgh. The seats were cramped, the windows small, the stewardess over-worked. He almost threw up twice. The coffee was cold, the little sandwich stale. His knees hurt, his legs cramped. In Pittsburgh, the plane refueled, exchanged some passengers for others, and finally left an hour later. It arrived, ultimately, at National Airport just outside Washington, D.C., at around 4:00 in the afternoon.

He took a cab to the Headquarters of the United States Marine Corps, at Arlington Annex, in Arlington, Virginia. It was a set of wooden buildings, shabby for so grand an institutional identity, behind barbed wire on a hill overlooking the capital. In the distance, a white rim of buildings and monuments could be seen, grandly suggesting the greatness of the country it symbolized, but out here, across the river, the warriors of that country made do with less. The only concession to ceremony was the presence of ramrod-stiff Marines in dress blues outside, keepers of a temple, but inside, he found no temple at all. It was merely a busy workplace of men in khaki humming with purpose. It took a bit, but finally someone directed him to the Personnel Records Branch of G1 Division, HQ USMC. A sergeant greeted him in the foyer, and he identified himself and was led in, past offices and work bays, to an inner sanctum; that is, what appeared to be miles and miles of shelves stacked with the manila envelopes that represented each of the men who'd worn the Globe and Anchor in this century. The sergeant took Carlo to a reading room, windowless and bright, where what he had requested had been put out for him.

"What time do you close?" he asked.

"Officer Henderson, we don't close. We're the Marine Corps. Take your time. We run a twenty-four-hour department here."

So Carlo, exhausted and bewildered, at last sat down alone with the ultimate clue in his quest.

Finally, shaking slightly—the effect of the hard day's travel, or his own apprehension?—he opened the battered file that contained the service record book of SWAGGER, EARL L., FIRST SGT., USMC (RET.)

With the service record book, he was able to watch the man progress from lowest grade to highest, across three continents, an ocean and the mightiest war ever fought. The book was a compendium of places lost or destroyed or forgotten about, of judgments tempered and faded but always accurate, and finally of obscure institutional relics and random facts, including fingerprints taken on enlistment, civilian occupation and education, prior service, promotions and reductions—including examinations and recommendations for advancement, pay matters including travel allowances; military justice including time lost through misconduct; inventories of residual clothing and equipment; enlistment and reenlistment data with supporting medical records; foreign and sea service; commanders' ratings on conduct and efficiency; marksmanship scores; specialist qualifications; and awards and decorations. It was in bad penmanship, in a language whose intricacies and nuances he didn't understand. But he did start noticing things: he noticed right away, for example, a discrepancy in birth dates. Earl joined the Corps in Fort Smith, in 1930, claiming to be seventeen, but Carlo now knew he was born in 1915; he was two years underage. That spoke of a boy in a hurry to get away from what Carlo knew was the hell of his life.

The book followed the boy from his first days as a recruit at the brutal Parris Island of 1930. Many of the scores were meaningless to Carlo, for they referred to tests he didn't understand in a numerical progression he also didn't understand. But he understood simple marksmanship, and noted that the boy shot expert in all weapons. PVT SWAGGER, E.L. was then sent to Sea School, at the Norfolk Navy Yard in Virginia, and then deployed as a rifleman to the Fifth Marines in Nicaragua, working with the Nicaraguan Guardia Nacional in something called M Company, with an enthusiastic unofficial endorsement from the officer in charge, one Captain Lewis B. Puller. "PFC Swagger shows natural talent for combat operations and is particularly proficient in running a fire team of four men in jungle patrol." Then it was two years on the old *Arizona* as a rifleman, later squad leader of the Marine Detachment aboard that craft whose wreckage now still oozed oil in Pearl Harbor. But rank was slow to come by in the tiny prewar Corps, even if his recommendations were uniformly excellent and each commanding officer would write, in what appeared to be an unusual number of unofficial letters of recommendation, something like, "This Marine shows leadership material and should be encouraged to apply for Officer Candidate School or even an appointment to Annapolis and a regular commission." But Earl never went; he just seabagged on, finally promoted to corporal and assigned as a squad leader, then an acting platoon sergeant, with the Fourth Marines in China, from June of 1935 until June of 1939. He was in the Marine Detachment at Balboa in the Panama Canal Zone as a straight-up three-striper when the war broke out.

Carlo read it quickly, almost afraid of what he might find. But the record was uncontaminated with sin. Earl was assigned as a platoon sergeant in Company B, Third Battalion, Second Marines, where he served from February of 1942 until August of 1944. In September of

1942, he landed on Guadalcanal. That was a long and hard campaign. It won him his first Silver Star, and a recommendation for a commission (turned down). After a period of reorganization and retraining in Wellington, New Zealand, he went into it again—Tarawa. There, he was a platoon sergeant, and after the horrible fuckup at Red Beach One, where the Higgins Boats foundered on the offshore reef and he had to wade ashore with his men, taking heavy fire every step of the way, he got his most severe wound, a chest shot from a Japanese sniper on D plus two. That was followed by a four-month recuperation. Nineteen forty-four was the year of Saipan and Tinian, and two more attempts to commission him. His refusal to become an officer was beginning to irritate some, as the battalion executive officer wrote tartly: "Platoon Sergeant Swagger again shows exemplary leadership skills, but his continual refusal to accept the higher responsibility of a field commission is troublesome; he's clearly capable of such responsibility, being not merely aggressive in battle but shrewd in organizational details; but he seems to reject the commission on some vague psychological ground, because his father was a (decorated) officer in the AEF in World War I, and he doesn't want to be of the same 'ilk' as his father. He does not explain this very coherently, but the feeling is clearly deep-seated and passionately held. When the war is over, it is highly recommended that this valuable Marine be offered some kind of counseling to overcome his resentment of the officer class. Meanwhile, he performs his duties with outstanding diligence." In November of 1943, he was promoted to gunnery sergeant and reassigned to Company A, Third Battalion, Second Marines, Second Marine Division, during retraining and reorganization at Camp Tarawa, Hawaii. He served with A/3/2 in the Saipan and the Tinian campaigns.

In September of 1944, he was reassigned to 28th Marines in the new Fifth Marine Division, whose cadre comprised veteran NCOs from earlier Pacific battles. He was also promoted to first sergeant of Company A, First Battalion, 28th Marines. February of 1945 was Iwo Jima. The medal citation was there and Carlo imagined Earl charging up that hill in a fog of sulfur and volcanic grit and gunsmoke, destroying those machine-gun positions, finally entering that concrete bunker for a final up-close battle with the Japs. He killed forty-odd men in a minute and a half, and saved the lives of 130 Marines caught in the bunker crossfire. Amazing. The big one. But he was wounded seven times in that engagement. A severe bout of malaria, accelerated by combat fatigue, didn't help. He was sent to a training command in San Diego in June of 1945, after release from the hospital.

In October of 1945, he was declared unfit for further duty because of his wounds and a disability in his left wrist, which still bore several pieces of shrapnel. He was retired medically with a small pension, in addition to receiving his 52-20 severance package (twenty bucks a week for a year) from the government. In February of 1946 the paperwork on his Medal of Honor citation finally was approved, and in late July of 1946 he was given the award in a small ceremony at the White House.

"Excuse me," he yelled out to the sergeant, "could you explain something to me."

"Yes sir." The young man ducked in.

"When I was in the Air Corps, we called it 'AWOL,' absent without leave. Is there a Marine equivalent?"

"Yes sir. We call it UA, meaning unauthorized absence."

"Now, this particular man, would a record of his UAs be kept here? I don't think I saw any."

"Yes it would. Theoretically. The company first sergeant maintains the service record book. So how diligent the first sarge was, that would determine how diligently the records are kept. Do you have a date or anything?"

"Yes. Third week in January, 1942."

The young man leaned over the service book and began to rifle through the pages.

"Looking here, I can say definitely he was with the Second Marines at New River, North Carolina, before the Second left for the West Coast, departed for the Pacific in July from San Diego and landed on Guadalcanal in September. He was assigned to a platoon all that time. There's no Captain's Masts, no UAs, no disciplinary action of any sort. He was there every day."

"What about, you know, temporary duty? TDY we called it."

"In the Naval Services, it's TAD. No, it would be unusual for a ju-

nior sergeant to go TAD at that point in his career, and this one certainly didn't. He was too busy getting ready to kill Japs."

"Leave, none of that?"

"No, sir. Not during the third week of 1942. Wasn't much leave at
all given in the Marine Corps in 1942. He was on duty, on station, doing his job."

Carlo felt as if an immense burden had been lifted from him. Involuntarily, his mouth curled upward into a smile, bright and wholesome.
He felt himself blushing.

"Well, listen, you've been a big help. I'm very appreciative."

"Yes sir."

He couldn't stop smiling. Suddenly the world seemed beautiful. His
future was mapped out: he'd return tomorrow, the team would finish
up its raiding, they'd all go back to their departments, the experience
would mark him as someone special, and his career would just go on
and on. Not out of ambition was he pleased, but out of something else:
reverence. He saw what he was doing as divinely inspired. He was doing God's Will. It would be the Just Man who enforced both the Law
and the Word, living to standards set by the Book and in the flesh by
heroes like Earl Swagger; in their honor, he would live a life of exemplary conduct and—

"Of course," said the sergeant, "you might still want to check with
the Historical Section and see what was going on in the Second Marines that week."

After a night in a motel comprising three hours of desperately dead
sleep and three hours of fitful turning, Carlo took the cab back to the
Arlington Annex to find the G3 (Operations) Division of HQ USMC.
Operations was in another of the shambling wooden buildings that
were the center of the Marine empire. The building showed hard use:
it needed paint and air-conditioning and a general sprucing up; or it
needed tearing down.

He walked in, introduced himself and showed his badge, and was
accorded a professional respect he somehow felt he had yet to earn.
The FBI connection worked here too, and he went without trouble to

the second floor, to the Historical Section. In here, a narrative of the Second World War was being officially compiled by a number of civilians and Marine retirees. He was eventually turned over to a man in civilian clothes who was missing an arm, referred to by everyone as Captain Stanton.

"What I need," he explained, "is the regimental record—I guess it would be a logbook or something—of the Second Marines, during the third week of January in 1942. Specifically, Company B, Third Battalion."

"They were mostly still stateside then," said Captain Stanton. "Probably still at New River. Sometime in there they would have moved to the West Coast. They didn't deploy until July for the 'Canal.

"I understand that, sir. I just have to see what was going on in the regiment that particular week. That company, that battalion if possible."

"Okay," said the captain. He retreated to the stacks, while Carlo waited, his suit rumpled, feeling sweaty and somehow uncomfortable. The office smelled of cigarette smoke and dead heroes. In stalls men consulted volumes, maps, made phone calls and took notes. Light streamed through the sunny windows, illuminating clouds of smoke and dust; the atmosphere seemed alive with particles and gases. Was this all that was left of all those young men who'd gone ashore on the beachheads of the Pacific, so many of them dying virgins, shot down in warm water or in cloying sand, never having felt the caress of a woman or the joy of watching a son take a first step? Now, they were here: in a large government-green office, full of old journals and files in cabinets and maps, where their sacrifice and heroism was reduced to words to be published in dusty volumes that nobody would ever read. Wake-IslandManilaGuadalcanalBetioSaipanGilbertsMarianasTarawaIwo-Okinawa. It all came to this, the lighting of cigarettes, the rumpling of paper, the tapping of the typewriters, the scratching, so dry, of pen on paper. There should be a Marine in dress blues, playing taps endlessly to salute the boys of the broken palms and blazing sunsets and long gray ships and jungles and coral reefs and volcanic ash. This room housed it all, and somehow there should be more, but this is all there was. It was another reliquary of the bones of martyrs, some of them so young they didn't know what the word martyr meant.

"Henderson? You okay?"

He looked up to see Captain Stanton, holding a thick volume under his one good hand.

"Yeah, sorry."

"You were sort of talking to yourself."

"I'm sorry. They deserve so much more than this room."

"Yes, they do. That's why we have to get it all written down, so that it'll be recorded forever. Anyhow, here's the logbook of the Second Marines, January through April, 1942."

Together, they paged through it, finding old orders, directives from command and staff meetings, training schedules, disciplinary records, and a narrative of day-by-day operations. It was the collective diary of thousands of men preparing for a desperate, endless war at the end of the world.

"15 Jan 41: 2nd Marines receives deployment orders from HQ-USMC for Camp Pendleton, California, prior to shipment overseas in Pacific Battle Zone. Operations ordered to commence planning of the redeployment."

Then, for the week of January 17 through January 24, "Elements of 2nd Marines in transit to West Coast"; it continued until early February.

"They were on the move for three weeks?" asked Carlo.

"Son, a Marine regiment is part of a division, which is a formidable amount of men. We're talking about a headquarters element, three infantry regiments of about 3,100 men each, an artillery regiment, an engineer regiment, a tank battalion, a special weapons battalion, a service battalion, a medical battalion and an amphibious tractor battalion. They were understrength, of course, but a division carried a paper strength of 19,514 men. So we're talking about a unit that's folded into a larger unit of at least twelve to thirteen thousand men. Plus all the vehicles and equipment, including the guns. It all has to work together. It's no small thing."

Carlo sat there. A worm began to gnaw at his brain. He rubbed his hand against his eye but it would not go away.

"I'm trying to envision this."

"Envision chaos. Barely organized, confusing, messed up, full of mistakes. You're moving a large body of men and equipment. It's 1942, the war has just begun. Everybody's in a panic, nobody knows what's going to happen next. You're working on a railroad system that's just been converted to troop-carrying duties. It demands coordinating with the railways, assembling trains, picking routes, routing the trains in and around other military traffic and civilian traffic, the coming of blackouts, the beginning of wartime regulation and austerity. The logistics are a nightmare. It's a mess, and none of the officers or NCOs have any real experience in it. Up till then the Marine Corps has pretty much moved only at the battalion level. Now you're moving in units of 12,000 men."

Carlo nodded, let it sink in.

"I take it you were there."

"In 1942 at that time I was a staff sergeant in the First Marines. We were also at New River but we didn't move west until July. Our baptism of fire came later, at Bougainville. It would help if I knew what this was about."

"It's a security clearance and a problem has come up. I'm trying to account for a sergeant's location in the third week of January. I already know he wasn't UA or on temporary duty or leave. He was officially with the regiment at that time."

"That should settle it, then."

"What were the routes taken west, do you recall?"

"Ah, there were many trains, many routes, depending. Since we were staging for the Pacific at Pendleton, outside of Diego, we usually went a southern route. Let's see. In my case, the train went from New River through Nashville, down to Little Rock, on to Tulsa, down through New Mexico and Albuquerque. We were hung up at Albuquerque a week due to a coal shortage, and then on into Diego."

Little Rock!

"Goddamn!"

Goddamn!

It was the first time in his life of virtue and service that he could remember swearing.

"You look like I just hit you between the eyes with a poleax, son."

"Let me ask you this. Is this theoretically possible? A guy has been in ten years. He's a sergeant. He's been around, in China, Nicaragua and the Zone. He's well-liked, even beloved. He knows all the other sergeants and all the junior officers and they know he really can do his job well. Now his unit is moving west by train, in that huge mess you described earlier. At some place—say, Little Rock—he jumps the train. He's from Arkansas, he has some family business to attend to before he goes to war. It takes him about a week, maybe less. He gets it done, heads back to Little Rock. Sooner or later another train bearing Marines comes through. He puts his uniform back on so he can mingle with them easily enough, and maybe he knows some of them and they know who he is. So he gets out to San Diego a week late. It's not that no one has noticed, it's just that they know this guy will be back, and when he quietly shows up one day, that's that. Nothing is said about it. I know it's against regulations, but this is a combat guy, the best, no one wants to give him any trouble, it's a sergeant kind of thing, something sergeants would let other sergeants get away with. Is that possible? Could that happen?"

"Theoretically, no. We do take attendance in the Marine Corps every morning at muster. But . . ."

"Everyone knows that when they go up against the Japs, this is the guy they want around in a big way. He's got leader and hero written all over him in letters a foot tall. And he's probably going to die in the Pacific. Guys like him don't come back from wars, unless it's by some wild statistical improbability."

"The truth is, what you describe, is it possible? Son, it's more than possible. It probably happened a lot. When we shipped out, we knew we weren't coming back. I did it myself."

CHAPTER

39

He looked like a kid in a movie, one of those things with Dick Powell where everybody sang in a real trilly voice, and the women's hair was all marcelled and they wore diaphanous gowns.

They didn't make movies like that anymore, but that's what the kid looked like.

"You're kind of young for this shit, aren't you, kid?" asked Owney.

Frenchy sat in an office inside the corrugated tin of the Maddox warehouse way out on the west side of town. He'd been cooling his heels with a mob of surly Grumleys who looked as if they'd just as soon eat him raw as oblige him by letting him live. They yakked at each other in Arkansas hill accents so dense and fourteenth-century, even accent-master Frenchy couldn't quite figure them out. They also spit a lot, the one thing about this godforsaken part of the country he could never get used to.

He wore gray flannels, a blue blazer with the Princeton crest, blue Brooks shirt, a yellow ascot and saddle shoes. And why not? What else would a man wear for such a ceremonial event? Overalls? He'd secretly sworn never to wear overalls again. That store-bought suit he had worn every day as one of Earl Swagger's boy commandos? That thing should be burned.

"I'm twenty," he said. "I have very smooth skin, which makes me look younger. My mother says it makes me look like a girl. Do you think it makes me look like a girl?"

"Is this some kind of fucking joke? Are they tryin' to pull my leg?"

"My, nasty, aren't we? They said you liked to pretend to upper-class manners but were really pretty crude underneath. I guess they were right."

"He's got you there, boyo," said Owney's companion, an Irish movie star who looked too much like Dennis Morgan for anybody's good.

"Sir, I don't believe I've had the pleasure," said Frenchy.

"You know who I am, kid."

"I'm Walter Short, of Williamsport, Pennsylvania. You can call me Frenchy, all my friends did, that is, back when I had friends, and even that wasn't for very long. And you would be—?"

"Ain't he but a charmer, Owney," said the Irishman. "Aye, he's a lad, I can tell. It ain't no joke to this one. He's got the look of a gentleman schemer to him, I can see it on him. It's a Brit thing. They love to look you in the eye and go all twinkly on you before they pull the bloody trigger."

"Never you fucking mind who he is," said Owney to Frenchy. "You sing, buster, or you won't be a happy kid much longer. You convince me you got the goods."

"Sure. Let's see: the leader of the outfit is a famous ex-FBI agent named D. A. Parker, one of the old-time gunfighters of the '30s. Killed a lot of bandits, they say."

"Parker!" said Owney. "D. A. Parker! Who's the goddamned cowboy?"

"His name is Earl Swagger. He's more a Marine sergeant than a police officer. Lots of combat experience in the Pacific. Won some big medals. Unbelievably brave guy. Scary as hell. You don't want him mad at you. Oh, yes, you already know that. He *is* mad at you."

He smiled.

"Earl and D.A. really are splendid men. You'd never stop them with those hillbillies you've got changing tires in the garage. If that's the best you've got, I'd suggest a career change."

"Cut the crap, wise guy. Keep talking."

"I'll tell you so much for free," said Frenchy. "You go check it out while I go out and get some dinner. Then, tonight, I'll tell you what I want from you. When I'm convinced you can give it to me, then I'll give you what you want."

"Son, Mr. Owney here could have his boys squeeze it out of your high fanciness in a few minutes of dark, sweaty work, you know."

"The funny thing is, he couldn't. He could beat me for a year and I'd never tell. I know what I'm doing and I know how the game is played. You don't scare me."

"Look at the balls on that one, Owney," said the Irishman, amused. "Lord, if I don't think he's telling some kind of truth. He don't always tell the truth, but this time he is. And he'd take what you give him, Owney. He's a smart one, and he's willing to risk it all to win what he wants. Give the little pecker that."

"Kid," said Owney, who had a nose for such deceits, "why? Why you doing this?"

This was the only time in the long night that Frenchy showed even a bit of emotion under his bravado. He swallowed, and if you looked carefully, you might see a brief, ashamed, furious well of tears in his bright eyes.

But then he blinked and it was gone.

"He should have done more for me. They all should have done more for me. I got a letter. A fucking letter."

And then Frenchy told them everything he could about the raid team except where it could be found and where it would strike next.

Once the original breakthrough had been made, it didn't take long. Owney called F. Garry Hurst with the names Earl Swagger and D. A. Parker. Garry Hurst called associates in Little Rock and within three hours Owney had in his hands files, complete with photographs, that verified against Owney's own memory and the testimony of the two managers who'd seen them the identity of his two antagonists. The picture of D.A. came from a 1936 issue of *Life* magazine, called "The Fastest Man Alive," in which then FBI agent D. A. Parker drew against a time-lapse camera with a timer and was clocked at a move from leather to first shot in two tenths of a second. Among the pictures, one showed the then much younger man holding a tommy gun and looking proud at the final disposition of the Ma Barker gang in Florida. Another revealed that he'd been a member of the team that had brought down Charlie "Pretty Boy" Floyd in Ohio. In a last picture, the man stood tall and lean and heroic as the great J. Edgar Hoover pinned the Bureau's highest award for valor on his chest. In a few years, fearing that he was growing too famous, Hoover would fire him, as he fired the great Melvin Purvis.

The Swagger picture appeared in the *Arkansas Democrat Times:* the Marine, ramrod-straight, in his dress uniform, as the president of the United States put a garland of ribbon and amulet around his neck, the Medal of Honor. Once it would have been the biggest news; by the time of the photo, July of 1946, that is, three months ago, just before all this began, it had only played on an inside page.

"Fuckin' Bugsy didn't know what he was up against," said Owney. "That guy's a war machine. Bugsy's lucky he didn't get himself killed. And I am unlucky he didn't kill Bugsy for me."

"And Earl Swagger is unlucky," said Johnny Spanish. "If we don't kill the poor boyo, then sure as Jesus Bugsy will."

· · ·

Frenchy was back from dinner, looking extremely pleased with him-self. The two men awaited him in the upstairs office, but all the Grum-leys had been sent home. Only one lurked outside, with a pump shotgun, and he stepped aside for Frenchy.

Frenchy's mood was peculiar: he had no doubts, no qualms, and he felt, at least superficially, good, even well. But he was aware that he'd crossed some kind of divide and that it really was tricky on this side. He needed to maneuver very carefully here, and keep his goal in mind, and not get hung up. He had to get out of here with something other than just his skin: he had to get something positive, something that would take him where he wanted to go.

At the same time, though he didn't feel it, a pain lurked somewhere. It left traces, like tracks in the snow, as now and then odd images floated up out of nowhere to assail him: how Earl had saved his life when he fell forward into Carlo's line of fire during the training, the rage he felt when he wasn't named first man on the entry team, the oddest sense of happiness and belonging he'd begun to enjoy on the raid team. It was so strange.

This time, Owney was more respectful and less suspicious. He seemed like a colleague. He sat at the desk smoking a cigar and the Irishman sat at his side. Frenchy could see a *Life* magazine article with D.A.'s picture in it and a newspaper clipping of Earl. Drinks were offered, twelve-year-old Scotch whiskey. Frenchy took a cigar and lit it up.

"It checks out, old man," said Owney, who had suddenly trans-formed himself into a stage Englishman. "But the problem, my new friend, is that it's not enough. Most important: where are they? Second most important: how can we get at them?"

"Oh, I've got that all figured out," said Frenchy, taking a big draft on the cigar, then chasing it with just a touch of the old, mellow Scotch. "I've designed something that's really sharp. I mean, *really* sharp." He raised his eyebrows to emphasize the point.

"Hadn't you best ask the lad his price, Owney?" asked the wise Irishman. "If it's cream he's givin' you, it's cream he'll want in return."

"What do you want, old man? Money? Filthy lucre? Judas got his thirty pieces, how many pieces do you want?"

"Money?" said Frenchy. "You're making me laugh, Mr. Maddox.

You have me confused with a greedy little schemer who wants to buy a new Ford coupe. I am *beyond* money."

"That makes him truly dangerous," said the Irishman. "He's bloody Michael Collins."

Frenchy leaned forward.

"I've done my homework. I know how big you were in New York."

"True enough, Owney was the tops," said the Irishman.

"You still know people back there. I mean, big people. Judges, attorneys, bankers. You know them or you know people who know them. People with influence."

Frenchy's blazing ambition filled the room. Or was it his despair or his courage? Whatever, it was almost a little frightening. He leaned forward even further, fixing the two of them with eyes so hot they unsettled. The two gangsters felt the power of his will and his inability to accept that he couldn't get what he wanted.

"I want you to get me a job with the government."

"Jesus," said the Irishman. "I'm thinking the boy wants to be an FBI agent! We should shoot him now."

"No," said Frenchy. "Not at all, not the FBI. It's called the Office of Strategic Services. It's the spies. It's very tony, very Harvard, very old law firm, very ancient brokerage. Most of the people who work for it went to the same schools and they sit and drink in the same clubs. They're special, gifted, important men, who secretly run the country. They're above the law. You think you're important? You think you're big? Ha! You only exist because you fulfill some purpose of theirs. You supply a need and so they let you survive. They answer to no one except their own cold conscience. They are the country, in a way. I want to be one of them. I *have* to be one of them."

"Jesus, Johnny," said Owney. "The boy wants to be a spy."

"You can do it. Earl and D.A. couldn't do it, because they're nothing in the East and no matter how great they are, nobody out East would notice or care. It's a club thing. You have to get into the club. I know you know people. I know you could make three phone calls and I've suddenly got someone going to bat for me. That's what I want."

"I could make a phone call."

"To an important man."

"I could make a phone call to an important man."

"He could go to bat for me. He could *make* them hire me. He could tell them—"

"Yeah, yeah," said Owney. "Wouldn't be easy, but it could be done. Your record, it's okay?"

"If you look close, it's spotty. But from a distance it looks good. Right schools, that sort of thing."

"So, what are you going to give me?"

"Okay," said Frenchy, taking a draft on a cigar. "I'll tell you how to get them."

"We're all ears, boyo," said the Irishman.

"You have to have good men, though."

"We have five of the best," said the Irishman.

"And you'd be one of them, Mr. Spanish," said Frenchy. "Or should I say Mr. John St. Jerome Aloysius O'Malley, armed robber extraordinaire, called Spanish for the olive cast to his skin. As I say, I do my homework."

He sat back, beaming.

"Ain't he the smart one," said Johnny. "A sly boyo, misses not a thing, that one."

"Kid, you're impressing me. You are making me happy. Now make me happier."

"I'm going to make you unhappier. They *know* where the Central Book is. Right now, they're trying to figure out how to hit it. So you don't have a lot of time."

This was Frenchy's specialty, as it turned out. He had a gift for conspiracy, but under that, and far more important, he had a gift for conviction. It was an almost autistic talent, to read people in a flash and understand how to beguile them along certain lines. He knew he had them now, and he even had a moment's pleasure when he realized he could play it either way: he could set these guys up for Earl or he could set up Earl for these guys. Any way he came out on top! It was so cool! He held his own life in his hands; he could do anything.

"How did they find it?"

"They didn't," said Frenchy. "They're not smart enough. *I* found it for them."

He quickly narrated his adventures at the phone company on Prospect Avenue.

"Fuck!" said Owney, devolving to East Side hoodlum. "That fucking Mel Parsons! I knew he was no good! I'll get that changed right away!"

"Barn door and all the animals fled, sport," said Johnny Spanish. "Listen to the boy here. He's smart, he's got some talent. See what he's got to offer."

"Okay," said Frenchy. "D.A. had us quartered at the Lake Catherine dam, in the pump house."

"Fuck!" said Owney, this elemental truth right under his nose at last revealed.

"But he won't go back there. He's smart. When he goes operational again, he'll find some other place. You'll never find it. And even if you do, what are you going to do? Go in with a thousand Grumleys, kill everybody? There'd be a huge stink, the governor would have to call out the National Guard. What does that get you?"

"Go ahead, sonny," said Johnny.

"So you have to ambush them. But you've got to do it in such a way that when they're finished, it's not going to be a scandal. It's going to be a joke."

"You have the floor, kid. Keep talking."

"What would be a temptation they couldn't resist? That Becker couldn't resist?"

"Now, see, Johnny was talking about that today too. You guys sure you ain't related?"

"Possibly his lordship's triple-great-grandfather fucked me triple-great-grandmother the scullery maid in her bog cottage in County Mayo in 1653," said Johnny.

"I don't think we ever had any Irish servants," said Frenchy, completely seriously. "Anyway, here it is: the Great Train Robbery."

There was a quiet moment. The two men looked at each other.

"Yeah, I thought so," said Frenchy. "That was the biggest thing that ever happened here. October 2, 1940. Five men take out the Alcoa payroll, kill four railway guards and get away clean with several million dollars. In the Hot Springs yard! Big news! Great job! It's even said that a certain Owney Maddox built the biggest casino in the world in 1941 on the proceeds of that job. It's also said that the great Johnny Spanish, the world's smartest armed robber, masterminded the job."

"Have another cigar, kid."

"Don't mind if I do."

Frenchy turned the lighting of the cigar into high drama. He sucked, he puffed, he drew the fire into the long, harsh tube of finest Cuban leaf, he watched the glow, he got it lit fiercely, and finally he expelled a huge cloud which rotated, Hiroshima-like, above his clever young head.

"If Fred Becker *stops* another train robbery and if he *nabs* the team that did it and that's the team that did the *first* robbery and he gets convictions on *them,* by God, then he's a national hero. He's the next governor. He's won what *he* wants to win. See, he only sees the gambling crusade as a vehicle. He doesn't believe in it a bit. It's just leverage to get him to the next level."

Owney appraised the young man. He had the gangster thing. Mad Dog had it. Bugsy had it. The Dutchman had it. It would change over the years to something mellower and deeper, into a strategic vision. But now, raw and unalloyed, this handsome upper-class boy had it in absolute purity: the ability to see into a situation and know exactly how to twist it, where to apply force, where to kill, how to make the maximum profit and get away with the minimum risk.

"So," continued Frenchy, "what you have to do is find some way to plant the possibility that another train robbery's being set up. That Johnny Spanish has been seen in town. Becker will go for it like crazy. He'll go for it fast and recklessly. That's his character, his defining characteristic, that ambition. He'll *order* Parker and Earl to intercede. He has to. They're the only men he's got he more or less trusts. You've got him. Only, when he lunges for the big prize, it's just bait concealing a hook, and you get him right through the gills. You lure the team into that railyard, and hammer it good."

He sat back, took another huge puff on the cigar. The smoke curled around his face, and he took a sip of the Scotch whiskey, but not too much, for he didn't want to blur his sharpness.

"I think he will make a fine agent," said Johnny Spanish. "He's pure Black and Tan, a night rider with a cunning for the devil's work."

"Why, that's the nicest thing anyone's ever said about me," said Frenchy, only partially ironic. He felt suddenly something he had never felt before: that he was home. He belonged.

But Johnny went on. "See, he's got so much upstairs, but in the end, he's a brick shy in the realm of experience."

"What's wrong?" asked Frenchy.

"A night ambush's a devilish hard thing to pull. I've been in dozens so I know. You get your own boys all mixed up with the other fella's. Everybody's shooting at everybody else. Then, you've got a big space like that railyard, with lots of room for maneuver, and it gets even more mixed up. And to put a final ribbon on it, see, they're wearing those damned vests, so they're not going down. By Jesus, boy, you've thrown the babe out with the bathwater. You've got to lure them into a contained area so there's telling what's them and what's us. That, or figure a way to let us see in the dark."

The smile began slowly on Frenchy's face. It flamed brightly, gathering force and power, becoming a ghastly apparition on its own. His smugness was so radiant it became a force of illumination almost on its own. He gloated like a man mightily self-pleased to discover that he'd arrived exactly where he intended all along.

"Old man," he said. "Consider *this.*" He reached into his pocket and removed a page clipped from the June 1945 *Mechanix Illustrated.* He unfolded it and gently put it on the desk before them.

UNCLE SAM CAN SEE IN THE DARK read the headline, above a picture of a GI clutching a carbine with what looked to be a spotlight beneath the barrel and one of the new televisions mounted atop the receiver, where a telescopic sight might otherwise go.

"It's called infrared. You beam them with a light they can't see. Only you can see it, through that big scope. They're in broad daylight, only they don't know it. You can hit head shots, and to hell with the vests. You pop a few of them, and the rest turn and run. You litter the place with carbine shells and you vacate. I can get you hundreds of carbine shells. Your police are there in seconds, report no sign of another outfit and that the raid team panicked in the dark and shot the shit out of each other. They're clowns, who's not to believe it? Since you control the cops, nobody will ever work the forensics. Hey, is it swell or is it swell?"

The phone rang.

"Goddamn!" said Owney, reaching for it.

"With Mr. Maddox's connections, it can't be too difficult to get a hold of a couple of these gadgets. You set up on a boxcar. The raid team comes into the yard. Bing-bang-boom! It's over."

"Yeah?" said Owney, into the receiver. "Goddammit, this better be impor—"

His rage turned to amazement.

"Be right there," he said. He turned back to his confederates.

"You work it out with him," he said. "You guys are a team, I knew that from the start. Tell me where to go to get those units and you'll have them next week. I've got to run."

"What's going on, boyo?" asked Johnny Spanish.

"A babe has just shown up and she'll talk only to me."

"Ah, Owney, many's the fine fella who's been undone by a lass. You wouldn't be that kind, would you now?"

"Not a chance. But this one's different," he said, closing the door. "It's Virginia Hill."

CHAPTER

40

"I hate to fly," said Virginia. "It hurts my butt. I hate those little johns. I hate it when you're stuck next to some joe who wants to tell you his life story."

"Virginia," said Ben, "you have to do it."

They were in the lounge at Los Angeles International Airport, sipping martinis. It was a very deco place, all chrome and brushed aluminum, filled with soaring models of sleek planes. Outside, through an orifice now being called a "picture window," planes queued up to take off on the long tarmac. They were silvery babies, their props buzzing brightly in the sun, most with two motors, some few with four. They looked, to Ben at least, like B-17s taking off for a mission over Germany, not that he had ever seen a B-17 or been anywhere near Germany while the shooting was going on.

Virginia took another sip of her icy martooni. The gin bit her lips and dulled her senses. She had to pee but she couldn't find the energy. Her breasts were knocking against her playsuit top, as if they wanted to come out and play. The drink made her nipples hard as frozen cherries. Her brassiere cut into her gorgeous mountains of shoulders. One shoe had slipped half off her foot. Every man in the joint was staring at her, or rather, at parts of her, but that was a necessary condition of her life. Ben's pal, a tough little mutt named Mickey Cohen, lounged nearby, as a kind of sentry. He sent out such vibrations of protective aggression that none would approach, or even admire too openly. Mickey looked like a fire hydrant on legs.

Airplane! Virginia Hill went by train, in her own stateroom, on the *Super Chief* or the *Broadway* or the *Century* or the *Orange Blossom Special!* Elegant Negroes called her "Miz Hill" when they served her Cream of Wheat in the morning, tomato aspic in the afternoon and steak in the evening, all with champagne. It was so nice. It was the way a lady traveled.

"Now tell me again what you're supposed to do."

"Oh, Christ," said Virginia. "Ben, I am not stupid. I know exactly what to do."

"I know, I know, but humor me."

"Ah. You bastard. Why do I put up with this shit?"

"Because of my huge Jewish pretzel."

"Overrated. You might try kissing me a little first, you know. It's not always so good when we try and do it in under ten seconds."

"I look at you and I just can't wait. When you get back, kisses, presents, dinner, champagne, petting. I'll pet! I swear to you on my yarmulke: petting!"

"You bastard."

"Please, Virginia. I am so nervous about this."

"Twenty hours or so, I get to Hot Springs. I check into the Arlington where I already have a reservation. I go to Owney. He of course has to have me up. I tell him I'm on a sort of a peace mission. Ben is worried that Owney will think he's shoehorning in on the Hot Springs business with this desert deal. I'm to assure him that that's not the case and that if Vegas even begins to look as if it might work, you, Ben, will invite him, Owney, out as a consultant and fellow investor. Owney is to consider Vegas his town as much as Hot Springs and as far as Ben is concerned, Owney will always be the father and Ben the son."

"Yeah, that's good. You can do that?"

"In my sleep, sugar."

"Okay, what's next?"

"Then I pressure him about the cowboy. Does he yet know who that cowboy is? Ben has been very embarrassed about what happened to him with the cowboy. It's gotten all around and Ben is being teased about it and being laughed at behind his back. Can Owney please hurry up and find out who the cowboy is?"

"Yeah."

"Ben, I'm telling you, even if he tells me I am not going to tell you. I will not be part of anything against that guy. He was just a guy who lit a cigarette. You swung first. He didn't know who you were."

"Virginia, how many times do I have to tell you? Forget the cowboy. It's got nothing to do with the cowboy. You don't have to protect the cowboy. But you have to put that move on Owney, because he will see through the father-son bullshit in a second, and will know you have a secret agenda. He will believe *that's* the secret agenda. We *want* him to believe that I'm obsessed with the cowboy, that I've sent you there to find out who the cowboy is. That way, he will discount what moves I'm making and consider me a noncompetitor, caught up in some grudge match that don't have nothing to do with business."

"Okay," she said, and took another toot on the martooni. "Too much vermouth. Bartender, gimme another, easy on the vermouth. And two olives."

"She likes fruit," Ben said to Mickey. Mickey didn't say anything. He hardly talked. He just sat there, working on his fire hydrant impersonation.

"Now," said Ben. "What's next? It's very important. It's the point!"

"The painting."

"Yeah, the painting. You might have seen it the first time, Virginia, if you'd been paying attention instead of rubbing your tits up against Alan Ladd."

"He hardly noticed, believe me. His old lady was watching him like a hawk."

"He noticed, I guarantee. Anyhow: look at it very carefully. Get its name. But remember *exactly* what it looks like. In fact, buy a little sketch pad and as soon as possible, sort of draw what it was like. Label the colors."

"This is stupid. I ain't no fancy artist like Brake."

"*Braque,* Virginia. It's French or something."

"This is secret-agent stuff. What do you think, sugar, I'm in the *O.S.S.* or something?"

"Virginia, this is important. It's part of the plan. Okay?"

"Okay."

"We have to know all about that painting. Go back a second time, and check your first impressions, all right?"

"I can't stand that creep *twice.*"

"Force yourself. Be heroic, all right?"

"*Ty!*" she suddenly shouted, rising.

A small, fine-boned dark-skinned man had entered the bar for his own bout of martoonis; Virginia waved, her voluptuous breasts undulating like whales having sex in a sea of the brand-new miracle product Jell-O.

Ben felt a wave of erotic heat flash through his brain as the two mighty wobblers swung past him, and turned to see the man toward which she now launched herself.

It was that movie star, Ty Power.

"Virginia," he said, "why, what a nice surprise."

"Martooni, honey lamb? Join us. You know Ben."

"Don't mind if I do, Virginia."

"How's the new picture? I hear it's swell."

Business. Ben sighed, knowing he had lost her for the time being. Then he retreated to his own private recreational world as Virginia pretended to be a movie star and Ty concentrated on her giant breasts and Mickey worked the fireplug routine. He thought about how he was going to kill the cowboy and enjoy every second of it.

41

Carlo finally reached D.A. late that night from a phone booth in Washington National Airport. It took a pocketful of nickels before the connection was finally established and even then D.A. was only at this mysterious number rarely. But this time he was, though he'd clearly roused himself from a deep sleep.

"Where the hell have you been?" the old man demanded.

"I'm in Washington, D.C. I was checking on Earl's Marine records."

"D.C.! Who the hell told you to go to D.C.?"

"Well sir, it's where the investigation took me."

"Lord. Well, what did you find out?"

"Sir, I have to ask you. Suppose—" He could hardly get it out. "Suppose there were evidence that suggested Earl killed his own father?"

"What?"

He ran his theory by D.A.

"Jesus Christ."

"Sir, if ever a man needed killing, it was Charles Swagger. Heck, it may even have been self-defense and the reason Earl didn't turn himself in was 'cause he knew he'd get hung up in Arkansas and miss the trip to Guadalcanal."

"You tell nobody about this. You understand? Nobody."

"Yes sir."

"If I find a chance, I may poke Earl a little bit on the subject. But that's all. Under no circumstances are we going to indict a man like Earl for something that can't be proven but by the circumstantial evidence in some forgotten Marine Corps file."

"Yes sir."

"Now you get on back here. We may be moving back into Hot Springs very shortly, and we need you."

"Yes sir."

Frenchy was gone. Carlo was still tending to a sick mother and would be back. Two others elected not to return, and after the heavy weapons were confiscated, Bear and Eff left the unit, saying the work was now too dangerous.

That left six men, plus Earl and D.A., no weapons, no vests.

"Y'all have to decide," Earl told them, "if you want to go ahead with this. We're operating on about two cylinders. You're young, you got your whole lives ahead of you. I don't like it any more'n the rest of you, but those are the facts and I ain't sending any man into action who don't believe in the job and his leaders. Anybody got any comments?"

"Hell, Earl," said Slim, "we started this here job, I sure as hell want to finish it."

"I will tell any man here," said Earl, "that all he has to do is come to me in private and say, thanks but no thanks, and I'll have you out of here in a second, no recriminations, no problems, with a nice letter from Fred C. Becker. We ain't fighting Japs. We're fighting gamblers and maybe it ain't worth it for men with so much yet ahead."

"Earl," said Terry, "if you could go through the war and come home and have a baby on the way, and still go on the raids, that's good enough for me."

"Well, ain't that peachy. You may feel different if you get clipped in the spine or get an arm shot off."

"Earl, we are with you. You lead us, dammit, we'll follow."

"Good," said Earl. "You goddamn boys are the best. Carlo will be back soon, that's another gun. Plus, we think we got a real fine idea on where to hit 'em where it hurts the most."

He issued orders: he and Mr. D.A. were going back to the Hot Springs area that night to find another place to hide the unit, and they'd send word for the others to join up in two days or so. For the rest, they were just to train under Slim's guidance, working with the remaining .45s and practicing their pistol skills.

. . .

Earl and the old man poked about in the far environs of Hot Springs, looking for a good hide. A trailer camp out by Jones Mills promised something, but was too close to the main road in the long run, and not far from a small casino and bar where surely the presence of a passel of hard-looking young men in the vicinity would be noted.

"A fine sity-ation where the law's scared of getting spotted or jumped by the criminals," fumed D.A. "Ain't never been in nothing like this before. Like *we're* the ones on the goddamned run."

They tried a hunting lodge near Lonsdale, to the north, cut over and tried a fishing camp at Fountain Lake, and still couldn't quite settle on a place. Off toward Mountain Pine was Grumley territory, so no further progress to the west was made; instead, they cut back, drove up the Ouachita toward Buckville; at last they located Pettyview, an agricultural community with almost no street life at all. A quick inquiry by Earl at the real estate office located a chicken farm, abandoned since before the war and up for rent. They drove out and found the site about the best: an old house, an empty barn, six long-deserted chicken houses, piles of bones and shit turned to stone out back, and no neighbor within four miles or so. The barn could easily enough conceal all the cars, lamps didn't have to be lit at night, and the place was available for $35 a month with an option to buy, month to month. D.A. forked over the $70 in cash, and they were in business again.

"Let's head back into town," said Earl. "I want to see how things are going in that colored whorehouse."

"Sure," said D.A. "Who knows what might come of it."

"Want to get there just after dark, so's nobody sees us."

Again D.A. said sure, and they drove on in silence, and D.A. fiddled with the radio, trying to line up on the Hot Springs KTHS beam, which played a lot of the jump blues and new bebop he seemed to have a strange affection for. He liked music with a little juice to it, he'd say.

"Say, Earl," said D.A., "been meaning to ask. Your daddy? He's killed in, where was it?"

"Mount Ida," said Earl. "Nineteen forty-two."

"They never caught who done it?"

"Nope."

"I'd think a man like you'd be gunning for whoever done it. Want to go back and track that dog down and make him pay."

"My daddy was looking to die, and had been for years. That mean boy done him and me and everbody else a damn favor. I'd give the bastard my big old star medal if I found him."

"Earl! Damnation! You shouldn't talk like that! He was your daddy, and a fine upstanding man. A law officer. Shot it out with some bad fellas. A hero in the Great War. I'm surprised to hear you talk as such."

"My daddy was a bully. He'd just as soon thump you as look at you, while he's sucking up to the quality. He always thought he was too good for what he got, and he was ashamed of who he was and who we were. He was a Swagger, from a long line of Swaggers descended from folks who settled this part of the country right after the Revolutionary War. I hope my ancestors weren't the bastard he was."

Bitterness seemed to swirl over Earl, as if he didn't like being reminded of his father. Now he was grumpy and gloomy.

"Could he have been somehow mixed up in any Hot Springs business?" asked D.A. "I mean, Owney and the Grumleys got a lot to answer for. Could that somehow be a part of it?"

Earl actually laughed, though there was a bitter, broken note to it.

"That's a goddamn hoot if I ever heard one! My old man was a drunk and a hypocrite and a whoremonger and crooked to boot and a bully. But see, here's the thing: nothing he knew was worth getting himself killed over. Absolutely nothing. He was a little man. Only thing he knew were all the back roads and paths in Polk County. He got that from all the hunting he done, and all the heads he put up on his wall. He cared more about them heads than he did his own children. What the hell could he have known to interest an Owney Maddox? Mr. D.A., you sure you're still on the wagon?"

"Okay, Earl, just asking. Thought I'd check it out."

Earl stopped.

He looked directly at D.A.

"Let me tell you something. Nobody knows a goddamned thing about my father, and it's best that way. Long gone, buried and forgotten. That's the way it should be. Now, Mr. Parker, I don't like to talk sharp to you, but I can't be talking about my father no more. It makes me want to drink too powerfully, you understand?"

"I understand, Earl, and I apologize."

"Fine. Now let's go check on them Negro people."

They drove on in silence, cruising down Central through South Hot Springs, turning right at the hard angle that was Malvern Avenue and following that up to the Negro section. Night had fallen and it was a jumping street, as usual, with the gals calling down from their windows and the crowds bustling into the beer joints, to run against the wheel or bet the slots. And when they got to it, it seemed even Mary Jane's had found some kind of new life. It was really thrumming, almost like some sort of tourist attraction like the alligator farm or the shooting gallery in Happy Hollow. It looked like old Memphis Dogood was having himself a time keeping up with his customers, and the lack of girls in windows suggested they were all making their night's nut and more on their backs.

D.A. drove around back, where it wasn't crowded, and parked the car. The two men got out, found the door open and a man out back smoking.

"You, boy," said D.A., "you go on in and find Memphis. You tell him some friends want to see him."

The boy looked at them sullenly, but then rose and obeyed. Soon enough three heavyset fellows escorted the large yellow whore called Marie-Claire out. She looked them over and then said, "It's okay."

"Where's your man?" asked D.A.

"Gone. They come git him. He ain't never comin' back. He in the swamp somewheres."

"Who got him?" asked Earl.

"White mens. Grumleys, mos' likely. Don't rightly know. They come by, tell him they need to see him. Thas all. A few days back. He ain't comin' home, I tell you."

Earl shook his head.

"Sister, maybe he just wandered off with another gal," said D.A.

"And leave his place? Memphis love this place, he ain't never gonna leave it 'cept to be underground, thas God's truth."

She glared at the old man, showing a surprising ferocity for a black woman.

"I think Maddox got to him. Grilled him, then dumped him. Or had somebody dump him, more his style," said Earl.

Then he turned.

"Sorry, sister. All this bad stuff come down on your place from white folks, sorry about all that. These are bad people and we're trying to clean it up and people get hurt sometimes. Very sorry."

"You was the one shot that Grumley hoozer had the gun to my throat, wudn't you?"

"Yes ma'am. That was me."

"Well, suh, tell you somethin' then. You want to know about Mr. Owney fancy-man Maddox? I know a man might could help you."

"Tell me, sister."

"Yes suh. Ol' man name Jubilee Lincoln. Live by hisself over on Crescent, little ol' house. Spirit call him late in life. He speak fo' God now, run the New Light Baptis' out his front parlor. You might wanna see him."

"Why's that?"

"He know about this. You go see him."

They got to the New Light Baptist Tabernacle half an hour later, finding it a wooden house that had seen better times in a run-down neighborhood that backed into the hills of East Hot Springs.

"Now, Earl, you s'pose that gal went to call Owney Maddox and the boys? And they're waiting for us in there?"

"Don't reckon," said Earl. "I don't see how she could help Owney after what he done to Memphis."

"Earl, you think of them as regular people, whose minds work just like ours. It ain't like that."

"Sir, one thing I do believe is that they are the same."

"Earl, you are a hard, strange fellow, I do declare."

They parked in an alley, and the dogs barked and scuffled. They slipped in a back gate and went up to the door and knocked.

In time, stirrings from inside suggested human habitation. Finally, the door opened a crack, and an old man's face peered out at them, eyes full of the fear that any black man would feel when two large white men in hats showed up knocking after dark.

"No need to worry, pop," said Earl. "Don't mean you no harm. Memphis Dogood's gal Marie-Claire gave us your name. We are what they call them Jayhawkers, trying to push the Grumley boys out of town."

The old man's face lit in delight suddenly. A smile beamed through the eight decades' worth of woeful wrinkles that had meshed his face into a black spider web and for just a second, he was young again, and believed in the righteous way of progress.

"Suhs, I just wanna shake your hand if I may," said the gentleman, putting out a cottony old hand that felt a hundred years old. Earl shook it, and it was light as a butterfly.

"Do come in, do come in. Lord, Lord, you are the righteous, that I know."

"We're just polices, sir," said Earl. "We do our job, and white or colored don't matter to us."

"Lord, that be a miracle on earth," said the old man.

He took them into his living room, which boasted a batch of old chairs and an altar. Up front was a cross. Two candles flickered in perpetual devotion.

"Lord, Lord," he said. "Lord, Lord, Lord."

Then he turned. "I am the Reverend Jubilee Lincoln, of the New Light Tabernacle. That was the niece of one of my flock them Grumleys done kilt. You remember?"

Earl did. The black girl. At the top of the stairs. Crying, her eyes pumping moisture. The shiver in her whole body, the shakiness in her knees.

"I'm sorry," said Earl. "We saved the ones we could. Wasn't nothing we could have done about that gal. It's messy work."

"Alvina was a wild gal, like her mama, suh," said the Reverend Jubilee Lincoln. "Her mama died in a 'hohouse too, sorry to say. The word of Jesus don't mean nothin' to either of them gals, and they paid the price. Her daddy is mighty upset too. That man ain't stopped cryin' all day, ever day, ever since."

"It does happen that way sometimes," said D.A. "Sin begets doom, often as not. But I'm sure she went to heaven. She was walking righteous toward the law when them Grumleys finished her."

"Amen," said the Reverend Jubilee Lincoln. "I want to thank you, suhs. You sent some Grumleys to hell, and specially you sent old Pap Grumley there too, even if you didn't shoot him yo'self. Ain't no white men take so much risk to save cullud gals, as I hear it."

"We tried, Dr. Lincoln," said Earl. "We saved most. It pains us we weren't able to save all."

He couldn't remember the girl's name even. But he remembered the bullets hitting her and how heavily she fell down the stairs and how she died in his arms.

"Them gambler fellas don't give no two nothin's 'bout no culluds," said the old man. "I cleaned toilets and spittoons in the Ohio for fifty years, till I couldn't bend over no more, and nobody never called me nothin' but Jubilee, and nobody never gave nothin' about any of mine or what happened to them, no suh. You two is the only righteous white peoples I ever met."

Earl took a deep breath. Then he looked at D.A. Then he said, "You say you were the janitor at the Ohio?"

"Yes suh. Yes suh, and a hard job it be, specially since they put all them damn phones inside and all them boys sit there takin' inf'mation and smokin' and spittin' and drinkin'. It was a mess most nights."

"Sir? Would you—?"

"Would I what, suh?"

"Would you sign a statement saying you saw a telephone room in the Ohio?"

"That Mr. Maddox and them Grumleys, they like to kill me dead if they find out."

"It would be dangerous, that's true," said Earl. "But we'd keep you protected until it's over."

"Suh, if them Grumley crackers decide to kill a Negro man in this town, nothin' but the Lord Almighty could stop 'em."

"Well sir, we're trying to end that kind of thing. End it for good and all."

The old man considered.

"I reckon, the good Lord's gonna call me to Glory anyhows, soon enough. Been around eighty-seven years. Hell, if it rile them Grumleys up, I be *glad* to do it!"

CHAPTER

42

You could not deny how beautiful she was. How a woman could have hair that red, maracas that melony, a waist that narrow, hips that round and legs that long was something on the level of the truly miraculous. Her lips were like strawberries, her eyes green and forever. Everywhere she went, it might as well be spa-ring.

"Virginia, you look so wonderful, darling," said Owney. "Cocktail?"

"Fabulous," said Virginia.

"Martini?"

"Absolutely dah-vine, sugar. Dip the olives in the vermouth, that'll be quite enough."

"Yes, my dear," said Owney. "Ralph, you heard Miss Virginia. Care to come out on the terrace? It's lovely and the view is quite spectacular."

"Of course. But I want you to show me around. What a fabulous place. It's so New York here. It's a little bit of New York in the heart of little old Arkansas, I do declare!"

"We try, darling. We try so hard."

"Oh, birds! I never would have guessed."

They walked to his pigeons, cooing and lowing in their little cages.

"They're adorable. So soft, so cuddly."

The word *soft,* pronounced by Virginia Hill above the two most perfect breasts in all of the white world, more beautiful than a Lana's, a Rita's, and Ava's, almost knocked Owney out. He needed a drink, and to focus hard.

Ralph arrived.

"Martini, m'dear?" said Owney. "Low on the vermouth, as you requested."

"Sweet as shoefly pie and apple-pan dowdy, I declare." She was really laying on her Scarlett O'Hara imitation with a trowel. She took the drink, winked at Owney through it, and . . .

Gulp!

"That was fabulous. Could Gin-gin have another winky?"

"Ralph, run get Miss Hill another winky."

"Yes sir," said Ralph.

Owney took Virginia to look at Central Avenue, hazy in the falling dusk sixteen floors below.

"Ain't it a sight? Sugar, that is some sight. Can't b'lieve it's in the same South where Miz Virginia done growed up. Winky makes Gin-gin feel good. Where Gin-gin growed up was pure Southern-fried dogshit, complete with them uncles couldn't keep them fingers to themselves."

She threw him a smile, and sort of scrunched her shoulders in a practiced way that seemed to crush the immense breasts together more poetically, as if to mount them on a silver platter and present them for his pleasure.

"Virginia, come sit over here, in the arbor."

They sat. Gin-gin's second winky arrived. Gulp!

"Another, Ralph."

"Yes, boss."

"Now Virginia, I suspect you have a message for me."

"Oh, Owney, you don't miss trick one, do you, honey?" She touched his leg and flashed a mouthful of teeth at him. He vowed that he'd have two of the best gals sent over from the best house tonight, and drown in flesh.

"Well," she said primly, "Ben is worried that . . ." and off she went, explaining how Ben worried that Owney would take offense at his, Ben's, plans in the desert, exactly as Ben had laid it out for her, with a few breathless giggles, and a few fleshy quivers of the mighty boobs thrown in here and there for emphasis.

"The thought"—Owney laughed when she was done—"that I would take *offense* at anything Ben did in Nevada, why, darling, it's almost *adorable*. Ben is my favorite son. Of all my boys, he's the best, the smartest, the quickest. I'm honored that he's chosen me as his hero and that he seeks to emulate me. Why, what he accomplishes in that desert will be a monument to me, and I'm touched. Virginia, sweetness, do you hear? *Touched.*"

"I sure am happy that you're so happy."

"I'm so happy too. I genuinely *appreciate* the way Ben keeps me informed. In our business, communication skills are *so* important. Why, good heavens, it's almost dinnertime. We'll dine at the Southern. There's a most amusing fellow you'll meet, a business associate of mine."

"Sugar, I can't wait. But can I run to the ladies' first?"

"Why of course, my darling. Wouldn't have it any other way."

She tottered off on her heels, that body that seemed to have stepped off a Liberator fuselage only barely shielded by the artful languor of her gown, her flesh undulating underneath its strictures.

Owney tried to think. He had no buzz on because his own martini was pure spring water. What does this mean? What is going on? What is the hidden message?

"Why, Owney. Why Owney, what on earth is *this?*"

Owney rose, walked in to see Virginia standing awestruck in front of his Braque.

"You didn't see that the last time, Virginia?"

"No, I was trying to make time with Alan Ladd to get a picture."

"Well, then, my dear, that is *art.*"

"There's something about it," she said.

"Ben said it reminded him of Newark."

Virginia burst out with a laugh so spontaneous it shook him.

"That silly!" she said. "That boy don't know a thing."

"No, I suppose not."

"Why's it all square?"

"It's called Cubism, darling. An early modernist movement, which broke down the convention of the narrative and the objective. It communicates the power of ideas over precise information. One can feel its power. Actually when Ben says 'Newark,' in his way he's not far wrong. Braque called it *Houses at L'Estaque.* But it's not about houses. It's really about the power of the universe and how its deepest secrets are hidden from us."

She looked at him all goo-goo-eyed.

"Why, honey, I never knew you were so smart! You sound like a regular Albert Einstein."

"It's not quite e=mc squared, but in its way it's an equally radical supposition, eh?"

He stood there, feeling the pride he drew from the picture. Knowing its secrets made him feel ineffably superior. None of the square Johns from the Hot Springs business community who frequented his soirees had an iota's worth of knowledge about this thing. At $75,000 it had been cheap for that thrill alone.

"Houses at L'Estaque," she repeated. "Ain't that a toot!"

CHAPTER

43

It was too hot for gardening—it was darned near too hot for *anything!*—but Junie wasn't the sort to be stopped by a little heat. So out she went, the baby huge inside her and kicking, her feelings a little woozy, but nevertheless determined.

Arkansas was not rose country. You couldn't get a good rose, at least not here, on this flat plain with its half-buried tubes of homes and no clouds in the sky and the sun hammering down, somehow bleeding the day of color. She hadn't even tried roses. She knew roses would fail in so much direct sunlight.

So she'd planted less aristocratic flowers in the little bed outside her hut on 5th Street in the Camp Chaffee vets village, a mix of hydrangeas, daisies, lilacs and lilies. Now some weeds had come into the garden and it was time to expunge them.

Of course she had no tools, and the dried earth was too hard to attack with a spoon, and so she rooted around and found a ghoulish Jap bayonet that Earl had brought home from the war. It had a long, black blade, a truly horrifying thing, but she put it out of her mind that it had once been used to kill men, and insisted to herself that it was only a tool. With its smooth sharpness, she could penetrate into the soil deeply, twist vigorously and uproot the ugly scruff weeds that had seemed to come up almost overnight.

It wasn't a big job and wouldn't have been beyond her in any circumstances except these, where the heat just pummeled her. But she worked onward, through her discomfort, through her sweat, and in an hour had culled most of them. But her back ached. And her feelings of wooziness suddenly increased.

So she sat back for just a second, wiped her brow, and gathered strength for the last few weeds.

Possibly a mistake. As soon as she did, she looked up. Life was livable as long as you simply concentrated on what was just ahead of you, and let your faith and your love steer you, and did your duty. That she knew.

But, looking up, she confronted a bigger picture: the rows and rows of Quonsets gleaming dully in the sun, lit up now and then with a wife's attempt to brighten them (as she had) with flowers. The attempts were heroic and doomed. The huts were still government housing, with laundry on lines that ran between them, hardscrabble, almost grassless dirt that lay in the lots, dusty gravel streets.

Would they ever get out?

What about the boom? Would it ever reach them and take them somewhere? But not if Earl was dead in some horrid battle for nothing against gangsters.

Don't think that, she warned herself. She had a deep belief in God, country and her husband, and would never allow herself any willing subversion. But later, more and more, evil thoughts had been creeping into her brain.

Is this it? Is this what I get? What about all the jobs that were supposed to open up after the war, the explosion in industry and finance, construction and communication? Shouldn't it somehow be for the men who'd fought the hardest, like her Earl? Instead, is he going to throw his life away for nothing?

The man who was her husband was still a considerable mystery to her. He didn't like to talk about the war or his past, but they deviled him savagely. He was a good man, an honest man, but he had a reservoir of melancholy deep inside him that would not come out. When he gets on his feet, she thought, it will be all better. But he was on his feet now, and what he loved best had nothing to do with her, but only with other men, some kind of mission, something that took him so far away not just in emotion but in distance. It would involve guns and killing. He loved her, she knew. She didn't doubt it, not a bit of it. But the question remained: what good was that kind of love, because it wasn't the love of somebody there, somebody to be depended on. It was love as an idea, not a messy reality, love from afar. He was still at war, in certain ways.

The baby kicked.

You stop it, you little thing, she ordered.

He kicked harder, and there came a sudden cramp so intense her limbs buckled and down she went, curling up.

Oh, Lord? Was it time?

But her water hadn't broken, so no, it wasn't time, it was just one of those rogue pains that sometimes happen.

She wasn't sure what happened next. It all went dark. She fell into pain, then numbness. Then she heard a voice and thought it might be Earl's.

"Earl, honey?"

"No, Junie, it's me, Mary, from next door. Honey lamb, you fainted."

Mary Blanton was kneeling beside her, fanning her with a copy of *Redbook*.

"Oh, my goodness," said Junie.

"I don't know anything about being pregnant, Junie, but I can't think weeding in ninety-five-degree weather is recommended."

Junie shook the confusion out of her eyes. Now she felt really icky.

"I don't know what happened," she said.

"Come on, honey, let me get you inside and into some shade. You can't lie out here and roast."

With Mary's help, Junie hobbled inside, where she lay down on her bed.

In the little kitchenette, Mary turned on all the fans, then threw ice into a glass and appeared with a large iced tea.

"Here you go, you sip on that till you get your strength back."

Junie sipped the tea and its coolness hit her solidly.

"Are you okay?" Mary asked.

"Yes, I'm fine now. Thank you so much, Mary."

Mary was the bluntest woman Junie had ever met, and she'd worked in war factories for years while her husband, Phil, was in the Navy. Now he was working in a radio shop by day and going to electronics school at night on the GI Bill.

"Well, I don't know about any husband like yours who'd leave a girl all alone as much as you are. A girl as pretty as you and as pregnant as you ought to be getting special attention, not all by herself in a tin hut, pining away."

"Earl's got a job he has to do. He always does his job. That's the kind of a man he is."

"If you say so, Junie. I never heard of such a thing. It's not how we'd do it up North."

Mary just didn't understand, not being from around here.

"I know he was a hero, but that only goes so far. A man ought to be home when his young wife is going to have a baby."

Junie nodded. Then she started to cry.

Mary held her, muttering, "There, there, sweetie, you just cry it all out, don't you worry."

Finally Junie looked up.

"I am *so* scared," she said.

"About your Earl?"

"Yes. But also about the baby. I can feel it. There's something wrong. I could lose them both."

CHAPTER
44

Earl and D.A. were not demonstrative men. But the confidence they now felt, armed with the Reverend Jubilee Lincoln's signed affidavit and his considerable courage, came through anyway, in the way they walked, in the way they talked, in the way they were. The men realized that something had happened, some breakthrough had been made, and the game was very nearly over, victory in sight. That filled everyone with hope and joy, and even the loss of the heavy automatic weapons and the bulletproof vests and six men seemed not to faze anyone; a general air of lightness and frivolity ensued as they broke down the camp at the Red River Army Depot, loaded up and headed out for the new quarters on the Pettyview chicken ranch.

It helped that the phrase "chicken ranch" was a well-known synonym for whorehouse.

"Hey, we're going to a chicken ranch. Whoo-eee!"

"Bear, would your mama 'low such a thing?"

"Hell, bubba, I was a champeen chicken rassler afore you'se even a glint in your daddy's eye!"

"Boy, the best part of you ran down your mama's leg. Tell you what, you need any help, y'all come to me and I'll show you the ropes."

"Yeah, you guys all talk big, lemme tell you when you get a dose your old dicks gonna swell up like a tire on a hot day. Shoot, saw a feller in Memphis so purple and swoll-up he couldn't get his zipper zipped. Had to walk around with it hanging out. But it was so purple, nobody thought it was a dick; they thought it was some kind of tube or something."

The joshing continued, and someone said to Earl, who was supervising benevolently, "Say, Mr. Earl, we are running low on .45 hardball."

Earl examined the ammunition cache. There was but one case of the .45 hardball left, that is, 1,000 rounds.

"Shit," said Earl. "Well, I doubt we'll need it anyhow."

"Yes sir."

"Lookie here," said Earl, figuring out a scrounger's angle. "I see we got plenty ball tracer we used in the training."

It was true. Four cases of the Cartridge Caliber .45 Tracer M26 remained.

"Look, load up two cases of the tracer in my trunk. Maybe I can work a trade with another agency or something, and lay off the tracer in exchange for some more hardball. Who knows? If we have to, we can always go to tracer, but I don't want to do it inside."

"Yes sir."

"On the 'Canal, I saw ball tracer from an idiot's tommy gun light up a goddamn cane field. It was full of Japs, but if the wind blowed wrong, I know a Marine squad would have been fried up real good."

"Bet you chewed him out, eh, Earl?"

"Hell, boys, couldn't chew him out. That idiot was me!"

They all laughed. It was the first time in anyone's memory that Earl had referred to the war or made fun of himself, a double whammy in the cult of Earl that he had spontaneously created.

D.A. came out of his little makeshift office with a briefcase full of papers, and said, "Y'all ready?"

It seemed they were.

There was a last-minute discussion of routes and timing, for it would be better if everyone arrived later, and after dark, and D.A. told them to keep their lights off as they traveled down the last half mile of dirt road before they reached the farm and not to make the turnoff if there were other cars on the highway.

Each car had an assignment: one would stop for ice, another for groceries and snacks, another for Coca-Colas.

But finally, there was nothing left to do.

"Okay, boys. We'll see you tomorrow," sang D.A., and the little convoy was off.

"Look, that's fine, but something else has come up."

The meeting was at an out-of-the-way ice cream parlor in West Hot Springs, well off the byways of the gambling town. Becker wore his usual suit and had his usual pipe; but this time, besides assorted clerks and functionaries, he had two blunt-faced State Policemen in not so plain clothes as bodyguards.

"Sir," said D.A. patiently, as if explaining to a child, "I'm telling you we can end this thing. We can end it just like we planned. We all agreed very early on that the Central Book was the key. Now we've got a plan that—"

"I heard the plan the first time, Parker. I'm sure it's a fine plan."

"We can do it fast. Our boys are very well trained," said Earl.

"They're probably the finest-trained police unit in the country today. We can do it and nobody gets hurt, and it's over. You win. You're the hero. You're the next—"

"Earl," said D.A. sharply.

"Yes sir," said Earl, shutting up.

"The raids still make me uneasy," said Becker. "Too many things can go wrong, too many people can get killed. The community doesn't like the raids. All the killing—it makes people nervous."

"Sir, if you're fighting rats, some rats are bound to die," said D.A.

"Something else has come up."

Earl and D.A. said nothing but exchanged a brief glance.

"A source I trust, not in the police department or the municipal government, says that he was dining with his wife in the Southern Club and he saw Owney with a beautiful woman and a man he recognized from the papers as an Irish mobster called Johnny Spanish."

Earl and D.A. ate their ice cream.

"Sir, there's lots of gangsters come to Hot Springs."

"Not like this one. I made some inquiries. It seems Johnny Spanish—real name John St. Jerome Aloysius O'Malley—is a noted heist expert. An armed robber. He learned his trade in the IRA in the '20s. He specializes in banks and factory payrolls. Very violent, very smart, very tough. He has a crew of four other men, and they do the heavy work but the mob scouts their jobs and puts up the seed money."

The two men were listening numbly. Each by now had an idea where this one was going.

"They say Johnny Spanish was in Hot Springs in 1940. Early October, 1940. Mean anything?"

"The Alcoa payroll job."

"Exactly. So I'm thinking: Owney used Johnny before to raise money for a project—the building of the Southern. Now, you've put a big crimp on Owney financially with your raids. He needs cash to keep operating, to keep up his payments. His empire runs on cash. This would be the *perfect* time for another big job."

"That seems like the sort of thing you'd need a big police operation for," said D.A. "We haven't trained for that kind of operation, Mr. Becker."

"But you have the element of surprise! Now let me finish. I made some discreet inquiries. Alcoa sure isn't coming through Hot Springs anymore, I'll tell you that. But tomorrow night, the Federal Reserve Board is moving over a million dollars in gold up to Fort Knox, in Kentucky, where they're consolidating the gold reserves. They dispersed them during the war, because they thought it was too big a target. A million bucks' worth was moved to the Federal Reserve Bank in New Orleans. Now it's headed back to Fort Knox, under guard of the U.S. Army, and that train is slated to run up the St. Louis & Iron Mountain tomorrow night to Little Rock, where it'll divert to the Memphis & Little Rock and on to Kentucky tomorrow night."

"They're going to stop a train guarded by troops?"

"No. But suppose a bridge would catch fire? You watch. Sometime tomorrow a bridge along the St. Louis & Iron Mountain will catch fire somewhere north of Hot Springs but south of Little Rock. Or some track will be torn up. Or a tunnel will collapse. Something will happen tomorrow. The feds will divert to Hot Springs because it's the biggest yard between New Orleans and Little Rock, and the closest. If that happens, I guarantee you, Johnny Spanish will hit that train, Owney will make a million bucks and he'll go on and on and on."

"You should call the FBI," said D.A. "It's a federal thing. They have the firepower to handle that sort of thing. I still know a few fellas in the Bureau. I'm sure they'd share the credit, Mr. Becker. That could make you look real good."

"Oh, I'd get muscled out. I know how the FBI works. You worked for Hoover. You know what an egomaniac he is."

The dull, pained look on D.A.'s face told the story.

"He's right," he finally said. "They'd push us out and it wouldn't have nothing to do with us. J. Edgar himself would come on down to get in all the pictures."

"Now," said Becker, "look at it this way. If our team does this, brings these fellows down, makes the nab, it has exactly the same effect as closing down the Central Book. Then we can hit the Central Book too, if we have to. But if we get Johnny Spanish and his boys, we link him to Owney, we save the gold, we pin the 1940 Alcoa job on him, just *think* of it!"

Earl said, "I don't like night operations. They're plenty tricky, especially on unknown ground. Everything looks different at night. You got bad communication problems, you have target-marking problems, you have terrain recognition problems. You need perimeter containment, you need experience. Lots of men died at night because their own boys got jittery."

But D.A. responded quickly. "Yes, but Earl, think of the reward. This might be it exactly. This would put us on the map for all time. I can see the look on J. Edgar's face if I showed up on the cover of *Time* magazine. Whoooeee, that chilly bastard would twitch his lips like the strange fish he is and wish to hell he'd gotten there first. Whooooeee."

Earl saw at that moment his argument was lost. D.A. had connected with the concept in some deep way that called upon his own bitterness and seemed to validate his derailed life. It was the poison of dreams.

"Yes sir," Earl said. "We are short on men."

"I'll call Carlo at his mama's and get him back fast. And hell, I'll go myself. I'm still the best gun in town. Ain't as spry as I once was, but I'm still damned fast."

"That's the spirit," said Fred Becker. "By God, that's the Marine spirit!"

CHAPTER

45

Somewhere along the way, Herman Kreutzer had picked up some expertise in electronics, so he understood Sniperscope M1 right away, and he was the one who talked Johnny Spanish through it, with guidance from War Department technical manual TM 5-9340, classified SECRET! Owney must really have had some juice to come up with something this special this fast.

The system consisted of two units linked by electrical cord: the Carbine, Caliber 30, T3 Modified, which wore the Telescope T-120 jury-rigged by special bridge mount to its receiver, and clamped beneath its forestock the infrared light source, which resembled a headlight, and behind that a plastic foregrip with the lamp trigger switch; and, three feet of cord away, the electrical power supply unit, a large metal box that supported the battery and various vacuum tubes. The whole thing weighed about eighteen pounds, loaded. The scope looked like a thermos jug, the headlamp like, well, a headlamp, and the electrical power supply like a large but utilitarian radio. You couldn't move fast with it, you couldn't maneuver, pivot, twist or switch angles or positions quickly.

"Ah, whoever came up with this gizmo never trekked the alleys of Dublin, that I'll tell you," said Johnny, feeling the heavy weight of the rifle but more peculiarly its awkwardness, for the scope was too large and the lamp completely threw off the balance of the little piece; and the fragility of the connection to the battery housing via the cord made the whole thing even more problematical.

"You'll get the hang of it, Johnny," said Herman, fussing with various switches and consulting the manual. "It's just for sitting in a hole and clipping Japs as they come over the ridgeline thinking everything is hinky-dinky banzai. Okay, I think we're set. Red, get the lights."

Red Brown hit the lights. Jack Bell and Vince the Hat put their cards down. The Maddox warehouse went dark.

"Throw the bolt," said Herman.

Johnny, in the kneeling position, snapped the bolt, lifting a round into the carbine's chamber.

Herman read by flashlight. "Okay, now with your front hand, hit the trigger switch up on the front grip."

Johnny did as he was told.

"By Jesus, it's broken," he said.

"Nah, it's invisible. Invisible to you, to the naked eye. Look through the scope."

Johnny obeyed.

"Nothing."

"Okay, I'm going to try a few of these switches and you keep looking and—"

"My God and sweet Lord," said Johnny. "The blasted thing's glowing like a horror movie. Where's Boris Karloff when you need him?"

"What's it look like?"

"All green."

"What do you see?"

"Hmmm," said Johnny, concentrating. "Why, I see them paint cans you set up."

"Is there a crosshair?"

"Indeed."

"See if you can hit anything."

"Hold your ears, boys."

Johnny loved to shoot and he shot well, as did his whole crew. He babied the carbine, locked it into his shoulder, his other arm braced on his knee, he steadied and waited and then popped off a shot. To his surprise, the carbine fired full automatic; a spray of five bullets launched themselves toward the target in the brief time that Johnny had his finger on the trigger. The burst was sewing-machine fast, a tap-taptaptaptap that stunned everybody.

"Yikes," Vince said. "The fuckin' thing's a machine gun."

"It's the M2 carbine," said Herman. "It goes full auto. It's supposed to fire that way. Did you hit anything?"

Johnny looked through the scope again.

"One of them cans is gone. By Jesus, I must have hit the bloody thing."

He fired four more bursts from the curved thirty-round magazine, and in the dark, even with the echo of the shots, they could hear the paint cans tossing and splashing and banging as the bullets tore through them.

"Lights," said Herman.

The lights came on. Johnny had hit all four cans, and the paint, red, exploded out of them, spattering across the corrugated tin walls of the warehouse.

Smoke floated in the air and faraway holes winked as they admitted outside light from the bullet punctures in the tin wall. The stench of burned gunpowder lingered. A red mist floated.

"Looks like bloody Chicago on a St. Valentine's morn," said Johnny.

. . .

Much fiddling and experimentation remained. Eventually, Johnny and Herman got the scope zeroed to the point of impact: the infrared lamp had a range of about one hundred yards, but at that range Johnny could put four shots in a target in a second, because his trigger control was so superb and the heaviness of the weapons system dampened the already light recoil of the carbine.

"They got a lot to work on with this thing," said Herman, his brilliance ever practical. "Needs to be lighter, tougher, stronger, with a longer range. They've got to mount it on something more powerful than a puny little carbine. They get it all jiggered up right, goddamn, they are going to have a piece of work!"

"Yeah, well, we can't wait till they get around to that. We go with what we got."

"Johnny, I'm just saying that—"

"Yah, ya big Kraut, you're thinking of them good old days mowing down people with your BAR in the trenches."

"Actually, it was a piece of shit called a Chauchat. Finally we got the BARs but not until—"

"Herman, *concentrate,* you bloody genius, on the night's work. Tomorrow we'll have a nice good visit with them wonderful old days in the AEF, all righty?"

The five men gathered around a plan of the railyard that Owney Maddox had supplied. It helped that they'd worked the same yard exactly six years earlier, although Jack and Vince weren't on the crew then. Quickly enough they came up with a sound plan, based on Johnny's cunning and Herman's sense of infantry tactics.

"We want them in a bunch," said Herman. "We want this over as fast as possible. It can't be a hunt, you know, a goddamn man-on-man running gunfight through the railyard. Get 'em into the zone, let Johnny hose 'em down, move in, mop up, dump a bunch of carbine brass and a few guns, and get the hell out of there. Get our money, go back to Miami."

"Owney'll be there too," said Johnny. "He wants to celebrate the finish."

"Damn, Johnny, that'll slow us down," said Herman.

"But you see, Herman, you smart fella, in this town, Owney owns the coppers. That means they ain't going to be responding to calls from people who hear the gunshots until we're out of harm's way. All right?"

Yes. It was all right.

Johnny Spanish's crew rallied at the deserted railyard canteen at about 10:00 P.M., under cover of dark. They looked like a commando unit, with faces blackened, in blue jeans and dark shirts and watch caps pulled low. They checked the weapons a last time, made sure all magazines were loaded and locked and that they had plenty of quick reloads. Vince had secured one of the larger old one-hundred-round drums for his Thompson 1928 from the Grumleys, who had plenty of drums but no more guns, and was busily cranking the spring—not easy—and inserting rounds to get the thing topped off. Herman and Johnny double-checked the infrared apparatus.

At 10:15, a scuffling announced the arrival of another player, and it was Owney himself, accompanied by his new Best Friend, Frenchy Short. Owney had no long gun, but carried a Luger in a shoulder rig.

"How do you know they'll come from west to east," said Owney. "Maybe they'll set up on the east side of town and come through from that way."

"Uh-uh," said Johnny. "Know why?"

"No."

"The dogs."

"The dogs?"

"All them black families live close up to the track over in the east side nigger section. They all got dogs, and them dogs set up such a racket when they're annoyed. Parker and Swagger are smart boys. They'll know that. They'll come like red Indians, from the west, I tell you. He'll read the land, Swagger will, and he'll see where our government train will have to be and he'll move from west to east, across the gap in the tracks, and that's where we'll hit him. Oh, it'll be a pretty thing. Caught a Brit squad in the open just like this, I did, yes sir, 1924, with me Lewis gun, and you should have seen them feathers fly that night!"

"Yeah, right," said Owney.

"Owney, lad, I'll want you on the flatcar with us. But you stay put once the fun starts, as I don't want to lose track of you and put a hot one between your beauty eyes. What a terrible pity that would be."

"That's encouraging," said Owney, "coming from an Irishman."

"You got any last comments, Judas Junior," Johnny Spanish asked Frenchy.

"The truth is, you should hit Earl first. If Earl goes down, the rest will lose their will to fight. He is the spirit of that unit. Without him, they're just Boy Scouts."

"Odd, but I think I understood that already," said Johnny.

A last watch check: It was now 11:00. The Grumleys had obediently set a bridge afire in Traskwood and the train—it was actually leased, at Owney's insistence, by his great customer, Jax Brewing, of New Orleans, Louisiana—would pull into the railyard around 1:00. Presumably at that time, Earl and his boys would move from their secret quarters and into the railyard, wait for the suggestion of mayhem, and then spring, only to realize in their last horror that they had been sprung.

"Think we'd better be goin', fellas. Good hunting to the lot of you; meet you back here at three and it's champagne for everybody, on his lordship Maddox."

But as Johnny prepared to lead his team out and Owney was consumed in some drama of his own, Frenchy took a moment to speak to the Irish chieftain.

"Yes, lad?"

"Earl? He's—he's actually a—"

"I know, boy. He's a hero. He's the father you never had. Could I cut him some slack? Could I take him in the legs, say? Could I just put him out of action? I've seen the lovesickness in your eyes, boy. But the answer is no, can't do it. As you say, he's the best. Kill the head, the body dies. He has to go first. I'll make it clean. A shame, in another life Earl and Johnny could be the best o' friends, and repair to a pub every night to talk over the gunfights of yore. But no, sonny: he goes first."

"Yeah," he said. "You're right."

"Look at it this way," said Johnny. "Bugsy Siegel has sworn to kill this fine fella. He even sent his girlfriend out just to get the name.

Bugsy's still mad. If we don't do it cleanly, Bugs might do it messily. That would be too sad an ending for a hero, eh? At least tonight he goes out like the man he is, a braveheart till the end, no?"

CHAPTER
46

The word came around 5:00; exactly as had been predicted, a bridge had caught fire up near Traskwood, and the St. Louis & Iron Mountain line was shut down until the fire could be put out and the bridge reinforced. All freights were to be diverted over to the Chicago, Rock Island and Pacific lines, which went east and west; a few would be shifted to the Hot Springs railyard.

"That's it," said D.A., getting the news from a messenger sent out by Fred Becker. "We go, then. It's all set. I'd get myself ready now. Becker says that northbound train won't be in until well after midnight, but I want us on site and ready to move well before then."

The men nodded and mumbled; most were glad to be moving out and into the last phase, since the chicken farm, such a joke in the abstract, proved to be a hot, dirty, dusty old place that smelled of hardened chickenshit anyhow, and they were anxious to move onward. Even Carlo Henderson, who'd just showed up that afternoon and hadn't had time to settle in yet, appeared ready to go and didn't need any rest from his journey back.

The teams drove in by different routes, and assembled just west of the railyard and station, on Prospect, behind a grocery store. There was less a need for secrecy this time, because, absent the Thompson submachine guns and the BARs, they were just men in suits with hats, completely nondescript in a town filled with men dressed exactly alike.

Earl checked his Hamilton, saw that it was nearly midnight. They were about a half mile south of fabulous Central, where the clubs and casinos were blazing up the night, so over here it wasn't nearly so busy.

"All right," Earl said. "I want you going out in skirmish teams, two men apiece. Don't go in a mob. Couple teams move on down the block. Don't get caught in the light of the station. Spend a few minutes in the dark and get your night eyes. Go into the yard and about halfway across it there's a little hollow and some open space, under the electric power wires. There's a switching house there, just a little shed, and set there somewhere. That's where we'll rally. We'll hunker up there and wait till the train arrives."

"Earl, suppose they gun the guards?"

"I know if we attack 'em while they've got the guns on the guards they will kill those boys. If we attack 'em before, we got no case and we stop the robbery, but we want a case. So we have to trust they go in and get out fast, and that's when we go. All set?"

They all mumbled assent.

"Anything to say, Mr. Parker?"

D.A., who usually wasn't with them at this point, said only, "You boys listen to Mr. Earl. He's right on this one. I'll be with you the whole way."

"Sure wish I had my tommy gun," Slim said.

"Hell, you couldn't hit nothing with it nohow," someone else said, to some laughter.

"Okay, fellas. Good hunting and be careful. Don't get yourself hurt. Everybody goes home."

They broke down by teams and one by one the teams departed, until only Earl and D.A. were left.

"Well, Earl, you all set?"

"Yes sir."

"Earl, this will work fine. I swear to you."

"I trust you, Mr. Parker."

"Now, Earl, trust me on one last thing."

"Yes sir?"

"When we get to that switching house, and when we get an indicator that there's a robbery going on, I will move out with the boys. I want you and Carlo to stay in the switching house."

"What?"

"You heard what I said."

"What the hell is—"

"Now you listen, Earl. This is going to happen one of two ways. It's going to happen easy or hard. If it happens easy, it's just going to be a matter of 'Stick 'em up, you bastards.' Now if it goes hard, it could be a sticky mess. Then I want you coming in where you can help out the most. You're the only one here with that kind of savvy. And that Henderson kid, he's a rock-solid hand too. So that's what I want you two boys doing."

"Mr. Parker, the boys are used to seeing me up front."

"The boys will be fine, Earl. You have trained the boys well."

"You're just trying to—"

"Earl, this is the way I have figured it out. This is the way I want to do it."

But Earl was worried. He knew the fight would be what it wanted to be, not what D.A. wanted it to be.

Now Frenchy had no place to go. It's the waiting that got to him. Best thing would be to find a whorehouse, get drunk and laid, and wake up tomorrow morning to see how it had gone.

But that wouldn't work. Tomorrow, early, he'd take the bus to Little Rock and from there a plane on to Washington, D.C. The day after, he would go to a well-appointed law firm on K Street where a senior partner named David Wilson Llewelyn would interview him, strictly as a formality. David Llewelyn had served in the OSS during the war and was a close personal friend of a man named Allen Dulles, who had run OSS. He was also a close personal friend of a man called Charles Luciano, recently deported, but a gangster who had made certain the docks ran well in New York during the war. Llewelyn owed Charlie Lucky a favor, particularly when Llewelyn couldn't get the deportation canceled. And Charlie Lucky owed Owney Maddox a favor, for some obscure service years back. Frenchy would be the favor, a prize in a transaction that would satisfy the honor of three important and powerful men, none of whom really gave a shit about Walter H. formerly "Shorty" and now "Frenchy" Short of Williamsport, Pennsylvania.

He felt utterly desolate. He sat in the bar of a place just down from the bus station, a honky-tonk full of smoke and mending GIs on out-patient status from the Army and Navy Hospital, amid girls of some-what dubious morality and hygiene. He nursed a bourbon, and tried not to see himself in the mirror across the bar. But there he was: a handsome young man in a spattered mirror, very prep-looking, as if he'd just stepped off the Choate campus. Looked younger than his age. Who'd look at such a mild, innocent kid and guess what grew in there? Who knew he had such dark talents, such a twisty, deviant mind, such raw guts, and such a total commitment to himself above all things? You could look at a thousand such boys and never pick him as the one like that.

Frenchy was busy doing something his training would teach him was utterly pointless. He was justifying.

It's not my fault, he was saying to himself. They betrayed me. They did it to me first. They should have fought harder for me. Goddamn that Earl, goddamn him to hell: he knew how good I was and he knew it wasn't my fault I stumbled in the middle of a gunfight and af-ter all I was the one who made everybody look good when I got those two bank robbers who I know were trying to move on me and would have killed me and maybe the whole raid team if I hadn't've stopped them.

His was the gift of self-conviction. In a little while he had recon-structed the past. This new version was much better. In it, he was the secret hero of the team. All the fellas looked up to him. He led all the raids. He got the two bank robbers. But Earl and D.A. were jealous of his success, of his natural heroic style and his cunning and nerve. After all *he* had found the Central Book. So they had to defeat him, destroy him, ruin his chances. The old and the corrupt always tried to destroy the fresh, the energetic, the talented. It happened all the time. It wasn't his fault.

The more he thought about it, the better he felt.

"Anything?" whispered Owney.

He crouched next to Johnny on the flatcar, and crouched behind them, guarding the delicate umbilical between the carbine and the light source, was Ding-Dong.

"I think they're there. I heard something. But I can't see anything yet," Johnny responded.

The only sound was the odd tinkle of running water, as if someone somewhere had left a faucet running. The smell of kerosene, oil and coal filled the air, making it unpleasant to breathe. Odd noises came: the scuttling of rats or possibly hoboes, the movement of yard bulls on their rounds, the clanks as brakemen greased up the journal boxes over the axles. But here, in the center of the yard, it was surprisingly clear: the coaling and watering docks were farther out, on the outskirts.

Johnny Spanish watched through the green glow of the infrared scope. It was strange. The world had been turned inside out, almost like a photographic negative. Light was dark and dark was light, with a crosshair superimposed.

He could see the switching shed, but there was no indication that anything was happening. Because he was looking into a lamp beam, the problem of shadow—though it was green, not black—was disconcerting. He wondered if he should have done more work on the scope, getting a better sense of what was going on in the glowing puzzle that was his night vision through the eyepiece. Could men move into his firing range and he not identify them as men?

No, not really. He could, after all, make out the shape and size of the switching house, could see the little dip behind it, could see the hard steel struts of the power wire pylons. There was no background, because the power of the lamp didn't penetrate that far. He couldn't see what wasn't illuminated, which gave the universe a completely foreshortened perspective, as if the world were but 150 yards deep or so.

"Do you see—"

"Shut up, goddammit! Shut up and be still!" he commanded Owney, who was shaky.

Owney said nothing.

Then, far off, they heard the sound of a train approaching.

"It's time," Johnny whispered softly.

"Ding-dong," said Ding-Dong Bell. "The party's about to start."

CHAPTER

47

Crouched in the dark behind the switching shed, they watched as the train pulled into the yard. It looked like any other train, leaking steam, hissing, groaning, like some kind of large, complex animal. When it finally came to rest, it clanked, snapped, shivered and issued steam from a variety of orifices. A lot of the boxcars said JAX BEER but that meant nothing; trains were thrown together out of all kinds of cars, everybody knew.

In the center of the train there was one long, black car, with lights beaming through from little slots. It looked like some kind of armored car, the exact center of the contrivance, a dark, sealed, menacing blockhouse on wheels.

"That's it," whispered D.A. to Earl.

"Yeah," he said.

It was nearly 2:00 in the morning. Before them for hours had been black nothingness, only the incongruous sound of water running from someplace close at hand, the stench of kerosene. A yard bull had come their way, carrying a lantern, but he was so unconcerned he simply looked into the shed, saw no hoboes hunkered there and moseyed on. But now at last, the train.

"Should we move in?" asked D.A.

"Nah. Wait for them to make a play. It don't mean nothing if you move too early."

"Yeah."

"I'll check the boys."

Earl separated from the old man, and slid almost on his hands and knees along the shallow embankment where each member of the team crouched, low and ready, each man locked in his own private drama.

"Okay?"

"All set, Mr. Earl. You give the signal."

"It'll be a bit yet, you just wait calmly."

"I'm ready."

He gave each man a tap on the shoulder, feeling their aliveness, their vitality. This was it. It would be over after tonight. They all knew it.

The last guy was Carlo.

"You okay?"

"Swell, Mr. Earl."

"Your mama okay?"

"She's fine."

"You get the word from D.A.?"

"Yes sir. But I don't like it much."

"I don't like it much neither but that's what the man says. When the men move out, you head on over to that shed and join up with me. We'll wait and see what happens."

"I got it."

"Good boy."

Earl squirmed back to D.A.

"It's not too late. I can lead 'em. You can come in where *you're* needed."

"No, Earl. This is my party. I've earned this one."

"Yes sir, but—"

Suddenly, a hundred-odd yards away, a door flew open, throwing a slash of light across the yard. There were two quick shots. Figures seemed to scurry back and forth in front of the dark car in the middle of the train, and men climbed in. Another shot sounded.

"Jesus," said D.A.

"That's it," said Earl. "They've done made their move."

"We should go now?"

"I'd give it a few more minutes. Let 'em feel comfortable."

"Yeah."

The door slid closed, and the light went out. Time ticked by, nearly two minutes' worth. Finally, D.A. said, "Okay. Let's do it."

"That's good," said Earl. "You want to be set up when they come out."

Earl scampered down the line.

"Time to move out," he whispered to each man, until he got to the end.

"Come on, Henderson."

"Yes sir," said Henderson.

The men scooched forward, then rose. D.A. was in the lead. Visibility was limited to maybe twenty-five yards at most, but they formed up in good order, a skirmish line with ten feet separating them.

D.A. moved to the center of the line, gave a wave that passed as a sort of signal, and they moved out, crouched, each with his .45 clasped in two hands in front of him, as they had been instructed.

Johnny saw them rise in the green murk.

"Okay," he said.

He felt Owney tense with anticipation.

Now they came. Seven men, like soldiers in the Great War, bent double, moving cautiously across no-man's-land. It reminded him of 1918 and the last big German attack, and the endless killer's ecstasy he'd felt experiencing the delights of the Browning .30 water-cooled, watching the bullets flick out and unleash a storm wherever they struck and in that turbulence knocking the advancing men askew like tenpins, so many of them, and the hot pounding of the gun, the furious intensity of it all, the star shells detonating overhead. This infrared thing: it was his own private star shell.

He tried to pick out Earl. Earl will be in the lead. Earl would be heroic. But the instrument couldn't resolve such details; he could only make out blurs moving with the sure, steady pace of human animation.

"Shoot 'em," hissed Owney as he watched the carbine barrel tracking ever so gently off Johnny's hold, as the Irishman measured his shots.

But Johnny had nerves of tungsten. That's why he did so well at this business. He let them come onward because he knew that after the first burst, the formation would scatter, and he'd have to track them and take the survivors down running. That meant the further they were from cover, the more time he'd have and the fewer who'd make it back to the switching shed.

He let them come on another minute. Then another. It had a curious, almost blasphemous intimacy to it. The men felt unobserved, he could tell, secure in their darkness. Now and then they'd halt and gently regroup and at odd moments in this process they'd strike poses so bored and languid and unselfconscious, it was as if he were observing them in the shower.

"Shoot, fer Chrissakes!" barked Owney, as the pressure of the stalk proved too heavy for his more brutal and direct style of gangstering.

"Now, now, boyo," crooned Johnny, "just another bloody second. I think I've got the leader all picked out."

It was the bigger fellow in the middle, a drooping, long-armed hulk of a man, who led the boys onward, a little ahead of them. That would be Earl, of course. He was so large. Odd that he'd be so large; the kid had never said he was a large man, but just a fast, tough one, sinewy and quick and raw.

He found his position, and the leader stepped into the crosshairs.

Now, he thought.

They walked slowly through the dark, seeing the train ahead of them in the dark, its flanks illuminated so slightly by the vagrant incandescence of Central Avenue far away, but filling the horizon with light.

There was no movement from the train. Whatever was transpiring was transpiring in silence. These guys were good: very professional, D.A. was thinking.

He glanced to either side, and could see the boys nearest to him and beyond that make out the shape of the boys further away. He was aiming to rally in the hitch of the armored car to the car behind it, then send two men down to the other end, and in that way set up a crossfire. He'd have one or two boys actually under the car too, in case Johnny's men tried to duck out that way. Those boys could nail them easily. He was quite willing to kill all of Johnny's boys. He knew in this business that you had to commit to killing early and stay committed. If you poisoned your mind with notions of mercy, it would cost you a moment's hesitation and that could destroy you in a flash. When the guns came into play, shoot fast, shoot well, shoot a lot: those were the rules.

They were so close now.

. . .

The line disappeared or at least got so indistinct Earl could not pick it out against the slight illumination of the train a hundred yards off. There was a sense of blur, of disturbance to the atmosphere, but that only.

"They're going to be okay, I think," said the boy.

"They're almost there. It's looking—"

Five short bursts fired so fast it sounded unreal. In the clear part of his brain, Earl made the numb note that somebody had extremely good trigger control and that the weapon's signature had an aching familiarity to it, something he knew so very well, and a fraction of a second later he identified it as an American carbine. But that part of his mind was very far away from the other part of his mind, which was hot and shocked and full of anger and fear and terror at once.

Ambush.

Perfectly sprung, perfectly set up, brilliantly planned.

Again the carbine: short, precise bursts, obviously an M2.

"Jesus, Earl," the boy said, and made a move to run to the aid of his friends. But Earl's first move was to grab the boy and haul him to earth.

"Stay," he hissed, for even though he had yet to articulate it in any meaningful fashion, a number of anomalies struck him at once. Why was the fire so precise? At night it was almost always a question of area fire, sweeping and intense; or it involved a star shell, throwing its illumination across the terrain, so that targets could be marked. Neither of these night-action features presented themselves and though, like the boy, he had a longing to run to the wounded he knew too that to do so was simply to enter the killing zone as defenseless as they.

And now he cursed the lack of a long gun. What he needed, he saw in a flash, was the BAR now locked in the State Police arsenal in Little Rock. With that powerful instrument he could suppress the battlefield, drive the shooters to cover, get his people a chance to get back.

"We need to—"

"No," Earl exploded, "you follow on me."

And with that Earl ran not to the killing zone, but rather to the switching shed, and set up a good supported kneeling position behind it, with just his head and shoulders and the pistol in a good two-handed position.

His ears found the zone and in a second a flash located the position. He could barely see his front sight, but he cranked up a good ten feet from the source of the fire, for he had to throw rounds in long arcs to get them there.

But it was a guessing game. He didn't know where you held to bring a .45 slug onto target from an unknown distance of about a hundred or so yards.

He fired, seven times quickly, put the gun down, and took Carlo's, who, smart as usual, had immediately understood the gist of it, and had prepared his own weapon for Earl, who then, with it, proceeded to lay out another magazine, exactly as Carlo inserted another magazine into the empty gun.

It wasn't much, but from far off came the splatter of shots hitting and kicking up dust and metal fragments, and maybe in that noise a kind of a sound of scurry or discomfort.

Earl had it now, and knew what would come next. He withdrew, knowing that he had but seconds. The boy was baffled.

"What are you—"

Again the carbine snapped out a short burst, and the astonishment came in where the bullets struck. Not near them, but exactly where they had fired from. Three bullets bit into the wood of the switching shed in exactly the location of Earl's foray, and three more spat across the dirt, kicking up clouds and filling the air with gun spray.

"Jesus!" said the boy.

"He can *see!*" croaked Earl. He thought for a second, realized he was zeroed in some sense. But he also figured the gunman would guess he'd move to the other side of the switching house. He didn't. He moved back to exactly where he'd been, took a sight picture, fired to the same point, and withdrew. A burst answered him, and he thought that was the last time that would work.

But next they heard a terrible groaning sound, and two figures spilled into the hollow just behind them. It was D.A., blood on his face, supported pitifully by the husky Slim.

"They done kilt us!" said Slim, and at that moment he made the mistake of rising too high out of the hollow as he addressed Earl, for three bullets popped dust, blood and hair off his head and he pitched forward.

Johnny watched them come, wondered briefly if he should try and hit the leader first but then decided they would scatter at the first shot and that he'd get more of them by going from right to left. He watched the man furthest from him come, settled into his rhythm, tracked him.

It was dead quiet.

He squeezed the trigger and a three-round burst pierced the night. The muzzle spewed burning gas brilliantly but on the scope the flashes registered only as interference across the bottom; he pivoted slightly and in less than half a second fired another squirt, then another, and then another.

It was not like killing.

It seemed to have nothing to do with killing. It was like some kind of ghastly fun, a game, to put the reticle of the sight on forms that had been reduced only to the green light of their heat, squirt them, feel the gentle shudder of the weapon and watch as they seemed to collapse into themselves.

By the time he got to the leader, that fellow had figured out what was going on. It couldn't have been but a second or two. He fired, and the bullets were off mark, one out of three hitting, he knew, by the way the man fell. He was about to squirt him again when another man came into the scope; he diverted and fired again. A hero. Running to his fallen boss! Johnny liked that loyalty in a man, any man, even this man, as he killed him.

Now it was mopping up.

The living had fallen to the ground, presumably confused over the weird accuracy of their antagonist, but still believing themselves to be safe in the dark. They didn't know they were flanked on two sides, or that two more gunners from the train would be moving on them, with instructions to circle around behind, trapping them completely in the hollow behind the switching shed, toward which their own instincts would dictate that they retreat.

He hunted and found a crawler in the dark.

The three-bullet burst centered the boy perfectly, kicking a spray of dust from his coat as the bullets skewered him. Another was intelligently moving not to the rear but to the extreme right, having figured that gunmen would cover the rear. Another good man; with pity in his heart, but not mercy, Johnny took this lad too.

"Are you getting them?" asked Owney, an idiot who wanted a report in the middle of a battle.

"In spades, bloody spades, boyo," he said, and veered back to the center, where the fallen, wounded leader must be. Another boy was now attending to the leader, one he'd probably missed.

Ah, now you two and the night's work is done, thought Johnny.

But detonations suddenly erupted too near them, with the sprang of bullets on metal, and worse, the spray of spattered lead, which lashed out and made them wince.

"By Jesus!" said Johnny.

"Where the fuck did *that* come from?" Owney said. "I think he hit me."

"Nah, he's shootin' from far off, you just felt a whisper of tiny fragments. Stay cool, buster."

The rounds had hit on the flatcar bed a good twenty feet from them, but enough to distract.

Johnny looked into the gloom and through the darkness could only see the flashes far off, in the lee of the switching shed. These seven rounds, however, hit a bit closer, kicking up their nasty commotion but ten feet away.

"He sees us!" said Owney.

"Not a bit of it! He's shootin' blind, the bastard," said Johnny, returning to the scope. He put the reticle on the last flash and tripped a six-round burst. The bullets struck dead on, lifting dust from the ground, pulling puffs of debris from the wood of the house.

"I may have got him," he crowed. "Right in the gizzard."

But he reasoned that the boy, if not hit, would move to the other side of the switching house, so he pivoted slightly, found that locality in his sight. The image was not so distinct as it was at the very limits of the infrared lamp, but he knew it was good enough to shoot. But the next seven shots came from the same side as the first fourteen, and he knew the fella had outguessed him. He pivoted back, saw nothing, but then a flash of motion. Something had slithered into the hollow behind the switching house and in a second, as if on cue, a boy rose, and Johnny potted him, three-round burst, head shots all.

"By Jesus, got another!"

"Is that all of 'em?"

"No, there's one, maybe two more at the shed. They don't even suspect that where they are now there's men all about them, ready to open up on command."

"Let's finish it."

"Give 'em a moment to think. They'll realize they're fooked, then they'll make a break and me boys will do them good and it'll be over. There's no place for them to go, except into the ground."

"You can't hit them from here?"

"From this range I doubt these little carbine bullets can carry into that shed. Herman's Browning rifle will make Swiss cheese of it, though, and de Palmo's Thompson should write an exclamation point to the night's fun."

The three men lay on the bottom of the switching shed, curled around the big levers that controlled the track linkages, breathing heavily.

"Oh, Christ," said D.A. "Oh, Jesus H. Christ, they had us nailed. They ambushed us perfectly, the bastards. Oh, Christ, all those boys, Earl, Earl, I lost all those boys, oh, Jesus forgive me, all those poor boys, such *good* boys, oh—"

"Shut up, Mr. Parker," said Earl. "Think about here and now!"

"He's hit bad," said Carlo. "He's losing blood fast. We've got to get him to a hospital or he'll bleed out."

"There's always a lot of blood. Stanch the wound. Apply pressure. It'll coagulate. If he's still kicking and he ain't in shock, he's got some time yet."

"Yes sir."

"Earl, they had us."

"Yes sir, I *know* they had you."

"What're we going to do?" asked the boy.

"Hell if I know."

"We could fall back on the low crawl."

"Nah. This old man can't crawl none. And they got boys on each side of us, and probably behind us by now. He ain't no dummy, whoever done put this thing together. The bastard."

"Earl, I am so sorry for getting all them boys killed."

"It's a war. War ain't no fun at all, sir," said Earl.

Carlo said, "We low on firepower too."

"Yes I know," said Earl, and reached to see if the old man still had his .45 but he didn't. He did have two full magazines in his coat pocket, however.

Earl calculated quickly. He'd fired three magazines, meaning twenty-one rounds were gone. He had one left, the boy had two left, and the old man two. That's thirty-five rounds in five magazines, with two pistols.

Shit, he thought. We are cooked.

"What're we going to do, Earl?"

"*I don't know!* Goddammit, I am thinking on it."

"We could split up, go in two ways. One of us ought to make it. We get cops and—"

"They ain't no cops coming," said Earl. "Don't you get that? They'd be here by now. This is it. This is all there is. And don't you get it yet? He can see in the dark."

"Earl I am so sorry about them boys I—"

"Shut up, the two of you, and let me think."

Above them, the wall on the left-hand side of the shed exploded, spewing fragments, high-velocity dust, and twenty .30 caliber bullets in a kick-ass blast, which went clean through and blew twenty neater holes in the right-hand side of the wall. The noise banged on their eardrums till they rang like firebells. The smell of pulverized wood filled the air, mingling with the kerosene and the oil.

"Browning," said Earl. "He's about twenty-five yards away over on the left. He can cut us to ribbons if he's got enough ammo."

"Oh, Christ," said Carlo. "I think we bought it."

"Not yet," said Earl. "Not—"

Another BAR magazine riddled the wall, this time six inches lower. A few of its shots spanged off the potbellied stove.

Then a voice called out.

"Say chums, we can finish you anytime." It was Owney, not far away, with that little twist of fake English gent in his words. "You throw your guns out, come on out hands high, and you can leave. Just get out of town and don't ever come back, eh? That's all I'm asking."

"You step out," said Earl to his companions, "and a second later you're dead."

"I'll give you a minute," said Owney. "Then I'll finish you. Make the choice, you bold fellows, or die where you stand."

But Earl was rummaging around in the shed. To Carlo he seemed a man obsessed. He cursed and ranted, pushing aside lanterns and crowbars and gloves, standing even, because he knew the BAR man wouldn't fire as the minute ticked onward until at last—

"*Ah!*" he said, sinking back down to the ground with a handful of something indeterminate in the dark.

"Now you listen up and you listen up good. Henderson, load up them .45s and get 'em cocked and locked."

Johnny dumped a magazine, even though it had a few rounds left, and snapped in a fresh one so he'd have plenty of ammo.

He went back to the scope.

In the green murk, he saw nothing except the outline of the switching shed sitting atop the little hollow. Some dust seemed to float in the air on the side where Herman had hammered two BAR magazines into it, but otherwise it was motionless.

"Maybe they're all dead," Owney said.

"They ain't dead," said Johnny. "That I guarantee you. No, they're in there like rats in a trap, snarling and trying to figure how to flee."

Owney checked his watch.

"You said a minute. You gave 'em two."

"I did," said Owney. "But I want 'em out. I want 'em found outside, not inside."

Once again he rose and yelled.

"I'm telling you for the last time. Come out and surrender or get shot to pieces in that shed."

The gunfire had provoked the dogs all through the Negro district and their barking filled the air. But no sirens screamed and it seemed as if the universe had stalled out, turned to stone. It seemed darker too, as if the townspeople, hearing the firing, had done the wise thing, turned out their lights, and gone into cellars. No yard bulls or brakemen showed; they too conceded the yard to the shooters, and presumably had fallen back on the control tower or the roundhouse for shelter from the bullets.

"I'm going to give the order to fire," Owney screamed.

"We're coming out!" came a voice.

"Now there's a helpful fella," said Johnny.

He bent into the scope and saw two men emerge, one supporting the other, their hands up. Then a third. The third would be the dangerous one. He put the scope on him, and his finger went against the trigger and—

Exploding green stars!

Brightness, intense and burning!

The hugeness of fire!

He blinked as the scope seemed to blossom in green, green everywhere, destroying his vision, and he looked up from it blinking, to see nothing but bright balls popping in his eyes as his optic nerves fired off, and heard the sound of gunfire.

"He's got night vision, see?" Earl said.

"Earl, ain't nobody got night vision," said D.A. "Talk some sense."

"No, he's got a thing called *infrared*. Some new government thing. They used it on Okinawa. I heard all about it. You can *see* in the *dark*. That's how he makes them good shots. That's how come he headshoots Slim from a hundred yards in pitch dark. He can see us."

"Shit," said Carlo.

"Now, way that stuff works, it sees heat. Your heat. It shines a light that only he can see. A heat light. But it sees all heat, or all light."

"Yeah?"

"So here's the deal. I give the signal, I'm going to light this batch of flares. In his scope, it's all going to white. He ain't going to see nothing for a few seconds. Then I'm going to lean around the back and keep that BAR boy down with a gun in each hand, fast as I can shoot."

"Earl—"

"You shut up and listen. You take the old man and you run to the sound of the water. You hear that water?"

Yes: the faint tinkle of water, not too far off.

"That water. That's where Hot Springs Creek goes underground. It runs the whole length of Central Avenue underground, about two miles' worth. You and the old man, you get in there and you keep going till you find a door. It's the secret get-out for a lot of places, and the bathhouses drain into it too. You get in there, you get in public and you get the hell out of here."

"What about you, Earl?"

"Don't you no nevermind about me. You do what I say. Here, I want you to take this crowbar too."

He held up a crowbar he'd scrounged.

"There'll be a boy out there, waiting for you. You should see him, his eyes should be blinded by the flares. You have about a second, you throw this bar and you smash him down, then you run on by to the culvert and you are out of here."

"Earl, how do you know about that culvert?"

"*Goddammit!* You don't worry about that, you do what I say."

Owney cried again.

"I'm telling you for the last time. Come out and surrender or get shot to pieces in that shed."

The two of them got the old man to his feet, keeping well away from the window. They came to lodge against the doorway, just a second from spilling out.

"Now are you ready? You ready, old man? I'm going to light these flares and —"

"I'm going to give the order to fire," Owney said.

"We're coming out!" screamed Carlo.

"Good," said Earl. "Look away, don't look into the flares. I'm going to light these things, then you hand me the guns and—"

"He hands the guns to me, Earl," said D.A. "I can't run nowhere. I got nowhere to run. Give me them pistols, boy."

"No!" said Earl.

"I'm *ordering* you, Henderson. Earl, light them damn things. Son, give me the pistols 'afore I pass out. You go, goddamn you, and don't you look back."

Carlo didn't think twice. He handed the two pistols to D.A., who lunged a little away from him and halfway out the door and seemed to find his feet, however wobbly.

"You old bastard," said Earl. "You go down and we'll be back for you."

"You do it, goddammit!" said the old man.

"Shit," said Earl, and yanked five pieces of tape in rapid succession, which lit the flares. He felt them hiss and burn and their explosive heat. But his eyes were closed, he didn't look into them, he edged to the door and then dumped them on the ground.

"Run!" he commanded, but Carlo was already gone. He followed, and he had a sensation of the old man spinning in the other direction, and he heard the .45s blazing, one in each hand, fastfastfastfast, the old man fired and as Earl ran he saw in the glow a man rising with a tommy gun but slowly, as if blinded himself and Carlo threw the crowbar from ten feet with surprising grace and accuracy and the heavy thing hit the gunman in the chest and hurt him badly so that he stepped back and fell.

The boy ran on and Earl ran too, out of the glow, and they heard the heavy blast of the BAR and answering shots from D.A.'s .45s.

Suddenly it was a dirt blizzard. Around them erupted fragments, dust and debris as the carbine gunner got onto them, and the boy stumbled but Earl was by him, had him, and pulled him down into the stream.

They heard the BAR. They heard the .45s. They heard the BAR. They heard no more .45s.

"Come on," said Earl. "Come on, Bobby Lee. You got to go *now!* It don't matter that it hurts, you got to go *now,* with me."

And Earl had the boy and was pulling him along, in the dark, through the low tunnel.

. . .

"Did you get them?" asked Owney.

"I think two got down in some kind of ditch. The one out back, Herman finished him."

"Shit," said Owney. "They'd better not get away. Goddammit, they better not get away. If one got away, you know which one it was."

Johnny yelled. "Herman, lad, circle around and see where them boys gone. You other fellas, you converge on the shed. We're coming ourselves."

Getting the cumbersome apparatus off the flatcar was not an easy thing but with Jack Ding-Dong doing the labor, they managed. Then Jack carried the heavy battery unit, and Johnny walked ahead with the rifle, scanning through the scope. Owney was just behind.

"On the right," said Johnny, and Owney looked and saw a Jayhawker, just a young kid, lying spread out on the ground, his dark suit sodden with blood.

"They're all over the goddamned place. We done a good night's work, we did," said Johnny.

"Over here," yelled Herman.

They walked on, past poor Vince the Hat de Palmo, who was conscious again, in the ministrations of Red Brown, though he gripped his chest as if he'd been hit by a truck there.

"Them flares blinded me," he said to Johnny.

"There, there, lad," said Johnny. "They blinded me too."

At last they reached a culvert, saw the water glittering through it.

"That's where the bastards went. Trust a rat to find a hole. Where does this go?"

"Under the streets," said Owney. "Goddamn. Goddamn, the cowboy got away."

"But he's running scared, probably hurt. He's no problem, Owney. Not for a time. He'll mend, he'll come for you. We'll find him first and put him down. Damn, he's as sly a dog as they come, isn't he? How in Jesus' name did he know of this culvert?"

"I know what I'll do," Owney said. "I'll call the police."

"Johnny, Johnny?"

"What is it?"

"He's still alive."

"Who's still alive?"

"The old man."

"Jesus Christ," said Owney, turning.

He walked with Johnny quickly back to the shed. In the hollow behind it, the old man had fallen. He lay soaked in his own blood, jacking and twitching with the pain. Herman must have hit him five times, and Johnny two or three times before that. But the gristly old bastard wouldn't die.

"He's a tough boyo," said Johnny.

The old man looked up at them, coughed up a red gob, then looked them over.

"So you're the fellows done this work? Well, let me tell you, Earl will track you down and give you hell on earth before you go to God's own hell."

"You old turkey buzzard, why don't you hurry and die," said Owney. "We don't have all night for your yapping."

"Owney, I marked you for scum the first time I laid eyes on you and I ain't never wrong about such things."

"Yes, but how come then I'm the man with the gun, eh, old man? How come you're lying there shot to pieces, bleeding out by the quart?"

"Takes a lot to kill me," the old man said. Then he actually smiled. "And maybe you don't have enough pecker-heft to get it done."

Owney leaned over him and shot him in the forehead with his Luger like a big hero.

CHAPTER
48

They ran crouching through the darkness and in a bit of time the slight illumination of the opening disappeared as the underground course of the stream turned this way or that.

"Jesus, I can't go on," moaned Carlo.

Earl set him down, peeled back his coat and his shirt. The carbine bullet had blown through him high in the back and come clean out the front. He bled profusely from each wound.

Earl tore the boy's shirt, and wadded a roll of material into each hole, the entrance and the exit, as the boy bucked in pain and tossed his head. With the boy's tie, he tied a loop tightly that bound the two crude bandages together. With his own tie, he quickly hung a loop around the boy's neck, to make a crude sling.

"Let's go."

"God, Earl, I'm so damned tired. Can't you go and get help while I rest?"

"Sonny, they will see you when you can't see them and they will kill you. If you stay, you die. It's that simple."

"I don't think I can."

"I know you can. You ain't hit that bad. Someone has to survive to talk for them boys that didn't. Someone's got to remember them boys and what they did and how they was betrayed."

"Will you pay them back, Earl? Will you get them?"

"Damned straight I will."

"Earl, don't. D.A. didn't want you in trouble. D.A. loved you, Earl. You were his son. Don't you get that? If you go down, then what he did don't mean a thing."

"Now you're talking crazy."

"No, no," said the boy. "He sent me to investigate you 'cause he was worried you had a death wish. And then when I found out about your daddy, he told me to get back and not say nothing about it."

"I don't know what you're talking about, but you're wasting your breath. My daddy's been dead a long time."

"Your daddy just died a minute ago and his last wish was that you live and have a happy life, which you have earned."

"You just shut that yap now, and come on."

"Earl, I'm so tired."

"Bobby Lee, you—"

"I'm not Bobby Lee, Earl. I'm Carlo Henderson. I ain't your little brother, I'm just a deputy."

"Well, whoever you are, mister, you ain't staying here."

With that Earl pulled him to his feet, and pushed him along through the hot, sloppy water in the darkest darkness either of them had ever seen.

Hot Springs Creek was a sewer and a drain. It smelled of shit and dirty bathwater and booze and blood. As they sloshed along, they heard the skitter of rats. There were snakes down here, and other ugly things that lived under whorehouses and fed on the dead. Maggots and spiders, broken glass, rotting timbers, all lightless and dank, with the stench of bricks a century old and the banks a kind of muddy slop that could have been shit.

"How much further, Mr. Earl?"

"Not much. I don't hear 'em trailing."

"I don't neither."

"That goddamned infrared gizmo was probably too heavy to carry along down here, now that I think about it."

"Earl, how'd you know of this place?"

"Shut up. Don't be talking too much. Another couple of hundred feet and we'll begin to think about getting out."

"Getting out?"

"Yeah. You'll never make it if we go all the way to the other end. You'll bleed out. It's another mile and a half ahead. But all the speakeasies, the baths, all them places got secret exits, just in case. We'll get through one of them."

"Earl, I am so tired. So goddamned tired."

"Henderson, I don't b'lieve I ever heard you swear before."

"If I get out of here I am going to swear, smoke a cigarette and have sexual intercourse with a lady."

"Sounds like a pretty good program to me. I might join you, but I'd add a bottle of bourbon to the mix. And I don't drink no more."

"Well, I ain't ever had no sexual intercourse."

"You will, kid. You will. That I guarantee you."

He pulled the boy out of the water and up the muddy bank, where he found a heavy wooden door. It seemed to be bolted shut. The boy sat sloppily in the mud, while Earl got out his jackknife and pried at a lock, and in a bit old tumblers groaned and he pulled the thing open two feet, before it stuck again.

He got the boy up, and the two of them staggered onward through a chamber, up into a cellar, around boxes and crates, and upstairs, and then came out into corridors. The temperature suddenly got very hot, and they bumbled toward a light ahead, and pushed through a door, and found themselves in a moist hot fog with apparitions.

"Get a doctor, get a doctor!" Earl hollered, but what he heard was screams as shapes ran by him, scattering in abject panic, which he didn't quite understand, until a naked old lady with undulating breasts ran by him.

He fell to clean tiles which he soiled with the slop on his shoes and pants as other women ran by, screaming.

And then a policeman arrived, gun drawn.

"Get this boy to a hospit—" he started, but the cop hit him, hard, in the face with the pistol barrel, filling his head with stars and pain, and he was aware that others were on him, pinning him. He heard the click as the handcuffs were locked about his pinioned wrists. Then someone hit him again.

CHAPTER
49

Earl lay in the city jail. No one interviewed him, no one asked him any questions, no one paid him any attention. They let him shower, and gave him a prison uniform to wear, and took his suit out for cleaning. He seemed to just brood and smoke and had trouble sleeping. Late one night, a decent bull who'd been a Marine led him from a cell into an anteroom and let him call his wife, to tell her, once again, he had survived.

"I knew," she said. "They didn't have your name in the papers with those other poor boys."

"That's the one thing they got right, then."

"All those boys, Earl," she said.

"It was just so wrong," he said.

"Earl, come home. That is the devil's own town. You've given it every last thing and what's it got you?"

"Nothing."

"Earl, it's not worth it."

"No, it's not. It never was. All them boys gone."

"Earl, you can't think about that. It'll kill you."

"I know. I should think of other things: how's that baby?"

"Kicking a bit. A little kicker, if you ask me."

"I'm coming home as soon as I can, sweetheart. I will be there when it comes."

"I know you will or die trying," she said.

He watched it play out in the newspapers over the next few days. He thought he was beyond surprise, but even he had trouble believing what came next. The *New Era* had it thus:

JAYHAWKERS AMBUSH SELVES

Seven Die in Railyard Mixup

Members of the Prosecuting Attorney's special raid team evidently got in a gunfight amongst themselves in darkness last night in the Missouri and Pacific Railyard.

Seven men were killed, including D. A. Parker, 65, a legendary FBI agent who shot it out at one time with the gangster chieftains of the '30s.

Sources indicate that Parker was the leader of the unit, known in local parlance as "Jayhawkers," after the Kansas brigands that bedeviled Hot Springs before the Civil War.

"I am exceedingly disappointed in Mr. Parker," said Fred C. Becker, Garland County Prosecuting Attorney. "He was a man of experience but evidently in his advanced age, his mind began to deteriorate and he made a number of bad judgments. Night operations are tricky, as I learned firsthand in Italy in the United States Army. I will forever hold myself responsible for my lack of foresight in not replacing him with more rational personnel. I feel the pain of this loss immensely. And I take full responsibility."

Sources gave this account of the night's events.

Acting on a tip, Parker took his unit to the railyard, where he suspected a train robbery, similar to the Alcoa Payroll Job of 1942, was being engineered.

In the darkness, his men got separated. For some reason, one of them fired and all the others began to fire at indistinct targets. When it was over, seven men, including Parker, lay dead.

The state papers in Little Rock were kinder, but only a little bit. In all, that seemed the verdict: an idiotic D. A. Parker leading his little ragtag band into the railyard on a fool's errand, where out of sheer stupidity it self-combusted. The Jayhawkers had killed themselves.

Earl knotted the rag up into a ball and tossed it across the cell. He lay all day and night. It was not unlike the war. He just stared at a numb patch of ceiling, trying to work out what had happened and why. He tried not to think of the boys and the brief spurts of fire that took them down so neatly, and how well planned, how ingenious the whole thing was. He tried to exile the grief he felt for the good young men and the rage he felt for Becker and Owney Maddox and this Johnny Spanish, the professional bank robber, who must have set the whole thing up.

He tried so very hard, and he tried hard not to think of the mute coffins, lined up and shipped without ceremony back to their points of origin.

On the third day, he was taken from the cell into a little room, and there discovered not Fred C. Becker but Becker's head clerk, a ferrety little man with eyeglasses named Willis O'Doyle.

"Mr. Swagger?"

"Yeah. Where's Becker?"

"Mr. Becker is working on important cases. He could not attend."

"That bastard."

"Mr. Swagger, attacking Mr. Becker verbally will not do you any good in this room."

"Am I being charged with anything?"

"No. Not if you cooperate."

"Jesus Christ, he gets seven men who fought and bled for him killed and I'm supposed to cooperate?"

"Mr. Becker is as upset as you at the outcome of the action. But he feels with more effective leadership from Mr. Parker and yourself this could have been avoided."

O'Doyle looked at him with placid ideologue's eyes, unaware, uninterested.

"Mister, you don't know much about things, do you?"

"Be that as it may, Mr. Swagger, I am here to inform you that the governor of the state of Arkansas has today officially required that the prosecuting attorney's special raid team officially cease to exist. Mr. Becker has decided to comply with that order. A news release to that effect will be put out this afternoon."

"He can still win, you know. He can still hit the Ohio, even with just a few state cops, close it down, and put it to Owney Maddox."

"I don't think Mr. Becker is interested in further dangerous activities, especially in the downtown area."

"He's given up."

"Sir, it does you no good to assail Mr. Becker."

"If he doesn't do something, he's a loser. He's gone. Nobody'll ever elect a quitter to anything in this state. It's the South, for God's sakes."

"Mr. Swagger, the city attorney was going to indict you on charges of malicious mischief, discharging a firearm within city limits, leaving the scene of an accident, and breaking and entering for that little trick of crashing into the Fordyce. You're lucky he didn't include pandering and sexual deviancy for entering the women's bathing area!"

O'Doyle was a prude; his little face knitted up in distaste.

"But Mr. Becker interceded in your behalf. All charges will be dropped against you and Mr. Henderson. The condition is that you sign a statement acknowledging the events in the railyard three nights ago, and leave town immediately, and never come back. This offer is on the table for the next ten minutes. Mr. Becker wants you gone. Gone forever, so that he can begin the healing. He has many more steps to make on his journey."

Earl just looked at him with contempt. Becker had made some kind of peace with the city, with, presumably, Owney. It was all to be covered up.

"What kind of investigation did they make at the crime scene?"

"It was never considered a crime scene, but an accident scene. The

Hot Springs city police cordoned it off, and set about to provide medical help. Unfortunately, so well trained was your team that all the bullets were fatally placed. Seven men were declared DOA. It's been a very bloody summer."

"You could pull that one to pieces with ten minutes' worth of investigation. Did they take up shell casings? Did they do forensics on the bodies? Did they talk to witnesses who heard different kinds of gunfire? Did they even find carbines in the area? Our carbines were taken away, along with every other long gun and our vests. How could we have shot each other with carbines if we didn't have no carbines—"

"I am assured that several carbines were recovered on site, Mr. Swagger. You had better get used to the idea that this is over, and that the best thing for you to do is leave the county and begin again elsewhere. I've spoken to Mr. Henderson. He's seen the wisdom in our suggestion."

"I don't know why you bastards always turn on the men you pay to do your killing for you," Earl said. "But that's the way it happens."

"You understand, you are also forbidden from making contact with Mr. Becker, from speaking to journalists or publishing an account of these events, of publicly identifying yourself as a member of what the newspapers called the Jayhawkers?"

Earl looked at him.

"You are also officially warned that any attempt at misguided vengeance against those you perceive as culpable in this case will be considered a willful violation of this agreement and the law as well, and you will be prosecuted aggressively and to the full extent of our resources. You are to leave town quickly, quietly and completely. You are never to set foot in Garland County again. Your ten minutes are almost over, sir."

Earl just shook his head.

"Mr. Swagger, this isn't merely the best deal you'll get, it's the only deal you'll get. I'd sign off on it, get out of town and get about my life's work, whatever that may be."

"He's just going to write all them boys off?"

"Mr. Swagger, I have other appointments. If this document is not signed in the next three minutes, I will direct the city attorneys to begin legal proceedings against you. With a wife on the verge of a baby, I don't think you want to spend the next few weeks in jail while this thing is painfully sorted out. By the way, your badge, which was in your effects, has been confiscated and destroyed. Furthermore, as you are no longer a bonded officer of law enforcement, you have lost the right to carry a concealed weapon. Sir, I would sign and vanish as fast as possible."

Earl's bull rage suggested to him that he ram the little man's skull against the wall, but he saw what paltry good that would do, and after he smoked a cigarette, he signed the goddamn thing, feeling as if he'd just sold out his oldest and best friends.

"Oh, and one last thing, Mr. Swagger. You will be billed seventy-five cents for the dry cleaning of your suit and tie and the laundering of your shirt and socks."

CHAPTER

50

Becker would see nobody. He canceled all appointments. He sat alone in his office, contemplating his ruin. Of course he lacked the nerve for suicide, and he enjoyed the self-pity too much sober to blur it with alcohol, so he simply stared out the window, sucked on his pipe, and blew huge clouds of aromatic smoke into the air.

Why did I ever try this idiocy? he thought.

What possessed me?

Am I merely stupid or am I colossally ignorant?

The newspapers were really piling on. Even his nominal allies in Hot Springs were distancing themselves from him. He'd been made to look like a bloody buffoon and now Owney would be bigger than ever.

It had all vanished: governor in '48, the youngest ever in the state's history. Maybe the Senate then. Maybe the national ticket. There is nothing more intensely bitter than a fantasy that has sustained one for a decade suddenly being snatched away and crushed by reality. How

could he daydream now? How could he settle back in the minutes before sleep and see himself exalted, vindicated, loved, propelled ever onward on good looks, charm and sheer affability? Postwar America was
going to take off like a rocket; television was going to rule and that
would give the advantage to handsome men; there would be change
everywhere, as the young replaced the old, as a new order took over for
an old one.

And he had lost.

He would not be part of it.

It seemed so unfair.

He loaded another ton of tobacco into his pipe and forgot himself in
the intricacy of the ritual for a while, then finally got everything
tamped and squashed in just right, and lit a match and drew in the
firecrackly explosion of dense heat. In that alone there was pleasure.

The door opened.

"Mr. Becker?"

"I told you I didn't want to be disturbed."

"It's your wife."

"I can't talk to her."

"It's the tenth time she's called."

"I don't care. Leave me alone."

"What about the two o'clock staff meeting?"

"Cancel it."

"What about your meetings with the mayor and the chamber of
commerce?"

"Cancel them."

"What about the newspaper people? The waiting room is full of
them. The columnists have tried to bribe me. They're annoying everybody and some of them don't flush the toilet when they're done
with it."

"I issued a statement. I have nothing further to add."

"Yes sir. Would you like a glass of water or some coffee or something?"

"No."

"Mr. O'Doyle is back."

"I don't want to see him."

"There are several matters that need—"

"Let the staff decide."

"Yes sir."

"Please go away."

"Yes sir. Oh, this came. I'll leave it here for you, sir."

Becker sucked in the pipe smoke, blew out still more ample clouds of smoke. He almost slipped off into his favorite fantasy, where he stands before a national convention, feeling the power of history as it approves him, and various people who denied him his specialness are seen below the podium, their faces crushed in bitterness. But then caught himself and returned to normalcy, and he was the one who was bitter and would be for a long, long—

This came. I'll leave it here for you, sir.

Now what the hell did that mean?

He looked and saw a large manila envelope on the floor, face down. What was *this?* Why would she leave it? What was . . . ?

His curiosity momentarily overcoming his lethargy and self-hatred, he went to the doorway and picked the envelope up.

It was first-class, special delivery, from Los Angeles, California, addressed to him personally, and marked HIGHLY CONFIDENTIAL.

What the hell?

He opened it and looked at the contents and—

"Miss Wilson! Miss Wilson! Get the Little Rock FBI on the horn! And fast!"

CHAPTER

51

Earl was escorted to his car by two Hot Springs plainclothesmen whose demeanor indicated they'd be just as happy to beat him to a pulp as to spit. He drove the seven blocks to the hospital with a black-and-white ahead of him and one behind him, and the plainclothesmen behind them.

He parked and went in, and found the boy sitting wanly in the waiting room. His left side was heavily bandaged and his arm immobilized by a sling, and his face appeared pale and forlorn.

"Well, ain't you a sight," Earl said, glad to see the kid was basically all right. That meant he hadn't lost them all. He'd saved one. He'd gotten one through it. That at least he'd done, when he'd failed at all else.

"Howdy, Mr. Earl," said Carlo. "Good to see you."

"Well, sir," said Earl, "guess my last official act is to take you to the station and see that you head back to Tulsa. Then I'm to get out of town and don't come back no nevermore, or these fine gents'll throw me in jail."

"Yes sir."

"Got the car right out here. Can you make it? Do you need a wheelchair?"

"No sir. I'm fine. I lost some blood, that's all, but the bullet passed through without breaking any bones. I been ready to leave for two days."

"Guess all them important boys had to decide what to do with us."

"Yes sir. Heard they was going to throw us into jail."

"But heroic Fred Becker stopped that. Yes sir, that's what I like about Fred, he always stands by his men."

"He's a real hero, that one," said the boy.

They walked out into bright sun, and all the cops were lounging on their bumpers. Earl waved.

"Howdy, y'all. We're going to the train station. Let me know if I get too far ahead of y'all now."

The cops stared at him grimly; now that he was disarmed and beat up badly, he didn't scare them a lick, no sir.

He opened the door for Carlo, then went around and got in.

The hospital was in the north end of town; they drove south down Central one last time to the train station. The eight bathhouses FordyceSuperiorHaleMauriceQuapawOzarkBuckstaffLamar gleamed on the left and on the other side of the boulevard, ancient, corrupt Hot Springs marched onward, the Medical Arts Building, the Southern, all the smaller casinos and brothels, on down to the Ohio.

"We could still shut that place down," joked Earl. "Two men without guns, with a cop escort. That would at least surprise 'em."

"Give 'em a good laugh, wouldn't it, Mr. Earl?"

"It sure would, Henderson."

Two blocks beyond they reached the train station. All evidence of the shootings of four nights earlier had vanished by now; the place hummed with pilgrims come to take the waters. The Missouri and Pacific 4:30 lay next to the station, cutting off the view of the railyard beyond, so at least they didn't have to look at the killing ground, the switching shed or the culvert.

Earl bought the ticket, one-way to Tulsa, $8.50, with just about the last of his cash. Supposedly the state would forward a last paycheck, or so he had been promised, but he'd believe it when he saw it.

The train wouldn't leave for half an hour, so the two men sat down on the bench. Discreetly, the policemen and the detectives set up a watch around them.

"You want an Eskimo Pie, Henderson?"

"Yes sir."

Earl went back inside, got the boy the ice cream and returned. While the boy ate his ice cream, he lit up a cigarette and stared at the train just ahead of him.

"Mr. Earl," said the boy. "How come you knew where that culvert was?"

"What?" said Earl.

"How come you knew where that culvert was?"

"Hmmm. I don't much know. Must have seen a map. What difference does it make?"

"How come you knew how steep the hill behind the Belmont was? How come you knew that street ran downhill not far from Mary Jane's? How come you knew where the manager's office at the Horseshoe was? Mr. Earl, was you in this town before you got here with D.A.?"

Earl didn't say anything. Then he said, "What difference does it make?"

"I have to have this out with you, Mr. Earl. Mr. Parker wouldn't want me to. But I have to know, Mr. Earl. If you murdered your father, I have to know, and then I have to work out what to do next. I can't let a murder pass, no matter that the man who committed it saved my life. I'm a police detective and that's what I'll be till the day I die."

"You are a good cop, Henderson. Wish I could say the same."

Earl lit another cigarette. The boy stared at him intently.

"It makes sense, Mr. Earl. You were going to the Pacific. You thought you were going to die over there. You had to have it out with your daddy, to punish him for beating your brother till he died, then hanging him up in the barn, and beating you till you ran away. But you couldn't disappear during normal duty, because the Marine Corps would keep a record. But when the division moved out for the West Coast from New River, that would be your time, Mr. Earl. You could disappear and come back and your sergeant pals would cover for you. You could get here and wait for him and recon the place and learn it up one side and down t'other. So you meant to beat him up and you shot him instead. You drive him out to Mount Ida, you dump him, you hop a freight, then another troop train, and you're on your way to Guadalcanal and who would know? Is that how it was, Mr. Earl?"

"Say, you are good, ain't you?" said Earl.

"You tell me, Mr. Earl. Mr. D.A. would let it pass as bad old business, but I have to know. I investigated it. I can't get it out of my mind. It kills me to think you done such a thing, but I can't look myself in the mirror if I don't know."

"Wouldn't that be some end? Survive the Pacific, survive all this and get the chair because some young cop has the genius to see into everything?"

"Some people need killing. No doubt about it. Your daddy, he's one of them, from what I can tell. I saw the pictures of that boy. I ain't even sure it's wrong, what you did. But I have to know. I just have to."

The mention of his brother hit Earl like a slap in the face.

"You are right," he said. "Some people deserve killing. And you got everything pretty right too."

He took a breath. "I will tell you this once and I will never speak of it again. I will never answer no questions on this and if you want to believe me or not, that is your decision, but you should know by this time I am not in the habit of telling lies. I only told one that I know of, when I told D.A. I had never been here."

"I believe you, Mr. Earl."

Earl took a puff, blew a blue cloud of smoke out before him. Passengers hurried this way and that, kids squawked, mamas bawled, dads lit pipes, traveling men read the paper, cops kept watch. It was America as it was supposed to be.

Earl sighed.

"I did decide to have it out with that old bastard. Didn't seem right for him to go on and on and both his sons dead before him for one damned reason or another. My topkick covered for me. I jumped train in Little Rock, and was here in Hot Springs for four days. I made it back to Pendleton just fine. Top understood. He was a good man. He didn't make it off the 'Canal, but he was a good man."

"I have it right?"

"Most of it. You only got one thing wrong."

The boy just looked at him.

"It's like everything you say. I learned the town, I learned all the casinos and finally I picked him up, b'lieve it or not, at the Horseshoe. The Belmont was too fancy for him. I knew about the hill behind the Belmont because I can read a goddamned map, that's all. But I followed my father from dive to dive, from joint to joint. It was a Saturday night and I was going to wait till the crowds died down, then jump him and beat the shit out of him. I wanted him to feel what it tasted like, to get a hard, mean beating. He'd never been beaten in his life, but that night, I would have cracked him a new head, that I swear."

The train whistled. It was time to go.

"You better get aboard," said Earl.

"I can't go till I hear it all."

"Then I better finish fast. You sure you're up to this?"

"Yes sir."

"Well, we'll see. The old man finally laid up at a place down at the end of Central. Just another no-name whorehouse at the cheap end of the row. I moved on down and waited. And waited. And goddamn waited. I seen him park his car, I seen him go in, and then nothing. Finally, 'bout four, I went in myself. There's something strange goin' on, but I'm not quite figuring it out. It's all dark, and the whores are just shocked-like. It's a run-down whorehouse, all dark, all crappy, all lousy. No johns nowhere, but some whores sitting in a little room, and I got to say, they's scared. They's almost in shock. 'You see a old man come in here?' I ask. I ask 'em, and they just run away, like they can't figure out what the hell is going on. Damnedest thing. I go upstairs. One by one I open doors. It ain't much different than Mary Jane's, and in a couple of rooms, I find other whores, some of 'em drunked up, some of 'em high on juju-weed, and I'm wondering what the hell is going on.

"Finally I get to a last door. Daddy's got to be in there. I kick the door in, and get ready for the fight of my life, because he was a big, mean sumbitch and he ain't going to stand still while his oldest boy goes to whip-ass on him. But he's just lying there and in the corner, this little gal is crying so hard, the makeup on her face is all run to hell and everything.

"I check Daddy. He ain't dead, but he's almost into the barn. 'Daddy,' I say. He reaches up and grabs my arm and recognizes my voice. 'Earl,' he says. 'Oh, God bless you, son, you come for your daddy in his hour of need. Son, I am kilt dead, get me out of this house of sin, please, son, I am so sorry for what I done to you and your brother, I was a wicked, wicked man. I done such evil in the valley and after and now the Lord has punished me, but for your sake and your mama's sake, git me out of this here house of sin.'"

"What was the valley?"

"Henderson, I ain't got no idea. Maybe he meant 'Valley of the Shadow,' that's all I could figure, and I puzzled on it for many a year."

"Go on."

"Well, I look, and he's shot. Shot above the heart. Had to be a little bullet, 'cause there's a little track of blood, not much. 'What happened?' I ask the girl, and she says, 'Mr. Charles, they busted in on him. They grabbed him and when he drew his little gun, they got it from him and shot him with it, right in the heart. They came to kill him and kill him they did.' This whore was crying up a storm. Mr. Charles, he was so good and kind, he took care of us, all that stuff. 'Who done this?' I asked. 'They done it,' said the whore. 'Gangsters done it. Shot him with his own gun and told me if I squealed they'd kill me and all the gals in the house.' 'Git me out of here,' he screamed. 'I am dying, Lord, I am dying, but son, Jesus, please, get me out of the house of sin.' So that is what I done. I come to beat the man and put the fear of God in him, and I ended up carrying him down two flights of stairs, him crying and telling me what a good son I was and all that, how wonderful I was, how proud he was. Things don't never work out like you expect, know what I mean? I was strong enough to carry him out. But I didn't want to go on the street, so the madam, she takes me down into the cellar, and through a big door and that's how come I got into the underground stream the first time. I carried him to the culvert. 'Thank you, son,' he said. 'Thank you so much.' I went back, got his car, drove it to the station and carried him to it. Time I got him to it, he's dead and gone. His last words was, 'I have been a wicked man and I done evil in the valley and so much evil come from that and I hope Jesus forgives me.' I didn't want him found there. I drove him to Mount Ida, dumped him, tore open the liquor locker behind Turner's. He had his Peacemaker in the car. I jacked off a round so they'd think it was a gunfight, I messed up all the tracks in the dust, and then I lit out cross-country. The next day, I hoboed a train. A week later, I reached Pendleton and four months after that, I hit the 'Canal. That's the true story. I was hunting him, but so was someone else."

"Jesus," said the boy.

The train had begun to pull out.

"Why'd they kill your daddy?" Carlo asked.

"I ain't never figured it. Who knows what that man had got himself into? He was a bad man. He beat and hurt people, he did terrible things. Someone finally caught up to him, I reckon. Before I did."

They rose, and went to the train, where a conductor was calling a last *"All aboard."*

"One thing maybe figures into this," said Carlo. "I only noticed this 'cause I was looking in newspaper files and I happened to make a connection. But you know that robbery? The Alcoa payroll job?"

"Yeah?"

"It was October 2, 1940. Your brother died October 4, 1940. There's something you might think on."

"Damn," said Earl.

Carlo got to the train, and hobbled aboard and for just a bit Earl kept with him as if he didn't want to let his one survivor from the wars escape his protection.

"Earl? Whyn't you let your father just be found in that whorehouse? Why take the risk? Would have served him right."

"You don't get it, do you, Carlo. Them whores. They wasn't like other whores. None of them."

The young man's face, still so innocent, knit in confusion.

"They was all boys," said Earl, stopping at last, spilling his last and most painful truth.

CHAPTER

52

She was an octoroon from the French Quarter, well schooled in the arts, with oval, wise eyes that bespoke the knowledge of ancient skills. So she had the thunderous savagery of the Negro race, but no vulgar Negro features. She looked like a white girl of special, almost delicate beauty, as if from a convent, but her soul was pure African. And she was extraordinary. She took him places he never knew existed. She took him to a high mesa that overlooked everything, and he could see the world from far away but in precise detail, and then she plunged him into a vortex so intense it made that world and its complications vanish.

"My God," he said.

"You like?"

"I like. I see why Miss Hattie charges so much."

"I am very good."

"You are *the best.*"

"I am so pleased."

"No. I am the one that's pleased."

Owney wasn't obsessed with the pleasures of the flesh like some, but now and then, in a celebratory mood, he liked to let go. And this one had really gotten him to let go.

"Ralph will take care of you."

"Thank you, Mr. Maddox."

"Thank *you.* Uh, you were—?"

"Opaline."

"Opaline. Thank *you*, Opaline."

Opaline, wrapped in a chartreuse silk peignoir, her white heels and beautiful shoulders flashing, walked out to dress. Owney rolled over, checked the clock. It was nearly 1:00 P.M.

He went into his bathroom and showered, then took his time dressing. He had no appointments today, the fourth day in the first week of the complete consolidation of his realm. Johnny Spanish and the lads were presumably still celebrating in some dive or other, on his tab, and he didn't begrudge them. All things considered, they had performed exactly as advertised.

Owney decided it would be a tweed day. He chose a Turnbull & Asser shirt in white linen cream and a red tie in the pattern of the 15th Welsh Fusiliers and, finally, a glorious heather suit from Tautz, the leading sporting tailor of the day. He finished with bespoke boots in rich mahogany. It took him some time to get everything just right, and finally, he enjoyed the construction. He looked like an English gentleman off for an afternoon's sporting. Possibly a partridge hunt, or a spot of trout fishing. He didn't shoot partridge and he'd never fished in his life, but in all, it was quite nice.

He walked into the living room.

"Ralph, I'll take my lunch on the patio, I think."

"Yes sir, Mr. Maddox, sir."

He went out, checked on his cooing birds, stroked one or two, attended to their feeding, then sat down. Ralph served him iced tea while the meal was being prepared.

"Telephone, Ralph."

"Yes sir, Mr. Maddox, sir."

He had one final *i* to dot. And the wonderful thing was: his worst enemy would dot it for him.

He reached into his wallet, and took out a note he'd received from the chief of detectives of the Hot Springs Police Department. It had a name and an address on it.

Earl Swagger
17 Fifth Street
Camp Chaffee, Arkansas

The cowboy. The cowboy had somehow escaped, but the police had done what no one else had been able to do: they'd captured the cowboy. He was released today, and ordered out of Hot Springs. But that wasn't enough for Owney. He mistrusted men like the cowboy, for he knew that the cowboy's anger would grow, and that he would never be safe until the cowboy was eliminated. But now there was peace in Hot Springs, and everybody knew it was time for the killing to stop and stability and prosperity to resume. A deal had been reached.

But he knew someone who hated the cowboy even more than he did.

He picked up the phone.

He dialed long distance, and the operator placed the call for him, and he waited and waited as it rang and finally someone answered.

"Owney Maddox here. Ben? Is that you, Ben?"

"Mr. Maddox, Mr. Siegel isn't here. He's in Nevada."

"Damn. I have some information for him. Information he wants very much."

"Do you want to leave it with me?"

"Yes. It's a name and an address for an Arkansas party he's most interested in. It's—"

But suddenly Ralph was hovering.

"Yes, Ralph?"

"Sir, there's some men here."

"Well, tell them to wait. I'm—"

"Sir, they's FBI. And Mr. Becker."

"What?"

At that point, Fred Becker strode onto the patio, with four FBI agents and four uniformed state policemen.

Owney said, "I'll call you back," and hung up.

He rose.

"What the hell is this all about? Ralph, call my lawyer. Becker, you have no right to—"

"Mr. Maddox, my name is William Springs, special agent of the Little Rock office, Federal Bureau of Investigation. Sir, I have a warrant for your arrest."

"What?"

"Sir, you own a painting by the French artist Georges Braque entitled *Houses at L'Estaque.*"

"I do. Yes, I bought it from a legitimate—"

"Sir, that painting was stolen in 1928 from the Musée D'Orange in Brussels. You are in receipt of stolen property which has been transported across state lines, which is a felony under federal statute 12.23-11. You are hereby remanded into custody and I am serving you with a search warrant for this property, for your office at the Southern Club, and for your warehouse complex in West Hot Springs, which agents and state policemen are currently raiding. Anything you say may be held against you. Sir, I am required to handcuff you. Boys"—he turned to his men—"rip this place up."

The cuffs were snapped on Owney.

He shot a look at Becker, who looked back with a smirk.

"You've been ratted out, Owney," said Becker. "You have some nasty enemies in Los Angeles."

"This is a two-bit fuckin' rap," said Owney, devolving to Brooklynese, "and you fuckin' know it, Becker! My lawyer'll have me outta stir in about two fuckin' minutes."

"Yes, perhaps, but we intend to search very carefully and if we find one thing linking you to the Alcoa payroll robbery or any of twelve to fifteen murders in Hot Springs since 1931, when you arrived, I'll put you away for the rest of your life and you'll never see daylight again. Say goodbye to the good life, Owney."

"Take him away, boys," said the FBI agent.

As they led him away, Owney saw his beautiful apartment being ransacked.

PART FOUR

Pure Heat

CHAPTER

53

Earl drove west, leaving Hot Springs in the rearview mirror. The road ran through forest, though ahead he could see the sun setting. The police convoy followed him to the Garland County line, and stopped there as he passed into Montgomery toward places beyond.

He told himself he was all right. Really, he told himself, he was swell. He was alive. His child would be born shortly. He had survived another war, an unwinnable one, as it turned out, but there was no changing things and there was nothing back there for him but probable death and guaranteed shame and humiliation.

I am not a goddamned avenging angel.

It is not up to me to avenge the dead.

I am not here to punish the evil.

I cannot go back to that town, one man alone, and take on a mob of professional gunmen, gangsters and crooked politicians.

My life is before me. I commemorate my dead by going on and having a good life.

He instructed himself in all these lessons hard as he was able, searching for a kind of numbness that would permit him to go on.

He tried to tell himself his wife and child needed him, this was over and finished.

But the road, darkening quickly, kept taking him back.

And maybe it was the hard truth he'd told the boy about his father.

He couldn't keep his mind in the present. His mind kept changing gears and he remembered that other night in 1942, his father dead in the seat next to him, much later, much darker at night, driving this same road toward Mount Ida, his mind racing, trying to figure out what to do, how to do it, feeling both cheated and relieved, wanting nothing now except to get over this thing, dump the old bastard and get back to the United States Marine Corps.

Then, as now, Mount Ida finally slid into sight, after such a long time, but then it was quiet; now it was much earlier and Turner's general store and liquor store were still open for business and some old boys stood or sat out on the porch before the old buildings.

Earl realized he had a thirst, and pulled off the road.

He walked up to the porch and heard the boys talking.

"Howdy," he said.

"Howdy, there, mister," came a reply.

"Got a Coca-Cola inside? A nice cold one? Got a long drive ahead."

"Yes sir. You go on in, and Ike'll git you a Coke."

"Thanks," he said.

"My pleasure, sir," said the man.

Earl walked in, found an old store with sagging shelves but well stocked, probably the only store this deep in the Ouachita forest, and folks from all around must have come here. He went to a red Coke machine, opened it up, and reached for a nickel. He didn't have one. He had only quarters.

He went up to the counter, asked a boy there for change, got it, went on back to the machine, and got his Coke. He was walking out and to his car when he heard one of the boys on the porch saying, "They say this'll make Fred Becker the governor."

"I thought that boy's all finished," said another. "But he beat 'em. He beat them Grumleys fair and square."

It took a second for this to register. At first Earl had the impression it was another Fred Becker they were talking about and that it was another batch of Grumleys, but then he realized that couldn't be the truth.

"'Scuse me," he said, "don't mean to butt in. But what's all that about Fred Becker and the Grumleys?"

"You from Hot Springs, sir?"

"Well, I done some work there. That's all finished and I'm heading on to Fort Smith."

"Hell, there's been a war there," said the man. "Fred Becker led a bunch of fellers against the gangsters in Hot Springs."

"B'lieve I heard something about that, yes sir," said Earl.

"Well," said the fellow, "today, he wrapped it up. Done arrested the gangster king himself, Owney Maddox, the big boss of Hot Springs."

"Arrested him?"

"That Fred done it by himself. Say, there's a fellow with some sand to him. They say he shot it out with the Grumleys at Mary Jane's and today he walked up big as life and arrested Owney Maddox."

"On what?"

"You must not have been listening to your radio. No sir, it's all over the radio. They're saying Fred's going to be the next damn governor. He got Owney Maddox on the charge of an art theft, for some kind of painting, and they searched Owney's apartment and they found some payroll slips from Alcoa, so they think Owney done masterminded that job. It's all falling apart on Owney Maddox. He's in jail and he's going to stay there and all them damn Grumleys he got working for him are squirreled good."

"Art theft?" said Earl.

"Some old picture he had. It was stolen, and Fred digged it out, and called the feds and made the arrest. Don't that beat all? It's just like with Al Capone. He's a bad man, but everybody's scared to go agin him, so they finally get him on tax evasion. So they get that Owney on art theft!"

"Ah," said Earl, as if he'd just learned something new.

"You okay, mister?"

"I'm fine," he said.

"'Cause you just look like a haunt walked through you."

"Nah, I'm fine," said Earl. He turned and went to his car.

He climbed in, but couldn't find the strength to turn the key. The Coke suddenly didn't interest him at all.

Fred Becker, hero? Fred Becker, the next governor? Hey, isn't it great about Fred Becker, how he got Owney Maddox?

He sat there, breathing hard.

What about them boys? What about that old man? They believed in their job and they risked their lives for it, and they got cut down in the night and nobody said Jack about it and a few days later it was as if it hadn't happened and nobody remembered a goddamn thing now that Fred Becker was a big hero.

In his head, one bitterness slid into and was absorbed by another. It was just like the war. All the boys go out onto the islands and they fight in battles so horrible it scars a man just to think about it. And they die, and by the time you get back everydamnbody's forgotten all about it and some joker's up front acting like a hero and he had nothing to do with it, not a goddamned thing.

He shook his head. The anger came over him so bad he could hardly stand it. He wanted to fight, to smash something, to howl at the moon, to kill something, to see it bleed and twitch out. It was a killing anger, a hurting anger.

He wanted to go back to Hot Springs and start shooting. But shoot who? They were all gone. Owney was locked up and whoever it was had hit the boys in the train yard, presumably that Johnny Spanish fellow, was off in some gangster hideout.

There was no one to kill. It was the same rage he felt when he went to beat his father and his father was already dying.

Earl got out of the car.

"You didn't drink that Coke up, mister."

"No, I didn't. Feel a need for something else tonight."

"You all right?"

"I am fine, sir."

He walked past them, but this time not into the general store but into the little liquor store next to it. There, in an old frame, was the front page of the Blue Eye newspaper with its story of the death of the great Charles Swagger, sheriff of Polk County, who'd died stopping a burglary over in Montgomery County, at Turner's liquor store, this very place.

"They never caught 'em," said the liquor store clerk, who was actually the same Ike who'd just stepped through a door.

"So I heard," said Earl.

"Hard to figure, that old guy fighting to save my uncle a few dollars' worth of beer."

"He wore the badge," said Earl. "He knew what he'd signed up for. Don't waste no time worrying about him."

"So what's your poison, sir?"

"You got that Boone County bourbon? Ain't had a lick of that in a time."

"You want the pint or the fifth."

Earl got out his wallet. He had seven dollars left and nothing else coming in soon.

"How much the fifth?"

"That'd be three dollar."

"Give me two fifths then. And keep the change, sonny."

CHAPTER

54

Nobody could believe how well Frenchy shot. Some of them were serious people. Some were ex-paratroopers, many ex-cops or FBI agents, some ex-Marines, all of whom who'd been in it, one way or the other. But Frenchy outshot them all, two-handed to boot.

"Son, who taught you to shoot like that?"

"An old guy, been in a lot of stuff. Worked it out, this system."

"It's not doctrine, but damn, it's so fast and accurate I don't see a point in changing it. Never would have believed it could be so fast, two hands and everything."

"You get used to it. It's rock steady."

"Wish I'd had you along on my team in Market Garden."

"Yeah, well, I was a little young for that."

"You ever in the for-real?"

"I was a cop in the South. I was in some for-real stuff. In it deep."

"Where?"

"Oh, the South."

"Oh, it's that way, is it? Sure, kid. You are a good hand."

"I was taught by the best," Frenchy said.

He was D.A.'s best pupil, really. The gun came from his holster so fast nobody could see it, was clapped by the other hand and outthrust even as his eyes clamped to the front sight and bangbang, he'd slap two holes in the kill zone, rotate to another, bangbang, and on to another, with the seventh round saved for just in case. These .45s had not been worked on like the ones D.A. had tricked up by Griffin & Howe, they were just old sloppy twenty-seventh-hand service Ithacas and Singers and IBMs, with an old Colt thrown in here and there for good measure, but they went pop every time the trigger was jacked and they felt familiar to Frenchy.

It was the shooting week of CIG training class 004, Clandestine Techniques, up on Catoctin Mountain in Maryland, where the old OSS had trained, a place called Camp Ritchie, maybe fifty miles outside of D.C. It still had a lot of World War II feeling to it, with the old LOOSE LIPS SINK SHIPS and INVEST IN INVASION BUY WAR BONDS posters turning yellow and tatty, the wooden barracks thick with the odor of men having lived in close quarters, all of it nestled safely behind barbed wire and guarded by Marines.

And of course Frenchy was just as good with anything; he could shoot the Thompson, the BAR and the carbine with extraordinary skill. It just seemed to come naturally to him, and it filled him with confidence, so that when the field problems arose, he seemed always to be the one who solved them fastest, even among men who'd been in combat. Soon he was an acting team leader, and he led after Earl's techniques, giving his boys nicknames (that is, nicknaming men who were ten years older than he was, Harvard and Yale graduates, and combat veterans), teasing them, cajoling them, always putting himself out front and when it came time to work, outworking them. He had a funny tic when he explained things to them: he'd listen, then say, "See, here's the thing," then gently point out the way it *should* be done.

Finally, toward the end of the course, an instructor drew him aside.

"You've done damned well, Short. You've impressed some people."

"Thanks."

"Now many of these guys will go under embassy cover to various spots around the world where they'll run agents, or recruit locals, or make reports. Some others will stay here, this'll be their only taste of the actual, and they'll be sent to headquarters, where they'll mainly be analysts."

"Both those sound pretty boring to me."

"Yeah, I thought so. You have a cowboy look to you. Are you a cowboy, Tex?"

"No sir."

"But you have a field operator's brain, I can tell. And real good shooting skills. Real good."

"Yes sir."

"You've been mentioned for Plans."

"Plans?" said Frenchy. "That doesn't sound like much fun."

"One thing you have to learn, Short, is that in this business nothing is what it sounds like. Okay?"

"Yes sir."

"Mr. Dulles sees Plans as a kind of action unit."

"Like a raid team?"

"Yeah, exactly. It'll be working in military or guerrilla-warfare situations, sometimes behind the lines, running operations. Probably high-contact work. Lots of bangbang. Lots of sentry-knifing, dog-killing, bomb-planting, border-crossing. That sound like your cup of tea?"

"Does it ever!"

"You have a problem with Army Jump School?"

"No sir."

"You have a problem with a commando tour with the Brits? Good training."

"Sounds good."

"You have a problem with language studies?"

"Ah—I speak French and passable German."

"Think about Chinese, Short. Or Indochinese. Or Greek. Or Korean. Or Russian, if the big one ever comes."

"Yes sir," said Frenchy.

"Good man," said the instructor.

And so Frenchy's course was set. He was to become a specialist in doing the necessary, not out of sentiment but out of hard, rational thought, carefully measured risk, a burglar's guts and a killer's decisiveness. But at this point he envisioned one more moment in his career with the Garland County raid team, a kind of a last thing that he owed himself. It came some months ahead in the week after he graduated from Clandestine Techniques OO4 at the head of his class and before he reported to Fort Benning for Jump School. He spent it in Washington, D.C., and for several days he roamed the city, looking for out-of-town newsstands, for copies of the Little Rock *Arkansas Gazette* or *Democrat*. He had no luck. But then he went to the Library of Congress and ordered up a batch of backdated *New York Times* and in that way, buried on a back page, learned of the fates of D.A. and the boys. EX-FBI AGENT SLAIN IN ACCIDENTAL GUNFIGHT. He did note that Earl's name was not listed among the dead, nor was Carlo Henderson's, so he assumed that somehow they had survived. It figured. You couldn't kill the cowboy. Maybe Bugsy Siegel would, as Johnny Spanish had predicted, but Owney hadn't been able to, not even with Frenchy's treacherous help.

If you saw him sitting there, in that vast, domed room on Capitol Hill behind the Congress, you would have seen a grave, calm young man, brimming with health and vitality, but already picking up a warrior's kind of melancholy aloofness from the workaday world around him. And at least at that moment—for he had not yet entirely mastered the art of completely stifling his emotions—you might have seen some regret too. Maybe even some sorrow.

CHAPTER

55

Earl started drinking almost immediately. The bourbon lit like a flare out beyond the wire and fell down his gullet, popping sparks of illumination, floating, drifting, pulling him ever so gently toward where he hoped the numbness was. No such goddamned luck. He drank only to forget, but of course the only thing the bourbon did was make him remember more, so he drank more, which made him remember yet more again.

He wasn't headed west on 270 toward Y City, which would take him over to 71 for the pull up toward Fort Smith and Camp Chaffee, where his wife and unborn child, his new life or whatever, awaited. He couldn't do that, somehow. He was in no state to face them and the emotions that he had controlled so masterfully for four days now seemed dangerously near explosion. He knew he was rocky. He turned south, down 27 out of Mount Ida, to 8, and then west on 8. He knew exactly where he was headed even if he couldn't say it or acknowledge it.

By the time he pulled into Board Camp it was nearly midnight. Wasn't much to be seen at all. It was never even as much as Mount Ida. He drove through the little town and there, a few miles beyond toward the county seat of Blue Eye, off on the right, he saw the old mailbox. SWAGGER it said, same as it always had.

He turned right, sank as the dirt road plunged off the highway, watched his light beams lance out in the darkness until at last they illuminated the house where he grew up, where his family lived, where his father lived, where his brother died. The light beams hit the house.

They illuminated broken windows, knocked-out boards, ragged weeds, a garden gone to ruin, peeling paint, the nothingness of abandonment. After his father died, his mother had simply given up and moved to town. He never saw her again; he was in the hospital after Tarawa when the news came that she had died.

Earl pulled into the barnyard and when his lights crossed that structure, he saw that it too had fallen into total disrepair. It needed paint and was lost in a sea of ragweed and unkempt grass. Daddy would shit if he saw it now. Daddy always kept it so nice. Or rather, Daddy directed that it be kept nice. It had to be perfect, and it was one of Earl's chores to mow the lawn and lord help him if he forgot it, or he didn't do it well enough. The lawn had to be perfect, the garden well cultivated, the whole thing upstanding and pretty, as befits an important man.

Earl turned off the lights. He opened the door. Crickets tweedled in the dark and the soft rush of the wind filled the Arkansas night, with maybe just a hint of fall in the air. The house was big, with four bedrooms up on the second floor. Once it had been the leading house in the eastern half of Polk County, maintained by a lot of good land, but somehow, some Swagger granddad or other back in the last century had gotten out of the farming business before really getting into it and committed to the law enforcement business, because the Swagger men were always hunters, always had a kind of natural instinct for the rifle, and a gift for reading the terrain. No one knew where it came from, but they'd been soldiers and hunters for as long as anyone could remember, just as long as they'd lived in these parts. They were never farmers.

Earl tipped the bottle up and felt the bourbon clog his throat and with a mighty gulp he took down two more harsh swallows. The illumination rounds went off in his guts, lighting the target. It made his eyes water. He stood, wobbling just a little, and faced the big house.

It scared him still. It was a house of fear. You walked softly in that house because you didn't want to upset Daddy. Daddy ruled that house as he ruled so much of the known world. Daddy's hugeness was something he could feel even now, his presence, looming and feary and cold and mad, that man who even to this day stalked the corridors of Earl's mind, always whispering to him.

"Goddamn you, Daddy, goddamn your black soul! Come out and fight!" Earl screamed.

But Daddy didn't.

Earl saw that he had finished the bottle. He returned to the car, now glad he'd bought a second one. He found it. He had some trouble with the cap because he was so damned drunk his fingers barely worked, but in a little bit, it came free. By now the bourbon had lost its taste. He swallowed, swallowed some more, and pitched forward. He passed out in the front yard.

Sometime later in the night, Earl awoke, still drunk but shivery in the cold. He was wet; he'd pissed his pants. No, no, it was dew, dampening him through his suit coat. He pulled himself up, shuddered mightily in the cold, seized the bottle and took another couple of pulls. But he didn't pass out. Instead he rose, and in the blurry darkness of his vision made out the car. He wobbled back toward it, unsteadily as hell, and made it all the way, falling only once.

"Goddamn," he cursed to no man, as around him the black world pitched and bobbed, as if he were on some merry-go-round that went up and down just as fast as it went around. He felt like he was going to puke. He flew off in all directions and all six of his hands reached for all six of the handles to the door of the vehicle, and somehow he got it open and plunged into the back seat, and collapsed with a thump as the blackness closed around him again.

He awoke again to a strange sound. His frayed mind stirred from unconsciousness. He seemed covered in grit somehow. Again the sound: loud, close, familiar. Again the grit, spraying downward on him like droplets of water, except it wasn't water it was—

BANG!

Another bullet tore through the window, puncturing neatly through, leaving a spackle of fractures, a mercury smear across the glass, erupting with a spray of grit that was pulverized glass which floated out in a cloud, then floated down upon him.

"Don't shoot!" he screamed and in a split second realized what had happened. Somehow Owney's Grumley boys had tracked him down. They had him nailed. They knew where he'd go and that's where he went and they found him passed out in the car and they worried it was a trick so they laid up until the light and when he still didn't stir after a bit they fired rounds through the windows and the windshield.

"Don't shoot!" he screamed again, knowing he was finished. He had no gun. He was aflame with pain, head to toe, from the ravages of al-

cohol. His mind was all jittery with fear. Goddamn them! They had found him!

Earl hated fear and worked hard at controlling it, at testing himself against it because it scared him so much, but now he had no preparation for it, and it just came and took him and made him its toy. He began to cry. He couldn't be brave. He couldn't fight. He was going to end up like his daddy, shot by killers and left dying and begging for mercy.

"You show us hands!" came the cry, *"or goddamn we will finish you good!"*

He looked around. Nothing to fight with. Another shot rocked through the window, blowing out a puff of sheared, shredded glass.

"I'll put one in your gut, mister, you come out or by God I will finish you."

Earl kicked the door open and as he rose felt the shredded glass raining off his body like a collection of sand. He blinked in the sunlight, showed his hands, and edged out. There were at least four Grumleys, all with big lever-action rifles, all laid up behind cover, all zeroed on him.

One of the men emerged from cover.

"You armed?"

"No sir."

"Don't trust him, Luke. Them boys is tricky. I can pop him right now."

"You hold it, Jim. Now, mister, I want you to shuck that coat and show me you got nothing or Jim will pop you like a squirrel. Don't you do nothing tricky."

Why didn't they just shoot him and be done with it? Did they want to hang him, beat him, set him afire?

Slowly with one hand, then the other, he peeled off the coat, and showed by his blue shirt and suspenders that he was unarmed. He kept his hands high. Two of the men approached while two others hung back, keeping him well covered. By the way they handled their rifles, Earl could tell they had handled rifles a lot.

"Turn round and up agin that car," commanded the leader.

Earl assumed the position. A hand fished his wallet out while another patted him down.

"What the hell are you doing here?" he was asked.

"I own this place. Been paying taxes on it for years."

"Hell, nobody owns this place, since old lady Swagger done up n' died in town. This is Sheriff Charles Swagger's old place, mister."

"And I am Charles Swagger's son, Earl."

"Earl?"

"By God, yes," came another voice, "according to his driver's license, this here's Earl Swagger hisself."

"Jesus Christ, Earl, why'n't you say so? Git them hands down, by God, heard what you done to them Japs in the islands. Earl, it's Luke Petty, I'se two years behind you in high school."

Earl turned. The men had lowered their rifles and gazed at him with reverence, their blue eyes eating him alive. Luke Petty looked slightly familiar, but maybe it was the type: the rawboned Scotch-Irish border reiver whose likeness filled the hills a hundred miles in either direction.

"Luke, I—"

"Goddamn, yes, it's Earl, Earl Swagger, who won the Medal of Honor. Where, Earl, Saipan?"

"Iwo."

"Iwo goddamned Jima. You made the whole damned county proud of you. Pity your daddy and mommy weren't around to know it."

That was another story. Earl left it alone.

"Sorry about the car, Earl. Folks is jumpy and we seen a car in an abandoned place and a man sleeping. Well, you know."

Earl didn't, not really, but before he could say a thing, another man said, "Earl, you look plenty wore out. You okay?"

"Yes, I'm fine. I now and then go on a toot, like the old man—"

"He was a drinking man, yes, I do remember. Oncet boxed my ears so hard made 'em ring for a month," one of the other men said fondly.

"Well, I have the same curse. I'm now living up in Fort Smith and I fell off the wagon. Got so drunk I didn't want the wife to see me. So I somehow turned up here. Sorry to rile you."

"Hell, Earl, it ain't nothing. You ought to move on back here. This is your home, this is where you belong."

"Don't know about that, but maybe. I have a child on the way and we will see."

Then he noticed the stars. Each of these boys was a deputy, each wore a gunbelt loaded with cartridges and a powerful revolver, each had the look of a rangy manhunter to him.

"What're you boys out huntin'? You look loaded for grizzly."

"You ain't heard?"

"How could I? Was drunked up like a crazy bastard last night."

"Earl, you best watch that. Can tear a fellow down. Saw my own daddy go sour with the drink. He died too young, and he looked a hundred when he's only forty-two."

"I hear you on that one," said Earl, who hoped he'd never drink again.

"Anyhow, we're hunting gangsters."

"Gangsters?"

"He ain't heard!"

"Damn, he did do some drinking last night."

"You know that Owney Maddox, the big New York gun what run Hot Springs these past twenty years? The one old Fred Becker caught?"

"Heard of him," Earl said.

"Five bastards busted him out of Garland County jail last night late. Shot their way out. Say it was just as bad as that Alcoa train job or that big shoot-out in the train yard. Killed two men. But Owney's fled, he's free, the whole goddamned state's out looking for him."

"Earl, you okay?"

"Yeah," said Earl.

"You look like a ghost touched you on the nose with a cold finger."

Owney. Owney was out.

CHAPTER

56

It was exactly the kind of operation Johnny Spanish loved. It demanded his higher skills and imagination. It wasn't merely force. On its own, force was tedious. Labor enforcers, racketeers, small-potatoes strong-arm boys, the common soldiers of crime, they all used force and it never expressed anything except force.

Johnny always looked for something else. He loved the game aspects of it, the cleverness of the planning, the deviousness of the timing, the feint, the confusion, the misinformation, and the final, crushing, implacable boldness. It was all a part of that ineffable *je ne sais quoi* that made Johnny Johnny.

Thus at 10:30 P.M. at the Garland County jail in the Town Hall and Police Department out Ouachita Avenue toward the western edge of the city, the first indication of mischief was not masked men with machine guns but something entirely unexpected: tomato pies.

The tomato pie was new to the South, though it had gained some foothold in New Jersey and Philadelphia. It was a large, flat disk of unleavened dough with a certain elastic crispiness to it, coated with a heavy tomato sauce and a gruel of mozzarella cheese, all allowed to coagulate in a particularly intense oven experience. It was quite a taste sensation, both bold and chewy, both exotic and accessible, both sweet and tart, both the best of old Italy and new America at once. Four tomato pies, cut into wedges, were delivered gratis to the jail by two robust fellows from Angelino's Italian Bakery and Deli, newly opened and yet to catch on, to the late-night jail guard shift. The boys hadn't ordered any tomato pies—they'd never even heard of tomato pies!— but free food was one of the reasons they'd gotten into law enforcement in the first place. Even those who had no intention of eating that night found themselves powerless in the grip of obsession, when the odors of the sizzling pies began to suffuse the woeful old lockup. Who could deny the power of the tomato pie, and that devilish, all-powerful, mesmerizing smell that beckoned even the strongest of them onward.

This was the key to the plan. Like many jails built in the last century, Garland County's was constructed on the concentric ring-of-steel design, with perimeters of security inside perimeters of security. One could not be breached until the one behind it was secure. Yet all yielded to the power of the tomato pie.

The guards—seven local deputies and warders and a lone FBI representative since the prisoner, No. 453, was on a federal warrant— clustered in the admin office, enjoying slice after slice.

"This stuff is *good.*"

"It's Italian? Jed, you see anything like this in It-ly?"

"All's I seen was bombed-out towns and starvin' kids and dead Krautheads. Didn't see nothing like this."

"Man, this stuff is good."

"Best thing is, they deliver to your doorway and it's piping hot."

"It's 'Mambo Italiano' in cheese and tomato. I love the toastiness. That's what's so good. I like that a lot."

At that point, two more men from Angelino's showed up, with four more pies.

"You guys-a, you love-a this-a one, it's got the pepperoni sausage, very spicy."

"Sausage?" said the guard sergeant.

"Spicy," said the deliveryman, who opened the flat cardboard box, removed a 1911 Colt automatic with a Maxim silencer, and shot the man once. The silencer wasn't all that silent, and everyone in the room knew immediately that a gun had been fired, but it reduced the sound of the percussion enough to dampen it from alerting others in the building. More guns came out, and a large fellow appeared in the doorway with a BAR.

"Get against the wall, morons," screamed the commander of the commandos—that is, Johnny Spanish at his best.

"Jesus, you shot—"

Johnny knew the tricky moment was in the early going where you asserted control or you lost it and it turned to nightmare and massacre. Therefore, according to his lights, he was doing the humane thing when he shot that man too, knocking him down. If he'd been closer he would have clubbed the man with the long cylindrical heft of the silencer, but that was the way the breaks went, and they didn't go well for that particular guard that particular day.

Herman grabbed the biggest of the men and said simply and forcefully, "Keys," and was obediently led to the steel cabinet on the wall, it was opened, and the keys were displayed for his satisfaction.

"Which one, asshole?" he demanded.

The man's trembly fingers flew to a single key, which Herman seized. With Ding-Dong as his escort, he headed into the interior of the jail.

Iron-barred doors flew open quickly enough and, deep in the warren, they came to the cage that contained Owney Maddox. That door too was sprung, and Owney was plucked from ignominy. He threw on his coat and rushed out, passing the parade as Johnny and his boys led the surrendered guards back into the jail to lock them up away from telephones so that he didn't have to shoot the lot of them.

"Good work," Owney cried. And it was. For his legal situation had collapsed and it appeared a murder indictment for the four guards slain in 1940 was in the offing. A gun had been found in his warehouse that had been used in that crime and the FBI test results had just come in. Meanwhile, all his well-placed friends had deserted him, and even lawyer F. Garry Hurst wasn't sanguine about his chances of survival. A life on the lam, even well financed as his would be, would be no picnic but it was infinitely preferable to life in the gray-bar hotel.

Johnny's team quickly completed the herding operation, locking the bulls back with the cons. Then they methodically ripped out all phone lines. Owney was bundled into the back of an actual Hot Springs police car, driven by Vince the Hat de Palmo in an actual Hot Springs police uniform and he disappeared into the night.

Johnny and his boys left in the next several seconds, but not, of course, before they'd finished the pizza.

Vince drove Owney through the night and at a certain point on the outskirts of town, they pulled into a garage. There, the stolen police car was abandoned, and Owney got into the hollowed-out core of a pile of hay bales already loaded on the back of a hay truck, which was to be driven by two trustworthy Negroes in the Grumley employ. The hay pressed in close around him, like a coffin, and the truck backed out and began an unsteady progress through town. It would only be a matter of minutes before sirens announced the discovery of the breakout, but the plan was to get Owney out of the immediate downtown area before roadblocks were set up. They almost made it.

The sirens began to howl just a few minutes into the trip. Yet nobody panicked. The old truck rumbled along and twice was overtaken by roaring police cars. Once it was stopped, cursorily examined, its hay bales probed and pulled slightly apart. Owney lay still and heard the

Negro driver answering in his shufflingest voice to the police officers. But the cops hurried onward when they grew impatient with the mo- lasses-slow drift of the driver's words as he explained to them that the hay was for Mr. Randy in Pine Mountain, from the farm of Mr. David- son in Arkadelphia, and so they passed on.

They drove through the night, though at about thirty-five miles an hour. Owney knew the city would be in an uproar. A certain code had been broken when the two police officers had been shot, which meant that now the cops would pursue him with all serious purpose, earlier arrangements having been shattered. But it could be no other way. Very shortly he'd be transferred to a sounder federal incarceration and there'd be no escape from that. Whatever, he understood, his Hot Springs days were over; his fortune had already been transferred, and the ownership of his various enterprises passed on, through the good offices of F. Garry Hurst, to other men, though the benefits to him would accrue steadily over the years.

But he did not believe that retirement was at hand. He would leave the country, live somewhere quietly in wealth and health over the next few years, and things would be worked out. He had too much on too many people for it to be elsewise. Somehow, he knew he wasn't done; possibilities still existed. It would be explained that he was abducted, not escaped; the deaths of the policemen would have nothing to do with him; a deal would be worked out somehow, a year or two in a soft prison, then he'd be back in some fashion or other.

He had to survive. He had but one ambition now, and that was to arrange for the elimination of Ben Siegel, who clearly was the agent of his downfall. It couldn't be done quickly, though, or harshly. Ben had friends on the commission and was said to be doing important work for them in the West. He was, for the time being, protected. But that wouldn't last. Owney knew Ben's impetuousness would make him somehow overreach, his greed would cloud his judgment, his hurry would offend, his hunger would irritate. There would be a time now, very shortly, when Ben was vulnerable, and he would be the one to take advantage of it.

In what seemed long hours later, the quality of the ride changed. It signified the change from macadam to dirt road, and the speed grew even slower. The vehicle bumped and swayed through the night and there was no sound of other traffic as it wound its way deeper and deeper toward its destination.

Finally, they arrived.

The hay bales were pulled aside, and Owney rose and stretched.

"Good work, fellows," he said, blinking and stretching, to discover himself on a dirt road in a dense forest, almost silent except for the heavy breathing of the drivers.

"Yas suh," said one of the drivers.

"You take good care of these boys," he said, addressing Flem Grumley, who stood there with a flashlight in a party of several of his boys, all heavily armed.

"I will, Mr. Maddox," promised Flem.

"The others arrive yet?"

"Johnny and Herman. The other two haven't made it in yet. But they will."

"Yes," agreed Owney.

The two drivers restored the hay and left with the truck. Meanwhile, Flem led Owney and Vince through the trees and down a little incline. A body of water lay ahead, glinting in the moonlight and from the lights of buildings across the way. It was Lake Catherine.

They stepped through rushes, and eased their way down a rocky incline toward the water, under the illumination of the flashlights guided by the Grumleys.

In time, they came to a cave into which the water ran and slid into it.

"Hallo, Owney lad," sang Johnny, rising to greet the man whose life he had just saved. "It's just like the last time, except we didn't steal any payroll, we stole you!"

CHAPTER
57

The deputies had gone, leaving Earl alone with his headache, his shot-out car windows and his bad news.

He shook his head.

Owney makes it out; he'll get away, he's got some smart boys in town with him, he'll get his millions of dollars out, and he'll go live in luxury somewhere. He won't pay. The dead boys of the Garland County raid team and their old leader pass into history as fools and the man they died to stop ends up living with a swimming pool in France or Mexico somewhere.

Earl felt the need to drink again. This one really hurt. This one was like a raw piece of glass caught in his throat, cutting every time he breathed.

The sun was bright, his head ached, he felt the shakiness of the hangover, the hunger from not having eaten in twenty-four hours, and the emptiness of no life ahead of him and memories of what was done stuck in his head forever.

He wiped the sweat from his brow, and decided it was time to go on home and try and pick up the pieces. Yet something wouldn't let him leave.

He knew, finally: he had to see the place one more time.

See the goddamned barn.

He'd seen it in November when he was discharged and stopped off here before going on up to Fort Smith and getting married and joining up with the rest of America for the great postwar boom. Hadn't felt much then. Tried to feel something but didn't, but he knew he had to try again.

He walked through the weeds, the wind whipping dust in his face, the sun beating down hot and ugly, a sense of desolation like a fog over the abandoned Swagger homestead, where all the Swagger men had lived and one of them had died.

The barn door was half open. He slipped in. Dust, cobwebs, the smell of rotted hay and rotting wood. An unpainted barn will rot, Daddy had always said. Yes, and if Daddy wasn't here to see that the barn was painted every two years, it would rot away to nothing, which is what it was doing. The stench of mildew and decomposition also filled the close dense air. The wood looked moist in places, as if you could put a foot through it and it would crumble. Odd pieces of agricultural equipment lay about rusting, like slingblades and the lawn mower that Earl had once used, and spades and hoes and forks. A tractor, dusty and rusting, stood mutely by. The stalls were empty, though of course a vague odor of animal shit also lingered in the air.

But Earl went to where he had to go, which was to the rear of the barn, under a crossbeam. That is where Bobby Lee had hanged himself. There was no mark of the rope on the wood, and no sign of the barrel he had stood upon to work his last task, the tying of the knot, good and tight, the looping of the noose, and the final kick to liberate himself from the barrel's support and from the earth's woe.

He had hung there, as the life was crushed out of his throat, believing that he was going to a better place.

Hope you made it, Bobby Lee. I wasn't no good to you at all. You were the first of the all-too-many young men I let down and who paid with it with their lives. There were legions of these beyond Bobby Lee, platoons full of them, from the 'Canal to the railyard in Hot Springs, all of whom had trusted him and there wasn't a damn thing he could do for them except watch them die.

A thought came to Earl. He could find a rope and do the same trick and that would solve a lot of problems for a lot of people, mostly himself. The faces of boys wouldn't always be there, except when he was in a gunfight, to haunt him and sour his sleep, his food, his life.

But Earl was somehow beyond that now. He had a vague memory of shooting himself in the head in a bathroom in Washington, dead drunk, and finding that he'd forgotten to load the chamber, the only time ever in his whole life when he had pulled a trigger and been surprised at what happened.

Bobby Lee hadn't been so lucky. He wanted to leave the world and no secret part of him intervened. He kicked the barrel and he left the world and went to a better world, where no drunken father would take his anger out on him, and beat him and beat him just to express his own rage at what lurked deep in his own mind. October 2, 1940. Earl had been in the Panama Canal Zone at Balboa, on jungle maneuvers, happy in his far-off mock war, his brain consumed with the tactical problems, the discomforts, the need to lead his men, his worry over a captain who seemed a little too fond of the bottle, the—

No, no. *Not* October 2, 1940. That was something else. That was something else. Bobby Lee killed himself two days later, October 4, 1940. Why had he remembered October 2?

Oh, yes. Now he had it: Carlo Henderson had pointed out that the Alcoa payroll job had been October 2. Five men shot and killed four railway guards in the same damned railyard, and got away scot-free with $400,000 that very quickly came back to Owney Maddox, who probably was going to live off it for the rest of his life.

Something nagged at Earl.

Suddenly he wasn't in the dust-choked barn anymore, where his brother died and where the general agenda was rot and ruin, but only in his head.

Daddy must have beaten Bobby Lee really bad on October 3 or October 4. He must have gotten completely drunk and angry and forgotten himself and beat the boy so hard the boy concluded there was a better place to be and it wasn't in this world.

Why October 4?

Well, why not? If it was going to happen, it was going to happen and any one date was as good as another.

Still Earl couldn't put it quite away. It *was* two days after the most notorious crime of the era. His daddy would have been busy on roadblock duty all that—

Well, what about that?

Why wasn't Daddy parked out on some roadblock? A robbery that big, leaving that many men dead, the roadblocks would have stayed out for a week at least. Yet somehow in all that mess, Daddy has a chance to get liquored up and comes home and finds his second son and cannot help but release his deepest rage and beats on the boy so bad that the boy decides this life ain't worth living no more and that he will stop the hurting.

Could Charles have had something to do with the robbery?

It almost seemed possible. For with Charles's secret life in Hot Springs, he'd certainly have come to the notice of Owney and the Grumleys. His weakness made him vulnerable to blackmail, as did his gambling debts. If they needed him, he'd have been powerless to stop them. He was made to order for the taking, with his rigidity, his pride, his secret shame, his alcoholism.

And maybe it wasn't till afterward he learned that four men had died and he hadn't just helped robbers but killers as well. And he'd been so overcome with disgust and self-loathing for what he'd done, he'd laid on a big drunk. The biggest. And God help his child when he got in that way.

But then Earl had a sudden laugh. Standing there in that rotting barn, breathing the choking dust and smelling the odor of rot and shit and rust, he laughed hard.

What on earth could my daddy have known to help those birds? Charles Swagger knew nothing! What the hell value was he? He knew how to sap a drunk and get the cuffs on. He knew how to fix an uppity Negro with a stare so hard it would melt a safe. He knew how to shoot, as he'd proved in the Great War, and in the bank in Blue Eye in 1923, but them boys didn't need shooters, that was clear; they knew how to shoot.

Earl turned, and slipped out of the barn. A cloud had come over the sun, so it was cooler now, and the freshness of the air revived him somewhat as he escaped the dense atmosphere. He allowed himself a smile. His father! A conspirator in a train robbery! That stubborn, mule-proud old bastard with his stern Baptist ways and his secret weakness and rancid hypocrisy! What could he offer such men! They'd laugh at him because they didn't fear him and without the power of fear he had no power at all.

Earl walked over to the porch and sat down. He knew he should leave soon. It was time to go. He had to make peace with his failures, to face the future, to go on and—

But: Who was my father?

Who was he? I don't know. He scared me too much to ever ask the question when the man was alive, and his memory hurt too much to ask it when he was dead. But: Who was he?

He turned and looked into the old house. If there was an answer maybe it was in the house that Charles Swagger inherited from Swaggers before and made his own little invincible kingdom.

Earl rose and went to the door. It had been nailed shut. He hesitated, then remembered that he now owned the place and the door only sealed him off from his own legacy. With a stout kick, he blasted the door open, and stepped inside.

Some houses always smell the same. He'd have recognized it anywhere, though now the furniture was gone, as were the pictures off the wall. The smell was somehow more than the accumulated odors of his mother's cooking and the generations of cooking that had come before; it was more than the grief or the melancholy that had haunted this place; it was more than the bodies that had lived here. It was unique and its totality took him backward.

He remembered himself as a boy of about twelve. The house was so big and dark, the furniture all antiques from the century before. If his father was home, the house would tell him: there'd be a tension somehow in the very structure of the universe. Daddy might not be angry that day, might merely be aloof and distant, but the danger of his explosiveness would float through these rooms and corridors like some sort of vapor, volatile and nerve-breaking, awaiting the spark that set it off.

Or maybe Daddy was drinking. He drank mostly on the weekends but sometimes, for unknown reasons, he'd drink at night and the drink loosened his tongue and let his demons spill out. Maybe he'd hit you, maybe he wouldn't, but it wasn't just the hitting; he'd be on you, like some kind of stallion or bull or bull rooster. He had to dominate you. He couldn't let you breathe.

What're you staring at, goddammit, he'd demand.

What's wrong with you, boy. You some kind of girl? You just stare. I'll knock that goddamned stare off your face.

Charles, the boy didn't mean nothing.

In my house, nobody stares at me. This is *my* house. Y'all live here because *I* let you. I set the rules. I provide the food, I pay the hands, I keep the law in this county, I set the rules.

Earl walked from room to room. Each was empty in fact but full in his own mind. He remembered everything, exactly: the placement of the sofa, the size and shape of the dining room table, the old brown pictures of Swaggers from an earlier time and place, he remembered them all.

Whoa, partner, he counseled himself. Don't let your hate just fog your mind.

He tried another approach. If you must understand your father, don't think about what made him angry, since *everything* made him angry. Think about what made him happy.

He tried to remember his father happy. Was his father ever happy? Had his father ever smiled?

He had no memory of such an event, but in time he realized that being occupied, his demons quelled momentarily by mental activity, was as close to happiness as Charles Swagger, sheriff of Polk County, ever got.

So Earl knew where he had to go.

Not into the kitchen or the bedroom or the cellar, and not upstairs where the boys slept, but back through the house to his father's trophy room.

That was his father's sanctum. That's where his father retreated. It was a sacred temple to . . . well, whatever. Who knew? Who could say?

Earl opened the door. The old woman had left the room pretty much intact when she left after his death. The guns were gone of course, presumably sold off, and the cabinet removed. Earl remembered standing before it as a child; in fact his one or two pleasant memories with his father seemed to revolve around the guns, which stood locked behind glass. The old man had some nice ones: Winchesters mostly, dark and oily, sheathed in gleamy soft wood, a Hi-Wall in .45-120, a whole brace of lever actions, from an 1873 he'd picked up somewhere to a '92 to an 1895 carbine, all in calibers nobody loaded anymore, like .40-72 and .219 Zipper and a beautiful old 1886 in .40-65; Daddy also had a couple of the little self-loaders, in .401. He had three shotguns for geese in the fall, and he had one bolt gun, the '03 Springfield, which he'd turned into a sleek and beautiful sporter. The guns were treated with respect. If Daddy approved—rare, but it happened—you were allowed to touch the guns. But they were gone. So was the desk, the volumes of works on hunting, reloading and ballistics, the liquor cabinet where the ever-filled bottle of magic amber fluid was kept. So was the map of Polk County, where he had painstakingly tracked his kills with coded color pins each year, yellow for deer, red for boar, black for bear, so that in the end, the map was a tapestry of brightly lit little dots, each signifying a good shot. A blank rectangular space stood on the wall, where the map had been taped for all those years and the paint hadn't faded. Now it was just emptiness.

And she had no stomach for removing the trophies themselves. It was as if Charles's powerful medicine still inhabited them, and looking at them on another wall, he saw they were dusty and ratty, beginning to fall apart like old furniture, their ferocity largely theatrical. Earl nevertheless felt the power of his father's presence.

Charles was a hunter. He stalked the mountains and the meadows of Polk and other nearby counties with his Winchesters, and he shot what he saw. He was a very good shot, an excellent game shot, and he learned the habits of the creatures. He was a man who could always support himself in the woods, and he had that Swagger gift, mysterious and unsourced, for understanding the terrain and making the good read, then finishing up with a brilliant shot on the deflection.

Earl remembered; his father took him hunting and taught him to shoot, and taught him to track, taught him patience and stoicism and a bit of crazed courage, the willingness to ignore the body and do what had to be done. And the odd thing was, they were skills that let Earl survive the dark journey that would become his fate. So he did in fact get something from his daddy, a great gift, even if he never realized it at the time.

He looked at the heads on the wall. Bear, boar, three deer, an elk, a cougar, a bobcat, a ram, all bearing either a graceful furl of horn or a mouthful of snaggly teeth. Like any trophy hunter, his father took only the best, the oldest animals, who had long since passed their genes along to progeny. The taxidermist was a fellow in Hatfield, and he too had the gift.

The animals seemed to live on that wall. They were frozen in expressions of anger or assault, their lips curled back, their fangs bared, the full animal majesty of their power exploding off their faces. It was all make-believe, of course; Earl had been to the shop and the taxidermist was a bald, fat little cracker who smelled of chemicals and had a shop full of marble eyes sent from 34th Street in New York, intricate replicas of the real thing that gleamed and seemed to stare, but were merely glass.

What does this room tell me?

Who was my father?

Who was this man?

He stared at the trophy animals on the wall, and they stared back at him, relentless, if locked in place, still spoiling for a great fight.

What did my father know?

On the evidence of this room, only the pleasures of the hunt. And the pleasures of the land the hunt was conducted upon.

That's what a hunter knows. A hunter knows the land. A hunter roams the land, and even if he's not hunting that particular day, he's paying attention, storing up information, recording details that some-day may come in handy.

That's what my father would know: the Arkansas mountain wilder-ness, as well as any man before or since.

That was the only place he was ever really happy.

CHAPTER

58

Owney was nervous. Across the way, there seemed a lot of activity. Searchlights and the pulsing flash of red gumballs cut the night as the cops stopped cars, threw up roadblocks, sent out search teams and dogs on the hunt for him. But the lake was serenely calm. It lay in the dark like a sheet of glass, glinting with illumination from the various points of light on the shore.

"Don't worry," said Johnny. "It'll be like the last time. It'll go with-out a hitch."

"I ain't worried about the lake," said Owney. "I'm worried about the forest. How can you remember? It was so complicated. It was at night."

"I have a photographic memory," said Johnny. "Certain things I don't forget and you can take that to the bank." He smiled, radiating charm. He held all the cards, and he knew it.

"And then we talk money."

"There's plenty, believe me," Owney assured him.

"That's the problem. I don't believe you. No matter what I ask for you'll cry-baby and try to jew me down. But I know you've got mil-lions."

"I don't have millions," said Owney. "That's a fuckin' myth."

"Oh, I've done some checking," said Johnny. "I have a figure in mind. A very nice figure. After all, we *are* saving your life. It seems like I should take you for everything, because I'm saving everything."

"Is this a getaway or a kidnapping?"

"Well, actually, it's a wee bit of both," said Johnny. "We won't leave you with nothing."

"No, you wouldn't want to do that," said Owney. "You want me to be your friend after all this is over. I'll get back, somehow, you know I will. I'm Owney Maddox. I ran the Cotton Club. I ran Hot Springs. This is just a little setback. I ain't going into no retirement. I'll be big in the rackets again, you'll fuckin' see."

"Yeah, sure," said Johnny.

"I think I'll move out to California. The opportunities are golden and I got a feeling there's about to be a change in management real soon. A certain party's luck just ran out."

It was almost time.

Johnny checked his watch and went to the mouth of the cave and looked across the lake. Owney followed and sure enough, out of the darkness they saw the white flashing sails of a large craft. That was the core of Johnny's plan. He knew that the law enforcement imagination was somehow drawn to the drama of the high-speed getaway. Thus cops thought of roads mainly, and of airplanes and railways. Crime was modern, fast-paced, built on speed. Who would ever suspect—a sailboat?

It was a beauty, owned by Judge LeGrand, a fifty-footer under two masts and a complexity of sails that pulled it gracefully and silently across the water. The judge entertained on it many times, taking visiting congressmen and titans of industry out for elegant sails across the diamond-blue water, under the diamond-blue sky, swaddled in the green rolling pine hills of the Ouachitas, where they sipped champagne and ate oysters and laughed the evening away like the important men they were, so that when they lost their hundreds of thousands at Owney's gaming tables, they still went home with wondrous tales of Southern hospitality and sleek nights under starry skies.

The boat drew four feet; she was a trim craft, pure teak and brass, with a crew of four to run her and an auxiliary engine—nobody knew about this, it was her secret—that could propel her through the water in the absence of wind and had the special gift of taking her along narrow passages under mechanical power if necessary, and it would be very necessary.

The boat was too cumbersome to dock, so it simply put up at anchor seventy-five feet out and a dinghy, propelled by two oarsmen, slid toward them.

"All right, you boys, let's get aboard," Johnny commanded as the small craft nudged ashore.

They left the cave, scuttled down the bit of hillside and ducked among the reeds until they reached the prow, which was being held steady at a taut rope's end by a crewman. Owney clambered aboard, shivering ever so slightly as the breeze picked up. The boat's insubstantiality annoyed him—he liked things solid—as he found a seat. He felt it continue to slipside and tremble as the others came aboard. But then, quickly enough, they were off and the progress to the bigger boat was easy.

Hands drew Owney aboard.

"Good evening, Mr. Maddox," said Brick Stevens, the boat's skipper, a hot local available bachelor who secretly (Owney knew) was screwing both the judge's daughter and his wife, "how are you, sir?"

"I'll be much better when I'm sipping a piña colada in Acapulco," he said.

"It'll just be a couple of days. The judge sends his best wishes."

"The judge better keep sending his money. I own this town, after all."

"I'm sure the judge realizes that, sir."

After Owney, the five gunmen, encumbered with their weapons, clambered aboard.

"All right, boys," said Brick, "let's go down below. Meanwhile, we'll be off."

They stepped uneasily down the teak steps into what was a stateroom, though not much of one, more a state crawlspace. But inside, yes, it was nice, more teak, with a small bar, lots of liquor.

Owney settled down on the sofa. The others took up chairs and whatever.

"I'm going to turn the lanterns down, fellows," said Brick. "It'll be safer that way."

"How long, skipper?"

"Can't be more than four hours. There's enough breeze and I'll go three sheets. I know these waters like the back of my hand. I'll have you where you want to be by twenty-two bells. That's ten o'clock for you landlubbers."

"We're all landlubbers here," said Herman Kreutzer, holding his BAR loosely.

"You will be careful with that?" requested Brick.

"Sure. But if a State Police cruiser tries to board us, you'll be glad I've got it."

"This is an antique, old man. We can't have it shot up."

"Then sail good, skip."

The skipper ducked back upstairs and in just a few minutes the boat began to edge forward in the darkness as its sails caught and harnessed the wind. It was like a train, in that it seemed to take forever to get going, but then, suddenly, had amassed enormous smooth speed, and flashed across the water.

Owney looked out the porthole. He could see a few lights, but wherever they were, the shore was mostly dark. There was no sound except for the snapping of the sail in the wind and the rush of the water being pushed aside by the boat's knifelike prow.

"We're okay on time?" asked Owney.

Johnny made a show of squinting at his watch, and then a bigger show of making abstract calculations in his head, and finally came up with an answer.

"Absolutely okay."

"Because the longer we hang around, the greater the chance of someone spotting me."

"I know it."

"And you've made the calls, it's all set up, these are reliable people."

"Very reliable. This is the soft way out. It worked before, it'll work again. Think of the last time as a rehearsal. This is the performance. Everything's set. The critics will love it. You'll be a hit on Broadway."

"I don't care about hits on Broadway. I care about hits in Las Vegas."

"It will happen."

"The fuck. Who the fuck he think he is! Braque! I bought that god-damn painting from a legit dealer. How's *I* supposed to know it was hot?"

"Owney, Owney, Owney," crooned Johnny. "You're home free. You'll have your freedom, your vengeance and your wealth. No man in America is better off than you."

The boat skimmed across the smooth water, and Owney settled down and watched as the lights of Hot Springs passed on the right and then got smaller and dimmer until they died away altogether.

Finally, a far shore grew near, nearer still until it seemed they were out of lake. They were, in fact. They had reached the northernmost point of Lake Hamilton. They were at the mouth of the Ouachita River.

Owney heard the captain giving commands. He cut sail and dropped anchor. It took his well-trained crew only a few minutes to rig for running by motor. Quickly they set up the Johnson outboard on the fantail, and ginned it up. It sounded like a sewing machine. Brick took the helm and guided them into the narrow mouth of the river.

But Brick knew what he was doing. It was said he'd run rum for Joe Kennedy in the old days, making a fortune before moving south and joining the horsey set. He was an adventurer too, and had skippered a PT boat in the war. He got a Jap destroyer, it was said, but maybe it was only a landing craft or a cargo scow. But he knew his art: he took the boat up the narrow strait of the Ouachita River, between darkened shores so close they could almost be touched, past the little river town of Buckville. Hot Springs was far behind, and then, up near Mountain Pine, the river shifted direction, widened, and headed west into the vast Ouachita wilderness. The boat gulled along against the current, and the men finally came on deck. Around them was only darkness and the sense of the forest so close and engulfing it almost had them. But they pressed on to the west, passing into Montgomery County. They were headed west toward escape.

In the vast quiet darkness, Owney began to relax at last. He was go-ing to make it, he finally believed.

59

Where was he? She couldn't put it out of her mind. He was in trouble. They had gotten him. He had survived so much, but he had not survived this last thing with the gangsters.

She called long distance to a newspaper in Hot Springs. Were there any incidents, any killings, anything involving a man named Earl Swagger.

The man said, "Lady, ain't you heard? We had a big prison break down here. The whole town's going crazy looking for Owney Maddox. You ought to call the cops, maybe they'd know."

Eventually she got to a lieutenant of detectives who chewed her out for interrupting them in their important work of capturing this escaped criminal, but he finally told her the last anybody had ever seen of that disagreeable individual, Earl Swagger, he was on his way out of the county and if she loved her husband, she'd make it clear to him he was never to return.

That was a night before.

Where had Earl gone?

She tried to settle herself down, but she just sat there, feeling nauseated and frightened in the darkness. There was nobody to help her. That was Earl's duty. Was he involved in the manhunt for this Owney, a gangster? He had told her he was off, he was out of that business, he'd been fired and he was coming home and that's all there was to it. He was coming home to work in the sawmill.

But she thought he was involved in the matter of Owney. The gangsters had finally caught up with him in some way. She thought of him off in the woods, the gangsters having executed him and dumped him in a grave that would go forever unmarked. Such a cruel end for a hero! It would be so unfair.

In her abdomen, her child moved. She felt it kick ever so gently, and that too was strange. Something about the child frightened her, although the doctor kept saying that everything was fine. But it wasn't fine; small signals of danger—her fainting spells, for example—

kept arriving as if the child, somehow, were sending her messages, warning her that he needed help already, that there would be difficulties.

She went to the desk, and got out the map of Arkansas. She looked at the highways. Clearly, it was no more than a few hours—maybe four or five at most—from Hot Springs to Camp Chaffee. There was no reason for Earl to be missing.

She couldn't stay put. She rose, nervous, not knowing what to do. It was near dark.

She went next door to Mary Blanton's and knocked.

Mary answered, a cigarette in her hand, and immediately read the distress on Junie's face.

"Junie, what on earth? Honey, you look awful. Is that critter kicking up a storm?"

"It's Earl. He was supposed to be back from Hot Springs last night and I haven't heard a thing."

"He's probably parked in a bar, honey. You give a man a day off and sure as hell, that's where he'll end up. My Phil'd waste his life among the Scotch bottles if I let him."

"No, Mary, it can't be that. He swore to me he was off the stuff forever. He swore."

"Honey, they all say that. Believe me, they do."

"I'm so afraid. I called the police and the newspapers, but they just told me he left late yesterday afternoon."

"Do you want to come in and wait here, honey? You're welcome. I'm just reading the new *Cosmopolitan.*"

"I'd like to look for him."

"Oh, Junie, that's not wise. The baby's due in two weeks. You never know about these things. You shouldn't be off on some wild-goose chase. And what if Earl calls?"

"But I'll go crazy if I just sit around. I just want to drive down to Waldron and then over to Hot Springs. That'd be the way he'd come, I know. We'll run into him and that'll be that. But I just can't sit there anymore."

"You can't drive alone."

"I know."

"Well, let me get my hat, honey. Looks like the gals are going on a little trip. Wouldn't mind stopping for a beer."

"I'm not supposed to drink, they say."

"Well, honey, there's nothing to stop *me* from drinking, now, is there?"

"No ma'am," said Junie, already feeling better.

"You just watch real good. You have a Coke, and you watch me drink a beer." She winked good-naturedly.

Mary got her hat and the two went out to Mary's car, a 1938 De-Soto that could have used some bodywork. Mary started the old vehicle, and they backed out of the driveway and headed through the maze of gravel roads in the vets village.

"Do you think we'll ever get out?" Mary asked.

"They say they're building more houses. If you had a good war record you can get a loan. But it'll still be a wait."

"All that time when Phil was in the Pacific, I kept thinking how wonderful it was going to be. Now he's back and"—she laughed bitterly, her signature reaction to the complexities of the world—"it's not wonderful at all. In fact, it plain stinks."

"It'll work out" was all Junie could think to say.

"Honey, you are such an incorrigible optimist! Oh, well, at least we won the war, we have the atom bomb, our men are back in one piece and we have a roof over our heads, even if it's made of tin and smells like the inside of an airplane!"

They laughed. Mary could always get a laugh out of Junie. Junie was so duty-haunted, so straight-ahead, so committed to the ideal, that Mary was a refreshment to her, because Mary saw through everything, considered every man who ever lived a promise-breaking, drunken, raping lout, and in her day had riveted more Liberator fuselages than any man in the Consolidated plant.

The camp vanished behind them as they hit Route 71 and followed that road's generally southward course as it plunged down the western spine of Arkansas.

There was little enough to see in the daylight and even less in the twilight. Traffic was light.

"You know, we could miss Earl's car. It would be easy to do."

"I know. Maybe this wasn't such a good idea."

"If it makes you feel better, you should do it. You get few enough chances in this lifetime to feel better."

Small towns fled by: Rye Hill, Big Rock, Witcherville, little dots on a map that turned out to be a gas station and a few outbuildings of indistinct size and meaning. It grew darker.

"Why don't we stop and get that beer," said Junie.

"Hmmm, now I'm not so sure. These boys out here, they may think we're fast city gals out larking about. See, all men think that all women secretly desire them and want to be conquered and treated like slaves. I don't know where they get that idea, but I do know the further you get from city lights, the stronger that idea becomes, although it's certainly very strong in the city too. And the fact that you're carrying thirty extra pounds of baby'll just get 'em to thinking you want a last adventure before you're a mama forever."

Junie laughed. Mary had such a bold way of putting things, which is why some of the other wives in the village didn't like her, but exactly why Junie liked her so much.

She looked at the map.

"Up ahead is a city called Peverville. It's a little larger. Maybe we'll find a nice, decent place where nobody'll whistle or make catcalls."

"Oh, if they don't do it out loud, they'll do it in their heads, which is the same thing, only quieter."

The land here was quiet and dark; it was all forest, and the gentle but insistent up and down of the road suggested they were going through mountains. Occasionally a car passed headed in the other direction, but it was never Earl's old Ford.

"I hope he's all right," Junie said.

"Honey, if all the Japanese in the world couldn't kill Earl Swagger, what makes you think some likkered-up cornpone-licking crackers from Hot Springs could?"

"I know. But Earl says it's not always who's the best. When the guns come out, it's so much luck too. Maybe his luck finally ran out."

"Earl is too ornery. Luck wouldn't dare let him down, he'd grab it by the throat and fix that Marine Corps stare on it, and it would give up the ghost!"

Again, in spite of herself, Junie had to laugh.

"Mary, you are such a character!"

"Yes ma'am," said Mary.

An approaching car looked to be Earl's, and both women bent forward, peering at it for identification. But as it sped by, a much older man turned out to be the driver.

"Thought we had us something for just a while," said Mary.

"You know, Mary," said Junie, "I think maybe we better head on back."

"Are you all right?"

"Suddenly I don't feel so good."

"Is that critter kicking up a storm?"

"No, it's just that I seem to be cramping or something."

"Oh, gosh, does it hurt?"

Junie didn't answer, and Mary saw from the pallor that had stolen over her features that it did.

"Do you want to go to the hospital?"

"No, but if I could just—"

She hesitated.

"Oh, I'm so sorry," she said. "I made a mess. I don't know."

Mary pulled off, reached up and flicked on the compartment light.

"Oh, God," she said, for Junie was soaked.

Suddenly Junie curled in pain.

"My water just broke," she said. "I am *so* sorry about the car."

"Forget the car, honey. The car don't mean a thing. You are going to have that damn baby right now. We have to find you a hospital."

"Earl!" screamed Junie as the first contraction hit, "oh, Earl, where *are* you?"

CHAPTER
60
The boat was behind them. They had left it at the River Bluff Float Camp, where the river grew too rough to be navigated.

Now they traveled through the darkness in a 1934 V-8 Ford station wagon, primer dull, which had come from the Grumleys' store of bootlegging vehicles. It had a rebuilt straight-8 Packard 424 engine, super-strong shocks, a rebuilt suspension and could do 150 flat-out if need be. Revenooers had called it the Black Bitch for years.

Forest was everywhere, and the narrow, winding road suggested that civilization was far, far behind.

Owney kept looking at his watch.

"Are we going to make it?"

"We'll make it fine," said Johnny. "I set it up, remember."

Now there was just this last, long pull through the mountains, along a ribbon of moonlit macadam; and then a final rough plunge down old logging roads, the exact sequence to which Johnny swore he had committed to memory.

"Suppose something goes wrong? Suppose we have a flat tire or have to evade a roadblock, and we fall behind schedule."

"If we're not there, he comes back next day, same time, no problem. It's flexible. I accounted for that. But we have clear road and we ought to keep going. The sooner we're out of here, me boy, the sooner you're enjoying the pleasures of them dusky Mex women."

"Okay, okay," said Owney. "I hate being nervous. I want to fucking *do* something."

"This is the hard part, old man," said Johnny.

"Say, Owney," said Herman Kreutzer from the back seat, "whatever happened to your English accent? It seems to have escaped too."

The gunman erupted in laughter. This annoyed Owney, but until he had reestablished himself, he was subject to such predations. His misery increased.

"Uh oh," said Johnny.

"Oh, shit," said Herman.

Owney felt the sudden infusion of red light as, just behind them, a police or sheriff's car had just turned on its lights and siren.

"Fuck, he's got us," said a gunman.

"We're going to have to pop this boy," said Johnny.

"No," said Owney. "I'll handle it. You guys, you been laughing at me like I'm nobody. I'll show you Mr. Fucking New York rackets."

"Oh, he's a tough one," said Vince the Hat.

"Let the boy operate," said Johnny.

Johnny guided the car to the shoulder and eased to a halt: Owney got out, raised his hands high.

The policeman—no, a sheriff's deputy, or possibly the sheriff himself, for the black-and-white's door read SHERIFF and under that MONTGOMERY COUNTY, ARK.—climbed out of the car, but kept his distance. He was not distinctly visible behind the haze of lights.

"I'm unarmed," called Owney.

He spread his coat open to show that he had no pistol. Then he started to walk forward.

"Y'all just hold it up there," said the sheriff.

"Ah, of course. Meant no harm, sir," said Owney in his best stage British.

"Who are you? Mite late to be pleasure-cruising through the mountains in a big ol' station wagon."

"We were enjoying the sporting possibilities of Hot Springs," said Owney. "Our money having run rather abruptly dry, we decided to head straight toward Fayetteville. We may have taken a wrong turn. Glad you're here, Sheriff. If you'd just—"

He took another step forward.

"You hold it," said the sheriff. "And tell all them boys to stay in that car. I am armed, and I am a good shot, and I'd hate there to be any trouble, because if there is, one or t'other of you and your boys is going to Fayetteville in a pine box."

"Yes sir. No need for violence. We'll show proper ID and you may verify our identities via your radio. I appreciate that people are jumpy tonight, what with that fellow escaping prison in Hot Springs. We've been stopped twice at roadblocks already."

He kept advancing.

"You hold it there, pardner," said the sheriff, putting his hand to a big gun in his holster, and at the same time looking quickly to the car to make certain nobody had stepped out and all the windows had remained rolled up.

"Sheriff, uh—?"

"Turner, sir."

"Sheriff Turner, I appreciate your nervousness given the drama of the evening. But I wish to assure you I am harmless. Here, go ahead, search me. You'll see."

Owney assumed the position against the fender of the police vehicle; the fellow gave him a quick pat-down and came to the conclusion he was unarmed.

But Owney also saw that he was a professional, and shrewd. He hadn't approached the Ford but stayed back by his own vehicle. No one in the car could get a shot at him, not without opening the doors and leaning out, and he was probably very good with his gun. If they all jumped out of the car, they might get him, but not before he'd gotten two or three of them. And he could then dip back into the woods, pop their tires and make it to a phone to call in reinforcements quick. Sly dog.

"What business are you in, sir?" asked the sheriff, somewhat relaxed that he'd found no gun on Owney.

"Well, I've been known to wager a penny on the ponies, the fall of a card or the roll of a die."

"Gambler, eh? But you didn't do too well in Hot Springs."

"Had a run of bad luck, yes. But I'll be back, you can make book on it."

"Well, y'all be careful. Ain't no speed limit here but you were moving mighty fast. Don't want to scrape you off a tree."

"No, indeed."

"Say, what was the name again?"

"Vincent Owen Maddox."

The sheriff's face knitted with a little confusion, for the name sounded so familiar.

"And you say you're headed to Fayetteville."

"Headed *toward* Fayetteville, old fellow."

"Well, Mr. Maddox—"

Then his face lit with amazement as he realized that the Owen became Owney, and his face set hard, for in an instant he knew who he was up against, and his hand flew fast and without doubt toward the big gun at his hip.

But Owney was faster.

In less than half a second he had a small silver revolver in his hand, as if from nowhere, as if from the very air itself, and he fired one bullet with a dry pop into the sheriff's chest. The big man never reached his Colt and stepped back, for the bullet packed so little impact it felt only like a sting, but in the next second the blood began to gush from his punctured aorta and he sat down with an ashen look, then toppled sideways to the earth.

"All right, you fellows," called Owney. "Get him in his car and get it off the road, chop chop now."

Johnny's gunmen got out of the Ford and dragged the dead police officer to his car. Vince started it, and began to creep along the road until he found enough of a hill to drive it over so that it would tumble off and into the underbrush.

"Say," said Johnny, "ain't you a fast piece of work. Where'd you get that little ladies' gun?"

"When they delivered my suit to the cave, it was tucked in a pocket."

"I don't mean that. I mean, where were you packing it? I didn't realize you were heeled. You sure got it out in a flash."

"I am a man of some dexterity."

"Where was it?"

Owney smiled, and pulled up his coat sleeve. His shirtsleeve underneath was unbuttoned and a black piece of elastic circled his wrist. Quickly he slid the gun under it, then drew the suit sleeve back down over it, where it disappeared to all but the most discerning eye. But Johnny could see it was an old nickel-plated revolver of the sort called a bicycle gun, a .32 rimfire from very early in the century, that lacked a trigger guard and had a one-inch barrel.

"It's a trick another sheriff once taught me," said Owney.

CHAPTER

61

My father knew the land. That's what my father knew. But what good is that? What value is that? What does that get you?

Earl walked out onto the porch, where he could see the sun setting to the west. But it was a quiet twilight in Polk County and no cars had headed on down the road in quite some time.

My father knew the land.

What does that tell me?

But the more Earl hammered against it, the harder it became.

He knew *this* land. What the hell good would that be to train robbers in Hot Springs, fifty odd miles away. He knew Polk County, an out-of-the-way spread of land, mostly mountain wilderness with a few one-horse towns far to the west, hard up against Oklahoma. What was there about Polk County that could be important to these men?

Well, maybe they could hide out in the mountainous trees of the Ouachitas. But there were plenty of trees, mountains and wilderness in Garland County itself or in Montgomery County. What would they need to come an extra county over here for?

He tried to recall what he knew about that robbery, what old D.A. had told him months back. Five armed men, an inside job, four guards killed, a huge payroll in cash taken, and they got away without a trace.

He applied his tactical imagination to it. It was a military problem. You have to leave an area. You are behind enemy lines. You are being hunted in force by all police agencies. How do you do it?

Well, obviously, you drive. But to where? Roadblocks are already out. You can't get far by road. Do you take a train? No, don't be ridiculous. Well, maybe you don't leave. Maybe you go to ground for a month and wait the manhunt out. You have, after all, friends in the area who can hide you. But . . . the longer you stay there, the more likely that somebody will notice something, somebody will talk, somebody will see something.

That leaves a boat. Could you take a boat? Could you ride up the Ouachita River to— well, to where?

That was interesting. You might go by boat, and possibly the cops wouldn't be covering the river or the lake because they'd believe you'd be on the road. But . . . a boat to where? You take the Ouachita to where? It would make most sense to take it south, toward the Mississippi, and he didn't even know if the Ouachita reached the Mississippi. And that took them into the flat part of the state, where—

This was getting him nowhere. It was pointless speculation. Maybe they did take a boat. Where would it get them, which way would they go, who could know now, six years later? And what difference would it make?

He heard a dry light whine from far off. It was so familiar he almost didn't notice it. He'd heard it in the Pacific a million times. He looked into the fading light and finally caught it, a plane, a silver speck up high, where the sunlight still commanded, glowing against the darkening sky, entirely too far to be identified.

An airplane, he thought.

They might go someplace where they could be picked up by an airplane. This suddenly seemed reasonable. You get into an airplane and you're free. It's 1940, after all. There's no radar, because it's still a secret; and the big wartime push hasn't begun, so the system of commercial aviation is haphazard and roundabout, planes come and go every day.

They go to an airplane.

What kind of airplane?

There are four men. They all have automatic weapons and presumably some supply of ammunition. They have clothes because they've been living in the area prior to their raid, and they have the trophy of their efforts, the payroll. Close to half a million, in cash. In small bills, in bags or a strongbox or some such. All that cash, maybe a hundred pounds of it. He had no idea how much a half million in small bills would weigh, but it would be considerable.

So: What kind of airplane?

Not a Piper Cub or any other small puddle-jumper, like the observation jobs he'd seen in the war. Maybe you could land all right, but it would be too dangerous to take off again with all that weight.

Therefore: it would have to be a multiengine plane, a substantial airplane that could carry five men, their equipment, their money. Something like . . . a DC-3? No, too big. But maybe some kind of Beechcraft, twin-engined, like the staff planes the brass had used in the war. You never saw them in combat zones, but behind the lines they were ubiquitous. Heavy, slow, low, but planes that were dependable and could land anywhere it was flat.

So where would you land such a plane?

Obviously, the airports were out, because they'd be watched by cops. You couldn't land that big a plane in a farm meadow, or anywhere near civilization because it would clearly be spotted, and you probably couldn't do it at night, because it would be too dangerous.

So: you had to find a big, flat field somewhere, but somewhere far from prying eyes, somewhere in the wilderness, in the mountains, somewhere safe and secure, unlikely to be stumbled upon. That would leave out a road, a farm, a park, it would leave out just about anywhere.

Where would you land a plane? And what on earth would his father the hunter have to do with it?

A memory came to Earl. It was indistinct at first, a blurred image from some deep pool where experiences had been recorded. It was from his childhood. He had a vision of a remote field, a valley, yellow and rolling. He was there with his father and a few other men. It was maybe 1927 or '28, he was maybe twelve or fourteen years old. He heard his father's voice, instructing.

"Now you pay attention," the man was saying, in that low rumble that was his voice, "because I don't want to have to say this twice, Earl. You want to look to the treeline. The mule deer is a creature of the treeline. He likes the boundary between the open and the closed. He also likes the wind to be blowing across the open, so that he can smell anything tracking him. He won't go into the full open, particularly during hunting season, because he knows he's being hunted. Don't know how, but he does. He's smart that way. He wants the tender shoots of the margins. This is where you will find him, in the dawn or possibly at twilight. You must be alert, for his moves can sometimes seem magical, and you must be patient, for there is nothing in his mind to distract him, as there will be to distract you, so you must compel yourself to stillness. Do you understand, Earl? Are you listening, boy?"

Of course he was listening. Who could not listen to Daddy? Daddy demanded respect, and Daddy got it. Earl sat with his rifle as his father explained to him, as he was introduced into the rituals of the hunt.

But now he remembered and he saw: a wide field, so remote that to see it was to feel oneself the first white man in the territory in the year 1650-something, and to marvel at it, its length, its yellowness, the low hills that encased it to make it a valley and the far, blue peaks of higher mountains.

A name came out of his memory.

Hard Bargain Valley, a splash of flat yellow in the mountains, called such because some westward pilgrims had thought to winter there and by spring all that remained was food for the crows. Earl remembered the crows wheeling overhead, back and forth, like bad omens. God had made a hard bargain with the pilgrims indeed.

Could you land a plane on Hard Bargain Valley?

Yes, he knew in a second. You could. Easily. A bigger plane too, not a Cub but a substantial twin-engined craft.

Now it came together in a moment, as if all the parts of the puzzle had been sunk in his brain all these years and at some darker deeper level he'd been working on them. Now they fit. They announced themselves with a thunderclap, a vision of purity so intense it almost knocked him back.

Five men, heavily armed, fleeing Hot Springs. They have to get to a remote spot where a plane can pick them up.

There's only one such place within a night's travel. But how will they find it? There're no paved roads in, only a hopeless mesh of old logging trails, some drivable, some not. Who would help them?

It would have to be a man who knew the territory better than anyone. Sheriff Charles Swagger, the great lawman and hunter.

And they'd know about Swagger. He had a secret life in Hot Springs. Once a month, he'd show up for gambling and whoring and sporting with the special, secret vice he loved the best. Owney Maddox, that champion of human weakness, would know this. He'd have the leverage on old Charles and there would be the man, a paragon of public morality for so long, suddenly caught in the grip and crushed into obedience by a gangster.

So Charles would draw up a route. He would then engineer the roadblocks so that the fleeing men could get through them when they reached Polk County. Then he would meet them deep in the forest, and take them the last few miles to Hard Bargain Valley, and it would be a good bargain for them, for the plane would come at dawn and pluck them away and they'd have disappeared forever. The $400,000 would be quickly enough laundered and it would return in a few weeks to Hot Springs, as working capital for Owney Maddox, who would use it to build the Southern, the most elegant and successful casino in America.

Earl could see the last melancholy act too. Charles hadn't known men had been killed in the robbery. He'd gotten in because it was just robbers stealing money from Big Business like Alcoa and the money would go to gamblers, it was just the way the world worked, victimless, corrupt, ancient. But four men had died and suddenly his father is an accessory to murder. It sickens him, and that's why he returns home drunk and bent with anger at himself, and who does he run into but his young son, Bobby Lee, and the boy becomes the focus of his fury, his deep disappointment in himself, all his failures. He beats the boy and beats him and beats him, then passes out. Maybe he beats him to death and strings up the body to hide the crime. Maybe the boy hangs himself. But that is how it had to be. The evil father, the helpless son, the one man who had a chance to stop it fled to another family called the United States Marine Corps.

It was at that point Earl realized that they would do tonight exactly what they did in 1940. Of course. It was the same problem, except the treasure wasn't a payroll, it was Owney Maddox himself. It had worked before. The same route, the same arrangements with a plane, the same destination. Only this time they didn't need a Charles Swagger because they were smart, one of them had paid attention and he could find Hard Bargain Valley on his own.

Earl looked at his watch. It was near 8:00 and the sun was almost gone.

They were going to get away with it, because nobody else knew where Hard Bargain Valley was or could get there in time.

He himself had no idea where it was. It was somewhere in the mountain vastness that even now was fading into darkness and that no one could find who hadn't been there before and didn't know the way and he didn't know the way and there was no map, the map was gone.

Then Earl remembered his daddy's room. The map was gone, yes, but its outline still was described by that bright patch of unfaded paint.

He turned swiftly, walked back through the house and entered the room.

He faced the emptiness.

Nothing. What had he expected? It was just a square of lighter paint, even now losing its distinction as the light failed.

He tried to remember what it showed. It showed Polk, one of Arkansas's most westerly, most poverty-stricken, most mountainous, most remote counties. He tried to think: What is the essential quality of Polk County? He tried to remember as he stared at the square: What did I see here? Remember what you saw. Remember what was here.

He remembered. A big map, with few roads and many creeks, and many blank areas marked UNMAPPED. The swirl of color depicting different elevations as the larger forms of the mountains were at least suggested. But what was the pure quality of Polk County by shape?

He remembered: it was very regular. It was, like the sheet of paper that documented it, almost perfectly rectangular, with only a flare to the northwesterly corner and the southwesterly quarter to render the shape irregular. But otherwise it was drawn as if with a ruler, by men who laid out counties from far away without any knowledge of what the land was and therefore in defiance of the land. The borders didn't follow mountain crests or rivers or natural forms in the land; they defied them, they bisected them, they conquered them.

So the rectangle on the wall, it almost represented the pure shape of the county, with those deviations in the corner that were largely irrelevant because neither of them contained unmapped areas.

Earl tried to remember. What else was there? What else marked the county? He couldn't remember anything, any roads, any mountains, any creeks or rivers. It was over sixteen years since he'd really been here. How could he be expected to—

Pins. Pins. The map was festooned with pins where Charles Swagger had taken game and over the years he'd taken a lot of game, and he loved mule deer most of all, mulies they were called, magical creatures of muddy earth color who exploded from stillness to grace to invisibility in the blinking of an eye, and if you even saw one, much less managed to kill one, you felt that nature had been benevolent.

Earl looked away, then looked back again, seeing nothing. Then he edged sideways so that he saw the blank space on the wall at an angle, and could read the texture of it and that's when he saw them.

Of course. The map was gone. The pins were gone. The Swaggers were gone, all of them, dead or cursed, especially this last one, but what remained after it all were the pinholes.

Scanning the empty space from an angle, Earl quickly began to pick them up, here, there, one at a time, little pricks in the plaster, perhaps visible only in this light, with its play of shadows to bring out the irregularities. A prick here, a prick there, two pricks close together and—

That would be it. That had to be it.

A large concentration of pricks lay in the northwest corner of the lightened space, maybe thirty-five or forty. Not in a cluster, but in two parallel lines, suggesting the margins of the treeline defining the valley itself. That's where Hard Bargain Valley would be. That's where Charles Swagger went every year and every year he tagged his mulie buck, in the margins, just off the flat, remote high field of yellow grass, over which crows heeled and cruised, like omens of ill chance.

Earl knew: it's in the northwest corner of the county.

He knew if he could get close enough by car, he could hump it in if he worked like the devil. He'd need a county map—there was an Arkansas state map in large scale in his car, and with it he could get close enough. It was maybe two hours' driving, maybe four hours of hard hike and climbing. He glanced at his watch. He could make it by dawn with an hour to spare.

He only needed one more thing.

He went into the third dusty stall and bent to the boards against the wall. He remembered hiding here in the long ago, from his father's rages. *Earl!* the old man would cry, *Earl, you get your ass in here, goddammit!* But Daddy never found him though it only forestalled the beatings a few minutes. No one else ever found him there either. He bet Bobby Lee had a secret place too, but this was Earl's.

With a few swift tugs he removed the boards from the wall. He leaned in—as he had when he stopped at the farm months ago, though then to emplace, not remove. He leaned in and dragged it out, a green wooden box wrapped in a tarpaulin, which bore the stamp SWAGGER USMC atop it, denoting that it was a sea chest that had followed its owner from ship to ship and battle to battle. He dragged the case into the barn, flicked on the bare-bulb light and pried it open.

More objects wrapped in canvas lay inside. He removed them, then unwrapped them, seeing each gleam dully in the yellow light. Each still wore that slick of oil that would keep it safe from the elements. He knew the parts so well. The frame and stock group, the barrel and receiver group, the bolt and recoil-spring group, the buffer and buffer pad. They all slid together with the neatness of something well designed. He knew the gun's trickery, all the little nuances of its complexity, where the bolt had to be, how the pins had to be set, when to screw in the bolt handle. Finally he slid the frame and stock group together and locked it in, and the thing assumed its ultimate shape. It took less than three minutes and he held his M1A1 Thompson submachine gun, with its finless barrel and its snout of muzzle, like a pig's ugly nose, its bluntness, its utilitarian grayness, its faded wood and scratched grip. He also had ten 30-round magazines and in the trunk of his car a thousand rounds of .45 ball tracer that he'd meant to trade to some other law enforcement agency.

Now, as in so many other nights of his life these past years, he had to get somewhere by the dawn. In the dawn, the killing would begin.

CHAPTER

62

At last, with a burst of energy from its 324 Packard horses, the Ford wagon got up a little hill and broke free from the trees.

"We're here," said Johnny Spanish, "with more than an hour to spare. Did I not tell you, Owney, you English sot, I'd have it done in time for you?"

Owney felt a vast relief.

He stumbled from the vehicle, taking in a breath of air, feeling it explode in his lungs.

The field seemed to extend for a hundred miles in each way under a starry sky and a bright bone moon. In pale glow it undulated ever so slightly from one end to the other. He could make out a low ridge of hills at the far side but on this side there were only trees as the elevation led up to it.

The last hours had been ghastly. Slow travel down dirt roads, at least twice when the engine seemed to stall, rough little scuts of inclines where all the boys had to get out and Johnny's deft skills alone, his gentleness with the engine, his knowing the balance and power of the automobile, when those alone had gotten them up and to another level.

How had Johnny known so well? It had been six years since, and in that experience that old sheriff had been the guide. He must have some memory. He was definitely a genius.

"You did it, lad," he said to Johnny.

"That I did. You're grateful now, Owney, but come the pay-up time it won't seem like so much. You'll come to believe you yourself could have done it and what I did will seem as nothing. Then you'll try to jew me down hard, I know."

"No," said Owney. "Fair is fair. You boys done two hard jobs in the last two weeks. I'll pay you double what I paid for the yard job."

"Think six times, Owney."

"Six!"

"Six. Not twice times, but six times. It's fair. It leaves you with a lot of what you've got."

"Jesus. It was a one-day job."

"Six, Owney. It was a five-day job, with lots of arranging to be done. Else you'd be looking at the rest of your time in an Arkansas Dannamora."

"Four and it's a deal."

"All right, Owney, because I don't like to mess about. Make it five, we shake on it, and that would be that."

Owney extended his hand. He had just paid $1.5 million for his new life. But he had another $7 million left, and beyond that, $3 million in

European banks that neither a Johnny Spanish nor a Bugsy Siegel nor a Meyer Lansky knew a thing about.

They shook.

"Boys, we're rich," said Johnny.

"Richer, you mean," said Owney.

"We're set for life. No more jobs. We can toss the tommies off the Santa Monica fishing pier."

"Believe I'll keep my Browning," said Herman. "You never know when it'll come in handy."

"All right, you lot, just a bit more to do. You know the drill."

They had to secure the field for landing. This involved reading the wind, for the plane landed against it and took off with it. As efficiently as any OSS team setting up a clandestine landing in occupied France, Johnny's boys picked some equipment out of the rear of the big Ford and went deep into the valley. There they quickly assembled a wind pylon and read the prevailing breeze. It was now only a matter of using a flare to signal the aircraft when she came, then turning her, then climbing aboard and it was all over.

While the boys did their work, and then moved the car to the appropriate spot in the valley, Owney took out and lit a cigar. It was a Cohiba, from the island, a long thing with a tasty, spicy tang to it, and it calmed him down.

He had made it. He, Owney, had done it. He was out; he would repair to the tropics and begin to plot, to raise a new crew, to pay back his debts, to engineer a way back into the rackets.

He had an image of Bugsy after the hit. He imagined Bugsy's face, blown open by bullets. Bugsy in one of his famous creamy suits, spattered with black blood, his athlete's grace turned to travesty by the twisted position into which he had fallen. He saw Bugsy as the centerpiece in a tabloid photo, its harshness turning his death into some grotesque carnival. When a gangster died, the public loved it. The gangsters were really the royalty of America, bigger in their way than movie stars, for the movies the gangsters starred in were real life, played out in headlines, whereas an actor's heroics took place only in a fantasy realm. A star in a moving picture could come back and make another one; a star in a tabloid picture could not, and that impressed incredible élan and grace upon the gangster world. It was glamorous like the movies but real like life and death itself.

Then he heard it. Oh, so nice.

From far off the buzz of a multiengine plane. She'd circle a bit, waiting for a little more of the light that was beginning to creep across the western sky to illuminate the valley, then down she'd come. It was a good boy, or so Johnny insisted. A former Army bomber pilot who could make an airplane do anything she could do and had set planes down on dusty strips all over the Pacific. But before that the boy had run booze and narcotics for some Detroit big boys, where he really learned his craft.

High up, the plane caught a glimpse of sun, and it sparkled for just a second, just like Owney Maddox's future.

Owney turned and before him suddenly loomed a shape, huge and terrifying.

It took his breath away.

Don't let me die! he thought, but it was not a man-made thing at all, or even a man. It was some kind of giant reddish deer, with a spray of antlers like a myth. The beast seemed to rise above him. His throat clogged with fear. In the rising light he saw its eyes as they examined him imperially, as if he were the subject. It sniffed, and pawed, then turned its mighty head. In two huge, loping bounds it was gone.

Jesus Christ, he thought.

What the hell was that?

He didn't like it, somehow. The animal's presence, its arrogance, its lack of fear, its contempt seemed like a bad omen. He realized his pulse was rocketing and that he was covered with a sheen of sweat.

"Owney, lad, come out of the field or you'll get cut to pieces by the props of your savior," called Johnny.

CHAPTER

63

The pain came every two minutes now. It built, like a worm growing to a snake growing to a python growing to a sea serpent or some other mystical creature, red hot and glowing, screaming of its own volition, a spasm, an undulation, a sweat-cracking, muscle-killing pure heat. Someone screamed. It was her. She screamed and screamed and screamed.

From her perspective, she could only see eyes. The eyes of the young doctor and they looked scared. She knew something was wrong.

"Let me give you some anesthetic, Mrs. Swagger."

"No," she said. "No gas."

"Mrs. Swagger, you're only a little dilated and you've got some hours to go. There's no need to suffer."

"No gas. *No gas!* I'm fine. I want my husband. Is Earl here? Earl, Earl, where are you? Earl?"

"Ma'am," said the nurse, looking over, "ma'am, we haven't been able to reach your husband."

"I want Earl. I want Earl here. He said he'd be here for me."

"Ma'am, he's got time. It's going to be a bit. We'll get you into the delivery room when you've dilated to ten centimeters. He'll get here fine, I'm sure. I just think you'd be more comfortable if—"

The pain had her again. The snake roped through her body. How could such a little bitsy thing hurt so much? She was so afraid of letting down Earl. But at the same time, where was Earl?

"Ma'am, I'm going to get your friend. She can be with you. That's all right, isn't it?"

"Yes."

Mary swam into view.

"Honey," she said. "I'll call Phil at the shop. He'll go straight home. He'll go to your house and wait on the front steps for your husband."

"Key," she said.

"What, honey?"

"Key. Key in the flowerpot to right of door, third pot. Answer phone."

"Yes. I'll tell him. He'll wait inside and if Earl calls he'll tell him where you are, so Earl can come direct."

"Where is Earl?"

"I don't know, baby. I'm sure he'll be there as soon as he can."

"I'm not strong."

"Oh, yes you are, baby. You are the strongest. You got through this whole thing without Earl, and you'll get through this if you have to. I know you've got the strength in you."

The pain had her again.

"What's wrong, Mary?" she said.

"There's nothing wrong," said Mary, but she flashed an uneasy look at the doctor. "You're having a baby. I have been led to believe it hurts a bit."

"I can tell something is wrong. Don't let them take my baby. They can't have my baby. I don't want the gas. If I have the gas, they'll take my baby."

"No, sweetie, that won't happen."

But again she had a guilty look.

In time the two women were alone as the doctor, the only one on call this late hour in the near-empty Scott County hospital, went on his rounds, such as they were. They weren't much because "hospital" was entirely too grand a word for this place; it was more a poverty ward with an operating room/delivery room/emergency room attached, because the quality went up to Fort Smith or over to Little Rock with their medical problems.

Mary came over with a conspiratorial look on her face.

"Baby, they don't want you to know, but they want you to take the gas."

"What's wrong? Oh, God, what's wrong?"

"It's called a posterior presentation. The baby is facing down, not up, and he can't come out down."

"Oh, God."

"With another doctor, they might be able to turn him when you dilate some more. Then they'd cut you a little and remove him and sew you up. But they need two doctors. They can't do it with one doctor."

"Don't let them take my baby."

"Honey, you may have to—"

"No, no, no. *No!*" Her hand flew to Mary's and grabbed it tightly. "Don't let them hurt my baby."

"Honey, if they can't get the baby turned, they may have to do something to save your—"

"No. *No!* Don't hurt my baby! Cut me but don't hurt the baby."

Mary started to cry as she held tightly to Junie's wan hand.

"You are so brave. You are braver than any man who ever lived, sweetie. But you can't give up your life to—"

"No," she said. "Earl will—"

"Earl would make the same decision. He wants you to be with him. You can have other babies. You can't give up your life for one baby. What would Earl do? He'd be by himself with a baby he wouldn't know how to care for."

"No," she said. "I don't want them to hurt my baby. They can't take the baby! Don't let them take the baby. Earl will be here. Earl will save us both."

"Honey, I—"

The pain had her again, and she jacked as it flashed through her.

Earl? Where are you, Earl? Earl, please come.

CHAPTER

64

Earl lay on his back. The dew had soaked through his coat. His hat was a pillow. He could see nothing but sky lightening as the sun came up. A cool wind rushed through the grass that concealed him. He could have been any man on a park bench or a camping ground, stretching, damp, a little twitchy as the dawn came up and a new day began.

But no other man would have a tommy gun cradled in his arms across his chest and no other man would carry nine other stick magazines loaded with ball tracer in the pockets of his coat or stuffed inside his belt—oh, for a Marine knapsack.

But Earl lay calmly, letting his heartbeat subside, letting his body cool. He was at the long end of a desperate journey across the northwest corner of Polk County, guided by an old map and his instincts. The car had taken him along dirt roads through vast forest and a nickel compass kept him oriented toward the section of the county where Hard Bargain Valley just had to be.

When he ran out of road, he took ten minutes to load up his magazines and his weapon, then he headed off on a track trending north by northwest, through strange forest, across swollen streams, and finally up a raw incline. It seemed to take forever; he thought of a night or two in the Pacific, the 'Canal especially, when the jungle had been like this, dense and dark and unyielding. You hated to be in it at night because the night belonged to the Japs, and them little monkeys could make you stew meat if they wanted. But there were no Japs in this jungle, except his own memories, his own fears, his own angers.

The worst part of the ordeal came at around 5:30 when the land, which should have been rising steadily to Hard Bargain Valley, instead seemed to straighten out. He kept his trust going in the cheap compass, but then he wondered if the presence of so much metal in the tommy gun and all the ammo had knocked it askew. But it held to a steady N and he kept orienting himself to the right of that pointing arrow, even though in the dark his doubts mounted fearfully. He had no other choice.

And then, as sweet a sound as he'd ever heard, there came the whine of a cruising plane, holding at about two thousand feet in a steady drone. That had to be it. That was Hard Bargain Valley and the plane that came for its human cargo.

Abruptly he ran into ridge, heavily overgrown, and made his way up it as quickly as he could. Thank God the tommy had a sling, for without one, the going would have been almost impossible. The gun hung on his shoulder, heavy and dense with that special weight that loaded weapons have, as he pulled himself up.

Then he saw it: the broad sweep of valley, flat and only gently undulating, pure natural landing strip, and on the other side other hills, and beyond them, presumably, mountains, for the darkness still closed out longer views.

Earl could see some kind of activity at the far end of the valley. He knew that's where Owney and his boys would be waiting for the plane to land.

Thus he edged down to the valley floor, still shielded for another few minutes by the darkness, and duckwalked out to the center. The plane had to land over him. When it did, he would empty a magazine into the nearest engine, concentrating all his firepower. That would drive it away. It would not land and then he would close with Owney and his boys, and although the odds were one against six it didn't much matter: business had to be taken care of, accounts settled, and there was no one else about to do it.

A shift in the pitch of the engines of the orbiting plane signified that enough light had arrived at last. Earl craned his head up a bit and saw the plane far off to the northwest, one wing tip high, the other low as it fluted in its approach to the landing path. It seemed to waver in the air as it turned, then straightened, then lowered itself. The gear was already down. It was some kind of low-winged twin-engine Beechcraft, a sturdy, prosaic aircraft. The pilot found his angle and seemed to come in on a string, bearing straight for Earl, coming faster and faster and lower and lower.

Earl's fingers flew involuntarily to the weapon's controls, to test them for the millionth time: the one lever was cranked fully forward to FIRE and the other fully forward to FULL. Then his fingers dipped under the weapon and touched the bolt handle on the other side, to check again that it was drawn back and cocked.

The gun seemed to rise to him and he rose from the grass. The butt plate found his shoulder and all ten pounds of the weapon clamped hard against himself as his vision reduced only to that narrow circle of visibility that was the peep sight. He saw: the flat of the receiver top, the diminishing blunt tube of the barrel and the single central blade of sight. The plane seemed to double, then double again in size as it roared at him, dropping ever lower. He knew that the increase in speed was a function of its closing the distance and it seemed to double again, its roar filling the air, and he pulled the gun up through it, sighting on the right-side engine, leading it, and when the computational machine in his brain so instructed, pulling the trigger and holding it down while running the gun on a smooth rotation from nine o'clock up to midnight and then over to two o'clock.

The gun emptied in one spasm, the sound lost in the roar of the plane. He could sense the empties tumbling, feel the liquid, almost hydraulic pressure of the recoil without a sense of the individual shots as it drove into his shoulder, but most of all he could see the tracers flicking out and extending his touch until he was an angry God destroying the world from afar. The arc of tracers flew into the engine and wing root and the plane trembled ever so slightly, then changed engine pitches again as it pulled up, banked right and flew out of the zone of fire. It seemed to dip, for flames poured from the engine, but then the pilot feathered it, and only a gush of smoke remained, a stain he pulled across the sky with him, and he waggled his wings and headed elsewhere.

Owney watched the plane come down. The pilot was good. He was very good. He had his course, his gear had been lowered, his flaps were down, he was coming lower and lower and seemed just a few feet from touching down.

Then a line of illumination cracked out of the darkness and lashed upward; it was so sustained that for just a second Owney thought it was a flashlight beam or some other form of light until he realized he was deluding himself. The streaking bullets caught the plane expertly, speared it, and the plane seemed to wobble. Owney thought it might explode. Smoke abruptly broke from the targeted engine and the plane quivered mightily as fire washed outward. Then the pilot yanked up and away and almost as if it had been a dream, the plane was gone. It reduced in size arithmetically as it sped away, trailing smoke.

"What the fuck was that?" asked Owney.

"It's him."

"Him?"

"The cowboy."

"AGHHHH!" Owney bellowed, a great spurt of anger uncontaminated by comprehensibility. "That fucking fucker, that fucking dog!" His rage was absolute and immense.

But Johnny spoke calmly.

"You just saw some tommy-gunning, old man. Isn't but one man in a thousand can hold the Thompson so perfectly on a moving target, leading perfectly, not letting it bounce off target. I suppose the tracers help some. They verify impact. But the bastard's bloody good, I'll tell you that. I know only one better. Fortunately it's me."

Around him the others had already unlimbered weapons and were quickly readying for action, the usual fitting of magazines and snapping of bolts. Hats and coats were coming off, automatics being checked for full loads.

"That fucking bastard," said Owney. "Oh, that hick bastard! I should have settled his fucking hash at the railway station. Who the fuck does he think he is?"

"Right now, he thinks he's going to kill all six of us, I should imagine. Owney, dear, you stay here. Johnny and his boys will take care of all this. Right, fellows?"

But there was no cheer from the boys. They had read the fine blast of sustained, controlled automatic fire just as surely as Johnny, and knew they were up against a professional.

"We've got the Ford," called Vince the Hat. "We could just get the hell out of here."

"He'd just ambush us. If he knows the way in, he'll know it out. Anyhow, we've got to deal with him now, or look over our shoulders forever. Evidently that railyard business upset the fellow."

"You bastard!" Owney yelled. *"We'll fuck you but good in a few minutes!"*

"Feel better, now, Owney? There's a good lad. You stay here while the men handle it."

"Johnny, what's your plan?" asked Herman Kreutzer, his BAR loaded and ready.

"He's probably slithering toward us right now. I'd stay wide, separated so he can't take more than one down with a single burst. I'd say let's move now and fast, because if it's only tracer he has, we'll be able to track them back to him better before the light is full up. Herman, you've the heaviest weapon, you'll provide sustaining fire. Take all your magazines. No point in saving them for a rainy day. It *is* the rainy day.

Let's form a line abreast and move in spurts. Stay low, keep moving. Look for the source of his fire. When you spot it, Herman, you must pressure him while we move in. Anybody have a better suggestion?"

No one did.

Earl knew they'd come quickly and they did. His every impulse told him to advance. Get among them, shoot fast from the hip, trusting instinct, their panic at his aggression, and luck. It never remotely occurred to him that he might die. His focus was entirely on destroying them.

All his voices were still. He did not think of the father who had failed him or the men he believed he had failed or the wife alone somewhere. He didn't think of D. A. Parker ordering him to get out or the long run through the sewer or the rage that the raid-team tragedy had been turned into farce for the good of a politician. He had no sense of failure at all, but only a sort of battle joy, hard and pure, and the need to get in close, put the bursts into them and punish them for their transgressions and for his own.

He squirmed ahead, low, sliding through the grass. The blood sang in his ears. The air tasted magnificent, like a fine wine, a champagne. The gun was alive in his hands, marvelously supple and obedient. He had never felt this way in the islands or in any of his other fights. There, fear was always around. Now he was shorn of fear.

A burst of fire came. It was duplicated instantly by three others, as Johnny's boys panicked, even though they were so professional. Bullets hurled through the grass, and where they struck, they raised a great destruction. Smoke and debris, liberated by their energy, rose in a fog, obscuring the field, but Earl saw his advantage. He quickly flicked the fire-control lever on his Thompson, setting it to single shot, rose slightly into a kneeling position even as the random bursts filled the air with a sleet of lead, found a good target and fired one round, its noise lost in the general thunder. He shot low, through the grass, so that his tracer might not be seen, and knew he'd made a good shot.

. . .

"Stop it! Stop it, goddammit!" screamed Johnny.

The firing stopped.

"Jesus Christ, don't panic, boys. You'll make it easy on him."

"Johnny, Johnny—"

"Shut up, Vince, you've got—"

"I been hit!"

It was so. Vince the Hat de Palmo lay on his side, astounded that he was bleeding so profusely. He'd taken it at the ligature of thigh to hip, and the wound spurted wetly, the blood thick and black across his suit. He looked at Johnny as his eyes emptied of meaning and hope.

"Take his magazines, boys," said Johnny. "We may need them yet."

"Johnny, I—"

"Easy, lad," said Johnny to the youngest of his men, shortly to be the deadest. "Don't fight Ding-Dong."

In his last motions, Vince cooperated with Jack Bell as the older man rolled him over and grabbed the two flat drums that were wedged between his belt and his back.

"You'll come back for me?"

"Sure, kid," said Ding-Dong. "You can bet on it." He gave the kid a wink, which Vince may or may not have seen before he slipped irretrievably into blood-loss coma.

In the interlude, Earl squirmed to the left, toward the low hill that rose at that side of the valley. He crawled and crawled and though he hated to crawl, this day it filled him with joy. The sun was now full on them, drying the dew from the stalks of grass.

The grass at the hill was drier, somehow, for the hillside drained more fluently than the flatland. As he drew near, a plan formed in his mind. This grass was of a different texture, possibly of a different species. He could tell because unlike the soft grass of the valley floor which merely hissed as he crawled through it or the wind pressed rills into it, this grass crackled like dry old bones and sticks in the breeze.

He stood.

He could not see them, for they too had sunk into the grass, or taken up concealed positions behind the odd bushes on the floor of the valley. He chose one such, leaned into his gun and fired a long squirt of tracers into it.

Then he ducked and squirmed away, as someone with a larger weapon than a Thompson brought fire to bear. These bullets whip-cracked through the sound barrier as they passed overhead, their snap echoing against the wind. It had to be a Browning rifle. Someone had a Browning at the railyard too.

He'll try and pin me, the others will work around and up the hill and the one other will go around me, yes. That's how it has to be.

"Do you have him?"

"Yes, he's in a gully at the edge of the hills, about two hundred yards off to the right. I saw the tracers come out."

"You keep him pinned, Herman. Red, you and Ding-Dong go high. Try and get to that hillside above him to get the fire down on him. I'm circling around to the back. You'll drive him to me, boys, and if you don't get him, I'll get him square in the belly."

"Let's do it."

Johnny scuttled off, beginning his long arc around to the rear. For Jack and Ding-Dong, it was an easier journey, for theirs was the straight shot to the hillside, and then a climb to bend around and get above him. The grass here was high and it concealed them; they didn't have to crawl but could run, keeping low, particularly as more gullies opened up the closer they got to the hill itself.

As for Herman, he waited a bit, then a bit more, and finally rose and began an exercise called walking fire, which was exactly what John M. Browning had designed his automatic rifle to accomplish. It was originally conceived as the answer to trench warfare and in this role it was the perfect instrument.

Herman was a big man, strong and fearless, and he loved and knew the gun he carried passionately. He could do amazing things with it. Now he rose, wearing two bandoliers with loaded magazines Mexican-style across his body over his suit coat, the gun locked into his side and pinned by his strong right forearm, which pressed it tightly against him. His reflexes were superb. He fired half a magazine and the burst sped exactly to the gully from which he'd seen the original tracers come. The burst lifted a stitch of dust. No man could do it better and the shame of Herman's life was that he'd not been a BAR man in Europe or the Pacific, for in that classification he'd have been a true genius. It wasn't that he hadn't tried; it was that he had too many felony convictions.

He finished up the magazine, stitching a hem of lead where he wanted it exactly. He dropped the empty mag, neatly and deftly inserted a new one, all the while walking, and was back putting out his bursts in less than a second. If that's where the cowboy was, he wasn't going anywhere.

Owney could hear the gunfire, but the men had disappeared into the grass. There seemed to be a lot of moving around. It was like chess with machine guns where you couldn't quite see the board.

He was nervous, but not terrified. Johnny's crew was the best; they seemed calm and purposeful. They had succeeded at every enterprise they had tackled, often spectacularly. They were the best armed robbers in America, fearless, famous, quality people, stars in their own universe. They would get him. He knew it. They would get him.

But they wouldn't.

He knew that too, at least somewhere deep inside.

Who was this guy? Where was he from? Why was he so good?

It unnerved him. He had been hunted by Vincent Mad Dog Coll. He was the ace of aces, Owney Killer Maddox, from the East Side. He had shot it out with the Hudson Dusters in 1913, one man against eight, and walked out unhurt, leaving the dying and the wounded behind him. He, Owney, had walked out spry as a dancer, stopped to reset his carnation in his lapel, and gone out for a drink with some other fellows.

Who could scare him? Who had the audacity? Who was this guy?

The BAR bursts ripped up clouds of dust and dirt. The gully filled with grittiness, so that you almost could not breathe. If Earl had been where Herman thought he was, he would indeed have been one cooked fella. The noise, the ricochets, the grit, the supersonic bits of stone and vegetable matter, the sheer danger—all would have shaken even the toughest of individuals.

But Earl had shimmied desperately forward only a matter of a few yards and found a rotted log behind which to hide, even if he knew it was wholly unable to stop the heavy .30s that might have flown his way.

He now did the unthinkable. Instead of seizing the opportunity to put distance between himself and the shooters who were closing in from all sides, he did exactly what they expected him to do, which was nothing. That's what they wanted him to do. He did it. He just didn't do it where they wanted him to do it, not quite. He knew that as the BAR fire kept him nominally pinned, some others would be entering the dry, higher grass of the hillside, in order to get elevation on his position and bring even more killing power. That's exactly what he wanted.

Methodically, he began to tug at the stem of a bush that had grown up just in front of the log.

Jack Bell and Red Brown reached the edge of the hillside, still well hidden. They were rewarded for their efforts.

"Will ya look at that," said Ding-Dong. "Just what the doctor ordered."

"If it was a dame, I'd marry it," said Red, who actually had several wives, so one more wouldn't hurt a bit.

What they saw was a kind of crest running vertically up the hill, one of those strange rills for which only a geologist could give an adequate explanation. What it meant for the two gunmen was a clear easy climb up to the top of the hill, well protected by the geographical impediment from the gunfire of their opponent.

"Okay," said Jack, "you cover me. I'm going to make a dash, then I'll cover you and you make yours."

"Gotcha," said Red.

Both men rose. Jack dashed the twenty or so yards to the beginning of the spine of elevation, even as Red stood and hosepiped twenty-five rounds down the line of the hill, into the area where Herman's bullets had been striking. His too tore clouds of earth upward, and sent grit whistling through the air.

As he fired the last, his partner made it, righted himself, set up close over the ridge, and fired a blast. Red rose under cover of the fire, and sprinted till he was safe.

Both men drew back, breathing hard.

They looked up the hill. Alongside the ridge, it was about two hundred feet up through tall yellow grass, though it was protected the whole way. About halfway was a small strange group of stunted trees, yellowed and sinewy, then another hundred feet to the crest.

"Johnny," Red cried. *"We're going up."*

"Good move," said Ding-Dong. "He'll wait for us, we'll get up there, we'll have real good vision on the guy, we can take him or we can pin him while Johnny and Herman move in on him."

"Johnny's a fuckin' genius."

Herman couldn't be but a hundred or so feet from the edge of the field and the beginning of the hill. His BAR was almost too hot to touch. He'd sprayed steadily for the past five minutes, until he got close enough. He'd seen nothing.

Maybe he's dead. Maybe I hit him. Maybe he's bled out. If he'd gone another way, he'd have run into Johnny.

Nah. He's in there. He got himself into a jam, he's scared, but he's waiting. He's a brave guy. He's a smart guy, but one on five was just too many. He's in there. He can't move. He's real close.

He heard the gunfire from far to the right and judged that it was covering fire from Red and Ding-Dong. Red's yell came a second later.

That was it. If they got above him, the guy was screwed. They could bring fire on him and if they didn't kill him, he'd have to move. Herman would bring him down if he moved.

Herman snapped in a new magazine, waiting for the guy to move. He stood in a semicrouch and was so strong that the fourteen-pound automatic rifle felt light and feathery to the touch. He looked over its sights, through a screen of grass, searching for signs of movement.

He saw nothing, but given the source of the fire, given the speedy response on his part and the volume of fire he had poured in, the man could not have gotten away, unless there were secret tunnels or something, but there were only secret tunnels in movies.

Be patient, he told himself.

Johnny worked his way around in a wide arc to the base of the hill. He was possibly a hundred yards behind the cowboy's position. He squatted in the grass. He hadn't fired yet. He had a full drum, one of the big ones, with a hundred rounds. He could fire single shots, doubles, triples, even quadruples and quintuples if he had to, so exquisite was his trigger control. He could hold one hundred rounds in a four-inch circle in a fifty-yard silhouette if he had to. He could shoot skeet or trap with a Thompson if he had to. He was the best tommy-gunner in the world.

He was a little anxious.

This fellow was very good. He'd obviously used a Thompson well in the war and could make it do tricks. But Johnny knew if it came to shooting man-on-man, he'd take it. Nobody was faster, nobody was surer, nobody could make the gun do what he could make it do.

He squirmed ahead, then heard the gunfire from Red and Ding-Dong. Red yelled something—he could not quite make it out—but knew what it signified. Red and Ding-Dong had reached the hill and were heading up it. When they got elevation, it was all over. It would be all over very shortly. It was just a question of waiting.

Owney heard the firing. There was so much firing from the right-hand side of the field, and then there was nothing. But all the guns that fired had to be Johnny and his boys. He'd only heard one burst that seemed to come from elsewhere.

He could see nothing. Though the floor of Hard Bargain Valley was relatively flat and hard, for some reason the grass grew at different heights upon its surface, and from where he was, it looked like a yellow ocean, aripple with waves. Toward the edges of the valley, small stunted trees appeared in strange places, randomly.

He thought the fighting was going on over there, maybe a half mile down, on the right side. He thought he could see dust rising from all the gunfire.

Suddenly a long burst broke out, and his eye was drawn to what he took to be the position of the shooter. Another came in on top of the first. Each burst chattered for about two seconds, though from this distance the sound was dry, like a series of pops, like balloons exploding, something childlike and innocent.

Then he saw movement. It was hard to make out, but he saw soon enough that two of Johnny's men, visible in their dark suits, were scrambling up the ridge. They seemed well under cover.

Owney grasped the significance instantly. If they got above him, the cowboy was finished. They could hold him down while the others moved in on him.

Johnny, you smart bastard, he thought. You are the goddamned best.

Herman waited and waited. Nothing seemed to be happening. He decided to move on the oblique and come on the cowboy's position from another angle.

Ever so slowly he moved out, angling wide, edging ever so gently through the high grass, keeping his eyes on the area where the man had to be. Once in a while he'd shoot a glance up the ridge that ran up the hill for signs of Red and Ding-Dong. But he saw nothing.

The sun was high now. A bit of wind sang in his ears, and the grass around him weaved as it pressed through, rubbing against itself with a soft hiss.

The grass seemed to be thinning somewhat as he drew near to the beginning of the incline. He slowed, dropped to his knees, and looked intently ahead. He could see nothing.

Where was the bastard?

He wiggled a little farther out, staying low, ready to squeeze off a burst at any moment. The silence that greeted his ears was profound.

He planted the gun's butt under his right arm, locking it in the pit, and stepped boldly out, its muzzle covering the beaten zone where haze still drifted. He expected to see a body or a blood trail or something. But he saw nothing. He saw a log ahead on the left and in the deeper grass some kind of bush and he directed his vision back, looking for—

Something to the left flashed. In the instant that his peripheral vision caught the motion, Herman cranked hard to bring his muzzle to bear on the apparition; it was a living bush and as it rose, fluffs of grass fell off it, the bush itself fell away and then Herman saw it was a man.

Earl fired five tracers into the big man in one second. They flew on a line and he absorbed them almost stoically in the center body, then sank to the earth, toppling forward, then trying to prevent his fall with the muzzle of the Browning Automatic Rifle, which he jammed into the ground. So sustained he paused, as if on the edge of a topple, his face gray and his eyes bulging, the blood running everywhere.

Earl didn't have time for this shit. He put seven more into him, knocking him down. The tracers set his clothes aflame.

Earl turned as fire broke out behind him. Two men with tommy guns lay at the crest of the ridge, and fired at him. But of course they had forgotten to adjust their Lyman peep sights for the proper distance, so while they aimed at him, the extreme trajectory of the .45s over two hundred downhill yards pulled their rounds into the ground fifty feet ahead of him.

Earl slid back to the earth, making a range estimation as he went. Bracing the gun tight against himself, he hosed a short burst high in the air, watched as it arched out, trailing incandescence visible even in the bright air. At apogee the consecutive quality of the burst broke up and each bullet spiraled on a slightly different vector toward the earth. Earl watched them, and saw that they hit just fine for windage but too far back. He needed more elevation. He corrected in a second, fired two shots and watched them rise and fall like mortar shells. They fell where he wanted. He pressed the trigger and finished the magazine, dumped it, quickly slammed another one home, found the same position in his muscle memory and this time squeezed off the entire thirty rounds in about four seconds. The gun shuddered, spewing empties like a brass liquid pouring from its breech, and the tracers curved through the air, riding a bright rainbow. Where they struck, they started fires.

It was Red who saw what was happening first. He felt okay, ducking back behind cover as a rainbow of bright slugs lofted high above him and descended, but without precision. It was absurdly raining light. Still, there was no real chance that any of the rounds could hit a target, as they dispersed widely as they plummeted.

Then he felt a wall of heat crushing over him, and the heat's presence seemed to distend or twist the air itself. To the right a wall of flame seemed to explode from nowhere. He'd never understood how fast a brushfire can burn, particularly on a hillside where the wind blows continually and there is no shelter.

The fire was a crackling enemy, advancing behind them in a human wave attack, throwing out fiery patrols of pure flame and crackling, popping menace. It sucked the air from them and its smoke closed on them quickly. They turned to run, but the fire was all around them and suddenly a lick of it lashed out and set Ding-Dong's sleeve afire.

He screamed, dropped his weapon and went to his knees to beat it out. But more flame was on him and soon he was lit up like a Roman candle, and if the power of the fire would drive him to run, the pain of it took his energy from him, and he fell back, his flesh burning.

Red didn't want that happening to him. He had just a second to decide, and then he scrambled up the ridge and leaped over it, escaping the hungry flames, but before he could congratulate himself, a fleet of tracers rose from nowhere and crucified him to the ground.

Earl spun, changed magazines again, and looked backward for another target. He could see nothing. If there was another man moving in on him from behind he was moving stealthily. Earl didn't have much cover here and in fact there was very little cover anywhere. He emptied another magazine, then another, hosing down the area where another man would be if he existed. That was sixty rounds in about ten seconds, and the tracers sprayed across the area before him like lightning bolts seeking the highest available target. They churned through the grass, setting small fires when they encountered dryness, but generally just ripping up earth and drawing a screen of dirt into the air.

He changed magazines a third time, moved out a little for a slightly different angle and squirted another batch out in another bright fan of searching bullets.

Johnny was too far to shoot when the thing started happening. Then it happened so fast and so unpredictably he was uncertain what to do. He watched the tracers arc out and descend behind the ridge. Smoke rose so fast in the aftermath it was astonishing. The ridgeline caught fire.

But by that time he had gone totally prone and begun to crawl, crawl desperately forward in the highest grass there was, hoping he could get so close he could count on his superior reflexes to carry the battle. He squirmed like a man aflame, whereas it was others who were aflame. Then the cowboy started shooting wildly. He listened as the man pumped out magazine after magazine, but behind him, where he'd been, not where he was now and where he was headed.

He crawled and crawled until the firing stopped.

By his reckoning he was now just twenty yards or so away, and the cowboy had no idea where he was.

He peered through the grass, rising incrementally higher for visibility and suddenly beheld a wondrous sight.

The cowboy had a jam. His empty magazine was caught in the gun and he tugged it desperately to get it free, his hand up toward the receiver. Then suddenly whatever it was gave, he pulled the magazine out, and dropped it, his hand reaching into his suit pocket for another.

"Hold it!" said Johnny, covering him with the muzzle.

The cowboy whirled but what could he do? He had an empty gun in one hand and a fresh magazine in the other. He was a good two seconds from completing the reload.

"Well, well," said Johnny, walking forward, his muzzle expertly sighted on the big man's heaving chest, "look who we've caught with his pants down. Jam on you, did it? Them damn things is tricky. You've got to baby them or you'll regret it, lad. Come now, let's have a look at you."

The man regarded him sullenly. Johnny knew he'd be thinking desperately of something to do. Caught like this, with no ammo! Him with the big fancy gun, him who'd shot all them other fellers, and now him with nothing.

"Cut me a break, will you, pal?" said the cowboy.

"And live the rest of me life looking over the shoulder? I should think not."

"I just want Maddox. I don't give a fuck about you. Just walk away and forget all this. You can live."

"Oh, now he's dictating terms, is he?" Johnny laughed. He was now about fifteen feet away, close enough.

"I didn't have to kill your boys. They were here, that's all."

"I should thank you for that, pally. Now the take's so much bigger. You've made me an even wealthier man. I'll drink many a champagne toast to you, friend, for your fine work. You are a game lad. You're about the gamest I've ever seen."

Earl just stared at him.

"I know what you're thinking. Maybe you can get the magazine into the gun and get the gun into play and bring old Johnny down. Why do I think not? No, old sod, you've been bested. Admit it now, you've been handled. Ain't many could handle the likes of you, but by God I'm the one man in a million who could do it."

"You talk a lot," said the man.

"That I do. The Irish curse. We are a loquacious race. Maybe I should walk you across the field and let Mr. Owney Maddox himself put the last one into you. He'd probably pay double for that pleasure."

"You won't do that. You won't take the chance."

"Well, boyo, that's the sad truth. But I won't be long. I'll just—"
His eyes lit.

"Say," he said. "I'm a sporting fellow. You're holding an empty gun."

"Let me load it."

"No thank you. But here's what I'll do." He reached under his coat and removed a .45. It was one of the Griffin & Howe rebuild jobs with which D.A. had armed his raid team.

He threw it into the dirt in front of Earl.

"That one's nice and loaded," he said with a smile.

"But it's five feet away."

"It is indeed. Now I'll count to three. On three you can make a dive at the gun. I'll finish you well before, but I might as well give you a one-in-one-thousand chance. Maybe *my* tommy will jam."

"You're a bastard."

"Me mother said the same. Are you ready, fellow?"

He let his gun muzzle drift down until it pointed to the ground. He watched as Earl looked at the gun on the ground five feet in front of him.

"See, here's the thing," said the cowboy. "Fights sometimes ain't what you want 'em to be."

"One," said Johnny.

He meant to shoot on two, of course.

The cowboy's tommy gun came up in a flash and there was a report and for just a millisecond it seemed a tendril of sheer illumination had lashed out to snare him.

The next thing Johnny knew, he was wet.

Why was he wet?

Had he spilled something?

Then he noticed he was lying on his back. He heard something creaking, like a broken accordion, an air-filled sound, high and desperate, a banshee screaming out in the bogs, signifying a death. He blinked and recognized it as a sucking chest wound. His own.

He could only see sky.

The cowboy stood over him.

"I slipped one cartridge into the chamber before I shucked the magazine," he said.

"I— I—" Johnny began, seeing that it was possible. The gun looked empty. It wasn't.

"Think of the railyard, chum," said Earl, as he locked in the new magazine, drew back the bolt and then fired thirty ball tracers into him.

CHAPTER

65

"Twelve," said the doctor.

"Yes sir," said the nurse.

"Mrs. Swagger, you are dilated twelve centimeters. You have another four or five to go. There's no need to endure this pain. Please let us give you the anesthesia."

"No," she said. "I want my husband."

"Ma'am, we've tried but we can't raise him. Ma'am, I'm afraid we've got a problem. You would be so much better off with the anesthesia."

"No, you'll take my baby."

She felt so alone. She could only see the ceiling. Occasionally the doctor loomed into view, occasionally the nurse.

The two put her gown down.

"We do have a problem with the baby," said the doctor. "It may be necessary to make a decision."

"Save the baby. Save my baby! Don't hurt my baby!"

"Mrs. Swagger, you can have *other* babies. This one is upside down in your uterus. I can't get it out, not without cutting you horribly and, frankly, I'm not equipped to do that and I don't know if I could stop the hemorrhaging once it got started, not here, not with two nurses and no other doctors."

"Can't you get another doctor?" someone asked, and Junie recognized the voice of her friend, Mary Blanton.

"Mrs. Blanton, please get back into the waiting room! You are not permitted back here."

"Sir, somebody has to stay with Junie. I cannot let her go through this alone. Honey, I'm here."

Good old Mary! Now there was a woman! Mary couldn't be pushed around, no sir! Mary would fight like hell!

"Thank you, Mary," Junie said, as another contraction pressed a bolt of pain up through her insides.

"Ma'am, there are no other doctors. In Fort Smith, yes, in Hot

Springs, yes, at Camp Chaffee, yes, but you chose a small public hospital in Scott County to have your baby during a late-night shift and I am doing what I can do. Now please, you have to leave."

"Please let her stay," begged Junie.

"When we go back to delivery, she can't come. You may stay here, ma'am, but do not touch anything, and stay out of the way."

"Yes sir."

The doctor seemed to leave, but instead he pulled Mary out into the hall.

"Look," he said, "we have a very complicated situation here. That woman may die. By my calculus, the baby's life is not worth the woman's life. The woman can have other babies. She can adopt a child. If it comes to it, I may have to terminate the baby's life, get it out of her in pieces. That may be the only way to save her life."

"Oh, God," said Mary. "She wants that baby so bad."

"Where is her husband?"

"We're not sure."

"Bastard. These white trash Southern hillbillies are—"

"Sir, Earl Swagger is not trashy. He's a brave man, a law enforcement officer, and if he's not here, it's because he's risking his life to protect you. Let me tell you, sir, if someone broke into your house at night, the one man you'd want to protect you and yours is Earl Swagger. That is why we have to protect his."

"Well, that's very fine. But we are coming up to decision time and I am not authorized to make this decision on my own and I could get in a lot of trouble. If I don't terminate the baby, that woman will die a needless, pointless and tragic death. She needs your help to decide. You help her decide. That's the best you can do for your friend."

CHAPTER
66

The screen of smoke blew across the valley, white and shifting.

Owney had a hope that Johnny Spanish and one or two of his boys would come out of it, laughing, full of merry horseplay, happy to have survived and triumphed. But he was not at all surprised or even disappointed when the other man emerged.

Out of the smoke he came. He was a tall man, in a suit, with his hat low over his eyes. He carried a tommy gun and looked dead-set on something.

Owney saw no point in running. He was a realist. There was no place to run to and if he got into the forest he would be easy to track and he'd be taken down and gutted.

It occurred to him to get into the station wagon and try and run the man down. But this cool customer would simply watch him come and fill him with lead from the tommy gun.

So Owney just sat there on the fender of the old Ford station wagon. He smoked a Cuban cigar and enjoyed the day, which had turned nice, clear, with a cool wind fluttering across the valley. The sun was warm, even hot, and there were no clouds. In the background, the hillside burned, but it seemed to have run out of energy as the flames spread and died, leaving only cinders to smolder.

The man seemed to come out of war. That's what it looked like; behind him, the smoke curled and drifted, and its stench filled the air; the hillside was blackened. There were bodies back there. Five of them. He'd gotten Johnny Spanish and his crew. Nobody ever got Johnny, not the feds, the State Police, all the city detectives, the sheriffs, the deputies, the marshals. But this one got them all in a close-up gunfight. He was something.

The cowboy was finally within earshot.

With a certain melancholy and an idea for his last gambit, Owney rose.

"*Lawman!*" he screamed. "*I surrender! I'm unarmed! I'll go back with you! You win!*"

He stood away from the car and took off his jacket and held his hands stiff and high. Slowly he pirouetted to show that he had no guns tucked in his belt. He rolled up his sleeves to show that his wrists were bare to the elbow.

He had the bicycle gun stuck in its sleeve garter against his left biceps, on the inside, just above the elbow. He'd ripped a large hole in the inside seam of the shirt, invisible from afar, so that he could get at it quickly.

Let him get close, he thought. Let him get close. Offer him respect. Show him fear. Relax him. Put him at his ease. When he lowers the tommy gun, go for the bike pistol and shoot him five times fast, in the body.

He smiled as the man drew near.

The cowboy was lean and drawn. His face had a gaunt look, exhaustion under the furious concentration. His suit was dusty, his eyes aglare, the hat low over them. He looked Owney up and down, taking his measure.

"I'm unarmed," said Owney. "You won! You got me!"

It just might work.

Earl was not surprised that Owney Maddox awaited him with his hands high, his arms bare. What else could Owney do? He was out of options, other than killing himself, and Owney wasn't that kind of boy. He was no Japanese marine, who'd cut his own guts out and die with a grenade under his belly so that when you turned the corpse over two days later, the grenade would enable you to join him in heaven. No, that was not Owney's style.

He stopped ten feet shy of Owney.

"You win, partner," said Owney, with a smile. "You are a champ. I'll say that. You are a pro. You handled the best there is, my friend. I'm outclassed."

Earl said nothing.

He raised his tommy gun, and holding it deftly with one hand let it cover Owney.

"You're not going to shoot me," Owney said. "My hands are up. I've surrendered. You don't have it in you for that kind of stuff. That's the difference between us. You can't make yourself squeeze on an unarmed man with his hands in the air. I know you. You're a soldier, not a gangster. You won a war, but you wouldn't last a week on an island with alleys and nightclubs."

Earl just looked him over, then transferred the Thompson to his left hand.

"Take your belt off and throw it over here."

"Yah. See. I knew you weren't the type," said Owney, doing the job with one hand.

"Thought you was English," said Earl.

"Only when I want to be, chum. Come on, tie me, let's get this over. I want to get back in time to hear Frankie on the radio."

But then he stopped. He looked quizzically at Earl.

"I have to know. You're not working for Bugsy Siegel, are you?"

"That guy?" said Earl. "Don't know nothing about him."

"You fool," said Owney. "You have no idea what you've done, do you?"

"Nope."

Owney joined his hands together for Earl to loop them with the belt. Earl knelt to retrieve the belt. As he rose with it, Owney stepped forward and seemed to stumble just a bit and then his hand fled to his arm. He was fast.

But Earl was faster. His right hand flew to the Colt automatic in his belt like a bolt of electricity shearing the summer air. It was a fast that can't be taught, that no camera could capture. He caught the pistol in his other hand and thrust it toward Owney even as a crack split the air. Owney had fired one-handed. Owney had missed.

Hunched and doublehanded, Earl knocked five into the gangster, all before Owney could get the hammer thumbed back on the bike gun for a second shot. The rounds kicked the gangster back and set him down hard as the little weapon fell from his fingers into the grass.

Now Earl knew who had killed his father. Now Earl knew what had happened to his father's little gun. But he didn't care. His old father meant nothing to him now. He thought of his new father, the man who'd died for him in the railyard. Now he'd tracked D.A.'s true killer down and paid out justice in gunfire.

Earl walked over to Owney. Five oozing holes were clustered in a slightly oblong circle on his white shirt under his heart. They were so close you could cover them with one hand, and they were wounds nobody comes back from.

"W-who are you?" Owney asked.

"You'd never believe it," said Earl.

67

She had borne so much pain she had become numbed by it. Her eyes were vague, her sense of reality elongated, her sense of time vanished. The pain just came and came and came, and had its way, though now and then a moment of lucidity reached her, and she concentrated on the here and now, and then it all went away in pain.

She heard someone say, "She's at fifteen. We've got to do it."

"Yes, doctor."

The young doctor's face flew into view.

"Mrs. Swagger, I have been on the phone all over the state trying to get an OB-GYN, even a resident, even a horse doctor over here. Someone can be here in an hour, I'm sorry to report. So I have to act now, or we will lose both you and the child."

"Don't take my baby!"

"You will bleed to death internally in a very short while. I'm sorry but I have to do what's right. Nurse, get her prepped. I'm going to go scrub."

She had fought so hard. Now, at the end, she had nothing left.

"It's all right," she heard Mary whispering. "You have to get through this. You'll have other babies. Honey, he's right, you've fought so hard, but it's time to move on. You have to survive. I couldn't live without you, I'm so selfish. Please, your mama, your papa, everybody, they are pulling for you."

"Where's Earl, Mary?"

"I am sorry, honey. He didn't make it."

Then she felt herself moving. A nurse was pushing her down the dimly lit hallway. The gurney vibrated and each vibration hurt her bad. A bump nearly killed her. She was in a brightly lit room. The doctor had a mask on. Then he turned away from her. A mask came and she smelled its rubbery density. She turned her face, waiting for the gas, and saw the doctor with his back to her. He was working with a long probe but she saw that it had a pointed end to it, like a knitting needle.

My baby, she thought. They are going to use that on my baby.

"She's ready, doctor."

"All right, give her—"

There was a commotion.

A woman had broken in. Angry words were spoken. Then she heard the doctor say, "I don't care about all that. Get him in here."

The doctor was back.

"Well, Mrs. Swagger, your husband just showed up."

"Earl!"

"Yes ma'am. And he has another doctor with him."

But there was something on his face.

"What's wrong?"

"This is your part of the country down here, not mine. You would understand better than me. I don't understand, but that nurse says if we let this doctor in here, there will be some trouble."

"Please. Please help my baby."

"All right, ma'am. I knew you'd say that."

"The doctor—?"

"The doctor your husband brought. He's colored."

Earl explained it once again.

"Ma'am, I don't care what your rules say. That's my wife in there and my child, and you need another doctor and this doctor has kindly consented to assist and he's delivered over a thousand babies through the years, so just step aside."

"No Negroes are allowed in this hospital. That's the rule." This was the hospital shift supervisor, a large woman in glasses, whose face was knit up tight as a fist as she clung to her part of the empire.

"That was yesterday. There are new rules now."

"And who has made that determination?"

"I believe I have."

"Sir, you have no right."

"My wife and baby ain't going to die because you have some rule that never made no sense and is only waiting for someone to come along and blow it down in a single day. This is that day and I am that man."

"I will have to call the sheriff."

"I don't give a hang who you call, but this doctor is going to help my wife, and that's all there is to it. I'll thank you to move or so help me God I'll move you and you won't like it a bit. Now, for the last time, madam, get the goddamned hell out of our way."

The woman yielded.

The two men walked in the corridor and a neighbor lady was standing there.

"You are not a man to be argued with, Mr. Swagger," said Dr. James.

"No sir. Not today."

A woman rushed to join them. She looked tired too, as if she'd been through it the same as Earl.

"Thank God you got here."

"You're Mary Blanton. Oh, Mary, ain't you the best though. I called and your husband told me what was going on. Dr. James was good enough to say he'd come along."

"Thank God you're here, doctor."

"Yes ma'am."

The young resident came out into the hall.

"Dr.—?"

"Julius James. OB-GYN. NYU School of Medicine, 1932."

"I'm Mark Harris, Northwestern, '44. Thank God you're here, doctor. We've got a posterior presentation and she's dilated all the way to fifteen and she's been in labor for twelve hours. That little bastard won't come out."

"Okay, doctor, I'll scrub. I believe I can flip the baby. I've managed to do it several times before. We'll have to perform an episiotomy. Then you'll have to cut the cord when I get into her so it doesn't strangle the infant in the womb. Then you'll have to stitch her while I resuscitate the infant. Make sure to have . . ."

Earl watched the two men drift away, and they disappeared into the delivery room.

He went back outside, to the waiting room, which was now deserted. The woman who had given him so much trouble was gone.

He couldn't sit down. He tried not to think about what was going on in the delivery room, or the hours since he'd dumped the bodies, called home, talked to Phil Blanton, driven to Greenwood, begged Dr. Julius James to accompany him, and driven here.

"I am worried about the doctor," he said to Mary. "This could be dangerous for him. He doesn't deserve all this bad trouble."

"Mr. Swagger, if they should move against him, they will be moving against you. I don't believe they will do that. They are bullies and cowards anyhow, not men."

"I do hope you are right, Mary."

In time, after Earl paced and Mary sat dumbly, a law officer approached, as if skulking. He wore a deputy's badge and had the look of the kind of old cop who sat in offices all day long.

"Are you the man that brought the Negro doctor?"

"Yes, I am," said Earl.

"You're not from around here, are you?"

"I grew up down in Polk County."

"Then you know this is not how we do things. We keep white and nigger separated. We have laws about it. I have to arrest you and the Negro doctor."

"I think you'd best go on home, old man," said Earl. "I do not have time for all this."

"Mr.—?"

"Swagger. Earl Swagger."

"Mr. Swagger, this is a great principle we are defending. It's bigger than your wife and your baby. We have the future of the nation at stake here."

"Deputy, possibly you know of my father, Charles Swagger? He was a man who done what he said he would do. He was famous for it. Well, sir, I am that kind of man only more so. So when I say to you, go away, go far away, then you'd best obey me or there will be hell for lunch."

The sheriff slunk away.

But he paused at the door.

"Your beefiness may work with an old man like me, Swagger, when all the deputies are out hunting Owney Maddox. But there are some boys at the end of the street getting liquored up who will take a different view."

"I'll deal with them when they come. If they have the guts. And don't you worry none about Owney Maddox. That bill was settled."

Another half hour passed. Mary sat, now hugging herself. Earl walked back and forth, smoking, like a man in a *Saturday Evening Post* cartoon. He kept glancing at his watch, kept looking at the door, kept trying to calm himself down. He was so desperately exhausted he could hardly think straight, but he was in that keyed up state where he couldn't sleep either. He was just a raw mess.

At last the door opened, but it wasn't a doctor. It was a janitor, a black man.

"Sir," he said.

"Yes, what is it, Pop?" Earl asked.

"They's coming. A mob. Seen it before. It happens oncet a while. They done got to set things back the way they was and when they do that, some boy's got to swing or burn."

"Not this time, Pop. You can bet on it."

He turned to Mary.

"I'll take care of this."

"Mr. Swagger, I—"

"Don't you worry none. I faced Japs. These boys ain't Japs. But just in case, I want you down on the floor. If some lead sails through, you don't want to catch a cold from it."

Earl walked out onto a porch.

He watched them come. The old man was right. There were about fifty of them, and from the groggy, angry progress, he could tell there had been much liquor consumed. The mob spilled this way and that, and shouts and curses came from it. He watched as supposedly decent people stepped aside, or stood back in horror, but he noted too that nobody stood up to these boys, nobody at all.

It was now four o'clock in the afternoon. He'd lost most sense of time and wasn't sure how long he'd been here, how long they'd been drinking, how mad they were. The sun was low in the western sky, and flame-colored. The mountains were silhouettes. A wind blew, and the leaves on the trees all shimmered.

On the boys came. He saw shotguns, a few rifles, a few squirrel guns, hoes, shovels, picks. They'd grabbed everything they could fight with. They were killing mad.

The leader was a heavyset man in overalls with a battered fedora and the hardscrabbled face of a fellow life hadn't treated kindly. His compatriots were equally rough, men who'd been purged of pity by bad breaks, brushes with the law, beatings from bigger men, and a sense of lost possibility. They looked like a ragtag Confederate infantry regiment moving out agin the bluebellies at some Pea Ridge or other. Earl had known them his whole life.

Earl watched them come, standing straight. His hat was low over his dark and baleful eyes. His gray suit was dusty and rumpled but not without some dignity to it. His tie was tight to his throat and trim. He calmly smoked a Chesterfield, cupping it in his big hands.

Finally they were there, and only his imperturbability stood between him and the doctors and his wife.

"You the feller brought that nigger here?"

"I brought a doctor here, boys. Didn't stop to notice his color."

"We don't 'low no niggers in this end of town. Bad business."

"Today, that changes. I'm here to change it."

In the crowd faces turned to faces and low, guttural exchanges passed electrically among them. Like an animal they seemed to coil and gather strength.

Finally, the leader took a step forward.

"Mister, we'll string you up next to that coon in a whisker if that's what you want. Now you stand aside while we take care of business, or by God this'll be the day you die."

"Boys, there's been lots of days when I could die. If this is the one at last, then let's get to it."

He flicked aside the cigarette, and with a quick move peeled off his coat.

He had a .45 cocked and locked in the shoulder holster that Herman Kreutzer had been wearing, another .45 cocked and locked in the speed holster on his hip that Johnny Spanish had been wearing and a third stuffed into his belt backward to the left of his belt buckle. His shirt pocket was stuffed with three or four magazines.

"I can draw and kill seven of you in the first two seconds. In the next two seconds I'll kill seven more. In the final two seconds, I'll get the third seven. Now if some of you boys in the back get a shot into me, you'd best make it count, 'cause if it only wounds me, I may get a reload or two in, and each time I reload that means seven more of you boys are going down. So I figure a sure twenty-one of you are dead, and probably more like twenty-eight or even thirty-five."

He paused. He smiled. His hand fell close to the gun on his hip, and there wasn't a lick of fear in him.

"Well, boys, what do you say? Are we going to do some man's work today? You will be remembered, I guarantee you that. You will go into history, you can bet on it. Come on, Fat Boy, you're up front. Is this the day you picked to get famous?"

The fat man swallowed.

"Ain't so much fun when somebody else has the gun, is it, Fat Boy?"

The fat man swallowed again, looked back to his mob and saw that it was leaking men from the rear. It seemed to be dissolving.

Suddenly he and four or five others were alone.

"Fat Boy, I am tired of standing here. You make your play or I just may shoot you so I can sit a spell."

The others left and the Fat Boy was alone. A large stain spread across his crotch as his bladder yielded to stress. But he didn't blink or swallow. He peered ahead intently at nothing.

Earl walked down to him.

He reached into his back pocket. The man stood stock-still, quivering.

Earl took out his wallet, opened it.

"I see your name is Willis Beaudine. Well, Willis, here's something for you to remember. If anything ever happens to that good doctor in there, it's you I'll come visit in the night. And Willis Beaudine, don't think you can run and hide. Many a man has thought that and they are now sucking bitter grass from the root end."

He dropped the wallet down Willis's overalls.

"Now scoot, Willis."

Willis turned and in seconds disappeared. Odd a fat man could move so fast.

Earl picked up his coat, threw it over his shoulder and walked back into the hospital waiting room.

Dr. James was waiting, along with Mary.

"How's my wife?" Earl demanded.

"Your wife is just fine, Mr. Swagger," the doctor said. "She's not bleeding anymore, and she's going to recover very nicely."

"And—"

"Yes," he said, "congratulations. You have a son."

1947

68

He didn't have any trouble finding Beverly Hills but Linden Drive proved difficult. Finally, he stopped on a street corner where a kid was selling Maps of the Stars.

"You're almost there, sir. Three blocks up to Whittier Avenue, then left and Linden is the next one on the left."

"Thanks, kid." He handed the boy a quarter.

The house was big. A star's house should be big. It had that Southern California Mexican palace look to it, with a crown of red tiles over white stucco, some kind of towerlike or churchlike assemblage in the front, immaculate gardens and lawns. He'd seen something like it in China, but the ones in China had all been smashed to rubble by Mao's Pioneers or Chiang's shock infantry.

He parked, checked his watch, saw that it was exactly 7:00 and went up the flagstone walk toward the dark wood front door, a massive slab of carved oak. It was still, and the sun was oozing through the trees toward the Pacific on one corner of the sky. It was so quiet here, the plush quiet of a very rich neck of the woods, where voices were never raised, dinner was served at 8:00 and the only noise would be the solidity of the Cadillac limo doors being gently shut by butlers or drivers.

He knocked, and a man answered.

"I'm here to see Mr. Siegel," he said. "I think he's expecting me."

"Yeah, come on in," said the fellow, some sort of flashily dressed Hollywood type. "I have to pat you down. Just to be sure. You know."

"No problem," said Frenchy.

He turned, assumed the position, and felt the quick, frightened run of hands across his body. It wasn't well done. He could have brought in at least three pieces if he'd wanted to.

"I'm a director," said the man. "I never thought I'd end up frisking guys. But if you're Ben's friend, you move in Ben's world."

"What would you do if I had an automatic?" asked Frenchy.

"I don't know. Probably scream, then faint."

Frenchy laughed.

"This way. I'll tell him you're here. He's upstairs with Virginia's brother and his fiancée."

"No problem. I'll wait. I've got plenty of time."

The man led Frenchy to some kind of living room at the rear of the house, or maybe it was a den. Who could tell in a house so big and plush? It was full of rococo touches, like a statue of Cupid, on tiptoes with his little bow and arrow in bronze. Some English dowager looked as if she were Queen Mab in an oil painting over the mantel but the coffee table had a French country look to it. Then a huge picture window displayed a rose trellis across the backyard about twenty-five feet, festooned with bright explosions of blossoming fire, like gunshots frozen, somehow. It was June and the roses were out. He studied the trellis in some detail, looked at the lay of the yard, the height of the wall, the location of the gate and even the lock on the gate. All very interesting.

In time, the man himself came into the room. Frenchy had never seen him before. He was shorter than he'd imagined, with a movie star's tan and white teeth, his blond-brown hair brilliantined back like George Brent's, his muscular, broad-chested body creamily bulging against the beautifully tailored glen-plaid double-breasted suit he wore, with a tie perfectly tied, perfectly centered. His eyes were bright and sharp and everything about him radiated sheer animal heat.

"I'm Ben Siegel," he said. "And Mr. Lansky said I should see you but not to ask the name."

"My name is a Top Secret," said Frenchy.

"You with the feds?"

"Not the feds that you need to worry about. Another outfit. We work overseas. Handling things. Very hush-hush. I just got back from someplace I can't even tell you about, or I'd have to kill you."

Ben looked him up and down.

"You're pretty young for that kind of thing, ain't you, kid? Shouldn't you still be sipping milk from a carton in the school cafeteria?"

"I'm smarter than I look and older than I seem."

"Okay, so? What's this all about? How're you in with Meyer?"

"I don't know Lansky. I know some people who know some people. Calls were made because favors were owed and I had something you might find useful. It happens also to be useful to me. That's why I'm here."

"Is this a touch?"

"It won't cost a cent."

"Okay. Sit down, Mr. Mystery Man."

"Thanks."

Siegel sat on a flower print sofa; Frenchy sat in a high wing chair, also flowery.

"So?"

"You want the name of a man in Arkansas. I happen to have some experience in Arkansas."

"You don't look like a country boy."

"I'm not. But I spent some time there and I worked for a law enforcement unit and I met the man you want to know about. I know all about him."

"How did you know I wanted to know about him?"

"You remember a guy named Johnny Spanish?"

"Yeah, whatever happened to Johnny?"

"Big mystery. But whatever happened to Johnny also happened to your old friend Owney Maddox."

"I hear Owney's in Paris," said Siegel.

"Somehow, I don't think so. I don't think he's in Mexico, Rio, Madrid or Manila, either."

"I've heard that too."

"Anyhow, Johnny Spanish told me of your interest in this individual."

"The cowboy. He packed a punch, I'll say."

"So I hear."

"Fuckin' yentzer hit me so hard I can still feel it. I sometimes wake up dreamin' about it. So what's the bargain?"

"I know who he is. I know where he is."

"What do you want in exchange?"

"A good night's sleep."

"I don't get it."

"Put it this way. This man and I were colleagues at one point. Then we had a policy disagreement and I was forced to make certain other arrangements. I don't know if he knows about them. I don't know what he knows. He could know everything, he could know nothing. It didn't matter when I was overseas, but now it looks like I'm going to be in the States for a bit, while I go to a language school. I don't want to worry about him showing up for a discussion."

"I get it."

"So our interests coincide. I give you him. You pay off your debt, and I don't have to worry about him coming to collect his debt."

Bugsy looked him up and down.

"You may be a guy who can handle himself but you really fear him, huh?"

"He is very good. The best. Better than me, and I'm very good and getting even better each time out. But I'll never get to his level. He's a natural. He's also capable of throwing everything in his best interest away on some obscure notion of honor. In other words, the most dangerous man alive."

"Maybe I ought to charge *you.*"

"No. You want him. I've heard the story a hundred times. It's a famous story. It'll probably end up in the *Saturday Evening Post* and then the pictures. You can't afford in your line of work to let something like that slide. That's why you've hired private eyes, bribed newspapermen, tried to infiltrate the Hot Springs police department."

"Say, you *are* informed, ain't you?" Bugsy was clearly impressed.

"I know some folks."

"Okay, spill it. Just a second. Hey, Al, get down here!"

The Hollywood gofer appeared a moment later.

"Yes, Ben."

"Write down what this guy says. Okay, go ahead, Mystery Man."

Al got out pad and paper and began to take notes.

"His name is Earl Swagger," Frenchy said. "He lives on Route 8, in Polk County, Arkansas, with his wife, just west of a little town called Board Camp, maybe fifteen miles east of the county seat, Blue Eye. The name is on the mailbox. It's his father's old place. He's got it painted up real nice now, I hear. And he and his wife had a little boy about ten months ago, so they're all very happy. He's just been appointed a corporal in the Arkansas State Police. You failed to find him on your own because part of the deal that was made when they closed down the Garland County raid team after Johnny Spanish blew it away was to destroy all the records, so that nothing exists on paper."

"Okay," said Ben.

"He's a former Marine first sergeant. He won the Medal of Honor on Iwo."

Bugsy's eyes squinted in suspicion.

"No wonder you don't want him on your tail."

"What else can I do? Perform some service for him and believe that it'll protect me from his wrath? Not in this world, pal."

"Yeah, well, this will make you real happy. I will send some guys out there. Very tough guys. They will jump this Earl Swagger with crowbars and smash him in the head. They will drag him someplace in the woods, and, on my instructions, they will break every bone in his body. Every single one. It'll take hours. They will smash his fuckin' teeth out, break his nose, blind him, punch out his eardrums. The last words he hears will be, 'Compliments of Ben Siegel, who remembers you from the train station.' Then they'll leave him there, and either he'll die tied to that tree or he'll be found and he'll spend the rest of his life in a wheelchair, blind, deaf and dumb. He will remember Ben Siegel, that I guarantee."

It was a little of Ben's famous craziness—the Bugsy part of him—that just leaked out.

Frenchy noted it, then stood. The two men didn't shake hands, and Ben walked him to the door.

"And if anybody ever asks you, kid," Ben said, "you tell them about the day you learned what kind of man Ben Siegel was."

"Yes sir," said Frenchy.

He went to his car and drove away.

Sometime later, Ben was reading the paper on the sofa. He sat with it in his lap, waiting for Chick Hill to come downstairs with Jerri. Al Smiley, his pal, sat next to him.

"This has been a very good day," Ben said. "A very good day. I get to scratch an itch that's been bugging me for over a year. The Flamingo is raking in the dough. I can pay off my debt to Meyer. Virginia will be back tomorrow. Hey, Al, life is good."

"Life *is* good," said Al.

"I always win. Nobody outfights me!"

Outside, the shooter steadied the carbine on the trellis. He wasn't trembling at all, but then that was his gift. At moments like these, he held together. Always had. Always would. It was what he was meant to do.

Front sight. That was the key.

Trigger pull. Squeeze, not yank. The carbine was light, a little beauty of a rifle, powerful as a heavy .38 or one of those Magnums.

He saw Ben Siegel's face against the front sight. Then the face faded to blur as the sight blade became hard and perfect.

The gun recoiled; he didn't hear the blast.

Ben had just the impression of being punched hard and also a brief awareness of glass shattering. Then he—

The gunman fired again, watched as blood flew from the neck. He wasn't aware of the man next to Bugsy collapsing in a heap on the floor.

He shot again and again into the face, watching as the whole beautiful head quivered each time it absorbed a bullet, then settled back, more broken, bloodier, the jaw askew, the cheekbone smashed.

A dog was barking.

The gunman left the trellis and walked up to the window itself, standing close to the eight bullet holes clustered in the heavy glass, each with its silvery webbing of fracture.

Ben lay with his head back on the sofa, his hands in his lap, a whole backed-up toilet's worth of blood corrupting the beauty of his suit and the flowers of the material of the furniture. His tie was still tight and perfect.

The dog barked again.

The shooter put the little rifle to his shoulder one more time, aimed carefully and squeezed the trigger. He fired through the punctured glass, and it collapsed like a sheet of ice. He hit Benjamin Siegel in the eye, blowing it out in a puff of misted blood and bone fragments, and it spun wetly through the air and landed with a revolting sound on the tile floor.

Frenchy lowered the carbine.

"That's for the cowboy," he said, "you fucking yentzer." Then he turned and coolly walked around the house, through the neighbor's yard, dropped the carbine into the back seat of his car, and drove away to the rest of his life.

CHAPTER
69

Earl sat with his son in the rocker on the porch. He held the boy close and rocked gently. The sun was bright and shone off the whiteness of the newly painted barn. He had done a lot to the old farm, including painting all the buildings that same brilliant white, mowing the high grass, planting a garden. He had a plan for plowing the field in the next spring, to put out a small crop. He wanted to buy some horses too, because he wanted his son to ride.

He checked his watch. He wasn't due on duty for another hour and Junie was in taking her nap. The State Police black-and-white was parked in the barnyard, next to an old oak.

A Little Rock newspaper with two items of interest lay on the floor of the porch, next to the rocker. BECKER SETS GOV BID one headline had read; and far below it, in the corner, another bit of news from the old days: WEST COAST MOBSTER SLAIN.

Neither had anything to do with him. Both seemed far away, and from another lifetime, not even his own. His life was now entirely different from that one, more settled. The rigors of duty, a necessary job; the effort it took to keep the farm running and to help Junie, who was still recovering from the strain of her labor; and the requirements of this new thing, which pleased him so much more than he could ever have believed, this business of being a father.

The infant squirmed against him, made some unidentifiable sounds, and looked him square in the eye. There was something about the boy that impressed his father. He looked at things straight on, seemed to study them. He didn't say much. He wasn't a crier or a bawler, he seemed never to get into accidents or do stupid things like putting his hand in a fire or grabbing the hot teakettle. He never awoke in the night, but when they went in, early, he was always awake already, and watchful.

"You are something, little partner," he said to his son.

The boy was ten months old, but he still had the warmth of a freshly baked loaf of bread to his father's nose.

The boy wanted to play a game. He reached out and touched his father's nose and his father jerked his head back and made a sound like a horse, and the boy's face knit in laughter. He loved this game. He loved his daddy holding him.

"Ain't you a pistol! Ain't you a little pistol, buster! You are your old daddy's number-one boy, yes, you are."

He had an idea for the boy. No one would ever raise a hand against him, and no one would ever tell him he was no good, he was nothing, he was second-rate. He'd already talked to Sam about it. This boy would go to college. No Marine Corps for him, no life of war, of getting shot at, scurrying through the bush. He would have a good life. He would be a lawyer or some such, and have a life he loved. He'd face none of the things his poor old dad had just survived. No sir. That wasn't for boys. No boy should have to go through that.

"Da—" said the boy.

"There you go, little guy! That's it! You know who I am. I am your old damned daddy, that's me."

The boy's teething mouth lit up in a smile. He reached out to touch his father's nose again, and the game recommenced.

But then Earl noticed the presence of two small boys standing just off the porch as if they'd just come sneaking out of the treeline to the left and were pleased with their stealth.

"Well, howdy," he called.

One was a slight youth, blond and beautiful; the other was bigger and duller, with the sad, slack face of someone vacant in the mental department.

"Howdy, sir," said the smaller, sharper boy.

"What you-all doing way out here?"

"We come out on our bikes. We's goin' 'splorin!"

"You find anything?"

"We's looking for treasure."

"Ain't no treasure out here."

"We gonna find treasure someday."

"Well, maybe so."

"You a police?"

"Why, yes I am. I am in the State Police. I haven't put my uniform on yet. You boys look thirsty. You want some lemonade?"

"Lemon," said the big boy.

"Lemon*ade*," corrected the smaller one. "Bub ain't too smart."

"Not smart," said Bub.

"Well sir, this here's my baby boy."

"He's a cute one," said the boy.

"What're your names, fellas?"

"I'm Jimmy Pye. This here's my cousin Bub."

"Bub," said Bub.

"Okay, you all stay there. I'm going to go in and pour you two nice glasses of lemonade, you hear?"

"Yes sir."

Earl walked into the house and set his son into his playpen, where the boy just watched.

He opened the refrigerator and got out a pitcher of lemonade that Junie always kept and poured out two tall glasses.

But when he returned to the porch, the boys were gone, having moved on in their quest for treasure.

Acknowledgments

In Hot Springs in 1946 there was indeed a veterans' revolt, in which returning GIs, led by a heroic prosecuting attorney, fought and ultimately vanquished the old line mob and gambling interests that controlled Arkansas's most colorful town. However intense it was—the old newspapers suggest it was very intense—it was not nearly so violent as I have made it out to be. Moreover the lawyer who led it—who as I write still lives and who had a most distinguished career—was in every way a better man than my Fred C. Becker. And even the English-born New York mob figure, reputed to be Hot Springs' secret Godfather, was far and away a gentler, better fellow than my nasty Owney Maddox, and is still thought well of in Hot Springs.

So I take pains to separate the real historical antecedents from my grossly fictionalized versions of them. *Hot Springs* is meant to reflect not the reality of the GI Revolt but only my fabrications upon its themes, with the exceptions of the real figures of Benjamin Siegel and Virginia Hill.

The rest is what I do, which is write stories, not histories, and whenever stuck between the cool plot twist and the record will choose the former. I am responsible for all of it, though I should mention those who helped me along the way.

Foremost of these is Colonel Gerry Early, USA Retired, of Easton, Maryland. Gerry, a personnel officer, volunteered to research Earl's Marine career and, with the help of Mr. Danny J. Crawford, Head, Reference Section, Marine Corps Historical Center, Washington, D.C., gave me the great pleasure of reproducing what I feel certain is Earl's record exactly as it would have been had he lived in a world outside my head. It's also a nice tribute to the professional NCOs of the United States Marine Corps in the '30s, who were to prove their worth (and earn glory) in the Pacific. This was long, hard work and I am indebted to them both.

My good friends Bob Lopez and Weyman Swagger were again there to help me. Lopez also introduced me to Paul Mahoney, who collects vintage cars, and Paul helped me with the cars of the '40s. And Paul, in turn, introduced me to Larry De Baugh, an eminent collector of vintage slots, who briefed me and showed me such devices as the Rol-a-Top and the Mills Black Cherry. My colleague Lonnae Parker O'Neal was generous in helping me get the nuances of Southern black speech patterns of the '40s. My *Washington Post* cellmate, the gifted Henry Allen, was of assistance in helping me work out the culture of the '40s, even as he was preparing his own millennium project for the *Post*, in which he attempted to and did in fact answer the following most interesting question: What would it have been like to be alive in each decade of the century? Our mutual supervisor, John Pancake, Arts Editor of the *Post*, was his usual helpful self in not paying terribly close attention to my comings and goings. I could just say, "John, you know, the book," and he'd nod, acquire a distressed expression, and then wearily look in another direction as I marched out.

Fred Rasmussen, of my old paper *The Baltimore Sun,* is a railroad buff par excellence, and he plied me with details on the mythic trains of the '40s, as well as with other railway details.

Some of Earl's comments on fighting with guns are drawn from the wisdom of Clint Smith, the director of Thunder Ranch, the firearms training facility in Mountain Home, Texas. They are used with Clint's permission.

I should mention some books, too. I helped myself with great enthusiasm and no permission whatsoever to the recollections of Shirley Abbott, whose wonderful memoir *The Bookmaker's Daughter* is certainly the most colorful record of the Veterans' Revolt and Hot Springs in the '40s we have, though of course that is not its primary focus. Her father was the head oddsmaker at the Ohio Club. There were many other books I consulted, on and off, most of them purchased at Powell's, the legendary bookstore in Portland, Oregon, where I was taken by Scott LePine of Doubleday, one of the best publisher's reps in the business.

Another book that deserves special mention: *Thompson: The American Legend,* a compendium edited by Tracie L. Hill. It's very expensive but every fan of these fabulous old beauties will get a great kick out of the sentimental journey into the gun's times and culture.

Then there's *Albion's Seed: Four British Folkways in America,* by David Hackett Fischer, which was so enthusiastically recommended to me by Paul Richard of the *Post.* It's an examination of the English roots of American culture, with a section on the Scotch-Irish borderers, who became the American Southerner, and ultimately, for my purpose, the Swaggers and the Grumleys.

In Hot Springs, Bobbie McClane, who runs the Garland County Historical Society, was unfailingly kind and helpful to me. So was Bill Lerz, who helped me find photos of those troubled days. On a less official note, Stormin' Norman, who rents motorbikes at the train station, took me on a wholly more salubrious tour of the town, pointing out where all the whorehouses and the casinos had been. That's something you can't find out from the GCHS, and it was most useful.

In the publishing world, I have to thank my brilliant agent, Esther Newberg; my publisher, David Rosenthal; and my editor, the legendary Michael Korda, who nudged me toward the true form of this book in the early going and kept me on track the whole way.

And of course my great friend Jean Marbella, of *The Baltimore Sun* and the rest of my life, was there to pretend to listen patiently as I bab-

ACKNOWLEDGMENTS *478*

bled about the cool new gunfight thing I'd thought up for Earl. As we say in Baltimore, thanks, hon.

Finally I should say that Mickey Rooney, whose presence in the upstairs of the Ohio Club was reported to me by a Hot Springs source, denies all connection with vice in the town. He says the only thing he remembers is the excellent barbecue.

ABOUT THE AUTHOR

Stephen Hunter was born in 1946 in Kansas City, Missouri. He graduated from Northwestern University and served in the United States Army. He has published ten novels and is a film critic at both *The Washington Post* and *The Tony Kornheiser Show* on ESPN Radio. He lives in Baltimore and is the father of two children.